THE ELEMENTALS

By L. M. Peralta

THE ELEMENTALS TRILOGY

The Elementals
The Council
The Creator

THE ARCADIAN STEEL SEQUENCE

The Wings of Heaven and Hell
The Seven Archangels of Heaven
The Seven Princes of Hell

United Trace

THE ELEMENTALS

BOOK ONE OF THE ELEMENTALS

L. M. PERALTA

First Paperback Edition: January 2013

Summary: When Sara discovers that she is the last surviving Water Elemental, she journeys to defeat a powerful element tyrant.

ISBN: 978-0-9888448-0-3

*This book is dedicated to
my family and friends
who encourage me in all that I do
and have helped me to find the right path.*

At a time when elements could be contained
Inside spheres, marble tombs, they were confined.

Their power taken, but essence not waned;
They were set in sacred places protected.

One could rule a mighty force of nature
But some with too much force did they wield it,
So the element in contrast must venture
To prevent the cruel command from rising.

The opposing tyrant may battle fierce,
But nature ultimately sets things right.
The elements that stand in battle will clash,
In this case, fiery flames must lose the fight.

Fire and brimstone rue the day
When an insidious leader was washed away.

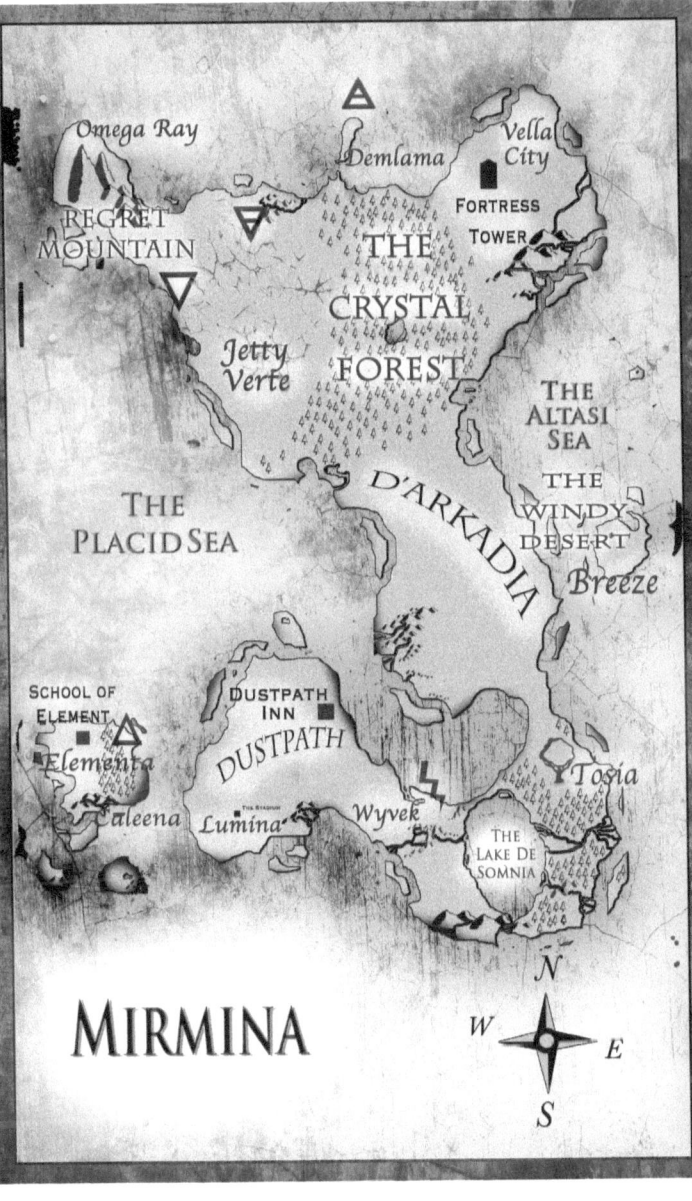

PROLOGUE

THE city that housed fire was black, and the illumination of the fire's surging brilliance did not extinguish the depth of the shadows. Darkness, alive and threatening, swept across the valley and the worn stone walls of the fortress at its center. Its dark fingertips crept along the cliff and jagged rock of the mountain with its shadow towering over the city.

At the city's core, the citadel huddled among the crumbling buildings. Inside the citadel was a castle made of stone from the surrounding structures. The power of the citizens kept the torches ablaze in the dim-lit streets. The mountains rose on the city's northern and southern borders, and the cliff rested to the east. Stones, fallen from the city walls, bruised the ground. The snow buried the wounds.

Stone houses clustered across the valley. Heavy blankets draped over the shutterless windows to keep out the cold. The doors needed to be replaced after every storm. The roofs wept frozen tears.

Soldiers marched through the mountain pass. Two of them dragged the body of a man. The arms of the men hung at their sides as they labored toward the dark city. The sentry sent a burst of flames into the air. The guards below opened the gate, allowing the soldiers to pass through the walls of the citadel.

The tired feet of the soldiers met the stone steps of the castle as servants opened the heavy wooden door from the inside. The soldiers walked into the ante room and through the doorway to the central chamber.

Within the central chamber was a wide expanse of cracked stone floor, and at the end of the broken stone mass, their leader, Hephaestus, sat on a stone throne. He stared at the men as they entered. He watched as the two soldiers dragged their prisoner.

The long body of the man on the throne hunched forward so that his pale face jutted out while the rest of his body lay hidden in the black folds of his clothes which blended into the dark stone. His long red cloak draped down like a trail of blood. His arms spread to the arms of the throne, and his hands clutched them. His golden-brown eyes fastened on the body of the man being dragged as the soldiers came closer.

Perditus stood at the side of the throne. His pale face and black hair matched that of his leader, but his eyes were gray, like storm clouds or the smoke of a rising fire. He wasn't yet fifteen years old. He would be in a matter of days, but the hours were heavy in this place, and time crept by slowly.

Perditus clenched his hands into fists. His head tilted to the floor, but his eyes strained upwards. He, too, focused on the man the soldiers held between them.

Sores and open wounds, thinly frosted over, covered the man's body. The assault had been the outcome of the dragging. Perditus wondered if they had dragged him all the way from his home despite the cries of those around him who dared not suffer the consequences of fighting back.

Perditus knew what the man was and knew why he had been brought to Omega Ray—so that Hephaestus could play with him as a cat does with a mouse.

Soldiers stepped to the side to avoid the direct gaze of the man on the throne. The two soldiers who held the prisoner remained in the center. One of them averted his eyes, but the other stared straight into the eyes of his leader.

He stood holding one arm of the prisoner. He was shorter in stature than the other soldiers, but his body was broad. He bore the partial weight of the other man with ease. He could have effortlessly held the man slung across his shoulders, but he wanted to drag him from the top of the mountain, across the snow, through the uneven ground of the city, and the stone of the fortress floor.

In contrast to the pale face of his leader, this man's skin was a reddish-brown. Right at the base of his jaw-bone, near the ear, he had a deep red birthmark.

The pale-faced leader turned to the red-faced soldier.

"This is not what I asked you to do," Hephaestus said.

The red-faced man did not avert his eyes.

"I understand that, Sir. But our given task proved once again impossible," he said. "Instead, we have brought this man. We found him near Lumina on Dustpath Road. He's a Water Elemental."

An offering, thought Perditus, so as to divert Hephaestus from thoughts of punishment.

Slowly Hephaestus's shoulders relaxed, and his body curled back against the throne.

"Is that so? I thought we would have gotten them all by now. Is he alive?"

"Yes." The red-faced man kicked the man he had been dragging, causing him to issue forth a loud grunt of pain.

Hephaestus placed his hands firmly on the arms of the throne and used them to prop himself up. He stood in front of the man.

"What's your name?"

"Elias," the man said.

Hephaestus stiffened.

"You know him, my lord," the soldier asked.

"No." Hephaestus's eyes turned back to the prisoner. "Lift up your head."

Elias did so. Bruises colored the skin around his eyes and along his jaw. His eyes were so swollen, Perditus doubted he could see what was in front of him. But he had seen worse off men find their way through the smoke.

The soldiers held Elias, and he could not wipe the dried blood from his lips. His finger moved ever so slightly. He begged, "Please, let me leave. I don't know what this man is talking about. I'm not an Elemental." Tears leaked from the slits surrounded by tortured flesh. "I'm just a man. A poor one. But I have a family, a wife and a son. I have to go back to them."

His eyes moved Perditus more than his words. He imagined that the man was found out when he took a drink from his hands absent any lake or stream. But Perditus had no desire to help the man. His sorrow was too sweet and poetic, and Perditus wanted to see what would happen.

"Fero, hold out his hand," Hephaestus demanded.

The red-faced man let the prisoner's arm slump to the ground before roughly grasping his wrist in both hands and stretching his arm out to present his palm to his leader.

Hephaestus's eyes focused on the hand of the prisoner, and the flesh caught fire.

Elias screamed and tried to pull his hand away, but Fero held it tight. With his hand ablaze, Elias closed his eyes and a mass of water, enough to fill three canteens, hung in the air and splashed down onto his hand, dousing the flames. The skin of his hand was pink, and some of it had burned away, leaving his palm raw and bloodied. The sweat on his brow mixed with the tears running down his face.

"Please, stop," he whimpered. His voice was pathetic and

desperate. He was a man with everything to lose.

"Stand him up!" Hephaestus demanded.

Fero and Dirge lifted the Water Elemental to his feet.

Elias stood unsteadily. He tried to touch his hand, thinking that might sooth it, but he flinched as his fingertips touched the burnt skin.

Hephaestus circled him slowly, eyeing him like a vulture considering its next meal. He stopped in front of him.

"Make Water dance for me," he ordered.

"What?" Elias asked, confused by this request. He had been dragged all this way to be a source of entertainment.? It was a cruel joke to be sure.

Hephaestus closed his eyes, and the prisoner's arm began to tingle with heat.

"Wait! Stop! Please!" Elias screamed like a man whose body was over the fire.

"You know the consequences," Hephaestus said, his voice even and calm. "Now, make Water dance for me."

Elias closed his eyes and concentrated. Slowly, a string of water began to twirl in the air in the wide space between the prisoner and the pale-faced man. It was the narrowest stream, without a bank, its source unseen. It spun into an orb and continued to twist in the air. The tiny strings of water twined around each other as Elias focused.

He was an artist in that moment, painting a picture like only he could. He had the eyes of the entire room on the moving water. It was so exceptional and so stunning.

Only Fero was immune to its charms.

It was a perfect watery chrysalis. Elias moved his hands as if molding it, but his flesh never touched it.

Perditus didn't know what he was thinking, but the prisoner had a smile on his face and tears in his eyes. They weren't the tears of a man fighting for his life, but a deeper sorrow that had happiness at its core.

Hephaestus gazed at the display like he had found some rare and beautiful animal.

He reached out to touch the watery orb with a trembling hand.

"Sir!" Fero warned.

"Quiet!" Hephaestus hissed.

His hand inched closer, the water hitting the light of the torches and reflecting it onto his palm. A breath away from the watery orb, his fingers grazed the cool water. But he flinched away as if afraid to touch it.

Perditus thought he heard a tiny gasp of awe escape his lips.

The Water Elemental opened his eyes wider than before despite the swollen flesh surrounding them, and a powerful jet of water from the core of the orb shot toward Hephaestus with profound speed. Hephaestus turned it to steam before impact.

Elias only meant to distract, not to harm. He knew he couldn't hurt this man. He turned to run, but Fero's auburn hand grabbed his shoulder and yanked him back.

Elias was on his knees again, struggling beneath the weight of Fero's hand.

Elias screamed. Smoke issued from his mouth. His insides burned, cooking his organs, filling the room with a rank, meaty scent.

Fero's eyes widened. A look of despair lighted upon his face. "No," he shouted. "We need him!"

But it was too late. Elias slumped to the ground. Smoke trailed from his lips like a serpent.

Fero, looking at his leader desperately, still held the man's limp arm.

"What do you mean we need him?" Hephaestus asked.

Fero continued to look at the dead man with a gaze that made Perditus think that he could stare at the corpse forever.

Hephaestus made a wide circle around the body as if death was a disease he could catch. He sat back upon his throne. "Why would I need him?"

Fero's eyes were anchored to the body, but he responded

to his leader's question. "The sphere sanctums . . . we have yet to see a Protector." At this, Fero looked up into the eyes of Hephaestus.

The light glanced off his golden eyes, making fire dance in his irises.

"Fear in my men?" Hephaestus leaned forward in his seat, like a python striking out at its prey.

Fero did not flinch. "Not fear, sir, but a barrier that we cannot break, not without a balance of the elements. The doors to the sanctums remain closed to us. A strange haze floats over them."

"Then tear them down."

"We can't. My men have tried everything. I exhausted my element trying to burn the doors down. Something is keeping us out."

"What?"

"Above the sanctum doors are the symbols for the elements, all of the elements."

Silence hung in the air.

"Go," Hephaestus demanded of the other soldiers.

They left, taking with them the body of Elias.

Only Fero and Perditus remained with their leader.

After the other soldiers had gone, Hephaestus didn't speak for a long time. Time had never crept slower in Omega Ray.

When he opened his mouth to speak it was like the flames had grown in his eyes. "So, you are telling me I need a Water Elemental?"

"That's what I'm saying, sir."

"That man's family?"

Fero shook his head.

Hephaestus put his head in his hands.

After years of taking Water Elementals to their graves, he needed one. The thought made Perditus smirk.

Fero interrupted the silence. Perditus wondered if silence was one of the few things too heavy for him to bare.

"The boy," Fero said, "he was taken to Element."

Perditus's fists tightened when Fero changed the subject. What right did he have to meddle in his joy?

Hephaestus drew his back away from his seat. "Are you sure it's him? It's been years since he ran away."

"Yes, sir. He is the reflection of his father. Should I bring him back?"

Perditus cringed.

"No," Hephaestus said.

At this, Perditus grinned. His down-turned face hid the smile.

"He could be useful in Element," Hephaestus said, "He is a brat, but he was always strong in his element. I'll have my men keep in touch with him. He can be my eyes in that place."

"You want me to arrange for that?"

"Yes, and soon. I don't want him getting too comfortable, thinking he has escaped me. There's nothing worse in a man than the thought of ease. It halts progress and self-improvement."

Perditus wondered if Hephaestus had ever suffered a moment of ease in his life. Maybe when he was a baby in his mother's arms, but Perditus could never imagine him as an innocent or vulnerable child.

He assumed that his cold, pale skin was hard as marble all his life and that the fire had always lived inside him, keeping his rage alive.

Hephaestus wasn't a person, but a monument. Something that could not be reasoned with and had no reason to be soothed.

"What about the sanctums? What do you need us to do?" Fero stood with his hands behind his back.

Perditus lifted his head, but neither Fero nor Hephaestus paid him a glance. He was like a shadow, warranting no consideration.

"Tell the men to search Mirmina for Water Elementals. I must have left at least one alive."

Fero looked at him without expression. He hadn't delivered that man all the way from Dustpath to serve as his leader's plaything. He sought him out. It wasn't Fero's cruelty alone that made him drag Elias to Omega Ray. Fero was angry that Elias had made himself so difficult to find. Fero didn't know that Hephaestus would dismantle his cargo without granting him a mere moment to explain its purpose. Fero had journeyed for years to decipher the secrets of the Sphere Sanctums. How many of those years were dedicated to finding that Water Elemental?

Perditus knew Fero would calm his rage on someone else. He wouldn't challenge Hephaestus. He couldn't blame him for his rash act.

Hephaestus twined his fingers together.

Perditus lowered his head. He watched Hephaestus's shadow upon the floor, and from that shadow came words.

"One day, I will get the spheres, and I will out balance everything."

1

THE FOUNTAIN

SARA curled her legs up so her feet could stay warm beneath the small blanket. Her bed creaked as she turned. Her eyes searched the room. The other girls rested in their beds. Some of them tossed and turned in an effort to get warm. Sara waited and listened to the rain outside. Drops hit her window in a steady rhythm.

The rain reminded her of fear, smoke, tears, and that singular night. She tried to overcome the rain's hypnotic power, but her eyes were drooping, and her mind was pulling her away.

The room filled with smoke, and the water in Sara's eyes blurred her vision. Her mother lifted her up. Glass shattered as her father smashed the back window with his elbow. Her mother helped her out the window, just large enough for four-year-old Sara to fit through. She told Sara to run. Crying and shaking, Sara ran from the house. She hid in the overgrowth near the forest and watched as the smoke became heavier and the fire surrounded the little cottage. Rain began to fall.

Thunder woke Sara. She sat up and pulled her blanket to her chin. Lightning flashed, brightening the room. Her eyes searched the space to find the other girls asleep. The thunder had not awoken them, and their tossing had ceased.

Sara tried to get out of bed as quietly as she could, but the bed squealed as she stepped down. She poked her head under the bed and retrieved a kettle full of water. She sat down on the floor and pulled the kettle toward her. Her eyes focused on the water.

"Please, please, please," she whispered.

Lightning flashed again, and for a moment, her face was reflected in the water. She never saw herself properly before. The orphanage had no mirrors. She wondered if she had grown to look like her mother. She was fourteen, yet shorter than other girls her age. Her mother was tall and slender, her movements fluid like the power she possessed.

She concentrated on the water.

"Come on, come on."

But the water didn't move. It didn't ripple.

Sara closed her eyes. Her mother's eyes were hazel, and her hair was light brown. Her voice was even and soft. Her father's eyes were green, and his smile made her feel at ease. Sara drew their faces in her mind's eye. She struggled to remember who they were, but being so young, she remembered only warm embraces, gentle words, sometimes harsh words, but more so the gentle ones.

Opening her eyes, she turned her attention back to the water. She glanced toward the window as lightning lit the glass.

Drop. Splash.

Water seeped over the edge of the kettle as ripples drifted from the center.

Sara focused more closely, hoping to send the water spilling again. But as she focused, a drop of water landed into the pot, causing the water to ripple and spill over the edge.

She looked up. Another drop of water dislodged from the ceiling and dropped down into the pot.

Sara sighed. She pushed the kettle back under the bed. She got her blanket and used it to mop up the water that had spilled. It was no use. The water continued to leak from the ceiling. The old pot could catch the drops, she thought. But that would only make the water in the kettle splash, causing more of a mess. Sara would go without dinner if Ms. Fiora discovered she took the kettle from the kitchen.

She crawled back into bed, carrying the wet blanket with her. She spread the blanket over the end of the bed to allow it to dry. Reaching under the mattress, she retrieved a necklace. The necklace had a blue gemstone in the shape of a raindrop hanging from a delicate woven cord. She clenched the gemstone in her fist and, colder than before, she tried to go back to sleep.

BLANKETS rustled against sheets as Sara awoke. The other girls were making their beds. She got up quickly to make her own. Taking the damp blanket from the end of the bed, she placed it over the sheets and smoothed out the dank wrinkles. As she bent over the bed, patting down the blanket, she caught the faint scent of rain.

Years ago, she overheard her father and mother as they talked in their dining room. Peering from behind the paneled wall, Sara watched her parents. Her mother sat at the small, pine dinner table, and her father stood across from her. He rubbed his forehead.

"I should go with you," she said. "I can reason with him."

"No, Sara needs you, and I have to protect both of you. He won't stop until he's killed us all."

Her mother knitted her brow. "I don't understand."

"No one can understand the mind of a madman."

"Sara?"

Sara was leaning over the bed. She turned her head. Miranda raked through her long hair with an old comb. The teeth of the comb were missing in places. "It's time to eat. You're not getting sick, are you?"

"No, I was thinking."

"About what?"

Sara sighed as she smoothed down the hem of her blanket and turned to take her dress out of the small drawer beside her bed.

"My mother. I don't want to forget her face."

"I don't remember my mother's face," Miranda said. "But she had long hair. I used to brush it for her and curl up in it at night. This was her comb." She held it up for Sara to see.

Miranda was twelve years old, but she was tall and thin. She combed her hair all day, and she flinched when any of the older girls offered to braid it for her.

The girls had their chores. The older girls helped in the kitchen and laundered the clothes and sheets, while the younger girls cleaned the floors and washed the dishes.

In addition to scrubbing floors, Sara walked to the market every three days. She used to go alone, but her thoughts brought her to her parents, their powers, and the question of why she lacked their gifts. She asked Ms. Fiora if Miranda could accompany her on the long walks into town.

The market lay in the center of town. Buildings sprawled around the market square. The school of Element sat on a hill, above the buildings. Its ivy-covered, stone walls stood stark against the pale sky. Element was where Elementals went to train. Elementals could manipulate and call the elements. Sara hoped to be an Elemental and to harness the power her parents had.

To block the sun, woven cloths covered the tops of the stands in the square. Various smells accosted market-goers, but the most prominent was the odor of dust and feathers.

Elementals stood between stands and performed tricks. A huge crowd surrounded the Wind Elementals, who played with the autumn leaves, making them swirl and dance. A Fire Elemental sent rings of flame into the air. He was middle-aged and had a scar going from under his ear, along his jaw, and down his neck. People made wide circles around him, giving him narrowed-eyed glances as they passed.

Sara noticed him before when she went to the market. In that mysterious way that people can feel the eyes of others on them, she felt his eyes bore into her back when she turned away from him. She bit her lip.

"Sara, there he is again," Miranda said, "Do you think he works for Hephaestus?"

"I don't know." Sara peered at him from over her shoulder.

"He sure looks scary enough."

Sara turned away from the Fire Elemental. At one of the stands, the merchant sold paper and charcoal. Sara jingled the money in her dress pocket as she stared at the paper.

She forced her eyes away from the paper merchant and walked to the stand that sold eggs and chickens. The chickens were frantic in their cages, causing loose feathers to fly into the air as they moved. The uproarious clucking of the distraught chickens, fighting in vain to be free of their cages, made this stand the loudest in the market. The merchant smiled as Sara approached. He was a calm man among chaos, with a pleasant smile on his face as the feathers of the chickens rested on his shoulders. Sara tried not to look at the struggling chickens.

"Half a dozen eggs, please." She held out the money. She memorized how many sparklings she needed.

"Aren't you one of the little girls from Ocean's Light? Half a dozen doesn't seem like enough to feed all of you."

"Ms. Fiora likes eggs in the mornings."

Sara's eyes drifted to the paper and charcoal.

"I see you're always staring at that paper," he said with a wink.

"I'm saving up for it."

"I didn't know you were given an allowance?"

Sara looked away.

The merchant handed her the eggs. Sara placed them one by one in the basket and covered them with a woolen cloth. She was careful not to let the eggs break. The girls whispered a story about a girl who used to live in the home. She tripped on the way from the market. The eggs cracked on the cobblestone path. After Ms. Fiora was done with her, the girl ran away from the orphanage and never returned.

On the road back, Sara took one coin from her pocket, knelt down, and slipped the coin into her shoe. Miranda combed her hair and hummed to herself as she skipped along the path.

She stopped and turned around. "Aren't you always the one who says Ms. Fiora will be mad if we're late?" Her hands were on her hips.

"I thought something got into my shoe." Sara stood.

"Just shake it out."

"It's fine now. You're right. Let's go."

When Sara and Miranda returned, Mari, one of the older girls, was crying on the steps in front of the house. Rosaleen, the nurse comforted her. "You'll see your father again. He's waiting among the Aethers in the heavens."

Sara and Miranda bowed their heads and climbed the steps to the door. Sara looked back at Mari before she stepped inside.

Ms. Fiora stood in her office, gazing upon the decorative box that rested upon the mantel. The girls believed Ms. Fiora kept the ashes of her late husband in that box.

Sara handed the money in her pocket to Ms. Fiora. Ms. Fiora stood tall, her shoulders back, and eyes at a constant downward tilt. Her dress was freshly ironed, the white collar pressed firmly down. Sara's skin tingled as Ms. Fiora counted the coins.

"Prices are still up, I see."

While the other girls did their chores, Sara returned to the bedroom. She took the coin from her shoe and opened her drawer. Inside, under an old handkerchief, was another coin.

She placed the second coin under the handkerchief and closed the drawer.

Weeks ago, she returned with fewer loaves of bread, telling Ms. Fiora she didn't have enough money for the extra loaves. The next time Sara went to the market, Ms. Fiora had given her extra sparklings for the bread. Sara could have taken all the extra coins, but decided that would be too risky.

That night, the wind beat against the window above Sara's bed. She thought of Mari who lost her father. She wondered what happened to him, if he died like her parents. She waited with her hands up to her chin clenching the raindrop necklace until she heard the gentle snoring of the other girls and felt confident they were asleep. She slinked down to floor, placed the necklace back under the mattress, and pulled the kettle of water from beneath the bed.

She stared into the water until her eyes hurt and clouds covered the dim light of the moon. Too dark to see, Sara replaced the kettle and climbed back into bed. She retrieved the necklace, and holding it, went to sleep.

HER mother woke her in the dead of the night. Her face was pink. Beads of sweat patterned her forehead. A strange and surprisingly loud sound came from outside, a crackling that roared. The fire surrounded the house on all sides. Her father tried desperately to put out the flames that filled the cottage. He drenched the flames with water flowing from his fingertips, but they would not go out.

"We have to get her out!" her father shouted.

Her mother ran, carrying Sara to the back of the cottage. Her father broke a small window. Her mother ripped the necklace with the teardrop gem from her neck and gave it to Sara.

"Always keep it close, my love."

Her father extinguished the flames outside the window. "Hurry," he said. "I don't know how long I can hold them back." Her mother placed her through the broken window. "Run, baby, and don't look back."

Sara ran. She tripped. She glanced toward the house. She expected her parents to climb through after her, but the flames rose in front of the window.

Sara felt warm tears rushing from her eyes aided by grief and smoke. A laugh resounded in the distance, and the fire rose from the cottage as the tears blurred Sara's vision. She did as her mother said and hid behind a wild shrub not far from her home.

The smoke rose and twisted in the night air. A cold, stiff rain fell, putting out the fire, but it was too late. The smoke smothered Sara's parents before the fire ever reached them.

Strong hands lifted her from among the leaves.

MARI was absent from breakfast the next morning. Sara stared into her bowl as Miranda talked and combed her hair. After breakfast, Sara carted the tray of bowls and dishes to the kitchen.

She rolled up the sleeves of her dress and dipped the first plate into the basin of water. Taking the bar of hard soap, she rubbed it between the palms of her hands. The soap would not lather. Sara stopped and put down the soap.

Faint sobs came from the back of the kitchen.

She dried her hands on the worn old dish rag and walked in the direction of the sobbing. Behind the large pots and sacks of potatoes on the floor was Mari.

Sara knelt down, took the handkerchief from her dress pocket, and gave it to Mari.

Mari looked up. Her sobs quieted. Embarrassment overcame her sadness for a moment. She took the cloth from Sara and wiped the tears off her cheeks.

"Thank you."

Sara got up to return to the dishes.

"Wait. Stay with me for a little while."

Sara knelt beside Mari. "Do you want some breakfast?" Sara asked. "I think there's still some porridge left over."

Mari shook her head. Her hand gripped the worn cloth.

Silence hung in the air for some time.

Sara struggled for words as if the silence would destroy them both had she not found them.

"What happened to your father?"

Mari glared at her.

Sara looked down at her hands.

"My father," Mari started. Her voice was softer than her glare. "My father died." More tears leaked from her eyes. "He was a soldier for the Resistance. Hephaestus's men killed him. I got the letter yesterday."

Sara was aware that Hephaestus was the Fire Elemental everyone in Mirmina feared, but she knew very little of what he had done. Her parents had sheltered her from it.

"The messenger gave me this." Mari held up a silver band for Sara to see. The band was large enough to be worn around the arm. "When he was alive, my father wore this as a symbol of his allegiance to the Resistance and to the protection of Mirmina." She balled up the material and threw the silver band across the room.

"Was your father an Elemental?"

"No." She sobbed. "He was just a man, but Hephaestus killed him like a beast."

Sara fought for something to say. "My parents died too. I was with them when it happened, but I don't remember much. I dream about it sometimes, but I forget the details in the morning."

Tears dripped into Mari's hands.

Sara touched her arm. "I'm sorry. No one can say anything to make you feel right again. I just wanted you to know you aren't alone. Everyone here lost somebody."

Mari stabbed her with her eyes. "My grief is cheap. That's what you're saying."

Sara shook her head. She stood. "I don't know what I'm saying. Please, forgive me."

Sara left the kitchen. She might get into trouble for leaving the dishes unwashed, but she failed to sooth Mari. *What was I thinking telling her her grief was on an assembly line?*

A crash came from the kitchen. Sara ran back inside.

A basket lay on its side. Cracked shells and egg guts littered the floor.

"What happened here?" Ms. Fiora stormed into the room.

Sara looked to Mari. Mari's lips trembled.

"It was me," Sara blurted out. "I broke the eggs."

Ms. Fiora grabbed her arm. "What happened, girl?"

"I slipped, backed into the shelf. The basket fell. I tried to catch it, but…"

"You know what eggs cost." Ms. Fiora pulled Sara out of the kitchen and dragged her to the anteroom where the girls read and played jacks and dice. The girls stopped their activities and looked up at Sara and Ms. Fiora.

Ms. Fiora left the room.

"Sara, what—" Miranda stopped and sank back into the crowd.

Ms. Fiora returned with the switch. "Palms up."

Sara slowly offered her hands.

Ms. Fiora snapped the switch across her palms. The pain stung and left heat. Ms. Fiora continued to strike her hands. Sara's palms burned and itched, but she held her hands out.

Mari ran into the room. Sara thought she would speak up and tell Ms. Fiora that what Sara told her was a lie. Mari was the one who broke the eggs. *Don't say anything*, Sara thought. *Ms. Fiora will finish with me. But if you say anything, she'll snap your palms and give me double for lying.* But Mari bit her tongue. Her eyes never left Sara's reddened palms until the punishment was done.

Ms. Fiora snapped the switch one last, biting time and moved away from Sara.

Sara tried rubbing her raw, itchy palms, but they stung worse. She left the anteroom and sat on her bed. Minutes later, Rosaleen walked into the room. "Let me see." She rubbed a gel on Sara's palms. The itching and burning dissipated.

"There," Rosaleen said. "It's not so bad. I've seen worse.

This should heal by morning."

Rosaleen patted Sara's arm. Mari entered the room as Rosaleen left. Her eyes were on the floor.

"You didn't have to do that for me, you know," Mari said.

"Why did you smash the eggs?" Sara asked.

"I was angry," Mari said. "You were right. All the girls here have lost someone. But my father . . . he didn't have to join the Resistance. He should have stayed with me. And now he's dead."

Sara looked at her hands.

"Why did you lie for me?"

Sara bit her lip. She was part of the reason Ms. Fiora was so upset about the eggs. Money was tight. Sara was stealing it. "I felt bad about what I said. You have just as much right as anyone to grieve your father. There shouldn't be a contest for who's in the most pain."

THREE days later, Sara and Miranda made the trip to the market. This time, Sara had put the two coins into her shoe. They slid back and forth as she walked.

"What was your mother like?" Miranda asked as they walked to the market.

Sara walked with her head down. "I don't remember much, but she was beautiful. She cared for me. She had powers like my father. They were Elementals."

"How come you aren't an Elemental?"

"I don't know."

Miranda took the comb out of her pocket. She stopped walking. Sara stopped too and looked back at her. Miranda was looking down at the comb. "This wasn't my mother's. When I was five years old, one of the older girls gave it to me before she left. I don't remember my mother. She left me outside of the chapel in Caleena when I was born."

Miranda cried, and Sara rubbed her arm. She wiped her tears with the backs of her hands.

Sara offered to hold the basket, and Miranda gave it to her.

Once in the market, Miranda's tears had dried. Sara suggested they split up to make fast work of their task and impress Ms. Fiora. She gave the basket to Miranda and told her to get the bread, while she would get the potatoes and beans. She handed Miranda coins for the bread and hurried off to the stand that sold the paper.

She stopped in front of the stand. She looked at her palms. Ms. Fiora's punishment had faded, but Sara remembered the sting. She looked back at the paper and charcoal. She swallowed her fear and approached the stand.

"I want three sheets of paper and a stick of charcoal, please," she told the vendor.

"That'll be three sparklings."

Sara took off her shoe and dumped the two coins into her palm. She retrieved one more from her pocket. As she felt for the coin in her pocket her fingers grazed the smooth surface of the teardrop gem of her mother's necklace.

The vendor grinned.

He looked down at the coins in her hand.

"You live in the orphanage, don't you?"

Sara nodded.

"Those aren't your coins."

Sara pressed her lips together and shook her downturned head.

"You shouldn't steal, not even from a bitter, old woman."

Without taking her coins, the vendor offered her a few sheets of paper and a stick of charcoal.

Sara looked at it tentatively.

"Go on, take it," he said. "When everyone in Mirmina wants one of your drawings, you can sign one for me."

"Thank you, sir."

Sara regrettably folded the sheets twice so that they would fit into her pocket. She hurried to buy the potatoes and beans and met Miranda at the fountain. Sara put the small sack of potatoes and the jar of beans into the basket at Miranda's feet. Miranda seemed to be mesmerized by the dancing of the Wind

Elementals, who were making leaves and ribbons twirl in the breeze around them as they danced.

"I wonder what it would be like to be an Elemental."

The Fire Elemental with the scar was watching them from a distance.

"It's time to leave," Sara said.

"Wait, I have an idea." Miranda took off her shoes and got up on the ledge of the fountain.

"What are you doing?"

"Take off your shoes."

Miranda reached down to give Sara a hand. "Come on, it'll be fun."

Sara sighed, but she took off her shoes and took Miranda's hand.

Once they both stood on the fountain's ledge, Miranda began to twirl and dance like the Wind Elementals in the square.

Sara looked down into the clear water of the fountain. Closing her eyes, she remembered the face of her mother. She danced, imagining that she could call Water to swirl around her. She moved her feet along the warm, gritty stone of the fountain's ledge. She felt a cool, light feeling on the underside of her feet.

The marketplace became very quiet.

Sara opened her eyes. The eyes of everyone in the market were on her. Miranda had gotten down from the fountain's ledge, and she too was staring at Sara. Sara's feet no longer touched the grainy stone of the ledge. Beneath her feet, the water glistened in the sun.

2

A NEW APPRENTICE

SARA stared at the glistening water beneath her feet. She curled her toes, and they dipped down into the cool liquid. All the years she tried to get water to move and failed left Sara thinking that she did not possess her parents' gift. Now she felt the full power of it.

It was strange. She hadn't concentrated like she had for hours, watching the stagnant water in that crude kettle, yet she stood on the clear surface as it was effortless.

She looked around to see if anyone else noticed her new-found power. The people in the market had stopped their shopping and stood around the fountain to watch Sara's dance. However, they did not watch her in awe and wonder as they had with the Wind Elementals or in fear as with the Fire Elemental. Instead, they stared at her as if she was a rare creature that shouldn't exist.

Tense because of the crowd's unexpected reaction, Sara stepped out of the fountain's cool, gently swirling water. Her feet, once flat against the water's surface, now moved out onto the warm, stone ledge and to the ground below. She stood next to the fountain and gazed at the water, swirling where her feet had left it and the watery footprints stamped on the fountain's edge.

A crowd of people gathered around her. "It can't be," she heard someone say among the whispering and sighs of surprise. The crowd was swelling to an overwhelming size. She hadn't remembered this many people in the market before she danced. Unable to see beyond the crowd, Sara began to panic. Someone grabbed her hand and pulled her through the sea of people. *The Fire Elemental!*

"Wait, what are you doing?" Sara tried to struggle out of his grasp. She remembered when Miranda suggested he might be a follower of Hephaestus. Her struggles were in vain. His grasp was too strong.

"Don't worry," he said, "I'm taking you someplace safe."

"Where?"

"To Element."

In Element, trainers helped young Elementals develop their skills. Sara had heard of it in stories. It was the oldest building in Elementa, older than the library or the marketplace.

"Why are you taking me there right now?" Sara asked.

"You belong there," the scarred Fire Elemental said.

Once they were far from the market, the Fire Elemental slowed his pace and loosened his grip on Sara's hand. Sara wriggled her hand out of his loosened grasp. Once free, she shook the pain from her hand. The skin was bright pink. Sara wondered if the color would ever fade.

They walked through the streets surrounded by towering buildings. The buildings stood fifteen feet high in packed rows, making the dirt streets narrow.

The Fire Elemental's scar was light pink against his dark skin, but had looked white from a distance. The scarred skin was uneven, and purple and blue veins were visible through the thin membrane. *Why had a Fire Elemental allowed himself to burn?*

"How do I know I can trust you?" she asked.

He looked straight ahead. His face was discerning.

"I'm Talon."

"Why did you pull me away from all those people? I'll have to go back soon. I can't leave my friend. We're supposed to go to the market together, and we're supposed to be back by a certain time or we'll be punished."

"You belong in Element."

"Wait." Sara stopped walking, and Talon turned around. "I can't leave."

"Do you want to go back?" His eyes looked stern, but not angry.

Sara looked back toward the orphanage and into the distance toward Element. Ms. Fiora was not an Elemental nor would she have any interest in helping Sara with her newfound power. *If I went back, would she let me go if I changed my mind?* Trainers worked at the school, other Water Elementals who could help her hone her skills. "No. I . . . I want to go to Element."

Talon looked at her for what seemed like a long time. But before she could read his expression, he turned back and continued on his way. Sara followed.

They walked two miles before meeting the steps of Element. Element was on the hill. Ivy covered the stone walls, and green moss grew between the cracks. On the oak door hung a brass knocker.

The Fire Elemental swung the brass knocker three times. It was an odd knock with uneven pauses in between. The door groaned as a short woman opened it. She had a small frame, and faint wrinkles gathered on her forehead. Her hair frizzed out in wispy curls. A smile brightened her face.

"Talon!" she exclaimed.

She smiled so widely and so quickly, her eyes glazed over. She looked like her mind might be in a haze, but steadily advancing on her face was a look of relief.

"It's like you've come back from the dead. Where have you been?" She smoothed out her hair.

"I don't have time," Talon responded.

"You're not leaving, are you? Please, stay longer this time."

Sara stood, half-hidden behind Talon and his long coat.

"Come in." The words rushed out of the woman's mouth and sounded like an order.

Talon and Sara entered, and the woman closed the door behind them.

"Who is this?" Her eyes pierced Sara. "Not your daughter? Doesn't look at all like you with your dark hair and her light brown. She must look more like her moth—"

"No," Talon said. "She's a new apprentice."

Sara looked at the ground. She knew what it felt like to be watched like a rare animal let loose from its cage. But this woman judged her for entirely different reasons.

"Oh," she said, "I'm sorry. I thought…" The woman stopped mid-sentence and smiled, "I'm Brina. Who are you?"

"Sara."

"It's not every day Talon brings in a new apprentice. In fact, you are only the second."

"Brina," Talon stopped her.

Brina smiled. "Would you like me to take your coat, Talon? You could stay awhile."

"I'm fine. I don't think I'll stay very long."

Brina's smile faded. She turned her attention to Sara. "I'll show you to your room."

"My room," Sara said, "as in singular."

"Of course," Brina said. She gave Talon a look that read: *Where did you find this girl?*

Brina turned to lead them to the room, but Talon grabbed her arm and leaned closer to her. "Give her one of the rooms on the top floor," he said.

"The top floor. We haven't been able to fill it since . . . Well, you know. She would be all alone up there."

Talon held her in his grasp and looked into her eyes. His stare was not menacing or fierce, but determined. He held that stare until she nodded.

Brina led Sara and Talon through the entrance hall and up the stone stairs. The stone steps felt hard beneath Sara's feet. *My shoes? I must have left them at the fountain.* They reached the top floor, and Brina opened the doorway to the hall. Rows of doors lined either side of the long hallway.

"Where is everyone?" Sara asked.

"At mid-day, the apprentices go outside to train."

"When will I be able to train?" she asked.

"You can start tomorrow. I'll set you up with a trainer. What is your element?" Brina asked, as they walked down the hall. Sara opened her mouth to answer, but Talon pulled Brina aside and whispered something in her ear. Brina's eyes widened. "No." She looked at Sara.

"I thought it best not to say it too loud," Talon said.

"Why?" Sara asked.

Brina gently pushed her along. "This room is unoccupied. It's yours."

She opened a door at the end of the hall. A large bed with white, satin sheets rested in the center, and blue curtains hung on the window in the back of the room. The cream-colored carpet felt soft under Sara's bare feet.

"We'll let you get more comfortable." Brina closed the door behind Sara.

Sara fell to her knees and ran her fingers through the soft carpet. She imagined that the bed must be twice as soft. She sat down on it. She touched cotton once in the marketplace. A vendor brought it from a village across the sea where he said it grew in a large field. The bed felt like that.

An end table sat on one side of the bed. Sara took the paper and charcoal out of her dress pocket and put them on the table. The charcoal had coated the inside of her pocket with black dust. She tried to smooth the paper out on the table to make the folds less apparent. She placed the charcoal and the paper in the drawer.

Reaching into her pocket, she retrieved her mother's necklace. She looked at the necklace for some time. She had never worn it as her mother had. Tying the woven string around her neck, Sara secured the necklace. She held the raindrop gem between her fingers and looked into its clear blue surface before letting it fall to her chest.

The window caught her eye. Outside, the field stretched to a tall, stone wall. On the field, apprentices practiced their elements. They ranged in ages. A group in the center made leaves dance on the Wind. Others summoned Fire to light torches. Earth Elementals stooped with their hands over the ground, causing saplings to sprout.

But no Water Elementals practiced their element. In the distance, was a lake where Water Elementals could train, but it was abandoned.

She was distracted by a boy who seemed to have greater command over his element than the others. He forced his element into the shape of a hand. The Lightning caused the fingers to look thin and wiry. Every time he clenched his own hand, the lightning hand clenched also.

He was a puppet master, and his puppet was bright and terrible. But it was also beautiful. Sara watched him for a long time.

AFTER Brina had shown Sara to her room, she walked back down the hall with Talon. She took his arm gently.

"A Water Elemental, it's impossible," Brina whispered.

He turned to her. "There is nothing impossible about it."

"You know as well as I do that Hephaestus—"

"Don't tell her," Talon said.

"She'll find out someday," Brina warned as they continued down the hall. "We can't keep her shadowed forever. One day she'll find out. She'll find out what she must do."

Talon stopped. "I did not send her here to die. She will not battle Hephaestus. I only wanted to bring her to Element so she could learn to protect herself. Nothing more."

"But we have no one to train her," Brina said.

"What about Spire?"

"Spire? She's a Wind Elemental."

"She protected the sphere, didn't she?" Talon said. "Spire's strong, and she'll know what to teach Sara."

Brina walked behind him, watching his labored steps. She touched his shoulder. "You should rest. I don't know where you've been, but you look exhausted."

Talon turned back to her. He had conditioned himself to avoid her eyes. Looking at the floor boards, he said, "Alright, I'll stay the night."

Brina had to control a smile from carelessly spreading across her face. "I'll get a room ready for you."

As she turned away, she felt Talon's eyes on her.

"Will you stay with me tonight?"

Brina's breath caught in her chest. She knew she had to respond to him before he thought too hard about what he had said.

"Of course," she choked out, trying to sound relaxed.

Brina led the way. Her room was on the second floor. She opened the door, and Talon walked inside. The bed was made, and nothing was out of place. Brina darted in after him to smooth out the smallest wrinkles on the bed quilt.

"I'm sorry. It's not the best." She stood from the bed. "I'll go now and let you get some rest before dinner."

"Wait." Talon's hands were at his sides.

"What is it?"

"I want you to stay. Do you still have the playing cards?"

"Yes. Yes, I do. They're in the closet."

She walked to the dresser in the corner of the room and opened the heavy, wooden doors. Reaching into the back of the dresser, she pulled out a worn box. She lifted the lid, careful that the contents were out of Talon's view. Inside the box were various trinkets, including an old ring, letters, and the playing cards. She took the playing cards out of the box, replaced the lid, and carefully returned the box to its place in the back of the dresser.

Sitting down at the table by the window, she waited for Talon. Talon made his way to the table and sat down. She handed him the playing cards. Talon held the cards in his hands gingerly. His fingers rounded the rough, burnt edges of the cards.

"They wouldn't be like that if you didn't get so upset when you lose," Brina said.

"No one likes to lose, but I always lose against you." He shuffled the cards and dealt them.

"This time I'll let you win."

"No, don't do that. I need to learn to win on my own. If you let me win, what's to keep me playing?"

Brina changed the subject. "I've been happy here."

"Good."

"I mean, it's comfortable. I miss home, but I've made friends over the years. I . . . I missed you, though."

Talon kept his eyes on the table. He stared at the grain of the wood for a long time before he put the cards back down and got up from his seat. "I shouldn't stay."

"Wait, Talon. Please sit back down." She got up, and crossed the room to stand in front of the door.

"I can't. I'm sorry." Talon stared at the floor.

"Please, I won't say anything else about . . . missing you."

"I'm sorry." His hands clenched into fists.

"Stop it." Brina stepped away from the door. "You can't just come and go like this. Where have you been?"

"I haven't been far." His voice came in a low growl.

"Where?" Tears started.

"Here, in Elementa."

"How long?"

"A few years."

"Years? And you never thought to come and see me?" She stood in front of him.

He avoided her gaze.

"Talon?"

"I have to go."

Brina put her hands on her hips. "Do you have a family now? Is that what it is?"

"No, that's not it."

"What is *it*?" Her voice was desperate, and she could feel the lump in her throat growing.

Talon kept his eyes away from her and walked out the door. His tattered coat flapped behind him, and his worn boots didn't make a sound.

Brina waited for some time. She could not hear his feet light upon the stairs. But, she heard the heavy door open and shut.

She rushed down the stairs and ran to the door, yanking it open.

Talon was at the foot of the stone steps.

Brina fought back the sob building in her chest.

"Talon, wait!"

He paused ever so slightly before continuing. But he didn't turn back.

The vines on the walls of Element grew as Brina watched him go.

3

FROM THE WINDOW

THE next morning, the sky was cloudless, and the sunlight shone in from the window of Sara's new room. Sara awoke to voices outside on the field. She made her way to the window. Elemental youths practiced below. The boy from the other day walked within the shadow of the building. He turned to wait for a friend when Sara caught his eye. She waved.

She thought he saw her, but he didn't wave back. He turned to his friend, who joined him in the shade. The other boy had light brown hair and dark skin from being out in the sun.

Sara jumped. A knock at the door pulled her eyes from the window. Before Sara could answer it, Brina opened the door and walked in. A tall, younger woman came in behind her. The woman was dressed in black, and her dark hair was tied back in a braid. A ring hung on a chain around her neck. Her lips were thin, and her deep brown eyes held a tint red that gleamed in her irises when they caught the light.

Brina bent and placed a basin bowl next to the door. She stood and clasped her hands in front her. "This is Lady Spire." She looked up at the tall woman. "Spire, this is your new apprentice, Sara."

Sara didn't know what to expect of her trainer, but she hadn't imagined she would look so severe. Spire reminded her of Ms. Fiora. Her palms tingled. They no longer burned, but the memory was fresh.

"I'll let you both get started." Brina left the room and closed the door.

"It's nice to meet you, Lady—"

"Call me Spire. Everyone in Element has been calling me *Lady*, and I don't want you to pick up the habit," the woman in black said.

Spire wasted no time.

"We should begin now," Spire said. "Show me what you can do." Spire went to the door to get the bowl and held it out in front of Sara.

Sara's eyes darted. "What do you mean?"

"Call Water into this bowl."

Sara stared at the empty bowl, not wanting to tell this new Ms. Fiora what she must inevitably tell her. "I . . . I can't."

Spire's eyes narrowed. "You can't?"

"I've started. I didn't know if I was going to get my element. I had been practicing, but—"

"What can you do?"

"Well . . . I danced in the fountain on the water like it was solid ground. But I've never called Water out of thin air."

"That's impressive. Highly impressive. But you can't *call* your element?"

Sara shook her head.

"How old are you?"

"I'm fourteen."

"I took you for younger, but old enough to know how to call your element."

"I'm . . . sorry. Is that bad?"

"It's unusual. I'm going to fill this water with water. You'll practice with that. In the meantime, Brina should be bringing your breakfast up. I expect you'll finish it, and after that we'll get started."

"Why can't I have breakfast with the others?"

Spire hesitated, not turning around. "That's a question for Brina."

She left the room and closed the door behind her. Sara wondered why Spire hadn't called Water into the basin herself, so she could save a trip down to the well. But she was glad Spire had left. Spire spoke in a terse, rigid matter, and Spire's presence was that of a stern disciplinarian to whom the smallest infraction would be a disappointment. *Will she punish me like Ms. Fiora did?* Her hands twitched.

Brina returned with Sara's breakfast. "I hope you like eggs and toast."

"I've never had eggs." Sara took the plate as Brina offered it to her. "Thank you."

"I think I can mend that dress for you," Brina said. "The stitches in the hem are coming loose. Where are your shoes?"

"I left them in the market. My other dresses are back at Ocean's Light. I could walk there later today to get them."

"No, that's all right. I'll get new ones made for you."

"What about my chores?" Sara asked.

"You don't have any chores. Elementals come here to train. Keep your room tidy, and that should be enough."

Brina opened the door to leave.

"When do I get to train on the field . . . with the others?"

Brina paused, her hand on the knob. "When your element is stronger." She closed the door.

Sara stared out the window across the field to the lake for several long minutes. She went to the door, expecting it to be locked. But as her hand touched the handle, the handle was turned from the outside. Sara backed away. Spire entered, carrying the basin of water.

"Have you finished eating?"

How long had Spire been gone? A few minutes perhaps. *Did she expect me to shovel the food into my mouth and swallow everything whole?* Maybe that was how Spire consumed her meals, swallowed whole like a serpent. Sara smirked.

"Something amuses you?"

"No." Sara shook her head. "Brina came in a minute ago. But I can wait."

"No, eat. You'll need all your strength."

Sara sat at the round table by the window, while Spire set the basin in the center. Sara wished Spire would leave. Nothing more than silence drifted between them.

"Do you normally train beginners?"

"No, I normally train the older students, ones who are no more than a couple years out the door."

"Why are you training me?"

"Do you not want to strengthen your element?"

"No, I didn't mean . . . I'm just embarrassed. I'm not at the level I should be. I've practiced everyday since I was six."

"Our element comes to us at different times. And, as for me, I think it will be worth the challenge to train a beginner." Spire smiled.

Sara smiled back. At least, Spire wasn't made of stone.

Once Sara finished her breakfast, Spire had her concentrate on the water in the basin. "Do what you can."

Sara concentrated for several minutes, but nothing happened.

"Listen to me," Spire said. "When you focus, relax your mind. Feel the water without touching it, think of its essence."

"I don't understand..." Sara stopped. She thought back to the fountain, to the soles of her feet against the cool surface of the water. She focused on her connection with the swirling depths, with her mother. Drop by drop the water gathered in the air above the basin. Sara smiled with relief. But the droplets seeped out of the mass of water floating before her.

"Control it," Spire instructed.

The water dropped from the mass back into the basin, where it splashed sending water over the edges.

"I can't," Sara said, and all of the water came splashing down. It coated the table, and spilled onto their laps before they could move away.

Sara mopped up the water from the table with her sleeve, not looking up at Spire. She felt a hand on her arm.

"It's alright. You're learning."

Spire left the room to get some towels.

She isn't prepared to teach someone like me, Sara thought.

Her eyes drifted to the window. The young Elementals practiced in small groups below. She watched as wind blasted down the field, vines and thick branches erupted from the earth, fire scorched the grass, and lightning lit up the sky in bright, quick flashes. But no one summoned water to the field. The lake rested under the willow, but no Water Elementals practiced at its waters.

When she returned, Spire helped Sara mop up the puddles from the table and the floor.

"Okay. Tomorrow, we'll start again. We'll work on getting you to manipulate water effectively, and then we'll move onto calling Water. I'll have a small tub moved into this room so you can practice."

Where are the Water Elementals? Sara wanted to ask, but she couldn't get the words out. Spire wasn't quite stone anymore, but she was focused and curt, which left no room for questions.

Before Sara gained the courage to ask her query, Spire had her hand on the doorknob.

"Rest for today. You'll be given no mercy tomorrow."

SARA awoke to find her breakfast on the table near the window. She got up and made her bed. She tucked the covers under the mattress. A new dress was laid out at the end of the bed. A pair of shoes rested on the floor. She put on the dress. The fabric was smooth, not coarse like the fabric of her old one. She slipped the shoes onto her feet.

She sat, ate her breakfast, and waited for Spire. Beside her plate was a glass of water. She tried to remember what it was like to dance on the water in the fountain. The glass moved. She pulled the water with so much force, that the glass fell over, and the water spread all over the table. Sara ran to the end of the bed and picked up her old dress.

Using the dress, she sopped up the water before it spilled onto the carpet. The table was dry, but the upper half of the dress was now soaked and dripping.

She bunched up the dress so that the skirt could soak up some of the water. Looking around the room, Sara found no place to put the damp dress. Her eyes rested on the window. Putting the dress onto the table, she eased open the window with both hands. Taking the dress, she hung it outside. The wind was strong, and it lifted the dress skirt and brought the wet fabric down hard against the side of the building. Sara lost her grip on the cloth. The dress slipped from her fingers. It caught the wind twice, and it landed on the ground a few feet from the building.

Sara sighed. The dress rested three floors down on the field. She decided to go down and get the dress before anyone noticed her clumsy mistake. When she tried the door, however, the knob would not turn. Sara tried again with no success.

She went back to the window and looked down. She was several feet from the ground floor. The bricks on the wall outside were uneven. Many of them jutted out from the others, creating tiny little ledges.

Sara took off her new shoes and got up onto the window sill. She stuck one leg out until her toes touched the ledge of one of the bricks. She reached her arm out and grabbed onto another tiny ledge. Taking a deep breath, she pulled herself out of the window and quickly grabbed onto another ledge with her once free hand. She placed the toes of her other foot upon another little niche. She clung to the wall. The wind forced her hair into her face, and, at first, she was too frightened to move. Once she was clinging onto the side of the building, she realized how senseless it was to risk a bad fall to relieve a little embarrassment.

But, she thought, she wasn't doing this for the dress. If she could do this, she could explore without them knowing. She could go to the lake at night and dance on the water.

She took another deep breath, and she slowly and cautiously climbed the rest of the way down. When she had less than two feet to go, she jumped down and quickly grabbed the dress. The warm breeze touched her face, and the grass felt soft beneath her bare feet. The field was unoccupied and still flooded with faint morning light.

The lake was closer than before but still several feet out of her reach. She was tempted to go to it, but if she didn't return, Spire would know, and she might never be able to sneak out again.

Draping the dress over her shoulder, she once again took ahold of the tiny ledges and climbed back up. The heaviness of the dampened dress made the climb more difficult, and the wind kept catching the fabric.

As she ascended, one foot slipped, scraping the grainy stone. Her fingers pressed into the stones above her head as her heart sharply descended into her stomach. One foot dangled dangerously. Sara regained her composure, brought her foot onto another stone and continued the climb.

Once up to her window, she threw the dress back in and grabbed hold of the sill. Placing one foot firmly down onto the sill, she managed to climb back in.

As she was closing the window, the door knob turned. Sara picked the wet dress up from the floor and put it on the table. She had closed the window on one of the curtains.

In came Spire followed by two men, carrying a wooden tub. The tub was shallow and round, and water glistened inside it. Spire directed the men to place the tub in the space between the bed and the opposite wall. After they finished their task, they gave a quick nod to Spire and exited. One of the men stared back at Sara before leaving.

Spire shut the door behind them. "Are you ready?"

"I think so," Sara said.

Spire paused and looked toward the window. Sara's palms prickled.

"You've been practicing this morning?" She walked over to the table to lift up the damp dress. She rested it against the back of one of the chairs.

"It was an accident."

"It's alright. I want you to keep trying." Spire gestured to the tub in the middle of the room.

Sara knelt by the tub and gazed into the water.

"Sometimes it helps to move your hands in the direction you want your element to go."

Sara looked up from the water. "Could you show me?"

Spire looked at the bed and moved her hand up through the air. The quilt on the bed fluttered in the air before falling gently back down.

Sara stared at the bed for a moment. "You're not a Water Elemental?"

"No."

"But I thought Elemental apprentices were trained by those with their element?"

"That's true, but there's no one else."

"No one else?"

"No other Water Elementals."

Sara slowly shook her head. "That can't be."

"You don't know?"

"Don't know what?"

Spire sighed and knelt beside her. "The man who brought you to Element, Talon, wanted us to keep you safe."

"From what?"

Spire's eyes looked hard, and the tint of red gleamed. "From Hephaestus."

"But why would he care about me?"

"Because he killed the others—the other Water Elementals."

Sara's hand went up to the raindrop gem against her chest. "Why would he do that?"

"Some believe he fears Water Elementals—that they are his particular weakness. The perfect adversary. That's why he's trying to eliminate them. By now, he probably thinks he has succeeded. But others hold out the hope that one last Water Elemental exists. They believe if she is as strong in her element as Hephaestus is in his, she can beat him."

Sara stared into the water, her fingers pinching the raindrop gem. "Do you believe that?"

"I believe Hephaestus is afraid of Water Elementals. I think for that reason alone it would be hard for him to go up against one who could match his strength."

Sara looked up at Spire. "Could I match it?"

"That's not what you're here for. You're here to get stronger so that you can defend yourself, not to be a martyr."

After three hours of training, Spire left for the day.

Sara slumped down onto bed. Her muscles were like jelly. Her eyes stared at the blank wall. *Did Hephaestus kill Mom and Dad?*

Talon brought me here to keep me safe. What if safe means being a prisoner forever? She would never be allowed to leave Element, and, if she did, she would never be able to use her abilities for fear of being discovered. The breath caught in her throat. The air around her became unfamiliar, and she wanted to be back at Ocean's Light where she slept in the small room with the other girls' beds so close to her own. She pulled the quilt up to her neck and brought her legs to her chest. She tried to sleep.

As the sun came up, Sara opened the drawer beside her bed and pulled out the charcoal and paper the vendor at the market had given her.

She walked to the table and tried to smooth out the sheets of paper. The attempt proved unsuccessful. Faint creases remained where she had folded pages to fit them in her pocket. She blew charcoal dust from the paper.

Picking up the charcoal, she pressed it against the paper and drew in soft, slow, uncertain strokes. She closed her eyes a few times to remember her mother's face. She held the paper out at arm's length. She failed to get the eyes right, and all together the portrait looked like a clumsy attempt. She smoothed the creases of a new piece of paper and started again.

Sara heard the voices of the apprentices on the field. Sara glanced outside. She made eye contact with the young Lightning Elemental. She knew it this time. He looked right at her, but this time she turned away and moved her chair further from the window.

OVER the next two months, Sara practiced her element under the watchful and stern eyes of Spire. She had learned to move water with a little less effort, but it was slow to do what Sara wanted.

"You'll get better," Spire encouraged her.

"I hope so. I feel like I don't quite understand, like I'm doing it by accident."

"The feel for it will come with time."

They sat at the table near the window.

"When I was young," Spire said, "I was unfamiliar with my element. Like you, I felt that it came by accident. It seemed unconnected to me. But one day, while I practiced, I felt as if it was a part of me, as familiar as my arm or my leg. Now, I can't imagine being without it."

Sara thought for a moment. "Why do so many people never develop an element?"

"Why are some people born with blue eyes while others are not? It has to be passed down."

"I wanted to be a Water Elemental like my parents. I tried so hard every day. Now that I have this power, I don't know what to do with it."

"One day you'll know."

*   *   *

SARA pulled the covers back and slipped into bed. She untied the woven cord from around her neck and placed the raindrop gem in the drawer. Inside the drawer were the drawings of her mother. Every sheet was covered. Sara had even started drawing along the sides of the pages to save paper. She sighed. *Where can I find more?* Pulling the covers up around her, she closed her eyes.

A knock at the door awoke Sara. Brina opened the door and walked in with Sara's breakfast. Sara waited for her eyes to adjust to the light from the window.

"Ms. Brina?"

Brina turned as if startled. She gathered herself. "You're awake early."

Sara rubbed the sleep from her eyes. "You don't have to keep bringing my meals up to me. I can go down and get them myself. I won't talk to anyone. I promise."

Brina lowered her eyes to the floor. "I'm sorry, but it wouldn't be safe for you to leave the room. Others might question your presence, and Talon wouldn't allow it."

"Is he here?"

"He comes by sometimes." She set Sara's breakfast on the table.

"Was he a trainer here?"

"Yes, how did you guess?"

"Spire said something about it." Sara got up from bed and went over to the table to eat her breakfast. "Why doesn't he train Elementals anymore?"

Brina sat in the chair opposite Sara. "Talon left Element a long time ago because his guilt consumed him."

"Why?" Sara asked.

"Years ago, he trained a young man, who excelled in his element because of Talon's guidance. He reached a level of mastery as high as Talon himself. But, he went astray and joined Hephaestus's army." Brina's eyes were distant. "Every death he has been responsible for, Talon has blamed on himself. He can never train another Elemental again."

Brina stood. "I should let you finish your breakfast. Spire will be up any minute."

Brina left like a mouse scurrying to the sanctuary of its humble hole in the wall.

Sara sighed as she heard Brina lock the door.

THAT night, Sara tucked the covers under her chin. Before she closed her eyes, something shuffled across the floor. Sara got out of bed to investigate. A folded piece of paper lay on the floor. She picked it up and unfolded it.

A Gift.

Following the folded note, several sheets of drawing paper flew from under the door. Sara went to the door. She picked up the sheets. "Who are you?" she asked whoever was behind the door, but no answer came.

THE water swirled in the tub. Sara's eyes trailed off listlessly.

"Maybe we need to move onto calling Water," Spire said, seeing Sara's indolent expression.

"Why can't I leave this room?" Sara's eyes focused on the window.

"I explained that to you."

"I want to go out. I want to go to the lake on the field."

"It's not safe."

Sara sighed and sat at the table. She watched the other apprentices as they trained on the field. "I'm starting to hate this little room."

Spire sat across from her. She picked up one of Sara's drawings. "You're getting good. Who is she?"

"My mother."

"You look like her."

Sara gazed out the window. If only she were brave enough to try climbing out of it again. She could dance on the lake.

"You're getting stronger every day," Spire said. "You won't stay in this room forever. But I want to make sure you can handle yourself outside it."

It felt like a false promise.

SARA waited in her bed as the sky became its darkest. She lifted the covers and walked to the window. Her hand went up to the glass, touching where she could see the lake off in the distance. The night air chilled the glass.

Sara eased the window open until she had enough space to fit through. Taking a deep breath, she grabbed the frame of the window and stepped out onto the first jutting stone. With caution, she climbed down.

The air was calm with only a light breeze to threaten her balance. Still, Sara clang tightly to the stones as she descended, her fingertips pressing into the grainy surface. With five more feet to go, Sara breathed a sigh of relief.

But as she continued, her foot slipped against one of the stones. She was unable to maintain her balance. Her stomach sank as she fell. Impact with the ground knocked the breath out of her. Sara lay on the grass. The night became darker. She blinked and tilted her head to the side.

The lake was several yards from where she lay. Moonlight glanced off the water. A willow stood at the edge. The tree's branches wept down and touched the silvery surface.

Sara stood, rubbing her sore shoulder. The hem of the curtains slipped outside her bedroom window and waved in the night air. They looked white in the night. Walking toward the lake, she felt liberated as the breeze played across her face.

When she reached the edge of the lake, she stooped down to run her fingers through the water. It was cool like the air, but more familiar. Yet, it was different from the water in the tub. The water in the tub had been gathered from the lake, but outside the water was alive. It had not been plucked from the root.

Sara stood and looked toward the middle of the lake. Drop

by drop, water gathered above the lake's surface, being pulled from its depths. Sara closed her eyes and thought of her mother, of the fire. When she opened them, a large sphere of water, the size of a pumpkin, floated in the air at eye level. She walked toward it, her feet meeting the surface of the water. She reached out to touch the sphere. It glistened in the moonlight, and the water wavered. Before her fingertips touched the surface of the sphere, the water crashed back down into the lake, and Sara's feet broke the surface. She lost her balance and kneeled beneath the water. Her knees sank into the soft sludge at the bottom of the lake.

Sara sank her fingertips and toes into the mud as she struggled to get back up. Her hands, feet, and nightgown muddied, she stumbled to the edge of the lake. She cleaned her hands and feet in the water. Mud caked beneath her fingernails.

Sara shook her head. She sat at the edge of the lake and let the water play with her toes. Her mind wandered. The mud crusted on the front of her nightgown.

From the corner of her eye, Sara saw a light. She hadn't noticed it before, being so mesmerized by the lake. The light came from a cottage several yards away and half-hidden by overgrown shrubs.

Although she feared being caught, curiosity grabbed Sara, and she made her way to the cottage. She slipped in between two gangly bushes covering a window. Inside was a worn bench beside a fireplace. Tools rested in one corner of the room, and a book lay on the floor with its pages ripped out and scattered around it. No one was in the room.

Sara moved through the bushes to the next window. Her heart stopped. Spire sat in an old chair inside.

Sara darted away from the window and pressed her back against the wall of the cottage. Gathering her courage, she leaned toward the window and peeked through.

Spire's gaze was on the double bed in the center of the room. She twirled a gold ring between her fingers. Her sleeveless nightgown revealed a golden band around her right arm.

Her eyes looked empty like they were searching inward.

The sorrow and loneliness in Spire's eyes made Sara ashamed that she had spied on her. Sara moved away from the window, upsetting the untrimmed plants, and hurried back to her bedroom prison.

SARA couldn't sleep, and the next morning her shoulder was still sore from her fall the night before. She wasn't sure when she would be able to make the climb again.

"What's wrong with your arm?" Spire watched Sara massage the pain from her shoulder.

"It's nothing. I slept on it last night."

Sara wanted to ask Spire about the cottage, but she didn't dare for fear that Spire might be suspicious or worse: she might show the same sorrow she showed the other night.

She caught Spire staring at the dirt under her fingernails.

That night, Sara clung to her the covers. She stared into the darkness, waiting for sleep to take her away from the small room.

Something shuffled across the floor.

Another folded paper rested a few feet from the door. She got up and snatched the paper from the ground. The sound of someone running down the hall reverberated through the wooden door.

She unfolded the paper. Inside was a silver key and a handwritten message. Sara held the key between her fingers as she read the note.

Because it's safer to take the stairs.

Sara stepped up to the door. She put the key into the lock and turned. Her heart hammered in her chest as a loud click sounded.

4

The Lake

SARA walked out onto the cool, familiar surface of the water. It wavered beneath her feet as she stared at her blurry reflection.

She had grown taller, but not nearly as tall as Spire. Her light brown hair grew down to her waist; her face became thinner and her features sharper.

For the three years that had lulled by, she had left her room in the cover of darkness to dance on the lake. The bit of freedom she gained from it felt good after being in that room for hours focusing on that accursed tub of water.

Everyday had been the same. Wakeup. Eat breakfast. Stare out the window. Focus on the tub of water. Have lunch. Stare out the window. Train some more. Have dinner. Turn the key. Sneak out at night. Dance.

Sara spun faster and faster, gliding on the water. What did

Spire know about freedom? What did any of them know, but her?

In mid-spin, she saw a figure close by. She dropped into the water, hoping he had not seen her. Sara held her breath. From beneath the lake's surface, the figure was a wavering blur of colors stretched across the water.

"Hey, are you alright?" the figure called. The water muffled his voice.

He dove into the lake, breaking the surface, and swam to where she went under. The lake was not very deep; he found Sara. He grabbed her hand, pulled her up, and lifted her from under her arms. Once her head above water, he carried her back to the bank.

Sara's body went limp. She allowed him to bring her to dry land. That's right. You didn't see me dancing on the water. I'm just a damsel in distress.

At the edge of the lake, he helped her to sit up as she pushed the wet hair from her face.

"I didn't know Water Elementals couldn't swim," he said.

Sara's eyes widened.

"So, you *are* a Water Elemental. I knew it. That's why you never come out on the field with us. You're always watching from the window."

Sara tried to recognize him. He had brown hair, and his skin was light, like the cream-colored napkins Brina brought with her meals.

"They keep me up in that room. For protection," she said, her eyes still searching his expression.

"It must be lonely."

Sara realized she had been staring too long, and her eyes darted to the ground. "I have Spire . . . but sometimes, I wish I was outside with all of you." *Not sometimes*, Sara thought, *always*.

"Lady Spire's training you?" he asked

"Yes." Sara squeezed water out of her hair. The water sank into the ground.

"You're lucky. Lady Spire is one of the best trainers in Element. She usually gets to hand-pick her students."

"I don't think she hand-picked me." She wrung the water from the skirt of her dress. "I'm Sara. What's your name?"

"Rodan."

"So, what's your element?" Sara asked.

But she knew. She watched him from the window call vines and leaves. Yet, it felt better to ask. It felt like she was part of something rather than a spectator watching from above.

"Earth," he said.

A seedling appeared in Rodan's outstretched hand.

"It must be amazing to create something living," Sara said.

"You can help. Needs water," he said.

Sara smirked. The saplings and seeds Earth Elementals summoned needed no water or sunlight to grow, but she played along. She focused on the lake. A droplet of water floated above the surface. Sara moved it toward her, and without touching it, she let it drop onto the seed in Rodan's hand. The seed split, the cover capsule cracking without a sound. Ivory petals emerged; the seed grew into a white flower.

"That's impressive," Sara said, watching the flower grow.

"I'm glad you think so. I had to learn it on my own. It's not something trainers waste their time teaching. I can crack open the ground, move boulders without touching them, turn sand to soil, but I wanted to be able to do something that required some finesse." Rodan placed the flower down at his side. Its roots sank into the ground where water from Sara's hair had fallen. "So, you've been sneaking out like this every night?"

"Yeah. Spire would kill me if she found out. I'm supposed to stay in that room until my element is stronger."

"How can your element get any stronger if you're not practicing out here by the lake?"

"Spire thinks a tub of water will have to do for now." Sara forced a smile.

"It won't do forever."

"No, it won't. I should go. I have to get some sleep." Sara stood. She walked toward Element, but stopped after a few steps. She turned to face Rodan. "I'm glad I met you."

"Same here. Will you be back tomorrow night?"

"I come here every night."

Sara ran across the field and opened the door to the building. She disappeared into its cold halls.

RODAN stood. He felt eyes on him.

"You met a girl." A man with blond hair stepped from behind the willow.

"You were spying on me, Bolton?"

The next day, Rodan and Bolton walked down the second-floor hallway and headed downstairs for breakfast.

"How much did you see?" Rodan whispered.

"Enough."

"You can't tell anyone she's a Wat—" Rodan stopped. He felt the presence of someone walking close behind them. He turned around.

"She's a what?" A bright-eyed girl with blond hair stood behind him. The green bird on her shoulder chirped.

"It's nothing," Rodan said.

"Rodan met a girl," Bolton betrayed him.

The blonde girl passed them and skipped backwards so she was facing Rodan.

"What's her name?"

"It's nothing," Rodan repeated.

"She doesn't have a name?"

"I can't talk about it."

They passed her as she put on an exaggerated pout, and the little bird on her shoulder chirped her disdain.

Rodan and Bolton stood in line to get their breakfast.

When he first came to Element, Rodan was the smallest of his peers. Now, he could see over the heads of everyone in the dining hall even his friend, Bolton. Sometimes he woke up thinking he was still that short kid, but he wasn't, not anymore.

Once they got their plates, they found a seat at one of the long benches in the great hall.

Rodan's knees hit the underside of the table. He picked up his spoon and dug it into the bean and pea pottage.

Bolton nudged his arm.

"A Water Elemental?" Bolton said in harsh whisper.

Rodan swallowed and eyed the crowd. "Keep your voice down."

"You're dating a Water Elemental."

"I've only just met her."

"And how often do you plan to meet her?"

Rodan looked for a sign of banter in his voice, but found none.

"I don't want to talk about this now."

"We're almost out of here. And you're hanging out with a Water Elemental . . . she's not exactly on the list you want to be on."

"List?"

"The extinction list."

Bolton had rarely ever been serious, but in that moment, he lost all his mocking and sarcasm.

"Don't say stuff like that," Rodan said.

"I want you to watch your back, that's all."

"I thought you had my back."

"Yeah, that's part of the problem. If you do something stupid, I'll have to get involved to save your skin." Bolton put his spoon down.

"What's she doing up there when she's watching us?"

"She's drawing," Bolton said.

"How do you know?" Rodan asked.

"When she looks down, her hand is always moving across the table. She's drawing."

"Do you think she's studying us? She's a Water Elemental. She must be thinking about fighting him."

"Why would she be studying us?"

"To build an army." Rodan looked down into his bowl and

stirred.

Bolton laughed, then stopped. "You want to be part of that?"

"That's not what I'm saying. But I think I would go if she asked."

"You barely know her, what her abilities are, what her motives might be."

"I know, but you would be crazy enough to join me, wouldn't you?"

THAT morning, the sun was free of the willowy clouds that overshadowed it the day before. Sara would have given anything to go outside. But instead, she was rippling water in a small tub in the confines of her room.

She needed water to be present to have any power at all. Although she had tried many times with Spire's guidance, she could not call it.

Spire sat in a chair nearby. Her eyes were distant, but her mind, though wandering was also sharply focused in the present. Spire often sat like that, thinking, and Sara had become accustomed to it.

When she first started training, she thought that Spire's wandering expression meant that she could take an unapproved break from her lessons, but Spire was watching when she didn't seem to be. Spire would instantly tell Sara to keep trying and then go back to her quiet thoughtfulness.

I'm boring her, Sara thought. I've been boring her for years.

Sara gazed across the room at the sky outside the window. "Spire, when will I be able to go outside and train on the field?"

"When you are ready."

"I'm seventeen. I'm tired of hiding. I want to meet other people. See other places, at least the dining hall if nothing else." Sara had seen the dining hall, she had explored every inch of Element, avoiding Brina's nightly patrols of the halls, but she didn't want Spire to know that.

"You can't call Water," Spire said. "You're not ready to go out there. And being seventeen doesn't entitle you to do whatever you want. It means that you have the responsibility to do what is right."

Sara's eyes darted away from the window, and she looked at Spire. "I don't understand. You're trying to protect me, but at the same time, I'm a prisoner. I haven't been allowed to leave this room in over three years."

Spire looked back at her. The look in Sara's eyes made something inside her coil up. She stood from her chair. "I think you need time to reflect. I'll see you tomorrow." Spire went to the door and left the room.

Sara sighed and walked over to the window.

Outside, Rodan had his hands on the ground. His eyes were closed. Branches sprouted around him.

Not far from Rodan was a man with blond hair. Sara had seen him many times before. He was the boy who captured her attention three years ago. With age, he had grown taller. His skin brown from the sun. He was a Lightning Elemental. Every time he used his element, a crash or boom followed.

He caught Sara staring at him. Sara turned away, and drew the curtain closed. She sat in one of the chairs near the window and couldn't stop the smile from spreading across her face. She shook her head and tried to focus on her drawing.

DOWNSTAIRS, Spire found Brina in her small library. "I have to talk to you."

Brina put the book of poetry she was holding back on the shelf. "What is it?"

"Sara. I'm losing her. She's becoming listless. All she thinks about is going out on the field with the others, and I can't get her to concentrate."

"She wants to go outside?"

"Yes." Spire sat in the armchair beside the window. "And I am tempted to let her."

"No, she can't. It wouldn't be safe for her." Brina turned away from the bookshelf. "Talon wouldn't allow it."

"Talon is never here. She isn't his responsibility."

Three loud, irregular knocks echoed down the hall.

"That's him," Brina said. Her face warmed to a rosy pink. "I'll talk to him about it." She hurried out of the room.

Spire looked out the window, across the field to the lake. She remembered when Water Elementals attended the school before she became a trainer, and she remembered that every holiday fewer and fewer of them came back until there were none.

Spire didn't want that for Sara, but she knew that the endless monotony of her life in that small room would catch up to her. Spire knew that Sara would grow out of that room. Her spirit was now filling the whole space and trying to stretch beyond it. She had only been waiting for Sara to have enough and do something beyond Spire's control.

BRINA went into the entrance hall and opened the door for Talon. "Come in. I'm glad you came."

Talon looked toward the stairs. "How is she doing?"

"Do you want to go up and see her?"

Talon shook his head. "No."

"You've come here every month for three years to check on her, yet you never want to see her. I don't understand you. Let me get your coat." Brina tugged on the shoulders of his coat, but Talon shrugged her hands away.

"No, I'm not staying long."

"Do you want anything to drink?"

"Water."

"Come with me."

Brina led Talon to the dining room. Rows of long tables and benches filled the room. The apprentices practiced outside. Brina went through the swinging doors into the kitchens to get a glass and pitcher of water. She returned, happy to see that Talon had at least sat at one of the benches.

"How have you been?" she asked as she poured the water from the pitcher into the glass.

"A glass? Am I some honored guest?"

Brina handed it to him. "Are you still begging in the market?"

"How did you know that?"

"I started visiting an old friend who lives on Earthshire around the corner from the market." Brina sat across from him. "You're better than that. I know you don't want to train anymore, but there are other things. You used to forge knives and tools. You're good. You could sell them."

"No."

"I'm trying to help."

"I know. Sorry," Talon said. He took in a gulp of water.

Brina rested her hand under her chin.

"What's wrong?" For the first time in years, Talon looked up at her.

Brina's breath caught in surprise. She hesitated for too long.

Talon, seeing her reaction, looked away again.

She composed herself and said, "Spire told me that Sara is unhappy."

"Is she?"

"She wants to go outside. She's talked to me too."

Talon gulped down what remained of the water in his glass. "You know I can't let her do that. I must protect her. Her father would have wanted me to."

5

REVEALED

TORCHES lit Hephaestus's crumbling bedchamber. The light glowed bright enough to leave long shadows on the walls. The shadows looked like people, unmoving, with their hands clasped and heads bowed as if at a funeral.

In the center of the room was a large bed, the funeral pyre. But no body rested there. The quilt was tucked in without a wrinkle in the fabric, and a thin coat of dust covered it. The pillows, also covered in dust, had long been unused.

In the corner was an armchair where Hephaestus sat. His elbow rested on the end table beside the chair. His eyes were closed, but he was not sleeping.

The musty smell in the air had long ago escaped his senses, and he had become accustomed to the sounds of rats scurrying in the corners.

The rats were ready to eat the flesh of his body when he

died. The thought didn't scare him nor did he long for death, but if death were to come, it was only right that the rats should get their feast.

He wondered about death, and what would happen after it. And he had seen it come to many, but for him he never thought death would really come. It wasn't a conscious thing that he said aloud in his mind, but it was something that he knew.

"Sicilia." The name escaped his mouth. He let it trail off until it was only the breath on his lips.

A knock sounded at the door, followed by the voice of one of Hephaestus's servants.

"My lord, Commander Fero is here. He says he has urgent news."

Hephaestus moved from his slumped position and sat up in the chair. "Send him in."

The red-faced man walked into the room.

"The boy has confirmed it. Element is harboring a Water Elemental," Fero said.

"You are sure this time?"

"He has seen her use her element. Do you want me to lead the men into battle, to storm Element and drag her out?"

Hephaestus's eyes became distant. He looked back at Fero. "Is she the last one?"

"We know of no others."

Hephaestus knew his number of loyal men was decreasing. The old and faithful had mostly died out, a few young heirs remained, but many of the battlements were abandoned.

"No. What if they find out that I need her? If I attack Element now, that would put a target on her back for the days to come."

"Your soldiers will keep any assassins away."

"Will they?"

He didn't like the look Fero was giving him. It was a look that he gave him more often now, the look that a sane man gives to the senseless.

"Let the boy . . . He's not a boy anymore, is he?"

Fero was silent.

"Let him figure it out. He knows what I want him to do, and he'll make it happen."

"You have a lot of faith in the dumb brat."

"He is his mother's son. He must have inherited something from her."

That look!

"Keep close to him, but not too close."

He knew what Fero was thinking: You're letting a seventeen-year-old boy devise a plan to get the last-surviving Water Elemental here? Isn't that beyond the boy's cunning? She was precious cargo and the only thing between him and spheres. But, after all, Hephaestus was a seventeen-year-old boy when he built his empire.

He had fire inside him, and the boy had it too, even if he didn't show it.

"Leave."

Hephaestus had his head in his hand. He didn't look up to see Fero go, but he knew he had gone because the heavy door shut on the silence.

His army was shrinking, and his soldiers didn't have faith in him anymore.

Hephaestus went to the window. The cold air did not chill his face. The flames inside him kept him warm.

Torches blazed outside the crumbling stone houses, but fewer than before.

Hephaestus had promised his people that Elementals would rise above all, even the Irradiatio and their Council, but the Irradiatio were gone. They were gone long before Hephaestus was able to wage war against them. And all the promises he made ended in death.

If he had the spheres, death wouldn't rule him anymore. He could grow his army again and draw the Irradiatio out of hiding, to face the punishment they deserved for their crimes.

His eyes glowed with Fire, and the once naked torches all

around the city burst alight with flames.

6

THE LIBRARY

L IGHT from the moon streamed into Sara's room, touching the side of her face. She clenched the key to her bedroom door. Once the hour was late enough, she slipped out of bed and tiptoed to the door.

She rotated the key until she heard the click signal the lock's release. She turned the knob, opened the door an inch, and peered outside. The hall was vacant.

She slipped out into the deserted hallway and crept to the stairs. The marble steps made no sound as her bare feet met them. Sara hugged the bannister, gazing around each bend as she rounded it. The steps led down to the entrance hall. Sara wandered across the cool, tile floor into the hall leading to the back entrance.

Light poured out of a room down the hall. Sara peered inside.

Brina sat in her armchair. She cradled a book in her hands. The spine was so worn that some of the pages were loose. Brina turned a page that had escaped the binding.

Every night, Brina would sink into that chair and read. Sometimes she would cry over the little book of poetry.

Sara wondered if she ever slept.

She took a deep breath and crossed the doorway, careful not to alert Brina. She turned the corner and made her way to the back door leading to the training field.

Sara opened the door. The chill night air met her as it took refuge within Element. She stepped outside and closed the door behind her.

Rodan waited in the distance by the lake.

She crossed the field to meet him. "You're always here before me." She sat next to him. "I get nervous and hesitant before crossing Brina's room."

"Not me," Rodan said. "My dad and I used to practice making our movements quiet in the forest. He cared about stuff like that. I guess I take it for granted sometimes."

Sara shivered. "I don't want to lose all this." She looked to the lake, to the trees, to the moon, and her eyes rested on him.

It did not escape Rodan's notice.

"She's always in the library reading," she said, "reading that same book. There are so many books in that library, but she's never tempted to pick up another."

"You know, that isn't the only library in Element," he said.

"It isn't?"

"Lady Spire never showed you the library? It's much bigger than Brina's."

"Of course not. Spire won't even let me leave that room."

Rodan stood and held out his hand to her.

Sara looked up at him. "I can't go. What if we're caught?"

"We won't be," Rodan said.

"We shouldn't."

"Shouldn't what? Live? Think? Breathe?" he said. "Come on, you deserve to see this."

Sara took his hand.

AS they made their way down the hall, Rodan leaned forward to peer into Brina's well-lit room. Brina had fallen asleep in her armchair with her book resting in her lap opened to the page she was reading.

Sara and Rodan crept to the entrance hall and down the enjoining corridor.

The hallway leading to the library was lined with portraits.

"Who are these people?"

"Trainers. They have a painting done once a year. They've been trying to get Lady Spire to sit for one, but she refuses."

Sara stopped in front of one of the portraits. "Talon."

The portrait depicted Talon dressed in rich colors, his hair short, and his face clean and unscarred.

"His eyes . . . he looks happy." Sara stared at the painting. She hadn't seen Talon in many years. She remembered him as guarded, scarred, and dirty.

"The library is this way," Rodan said.

Sara nodded and tore her eyes from Talon's portrait.

Rodan led her to the large, oak doors at the end of the hallway. As he opened one door, it made a loud screech.

Sara's eyes darted down the portrait-lined hall.

Rodan took her arm and drew her toward the room. They passed through the small opening, and Rodan tried to close the door, but Sara stopped him.

"Wait!" she whispered. "It might squeal again."

"I'll close it softly," Rodan said. "If Brina glances down the hall and notices the door open, she'll investigate."

He eased the door closed. It creaked, but didn't squeal.

"This way," Rodan said.

They passed rows and rows of books.

"So many," Sara said. "Ocean's Light only had three. The girls always fought over them."

Rodan went down one of the aisles and pulled an old book from the shelf. "This is my favorite." He opened it.

The pages were yellowed, and the book had a musty, cozy smell.

"It's about the Creator," Rodan said. "It started an uproar because it questioned the Creator's purpose in making the spheres."

"What does it say?" Sara asked.

"That the spheres were created so that we could transcend Nature."

"Do you believe that?"

"I believe Elementals exist to forward Nature's goals. Nature trusted us with her gifts. We do transcend humanity, but I don't say that out of pride. We were given greater power for a reason, and what we do with that power matters. Working against Nature has historically brought harm. We need to find the balance between Nature and our own desires."

"A balance. That's interesting." Sara's voice trailed off as her eyes rested on a blue book marked with the symbol for water, an inverted triangle.

Rodan put the book back on the shelf. "No one knows for sure, but it is fun to think about." He didn't notice Sara's attention had turned elsewhere.

She struggled to support the book's weight as she brought it down from the shelf.

Sara held the book in her arms and turned the pages. Inside were various Water Elemental abilities, detailed and described. One illustration depicted a Water Elemental pulling the water from the body of another.

"These must be battle techniques," Rodan said.

"Or torture techniques, but some of these would be useful in battle, I guess. I wonder why Spire hasn't taught any of this to me."

"She isn't training you to fight," Rodan said, "Trainers usually save the combat training for Elementals who want to become Resistance fighters. Abilities like these are difficult to control. My dad taught me how to fight."

"So, you can perform abilities like these? Ones meant for

battle?"

Rodan nodded. "Because of my dad, I've had a lot of practice. My friend, Bolton, too."

"Bolton?"

The door squealed open.

Sara shoved the book back on the shelf.

Rodan grabbed her hand and led her into a crevice between the shelves. Sara backed into it, and Rodan leaned against her so they wouldn't be seen.

Sara was breathing heavy. *I'll be caught, and I'll never dance on the lake again.* Sara looked up at Rodan. This might be the last time she would see him.

Rodan put a finger to Sara's lips, and her breathing slowed, but her heart still hammered against the walls of her chest.

Footsteps echoed through the library. The footsteps got louder as they approached the place where Sara and Rodan hid.

Rodan leaned his forehead against Sara's. Her hands trembled.

The footsteps against the tiled floor became more distant, and the door screeched shut.

Sara took a deep breath.

Rodan let out a nervous laugh. "That was close."

Sara nodded. "We should go."

"Right," Rodan said and, not wanting to, he stepped away from her.

7

NO MORE HIDING

SARA sat at the table. She gazed out the window at the Lightning Elemental with the blond hair. Her charcoal outlined the contours of his face onto the paper. She focused on his eyes. When he caught her gaze, she looked away.

Spire opened the door, and Sara folded the drawing and put it into her dress pocket. Spire walked in and closed the door behind her. Sara looked back out the window.

"I know you've been angry with me these past few days," Spire said. "I was too hard on you last week. I don't like standing in your way, but I'm afraid for your safety. It's one thing to keep a secret inside the walls of Element. But it is quite another to keep one out in the world."

Sara looked at Spire. "But I can stop using my element. Hephaestus won't know I exist."

Spire sighed. "I know you've felt the pull. You can't stop using your element. It urges you. No one has abstained for long. One day, your will would wane, and trouble would find you."

"But I can't stay in this room anymore. I haven't spoken to a living soul, except for you and Brina, in three years. Please, you have to understand."

"I do. But as long as Hephaestus lives, he will pursue you. He will find you. But if you stay in Element, you'll be safe. I want you to stay." Spire turned and left the room. She shut the door behind her, and the sound of the key turning in the lock met Sara's ears.

Sara folded her arms, rested them on the table, and sank her head down onto them. She wet her arm with her tears. She beat her fists against table.

The other apprentices had gone inside for lunch, and the field was clear.

As she gazed out the window toward the lake, she heard something sweep across the floor. Something hit the leg of her chair. On floor rested a folded note like the ones she had received years ago. She unfolded it. The handwriting was a bit better. The writer had been careful with this message. It read:

If you want to be free, you know what you must do.

Sara waited for the halls to clear. She unlocked the door of her bedroom and slipped out. Rodan was expecting her.

He sat at the edge of the lake, waving his hand through the blades of grass and making them grow taller. He looked up when Sara's footsteps disquieted the grass.

She knelt beside him.

"It's been a long day," he said.

Sara nodded.

"My dad's visiting tomorrow. He's always busy. He hardly ever has time for me." He snorted. "I don't know what to say when I see him."

"You should say you're happy he could make time to see you." Sara stared across the lake to the ivy-covered walls surrounding Element. She thought of her father, the water flowing from his fingertips. She had no right to tell Rodan how he should feel about his father just because she lost hers. "I'm sorry. I have something on my mind. That's all."

"What's wrong?"

"There's something I need to tell you." She stared over the wall surrounding the field to the dark trees. She thought it would be easy to tell him, but it wasn't. She wanted to explain everything in one breath. She couldn't. "I'm leaving."

"What?"

"I have to. I'm not staying in Element anymore. I'm going to fight Hephaestus. No more hiding."

"But, Sara…" He smirked. "You can't be—"

But she didn't smile back.

"I knew this was coming," he said.

"What do you mean?" Sara asked.

"You're serious? You want to fight him?"

"What choice do I have?"

"Well, you have lots of other choices." Rodan looked at her. Her resolve never faltered. The wavering sea-green of her eyes turned to emerald stone. "But, if this is what you have to do, I'm going with you," he said.

Sara held his gaze. Every night she had met him by the lake since the day he saw her on the water. They had shared stories and laughed together. He had been her companion when she was hidden from all others. But this was a favor she couldn't ask of him.

"No, this is my fight," she said.

"Why? Because a bunch of hacks think Hephaestus is afraid of Water Elementals?"

"No, because he's after me and won't stop until he finds me. So, I'll come to him and fight him on my terms."

"You can't go alone," he said. "I have friends who can help."

"This isn't your fight."

"This is everyone fight."

Sara stared across the lake.

Rodan grabbed her hands. She turned to him.

"If you're going to leave this place to fight him," he said, "you need people you can trust by your side. If there's one thing I've learned from my father it's that fighting with four fists is a hell of a lot better than fighting with two. If you are our best shot, you need to give it your best and that means bringing an army."

"You think you can raise an army for me?"

Rodan sighed. "No, but I can build a team."

Silence lingered between them. Sara looked at him. She looked for some sign of wavering, a gulp maybe or the twitch of an eye, but Rodan's eyes were steel, and his expression unchanging.

Sara's hands tightened around his. "Okay. Can you be ready tomorrow night?"

"So soon?"

"I can't wait another day."

SARA stood beside the willow. The moon was getting higher in the sky, and she began to pace, wringing her hands as she walked. She was leaving the place that Spire had told her would keep her safe and going into the world that she warned her against. Her resolve weakened a little. What if she was being rash?

But as Rodan approached, her will strengthened.

Two others followed him. By Rodan's side was a girl, younger than Sara. Her hair was canary yellow, and her green eyes were bright like limes. The other was Rodan's age. He had a shock of blond hair. Sara's breath caught. He was the apprentice that had seen her from her window.

"This is Farah." Rodan directed her attention to the girl. She gave Sara a smile, picking up only one corner of her lips.

"And this is Bolton."

Bolton had a thick, woven string around his neck, but whatever was hanging from it was hidden inside his shirt.

The night loomed above them; the stars and the moon shone in the dark sky, but day was approaching, and a light rain fell.

"Is everyone ready?" Rodan asked. "We have to hurry."

"Wait," Farah said. "Orka's not back yet."

"Orka?" Sara asked.

Farah put two fingers in the corners of her mouth and let out a loud, screeching whistle.

"What are you doing?" Bolton hissed. "You'll wake everyone."

A green bird landed on Farah's shoulder. The bird nuzzled its head into Farah's hair.

Farah pet the bird and offered it a piece of dried fruit. "Okay," she said. "Let's go."

From the lake, they crept across the training field. They stayed low, close to the shadows and away from peering eyes that might be watching from the windows, to the stone wall that enclosed Element. The wall was seven feet high, and the stones were smooth, creating even lines without ledges or crevices to stick one's foot in and climb up. Rodan sent a thick, leafless vine over the wall.

The vine stretched over the stone wall. The light issued from her window on the top floor of Element.

Sara was still looking up at the window of her prison room when Farah put a hand on her shoulder.

"Don't worry. It's easy," Farah said.

Farah grabbed the vine and placed her feet against the stone wall. She pulled herself up and climbed to the top. Her feet hit the ground with a soft thump on the other side.

Sara sighed.

"Are you okay?" Rodan asked.

She smiled. Any falter might make Rodan second guess his decision and discourage her from her plan. "I'm fine," she said. She climbed up the vine and went over to the other side of the wall with ease. After all, she had climbed much worse.

"See, I told you," Farah said as Sara met her on the other side. A dense forest waited for them behind the wall.

Rodan and Bolton joined them, and they proceeded through the unruly trees, Farah putting a protective hand over Orka.

8

AS SHE KNEW SHE WOULD

SPIRE walked across the training field to the entrance hall. The rain the night before left the grass dewy. The folds of Spire's dark dress waved in the breeze. She returned from a place of solitude, a cottage where the previous groundskeeper used to live. She made Brina promise to house the new groundskeeper inside the manor. She wanted to keep the cottage sacred.

She thought of Sara's resolve, that she might leave Element, with or without Spire's consent. Spire was once headstrong like that, believing that nothing could hurt her, that she, above all others, would beat the odds. She was foolish like that once.

As Spire grabbed the bannister to ascend the steps within the entrance hall, Brina stopped her.

Sweat painted Brina's brow, and her hair was messier than

usual.

"What's wrong?" Spire asked.

Brina drew closer to Spire and whispered, "Hephaestus's men were seen outside Wyvek temple. You know what that means."

"The spheres?"

Brina's small frame shook. "Spire, you know where the Water Sphere is," she said.

"He won't get to it. He doesn't know where to look."

"What if he does?"

"We'll fight."

"Fighting him and stopping him are two very different things," Brina said. "No one has been able to put an end to his tyranny. Our apprentices are well-trained, but not enough to stop Hephaestus's whole army if he decides we're next. And what about Sara? What will he do to her?"

"No more than we're doing to her."

"What do you mean?"

Spire looked away.

"Spire?"

Spire took a deep breath. "Sara wants to leave more than ever. I don't know what to say to her anymore."

"But surely you don't want her to go."

"I want her to be happy."

"You've been like a sister to her. You wouldn't want any hurt to come her way."

Spire stiffened. She wanted to tell Sara to leave Element, to be free in the world. But doubts concerning her safety stopped Spire from saying this. She changed the subject. "Why is Hephaestus trying to gather the spheres? Why risk his men to scare us? The Protectors will give them a deadly challenge."

"It's the myth," Brina said, "the one about combining the power of the spheres. He wants them for that."

"But that's a story."

"No one has proven it untrue."

"I guess he'll have to prove it to himself."

"But not before he kills anyone who stands in his way."

"If not for this, he would find another reason to kill those defenseless against him. I don't want anyone to die. It's not the spheres we should be worried about. Not unless…" Spire stopped and reflected.

"Unless what?"

"Unless he destroys them." She stared ahead, into the all too imaginable future. "He could destroy them."

"What should we do?"

"Find Talon. I need to speak to him."

WAITING for Brina to send the message to Talon, Spire sat in the armchair in her room and contemplated. Sara would leave; that was inevitable. Whether she would help her or not, Spire still didn't know. She put her elbow on the arm of the chair and rested her head on her hand. She stared around the room, wondering what it would be like to be trapped within its four walls.

Spire's room was bare, no paintings, shelves, or curtains. Anything personal she kept tucked away in the drawer beside her bed so she wouldn't have to look at it every day. In the drawer were letters she hadn't read in a long time. On top of the letters was a ring.

Sara will leave, Spire thought, as I did.

Spire's breath caught. She had to be sure.

She hurried from her room and took the steps two at time, grabbing the bannister as she pulled herself up to the top floor of the manor. The hallway stretched in front of her as she rushed down it.

Spire stopped outside Sara's room. From the moment, she reached the door, Spire sensed she would find nothing behind it. She could no longer envision Sara sitting at the table and gazing out the window. Sara was beyond that window. She knew it. So, when she unlocked the door and the truth revealed, she was not surprised.

Sara's drawings no longer decorated the walls. Her bed was

made as if no one had slept in it the night before.

A note, written in charcoal, lay on the desk beside the bed. Spire snatched it from the table and read:

Dear Spire,

You must be very angry to find me gone. Please, forgive me. Element was the one place where I felt safe, but it also felt like a prison. Maybe you won't understand. But you were right. I also can't live in constant fear. I can't always be looking over my shoulder and waiting for the snake to strike. To be free, I must fight him. Don't worry. I'm with friends.

I'll do my best, and I will win.

Sara

Spire's heartbeat stilled. She had imagined that Sara would leave, but she had never thought that she might fight Hephaestus. Spire had hoped she would find a way to stay safe and hidden. But Sara didn't want to hide anymore. Spire had to find her.

She ran downstairs and tore open the door to her room.

Her fingertips were blackened from the charcoal smudges on the clean, white paper as Spire grabbed her coin purse and shawl. She had her hand on the door when she stopped and looked back into the room. She darted to her bed and ripped open the nightstand drawer. She rummaged through it until she found the golden ring. She dropped it into her coin purse and rushed out of the room.

Spire departed without saying a word. She left Sara's letter on the nightstand.

9

TRAGEDY FROM ACROSS THE SEA

SARA rested in a clearing among the trees. Rodan settled on the flat surface of a worn stone. Farah sat cross-legged across from them, looking up at the canopy of leaves. Bolton leaned against a nearby tree. Of the four to them, no one had traveled from Elementa to Caleena through the forest. Farah sent Orka, to fly above the trees and help them find their way to the next town, but the green parrot had been gone for hours and had not returned.

"Where are we?" Farah groaned.

"I don't know." Rodan scrutinized the old map he had taken from the library in Element. "A lot has changed since the cartographers made this map."

"We'll be fine." Sara adjusted her bag. "It's like you said, Farah, Orka knows the trees. She'll find a way out."

Farah poked at the ground with a stick and shrugged.

Bolton unhinged himself from the tree and looked at Farah. "You lied," he said.

"I exaggerated," Farah said. "Orka knows enough. Plus, she can see above the trees. But I'm worried she's been gone too long. That's all. She could be distracted."

"Great." Bolton slumped to the ground. "I guess I'll get comfortable in my new home."

"Now you're exaggerating," Rodan said.

"Me? Exaggerating? We're planning to march into Omega Ray and fight the most powerful Elemental in Mirmina, and we can't find our way out of a forest. We're relying on a bird to report back to us. But it's not coming back, is it? It probably found a nice berry shrub to nest in."

Sara hands tightened on the strap of her bag. Bolton was right. She was so focused on getting out of Element and on taking a breath of fresh air, that she had forgotten that her freedom came at a price. She had to fight a dangerous man, one who wanted her dead.

Her little group wasn't doing so well. Only hours away from Element, and they were fighting. She needed to calm the rising storm or the wind would tear through the trees while the lightning cut through the wind.

"Can you tell me about your elements?" Sara asked.

A medallion was attached to the woven string around Bolton's neck. It had fallen out of Bolton's shirt when he came down from the wall. The silver medallion had a strange symbol on it. The symbol was made up of lines, etched into the medal, forming no particular shape. Upon closer inspection, the lines appeared to belong to the sphere symbols one drawn atop another until each was lost in an intricate web of lines. Bolton catch Sara looking at the medallion and tucked it away under his shirt.

"Well," Bolton said, "our elements are obviously not of the kind that can help us find our way out of a forest. I guess that's why we have to rely on someone's pet."

Farah rolled her eyes.

She turned to Sara. "I'm a Wind Elemental." Farah called the breeze to pick up some dry leaves from the ground and twirl them in the air.

"Lightning," Bolton said. But Sara didn't need that revelation. She didn't want him to know how often she had watched him from the field, that she was so fascinated by his element that she had taken the time to draw him.

"Lightning Elementals have power-swollen heads and twitchy fingers," Farah said.

"Whoa, when did I earn that reputation?" Bolton asked.

"A few years ago, a Lightning Elemental sent bolts at me because I was a challenging target. He was kid, but he knew what he was doing. I could see it in his eyes. He tried to hurt Orka. For years, I thought maybe it was just the one. But when my dad sent me to Element, I realized you're all a bunch of baboons with a bit of stick."

Bolton smiled.

"What are you smiling at?"

"Nothing," Bolton said.

Orka flapped down from the trees to Farah's shoulder. She chirped and bobbed her head. She left her perch and flew north.

"Come on. She knows the way," Farah said.

WORKERS loaded crates onto ships set to sail for Lumina Port the next morning. Men fished, laughed, and drank. Mothers sat in the sun as their children played along the pier.

Sandel watched them through the spyglass. He camped on the small, uninhabited island across the water from Caleena. He mopped the sweat from his brow, spread his fingers, and sent the breeze to waft against his face.

Sandel's army of Wind Elementals anchored their large ship off the side of the island. They slept under the trees the night before and swatted mosquitos that bit them in the dark, humid air.

"Commander, the troops are prepared to attack the village." Cato stood by the rocks.

"Good." Sandel dismissed the breeze. He would need that energy soon. He handed the spyglass to Cato. "We attack once to inspire fear. We attack again when we get the signal."

Cato lifted the spyglass to his eyes. A mother grabbed her toddler's hand as he neared the end of the wharf.

Cato dropped the spyglass to his chest. "Why does Hephaestus want us to do this?"

Sandel looked off into the distance toward the small village. The people were specks, tiny as ants. *Because he knows she will be here*, Sandel thought, *and he wants to see how powerful her element is*. "You don't ask questions, solider."

Sandel had been trained in Breeze. He used to be father to three boys. His family suffered the friendly fire of Breeze's army when their mechanical catapult malfunctioned, firing into the city and crushing them and many others beneath piles of metal, stone, and dust.

"You can't keep happiness," he whispered as he stared out across the sea.

He closed his eyes. His element stirred inside him, like a tornado ready to be released upon the world.

As mothers and children played and workers loaded crates, a tsunami carried by Wind came upon the village with a roar and toppled the wharf ends and the pier.

The tremendous fall of the sea-salted water washed away the boards, and the pressure of the wave took lives.

Sandel didn't cry for them, no more than a boy cries when he disturbs an ant hill.

10

BRINA'S LOSS

BRINA put on her coat. Her hand reached for the door-knob when she realized she had forgotten her hat. She went to her room and took the hat from off the mantel.

The old, burnt playing cards rested on the table. She had taken them out last night, musing at memories. But Talon would not be glad to see her. He had become like a walled castle and she an intruder.

As she passed Spire's room, she felt an unnatural stillness in the air. Brina hesitated at the door but continued down the hall. As she neared the end of the hallway, she looked back. The air was too still. Brina could sense something was wrong. She walked up the stairs to Sara's room.

"Spire, I need to talk to you."

She knocked on the door. "Spire? Sara?" She knocked harder and retrieved the ring of keys from her dress pocket.

She opened the door to find an empty room. Sara's letter was on the table beside the bed. The drawer was opened, and notes curled inside. Brina opened the drawer wider and found the notes someone had been slipping under Sara's door.

Brina stuffed the letter and the notes into her pocket. She hurried to find Talon.

FIRE flew through the air as villagers watched, eyes wide, mouths open. Others passed in disgust. Customers pushed, gossiped, and shopped.

Talon threw rings of fire, both amazing and frightening the onlookers. Spectators dropped coins in the bowl five feet away. Talon used to place the bowl at his feet to prevent robbery, but the villagers were too scared to get close to a Fire Elemental.

Brina broke through the crowd. She held a piece of paper above her head.

"Talon," she said, "She's gone."

Talon dismissed the flames and pulled Brina aside. His hands were hot from the fire that had hovered over his skin. "What are you saying?" he whispered.

"Sara and Spire are both gone. I found her note." She handed the paper to him. "And I found others. They were written by someone urging Sara to leave."

Talon took the letters from her. He rifled through them, scanning them and wrinkling the delicate paper with his rough hands.

He stared at the last letter. You know what you have to do…

"This isn't good."

"It's worse. Three other apprentices are gone too. Your nephew is one of them."

"Bolton?" Talon said.

"I'm sorry. I tried to keep her safe. I did what you asked. I don't know what to do. I need your help."

"They'll have to board a ship in Caleena. I can track them."

"No." Brina held onto his arm. "I don't want you to go. Please, not like last time."

Talon turned to her. He held her face in his hands. What had she expected of him? That he would send someone else?

Her eyes were hypnotic, two black wells surrounded by rings of golden brown.

She was older. Lines wrinkled her face, but they didn't run deep. *It's because she hasn't smiled enough*, Talon thought.

He could sense the vines inching toward him.

"I have to go." Talon pulled his arm away from Brina's grasp.

He tore through the crowd. He hurried down an alleyway and to the place he had been living for ten years. It was a tent made of an old, woolen cloth, rotted wood, and empty barrels. From the back of the tent, he retrieved something wrapped in heavy sheepskin. He undid the wrapping to reveal the sword he had forged the day he first left Brina's side.

11

UNNATURAL WIND

SARA filled her water canteen at the stream. Orka rested on a branch. Farah examined a forked twig while Bolton picked at his fingernails. Rodan compared the map to their location. "There's no stream on the map."

"That map's useless." Farah tossed the twig into the water. "We should keep following Orka."

They had walked through the night and through the next day. The sun was getting low in the sky.

"It's a bird," Bolton said.

Sara glanced at Bolton. He might be a skilled Elemental, but he does complain a lot.

Farah stood. "A trained bird."

"What other choice do we have?" Sara asked. "The map is wrong. Unless you want to wonder aimless through the forest sans guide."

Bolton held up his hands. "We'll follow the bird."

Sara capped her canteen. Orka rustled her feathers and flew west. They followed.

Their feet dragged. If they didn't reach Caleena soon, they would have to camp out in the forest for the night.

"We've been walking for hours," Bolton said, "and that tree with the green ivy looks awfully familiar."

"I've been marking the trees," Rodan said. "I'd know if we were going backwards, but it is getting late."

Orka flew above them. The bright green of her wings ended in blue feathers at the tips.

"We should zap down these trees." Bolton said. "We could see clear across."

"Don't," Rodan said.

"What? It's not like you planted them. And besides, you could bring them back after I've destroyed them." He knocked Rodan's arm with his canteen before taking a swallow.

The ground was uneven. The shrubbery grew dense among the tall, packed trees. Patches of dark sky were visible through the canopy of leaves.

"What would be the point of that?" Farah asked. "Sure, a Lightning storm could fall a few trees, but if we're in the middle of the forest, there's no way a handful of fallen trees will give us a clear view."

"It'll have to be more than a few," Bolton said.

"More than a few would tire you out," Rodan said.

Sara doubted a Lightning storm would tire Bolton out. While other apprentices recovered in the shade, he was still in sun and sending more than sparks.

"At least, we would know where we're going," Bolton said. "We should stop. We barely have light."

Farah whistled, and Orka flew down and settled on her shoulder.

Rodan rested his back against the tree. Sara sat next him, and Farah lay among the leaves. Bolton sat where he stood, laid out and put his hands behind his head. Orka flew up to a tree and settled on a branch. She curled one foot into the feathers of her belly and closed her eyes.

LIGHT played behind Sara's eyelids. As her eyes jumped open to meet the sun, she squeezed them shut to avoid the stinging brightness. The open air gave her goose bumps.

"Good morning." Rodan's voice met her ears.

Sara sat up and let her eyes adjust to the light.

"Morning."

Bolton and Farah stirred in their sleep.

"They won't be awake for a while. I have to bang on Bolton's door to get him up in time for breakfast."

"We should let them sleep," Sara said. "We probably have another long walk ahead of us. And even more after that."

"Why now?"

"What?" Sara asked.

"I mean, why did you decide to run now after three years?"

The light danced on Sara's hands as the wind rustled the tree leaves blocking the sun.

"I had enough. I want a life."

"You know, this isn't the only way," Rodan said.

"I'm not sure it isn't," Sara said. "I'm being hunted. If I try to suppress my element, it will call to me. If I go into the open, Hephaestus will find and kill me. If I stay in Element, I'll go insane. This *is* the only way. He doesn't know I'm coming."

Farah sat up. "What are you two whispering about?" She rubbed her eyes.

Bolton got up and stretched. "They were probably making plans to leave us behind," he said.

"We didn't want to wake you." Sara stood and shouldered her bag.

"Wait, we haven't had breakfast yet." Farah opened the bag slung across her chest. She retrieved four rolls of bread and a hunk of cheese. She sliced some of the cheese with her pocket knife and handed a piece of bread and cheese to each of them. "This is all I have left for the road, so we'll have to get more food in Caleena." She ate some bread and took a sip of water from her canteen.

Orka flew down to her shoulder, and Farah offered her a piece of bread.

Once they finished eating, Orka soared above the trees to seek out the neighboring town. They followed her until she came fluttering down to Farah's shoulder. She chirped, and Farah rubbed her head.

"What now?" Rodan asked.

Farah pushed aside the branches as she stepped through the trees. "This way."

Sara followed.

Below was a village near the water. A series of wharfs and small bridges led to shops and homes. Caleena was smaller than Elementa. Hut-like houses on tall stilts towered over the wharfs. Banners hung on the rails of bridges and from roofs. The banners displayed the element symbols, but Fire was absent.

On the eastern side of the city, workers were repairing the wharfs, but on the western edge, the pier was intact, and men loaded crates onto ships.

"This is Caleena?" Bolton asked.

"Yes."

A tall woman in a black dress stood behind them. Her long, dark hair was braided tightly, and she had a travelling bag.

"Spire," Sara said.

"You thought I wouldn't find you?" Spire said. "You'll put Brina in a panic when she finds out what happened."

"She was never going to let me out," Sara said, "and nether were you. I guess you came to take me back."

Spire's lips formed a thin line. "No," she said. "But I'm coming with you."

"You think you'll talk me out of it?" Sara asked.

"No, I don't." Spire said. "There's little one can say when someone thinks she's invincible."

* * *

BOLTON stood at the end of the wharf overlooking the sea. He took the medallion out from under his shirt. The sunlight glanced off it.

"Hey, Bolton, what are you doing over there?" Farah stood further up the wharf near the buildings. "We're going to check the shops for supplies."

Bolton tucked the medallion back into his shirt and followed Farah.

They browsed the shops looking for necessities. They bought apples, cheese, and more bread.

After they bought the food, they stopped at an antique shop. Orka fluttered down from Farah's shoulder to examine the pearls and colorful stones, but when the shopkeeper noticed her, he shooed her away.

"Come on," Spire said. "We didn't come to browse."

A loud roar shook the hut. Jewels fell to the floor. The shopkeeper scrabbled to pick them up.

"What's going on?" the shopkeeper asked. "Twice in a day?"

"Run!" a voice shouted from outside.

"Not again!" Another screamed.

Farah and Bolton rushed out. Spire was behind them. They met Sara and Rodan on the deck. Villagers ran past them as the wind swept banners and crates along wharf.

The wind tore the banners from railings and houses. People hurried toward the forest.

Orka clung to Farah's back so the winds could not force her away.

Farah ran to the edge of the wharf. Bolton darted after her, followed by Sara, Rodan, and Spire.

Swirling storms rose above the sea. Water washed over the pier.

"Hurricanes," Spire said.

"This isn't Nature," Rodan said.

"No," Spire said, "I don't think it is. Sara, keep the water away from the village. Farah, help me calm the wind."

Farah stretched her hands out and focused. Spire joined her.

Sara concentrated on the water. Her head began to hurt. The tempests crept toward the village. Waves formed.

Teeth ground, Spire and Farah forced the Wind back. The spirals surged forward.

"There are too many of them." Water sprayed across Spire's face.

A wall of water rushed toward the village. The winds died down.

"They stopped," Farah said.

The wave cast its shadow over them. The wind no longer carried it as it hovered over the village. The water roared. Sara tensed.

Brave villagers wandered onto wharfs.

Sara closed her eyes. *I can do this.*

She could sense the water wavering as the wave leaned forward.

"Do something!" Bolton yelled.

Sara's eyes snapped open.

"Don't break her focus," Spire said.

"Fine, I'll do something." Bolton sent streaks of lightning through the wave.

Farah cowered behind Spire.

"That won't stop them," Rodan said. "It must be more than twenty Wind Elementals."

"Then I'll send more bolts." Bolton shot wildly into the distance.

"Wait." Spire placed her hand on Bolton's shoulder. "You could kill them, but you won't stop the wave. The wind isn't carrying it. It will come down upon us no matter how many Wind Elementals you kill."

The wave's shadow covered the village. Villagers who had braved the wave to witness the outcome ran as the water came crashing down.

For Sara, the wave crashed in slow motion. The top of the

wave curled as the water eased forward. It bent like a cat taking a stretch. The foam at its crest sparkled. The body of the wave danced in hues of green and blue.

Droplets of water stopped in midair in front of Sara's face. The wave ceased its forward lean.

The villagers looked back.

The water wavered within an isolated space.

Sara's breath fluttered from her lungs as she held out her hand to the wall of water. Sweat beaded on her brow. She pressed her lips together and pushed the wave. The water swept away from Caleena and left ripples upon the shore.

Sara turned to the man who doubted her. Bolton's mouth hung open. The villagers stared.

Sara's head was hot. Her muscles went slack, and she hit the wooden boards.

SARA opened her eyes. Above her was a bamboo ceiling. Spire cooled her head with a wet rag. Sara tried to sit up, but Spire pressed her shoulders back against the mattress.

"One of the villagers offered us her home," Spire said. "You put on quite a show."

"I had too," Sara said.

Spire nodded. "Yes. But now everyone in Caleena knows who you are. Something like this will surely get to Hephaestus."

"You asked me to stop the wave," Sara said. "But I would have anyway. I couldn't let these people die to hide my secret."

"Of course not," Spire said. "You did the right thing, but consequences will follow your actions." Spire dabbed at Sara's face with the rag.

"Is she okay?" Rodan's voice came from behind Spire.

Sara strained to see him.

"She's awake," Spire said. "She just needs rest."

Sara sat up. "I think I've rested enough."

Farah entered followed by Bolton. Orka perched on Farah's shoulder.

"After that, I thought you'd be out for three days," Farah said. "You hit hard."

"I'm fine," Sara said. "Do we know why the Wind Elementals attacked the village?"

"I talked to some of the villagers," Farah said, "but they don't know anything. They couldn't stop talking about you. The way they talk it's like you've already stopped Hephaestus."

"Well, I'm working on it," Sara said.

"They could have only been after one thing," Bolton said. "And since you only just arrived, it had to be—"

"The Fire Sphere," Rodan said.

"Why would Wind Elementals want the Fire Sphere?" Sara asked.

"Isn't it obvious?" Bolton said. "They work for Hephaestus."

Farah narrowed her eyes at Bolton. "When we first arrived, you asked where we were. How do you know so much all of a sudden?"

"Everyone knows where the spheres are," Bolton said. "But I've never been to Caleena."

"That would be a good theory," Spire said, "if Hephaestus could get the sphere."

"What do you mean?" Sara asked.

"Hephaestus has tried for years to obtain the element spheres," Spire said, "but he has failed. He sent men to Caleena before. When the guardians of the chapel tried to stop them, Hephaestus's men killed them and hung their bloodied robes over the town banners. Hephaestus has a particular distaste for Lightning Elementals," she said, looking at Bolton, "and Water Elementals. To get into the sphere sanctums, he would need a balance of the elements. Without this, he will never get in."

"But what if he has figured that out?" Bolton said. "Hephaestus might swallow his hate to the get the spheres. What if more than Wind Elementals come? What if they sent that wave as a distraction or a way of hampering the village's defenses so they can sail over here and take the sphere?"

"I've studied the sphere sanctums," Spire said. "He needs a Water Elemental."

"But…" Rodan said. "We're assuming Sara is the only one. *Is* she the last Water Elemental? How did that wind pick up that much water?"

"She is the last Water Elemental," Spire said. "We would know if there were others."

"Another Water Elemental," Farah said. "Sara's the first one I've seen in my whole life."

Bolton turned to Spire. "And you managed to hide her away for three years. Hephaestus lives in place far from the eyes of Mirmina. Don't you think he might have an easier time hiding a Water Elemental? Especially, if he held him against his will in the dungeons below the city."

They went back and forth, arguing of the possible existence of a second Water Elemental. Sara's head ached. She couldn't hear their individual voices anymore. It was a mass of voices, creating one sound and rising and rising until silence settled over the room.

"How do we get the sphere?" Sara asked.

12

SPHERE PROTECTOR

THE chapel of the Fire Sphere was on Cal Hill above the forest. The building was hundreds of years old and existed long before people settled in Caleena.

A path through the trees led to the chapel. The people kept the path free of stones, pebbles, weeds, and bushes. The sun dried the dirt.

The guardians had been responsible for the chapel's upkeep, but after Hephaestus killed them, no one attended to the chapel. The statues within the chapel's vaults gathered dust, and the floors were dirty.

"Why is Hephaestus after the spheres?" Farah asked.

They approached the chapel.

"Probably because of the myth," Rodan said. "If you combine the spheres, you can absorb their power. The binding circle is under the ruins of Omega Ray. Each sphere must be placed in the circle. If one is missing, the enchantment won't work."

"That's a fairy tale," Farah said.

"It is," Spire said. "But the power he would gain from the spheres may not come from the orbs themselves, but from the people who will fight alongside him to avoid their destruction."

"Hephaestus wants to control us," Rodan said. "But why? To what end?"

"Control the Elementals," Spire said, "and you control all of Mirmina. Everyone would bow to him."

"But if we gather the spheres," Sara said, "he can take them from us."

"Not if we take them to Fortress Tower," Bolton said. "Hephaestus wouldn't be able to use them to control anyone. If you set the spheres at top of the tower, they can't be touched."

"We don't know if what the Council built will work," Spire said.

"The Council?" Sara asked.

"A group led by Thomas Morica." Spire said. "They created a binding circle in Fortress Tower to eliminate the need for Sphere Protectors. They said it was a better way to protect the spheres. It's never been tried. Morica's people couldn't fight a Sphere Protector to save their lives much less retrieve the spheres."

"If we leave them where they are," Bolton said, "what if he finds a way to take them? It will be too late to stop him. We'll have to bow like everyone else."

"You're right," Sara said. "Hephaestus may find a way to get them himself. But if we have them, it will slow him down."

Farah fed Orka seed from the pouch slung across her shoulder. She stroked the bird's back. "You wait in a tree down the hill for me. I'll be back."

Farah didn't want any harm to come to Orka. Spire told them of the danger they would encounter in the chapel. They would have to battle the Protector of the sphere. The Protectors guarded the spheres, and they drew their essence from the core of the pedestal. They were powerful and unyielding, having only one purpose in life: to protect the spheres at all costs.

Orka flew from Farah's shoulder.

They continued up the granite steps to the chapel. Marble pillars lined the chapel entrance. Fire blazed from their peaks.

"The fire never goes out till the sphere is lifted from its pedestal," Spire said.

They entered the chapel. It was cold and dark inside.

"We need light," Spire said.

"I'm on it." Bolton snapped his fingers and a small, condensed bolt of lightning appeared. The Lightning glowed and sent a path of light five feet in front of them. Farah stepped back into the darkness.

Dusty statues of creatures with the bodies of men and the heads of bulls decorated the circular room.

"This is creepy," Farah said.

A path trailed from the room. Heat came from the inside.

"No one to light the lamps anymore," Bolton said.

The narrow pathway sloped down into the darkness. They started down the path. As they got farther from the entrance, the air got stuffy and hot.

"How far down are we?" Rodan asked. "Are we below ground level?"

"Probably," Bolton said.

The path widened, and they came to a door. The door was ten feet high and half as wide and glowed with a light strong enough that Bolton dismissed the Lightning.

"Why couldn't we see this light from further back?" Rodan asked. "It's so bright."

Bolton went to open the glowing door, but jumped back when a white-hot sensation burnt his hand as he touched the handle.

"Damn it!" He tried to shake the pain from his hand. His palm was red and stinging with heat.

"Sara, can you cool it down so we don't have to use the

water from our canteens?" Rodan asked.

Bolton reached for his canteen, but he couldn't get the cap off with one hand.

"I can't," Sara said.

"What you mean?" Rodan asked.

"She can't call Water," Spire said. "She can only manipulate it."

Rodan turned to Sara. "You didn't tell me that."

The silence put Sara's heart in the pit of her stomach. It was like she had taken them out to sea on a ship to later tell them that it had no lifeboats. No. It was more like the ship had no sails, oars, or a wheel to steer. They floated in the middle of the ocean, helpless.

"A little help," Bolton said through his teeth.

Farah took the canteen from him and uncapped it. She poured the water over Bolton's hand. Bolton cringed.

"Grab me that," Rodan said.

Farah passed the canteen to Rodan.

Rodan poured water over the handle. The hot metal hissed as the water hit it. Rodan touched the handle with his fingertips. He grabbed it and pulled, but the door didn't give.

"We don't have a Fire Elemental. Maybe only a Fire Elemental can open the door." Sara said.

Spire looked around.

"How bad is your hand?" Rodan asked Bolton.

"It's been better."

"Do you think you could help me?"

Rodan and Bolton placed their hands on the large handle and pulled. Their efforts were in vain.

"It must be locked," Rodan said. "But there's no keyhole."

"Sphere sanctums have their protections," Spire said.

"Look," Farah said. "Isn't that the Wind symbol?" She pointed to a symbol in the upper corner above the door. Time eroded the engraving, but Sara could make out a triangle with a line through the middle.

Spire examined the symbol.

"Why would the Wind symbol be in the Fire Sphere sanctum?" Rodan asked.

"It's not just the Wind symbol. Look," Farah said.

Alongside the Wind symbol were other faint engravings, the symbols for Water, Lightning, Fire, and Earth. Beside them were two unknown symbols. One was a square with a tilde through the center. The other was a darkened circle.

"What are those for?" Sara pointed to the two symbols on the end.

"Lost elements," Spire said.

The Fire symbol glowed against the stone, but the other symbols were dark.

"Maybe each symbol is like a latch," Farah said. "If we use our powers on them, they might open."

"Fire is glowing," Rodan said, "but we don't have those other two."

"We have a balance," Spire said. "We shouldn't need the lost elements because their spheres are broken and their essence flows freely, unharnessed by anyone."

Spire stepped forward. "We should touch the door. Together."

They joined Spire. Together they touched the door below their element symbol. The symbols glowed.

"Did it work?" Rodan asked.

The door blazed brighter. They backed away from it.

The handle melted, and smoke wisped from the narrow space between the door and its casing. The door eased open to reveal a circular room with intricate patterns on the floor. The patterns looked like smoke swirling in the air. Painted on the ceiling were flames of blue, orange, red, and yellow.

As they stood at the entrance, Sara thought of the smoke and flames the night her parents died. A tear dripped onto the smoke-patterned floor. The salty water made the smoke appear thinner. Sara wiped her face, hoping no one saw the tears.

In the back of the room was another door. This door did not glow.

"The sphere must be in there." Farah ran to the door.

"Wait, don't." Spire held out her hand.

Wind pushed Farah onto her back.

The flames on the ceiling jumped to life, embers floated to the floor. The ground shook and split in half.

Bolton jumped across. He took Farah's arm, and they leaped forward and fell to the floor as a bull with bronze hooves emerged from the tear in the ground.

Two long, curved, black horns grew from its head. Its front arms ended in massive bronze clawed hands. It had dark brown fur, and flames surrounded its body.

"The Protector of the Fire Sphere," Spire said. The words were like breath leaving her lips. Only Sara who stood beside her could hear them. Spire spoke them with such reverence and fear that Sara could feel it too.

The beast roared, arching its head up and straining its corded neck muscles.

Rodan threw Sara the water canteen. "Weaken it!"

Sara, Rodan, and Spire stood in front of the monster. Farah and Bolton were behind it.

Sara looked down at the canteen. *It's not enough.*

The beast pinned its eyes on her.

But it will have to be.

Sara pulled the water from the canteen like water running from an inverted spigot, stopped it in mid-air, and shot it at the beast's chest. He howled as the water stung him and extinguished the flames around his middle.

Spire sent Wind and knocked the beast off its feet, but the monster got up, its bronze hooves sounded heavy and metallic against the stone floor.

The beast growled. The inside of his mouth was coated with bronze, and fire issued forth from it. He opened one clawed hand and breathed the fire into it. He swung his arm back to throw the ball of flames, but vines wrapped around his wrist and anchored it to the ground.

Rodan focused. Thorns wound around the monster's

chest, and vines swept across its back pinning it to the ground. The vines burned away, but Rodan sent more to hold the beast down.

The creature's eyes glistened. *It's hurt because it failed*, Sara thought.

"I'll hold it down," Rodan said. "Farah! Bolton! Get the sphere!"

Farah and Bolton ran to the back door. The door screeched as they dragged it open.

Inside the room on a glowing pedestal rested the Fire Sphere. Farah grabbed it. As she took it from its pedestal, she felt a pulling sensation on the sphere as if a link was being stretched. The sphere felt heavier the farther she took it from the room.

The monster turned to dust as if all its energy was zapped with the loss of the element sphere. The dust fell into the cracks in the stone floor.

Farah and Bolton joined the others. Farah grinned and held up the Fire Sphere. Rodan went to pat Bolton on the back, but stopped. He nodded to him instead. They left the room and sauntered up the pathway. Sara stared up at the peaks of the pillars. The flames had gone out.

"CATCH." Farah tossed the sphere to Bolton. "Feel that?"

The sphere was warm. It fit in the palm of his hand. Fire swirled inside. He could break it. Fill it with Lightning and destroy it.

"Are you alright?" Rodan asked.

"Yeah," he said. "You take it." He handed Farah the sphere, she and deposited it into her bag.

An orange haze fell on Caleena as evening came. They needed to go to Wyvek Temple to get the Lightning Sphere. Wyvek Temple was across the Placid Sea beyond the City of Lumina. They would have to find a ship set sail to Lumina Port.

On the wharf, a trade ship was docked and people in amber-colored vests loaded it with crates. The breeze rustled the sails and rocked the ship. The sunset gave the wood of the ship an auburn glow.

The captain stood on the docks and watched the crewmen load crates onto the deck. He wore a bronze band around his left arm.

Bolton approached him.

"My friends and I need a ride to Lumina Port," he said.

The captain looked Bolton up and down. "And who are you?"

"We're the people who saved the village." Farah stepped forward.

The captain turned. His eyes rested on Sara. "You're the Water Elemental, aren't you?"

Spire grabbed Sara's arm.

"Yes," Sara said.

"You can come aboard," the captain said. "I'm Captain Medlow. We set sail for Lumina shortly. Get what you need and be on the ship before the sails rise."

NIGHT fell, and stars speckled the sky. The water was dark with streaks of moonlight. The ship rolled and dipped on the sea.

Sara stood on the deck and leaned on the railing. Flecks of peeling paint stuck to her arms. She stared at the sea. Never had she seen water so still and black. It slept.

She shaded in the dark waves in her drawing. She used the railing as a surface. The grain of the railing disturbed the smoothness of the waves. Sara frowned.

Rodan approached and stood beside her.

"Are you alright?"

"The Protector of the element sphere," Sara said, "did we have to kill him? He only did what he was created to do. He guarded the sphere."

"We did what we had to do. He would have killed us, and we needed the sphere."

"It feels wrong. I didn't know he would die like that."

"At least once we have the spheres, Hephaestus can't use them to hurt anyone."

How can you be so sure? "You're right." Sara smoothed out the texture of the waves with her finger. "What do the bands mean? The ones people wear around their arms? The Resistance wears silver ones, right?"

Mari's father left her a silver band. *What happened to Mari and Miranda?* What happened to any of the girls once they left the care of Ms. Fiora? Women begged in the market square, but people ignored them in favor of the Elementals who had talents the women didn't possess. What talents did those women have to rely upon to survive?

"Earth Elementals wear green to honor the Creator," Rodan said. "Purple is reserved for the Morica Council, though no one has seen them in years. Red is for the Scholars. Black for criminals and traitors. Bronze for leaders, like the captain. And gold, gold is a symbol of a great deed, something of great impact."

"Gold." Sara, gazed at the water.

"Spire has one," Rodan said.

"She does? I've never seen her wear it. Wait . . . I did see it once, a long time ago."

"She hides it."

"Why?"

"I'm not sure," Rodan said. "Modesty, maybe."

"What did she do?"

"She protected the Water Sphere."

She's the reason I'm here. "She didn't tell me," Sara said. How do you thank someone for something like that?

"You need the rest," Rodan said. "We all do."

"I'll catch up."

He was hesitant. "Goodnight."

"Night."

Sara imagined hoisting herself over the railing and splashing into the water. Sea rolled as she danced. Everything melted into the moving, impermanence of water.

"Hey, what are you doing out here all alone?"

"I'm not alone. I'm with you."

"Alright then." Bolton leaned with his elbows against the railing.

Sara bit back a smile.

"I never asked," Bolton said. "What made you want to do this? You're not afraid?"

"Afraid? I'm terrified. Anxious. Eager."

"Eager?" He narrowed his eyes.

"I know how it sounds," she said. "But I want to face him. I want him to answer for what he has done. Still, it's like a fantasy. It all feels so . . . distant."

"So, what are you going to do after you overthrow Hephaestus?" Bolton asked.

"You say that like it's for sure."

"Well, I certainly don't want to talk as if it's not for sure."

"I don't know what I will do after. But when Hephaestus is gone, I won't have to hide anymore."

"Yeah." Bolton looked down and shifted his weight.

"What's wrong?" She placed her hand on his arm.

Bolton looked at her hand like he wanted to burn it away.

Sara moved it. "Sorry."

"It's okay," Bolton said. "I'm not used to—Never mind."

"Maybe you should rest."

"I'm not sure that will help." His eyes stared into the distance, somewhere beyond the sea.

"What we did to that Protector," Sara said, "I didn't like it. But I did like what you did for Farah."

"It was nothing," he said.

"Saving someone's life isn't nothing."

"That's not what I meant," he said. "Saving her was easy. I don't deserve a medal."

"And no one's offering you one. But that's just it. Easy or not. You saved someone and expected nothing in return. Not everyone is like that."

Bolton smirked and shook his head.

"What?" Sara asked.

"I'm afraid you're making me into something I'm not."

"I don't think I am."

"Yes, you are. You're making me out to be the guy who always does the right thing. That's a lot to live up to."

"Sure," she said. "You don't want people to expect good things of you?"

"Makes it easier if they don't."

"What are you going to do when this is all over?" Sara asked.

"Go home," he said.

"Back to Element?"

"Element's not home."

"Where's home?"

"That's a whole other time and place."

"So, how will I visit you? I can't cross time. I can only go in the direction it pushes me."

"After all this? You wouldn't be too busy signing autographs?" he asked.

"My hand's bound to cramp up sometimes."

"I'll tell you about home when I feeling nostalgic." Bolton stretched.

"It's a deal." Sara folded her drawing and walked to the cabin of the ship.

BOLTON stayed on the deck. He let out a deep breath and propped his head up with his hands.

Rodan leaned his arms upon the railing.

"I thought you went to bed."

"I decided to stay up a while longer." Rodan stared at the line where the sea met the distance mountains. "You're getting to know Sara."

"Yeah," Bolton said. "She's interesting for someone who's been living under a rock for three years."

"She asked about you."

"Me? Why?"

"She asked about everyone," Rodan said. "She wanted to feel like she was on the training field with us."

"I'm not going to pity her for being locked in a room," Bolton said. "Some people have gotten way worse."

Rodan nodded. "But she's strong. That's why I asked you to come with us."

Bolton turned to his friend. "I told you not to get involved with her. This is a death march. I don't like having to mitigate other people's problems."

"She's going to save the world."

Bolton pressed his lips together and shook his head. "Then she doesn't need. I'm not fooled by her pretend modesty, are you? She thinks she going march into Omega Ray and demand an apology. Make him answer for his crimes. She's living a fairy tale."

"She's the last Water Elemental," Rodan said.

"Who cares?" Bolton asked. "She's feels sorry for a Protector. Even if she could fight Hephaestus, she wouldn't kill him."

"You don't like her."

Bolton smirked. "Everyone in Mirmina can like her, love her. It doesn't matter. I'd rather hate her and know she will do what it takes to get the job done."

"What are you so angry about?" Rodan asked.

"You dragged into this. I have to make hard decisions."

"What? The decision to stop a dictator? Why did you agree to come? Why don't you leave?"

Bolton approached Rodan. "Because you've made that impossible." He left the deck and entered the cabin below.

13

STRENGTH

THE streets of Omega Ray were empty. The soldiers were on missions. A few ran back to their families, and Hephaestus sent others to kill them for their disloyalty. Those who remained trained in the snowy fields behind the broken city walls.

Servants mended the walls stone by stone. One worker's face was red from the cold. His hair was auburn brown. He was stronger than the others and had repaired walls before.

A soldier ascended the stairs of Hephaestus's stone citadel. He brought a report from Sandel's army. "My lord, the plan of attack on Caleena was successful. She showed her power," the soldier said.

Hephaestus's cold eyes were on the soldier. "How was it?"

"Her power is . . . substantial. She broke down the Wind Elementals' typhoon in seconds."

"Is Fero stationed in Lumina?"

"His ship left a week ago. I watched the ship set sail. It was difficult to melt the ice to let the ship pass through, but he should arrive in Lumina Port by tomorrow."

"Good. He'll distract them. Everything must line up perfectly."

Perditus watched from the hallway where he was not visible to Hephaestus. He listened to the news from the soldier with eager ears.

His rivals were across the seas. But that didn't mean he would be any more loved.

Perditus removed his slender, black gloves.

He looked at his hands. They were shiny and pink. The skin was slick instead of soft. His father had burned him again and again, trying to teach him to stop the flames. "Control them!" he shouted. It was so important that he learn to harness his element or he wouldn't be his father's son.

But his father had given up on him years ago.

14

ATTACK AT SEA

THE next morning, the sun brightened the waters to cerulean blue. The scent of sea-salt wisped through the breeze. The ship rocked on the waves.

"You smell that, Orka?" Farah asked. "It's the smell of the ocean."

The green bird on Farah's shoulder bobbed her head.

"Orka and I like this smell. We should be pirates."

"Why be thieves?" Rodan asked. "Why not sailors?"

Kill joy, Farah thought. Pirates are exciting. Rodan was trying to impress Sara. But Farah wasn't amused by his saint-like proclamations.

Orka screeched.

Farah covered her ears to deafen the sound. "What is it?"

"Will you shut her up?" Bolton raised his voice to be heard over the chirping.

"She doesn't carry on like this unless she feels threatened. She must sense something . . . something not good."

Sara glanced over the railing. "The waves look calm."

Spire looked around toward the sky. "Something is wrong."

The ship jolted to the side as harsh winds assaulted it, and water splashed onto the deck. The crewmen started taking down the sails, so they could not catch the wind.

Water spilled across the deck.

Sara gripped the railing as the waves tossed.

"No." Spire stopped her. "Save your energy."

A larger ship approached them. It appeared over the horizon. The sails displayed a triangle with a horizontal line through the center.

"Who's that?" Rodan asked.

The ship rocked, sending more water onto the deck.

"Wind Elementals," Spire said as the ship proceeded to sway.

"More of them?" Bolton asked.

"What if they followed us from Caleena?" Farah shielded Orka's body with one hand.

The ship took on more water. Captain Medlow came up from the cabin. "What's going on?" He rubbed his side. "All this rocking made it hard to get up the ladder."

"They're trying to sink us!" one of the crewmen yelled.

"Who?"

"Wind Elementals."

Spire and Sara were at the foremast. The water threatened to overwhelm the ship. If they didn't keep the situation stable, the ship would sink or turn to splinters.

Sara lifted the water above the deck and sent it overboard with a splash. The ship stopped rocking. The waves settled. The wind died down.

Deep breaths went around, but all on deck clung to parts of ship.

Farah rose from her crouched position and looked over

the railing. Her clothes were drenched, as were Orka's feathers. The water swirled. The wind twisted above it in a cyclone.

"Not again," Farah said.

She commanded the wind to push the hurricane farther out to sea. Farah struggled beneath the weight of the Wind Elementals' power. Spire rushed to her side and helped to send the cyclone away from the ship.

"Let's send it back with a little kick in it." Lightning spiraled around the tempest as Bolton held his hands out and pinned his lips together.

Who is he trying to impress? Farah thought.

The storm raged between the ships.

"They're too strong," Farah said. "There are too many of them."

The cylinder inched away from the ship, but rushed back, causing thick waves to splash upon the deck.

"We're going down," Spire said.

Farah glanced at Orka, who perched upon her shoulder. Were her feathers too wet for her to fly?

Sara pushed past the crewmen as the hurricane spiraled toward their ship. Spire tried to grab her as Sara rushed past her. She stood with her hands on the railing and faced the storm.

Sara closed her eyes as water sprayed across her face. Beyond, the water plunged toward the sea bottom. The ship lurched down with the water. Sara staggered and knelt on one knee. She pulled herself up. "Try!" she shouted.

Farah focused on the cyclone. The influence on the storm lightened. She pushed. The funnel hit the ship, water-logged and shaky from Sara's attack. The mast of the ship cracked. The sails tore. The ship was a mass of boards swallowed by the sea.

Farah gulped. She was dizzy. Orka nuzzled Farah's face with her head. "That was close." Farah petted the little, green bird. Maybe a career at sea wasn't for her after all.

15

THE ELEMENT GAMES

SAILORS docked the ship in one of the three empty docking stations in Lumina Port. Workmen loaded and unloaded ships and hauled crates onto wooden-wheeled carts. Seagulls flew above the ships and landed on the crates. The crewmen shooed the birds away.

As Sara stepped off the ship, Captain Medlow offered her his hand. "My Lady." Sara gave him a thin-lipped smile and took his hand. She descended the ramp.

"Thank you, Captain," she said.

"When you see the Big Bad, punch him in the throat for me," Medlow said. "He could have cost me my ship." The captain turned to one of his crewman.

Rodan joined Sara on the dock.

"So, this is Lumina," Sara said.

"Yep. Largest city in the world," Rodan said. "Well, inhabited city. Vella City is larger, but it's been abandoned for years."

Farah ran past them.

"Where is she going?" Spire asked.

"Probably to get her fill of the city," Bolton said.

"We don't have time for that," Spire said. "We must gather the spheres before Hephaestus discovers us."

"Good luck with that," Bolton said.

Rodan narrowed his eyes at Bolton.

"This is the city of distractions," Bolton said. "People don't come to Lumina to plan the demise of element tyrants."

They followed Farah as she weaved through the crowd.

The buildings were taller than those in Elementa. They soared into the sky. Crowds pushed through the city. People browsed shops and wore bright colors. The buildings, the floors, and the city walls were made of marble.

The wild colors and festive dancing drew Farah deeper into the city. The place had caught her like a magnet. She wandered without aim.

They followed Farah under the overhanging ceiling, supported by marble columns. They crossed a large, marble pathway, sloping up above the water. People congested the marble floored plaza.

A fountain sat in the center of the square, but no water flowed. Grasses and red flowers filled the fountain. A chill ran through Sara. Water must have once danced in the fountain before the fountain served as a symbolic graveyard for Water Elementals.

Colorful banners hung from buildings and sky rails. Like in Caleena, the banners depicted the symbols for Fire, Lightning, Wind, and Earth.

"What are the banners for?" Sara asked.

"The Element Games," Rodan said.

"What is that?"

"The contest is held once a year," Spire said, "and is comprised of a series of battles, a marksmanship challenge, and an artistic talents category. Whoever wins earns the prize of the jewel orb priced at twenty-five hundred sparklings."

"Sign me up," Farah said.

"We don't have time to waste," Spire said.

"Waste?" Farah said. "If I win, we could sell the orb in town. Twenty-five hundred sparklings can buy a lot of supplies."

"If you win," Rodan said.

Farah put her hands on her hips.

"Why not?" Bolton said. "It would be a perfect time to train. There's a practice facility near the Stadium."

"You're not going to watch me win the orb?" Farah asked.

"You'll have more than enough of an audience," Bolton said.

They left the marble plaza to find the registration desk. They passed groups of people gossiping and betting.

"My bet is on Jacopo," one said.

"That nasty Fire Elemental. I heard he was one of Hephaestus's fiends," another said. "You never can tell anymore, but lots of Fire Elementals sympathize with Hephaestus."

"Not only Fire Elementals," the one said. "Three years ago, Hephaestus's men went to my sister's village. They were looking for more soldiers to join his army. When no one volunteered, they attacked the village. My sister saw Wind Elementals and Earth Elementals too."

Farah discovered the ticket booth. Sara followed her. People lined up to purchase their tickets. Farah got in line and waited. Once at the front of the line, she asked the ticket salesman where registration was taken.

"That's not my department," the man said. "Besides registration ended weeks ago."

"Look," Farah said. "There must be a mistake. I registered last month, but I never got my paperwork."

"Paperwork?"

"Is there anyone we can talk to?" Farah asked.

"Ask Dabert at the bar," the man said. "Maybe he can help

you."

The bar was across from the ticket booth. The ticket salesman pointed it out to them.

Patrons filled the bar. They talked about the Games and bet on their favorite contestants. Behind the bar, Dabert wiped a glass with a worn rag and smoked a roll-up.

Farah stepped toward the bar, but Rodan put his hand on her shoulder. He approached the bar.

"We want to register for the Games," Rodan said.

"Registration ended a month ago," Dabert said.

Farah walked to the bar before Bolton, Sara, or Spire could stop her.

"We came to see if you can help us find a way around things," Farah said.

"It'll cost you." Dabert placed the glass on the rack behind him.

"Let's get out of here," Spire said.

Farah turned to Spire. "This is twenty-five hundred sparklings we're talking about."

"Spire's right," Sara said. "We don't have the money."

Farah turned back to the bartender. "How much?"

Dabert put his hands on the bar top. "Five hundred. For one of you."

Farah slapped five coins down on the bar. They were large, silver coins. "That should cover it."

Sara glanced at Spire. Spire shook her head.

Dabert ran his hand along the bar and dragged the coins toward him. He examined the coins and pocketed. "See that's done."

Farah smiled and turned away from the bartender.

"You need to be at least fifteen to compete, shrimp." A man at the bar turned in his seat. He had a dark tan and a peculiar deep red birth mark that ran from his jawline down his neck.

"I am fifteen," Farah said.

Orka chirped.

"And no pets allowed."

"Hey." Bolton stepped up to him. He hesitated. A meaningful look arose in his eyes like he was trying to work his way out of a labyrinth.

The man stared at Bolton. He laughed. He stood. The man was short, but he was nearly double Bolton's mass. Flames gathered in his open hand.

Dabert slammed his rag onto the bar top. "Enough of that or you all can get the hell out of my bar."

The man dismissed the flames and sat. He reached into the pocket of his coat and withdrew five silver coins. He slid the coins across the bar to Dabert. "Sign the boy up too."

Bolton pinned the man with his eyes as they left the bar.

"You know him?" Rodan asked.

"No," Bolton said.

"We have to get a couple rooms at the inn," Farah said. "The Games don't start until tomorrow. Look." She pointed to the banner above the Stadium.

They rented two rooms. Spire left to get supplies and food for dinner. Sara sat at a table with her paper and charcoal. She drew a sketch of the city.

"You're good." Farah watched as Sara traced the contours of Lumina Stadium and the surrounding buildings. "I've been here half a dozen times, and I wouldn't have been able to remember that much detail."

"I've had a lot of practice," Sara said.

Farah slid down into the chair across from Sara. "So, you and Rodan."

Sara looked up from her drawing. "Rodan and I?"

"He told me he met you at the lake."

"He told you?"

"Well, not exactly."

Sara returned to her drawing. "We're friends."

"I don't think he feels the same way you do," Farah said.

"He's not my friend?"

"I wouldn't say that. But I think maybe he wants more."

Sara gazed down at her drawing and smirked. "I don't know."

"How long were you locked in that room? He came all this way with you. He's willing to fight the man himself for you."

Sara looked at her. "Why are you here?"

Farah frowned and tilted her head side to side. "I'm like you, I guess. My dad sent me to Element nine years ago. I'm sick of the place."

Orka chirped from her perch on the headboard of Farah's bed.

"Orka's sick of it too," Farah said. "Dad said he wanted me to get a proper education. But I know better than that. He wanted to get rid of me so I could be somebody else's problem for a while."

"That's bleak," Sara said.

"I'm used to it." Farah put her feet up on the table.

Sara's hands tingled. "Can I open the window?"

"It's fine."

Sara opened the shutters. The evening air drifted into the room. Sara took a deep breath.

"You okay?"

"Yes, the room felt a little stuffy, but it's alright now." Sara put her drawing into her bag.

BOLTON walked through the passageway. The stones muffled the cheers of the crowd. He remembered fighting an Elemental far older than him. The cheers of that crowd were more like jeers.

He stopped. His hands were balled into fists.

"Are you alright?" Farah asked.

Bolton wrung out his hands. "Yeah."

The other contestants walked alongside them. A few were pale with sweat-stained brows. Only one man didn't appear troubled by the coming events. The man they met in the bar. The short man. But he was stocky. He wasn't wearing the long coat Bolton saw him in at the bar. His arms were muscled, nearly as thick as his neck.

Bolton used to criticize Rodan for doing pushups after training. What was the point of having all that muscle when you had power beyond the physical?

The cheers of the crowd faded.

"Ladies and gentlemen, welcome to this year's Element Games."

An assistant pushed past them and began to organize the contestants into groups and line them up. He pulled Farah away from Bolton and placed her at the beginning of the line.

"As we all know these times can be trying," boomed the announcer.

Bolton scoffed.

"But the Games have always reminded us that there are heroes! Heroes that will rise up and show their skill and their strength."

Bolton glanced around him. Which one of these games-mad idiots ever tried to fight Hephaestus?

The assistant moved Bolton to the back of the line.

"And so, good people, I give you your contenders!"

The doors heaved open. The light stung Bolton's eyes. The screams of the crowd funneled down the passageway. Farah strolled out into the light.

"Farah. Wind Elemental. Heiress of Breeze."

Did he say Heiress of Breeze?

"Taryn. Wind Elemental from the Windy Desert."

Bolton swallowed as he watched the other contestants file out.

"Dema. Lightning Elemental of the Isle of Elementa."

Cheers erupted.

"Jacopo. Fire Elemental from Omega Ray."

The crowd booed.

Bolton glanced around. Fire Elementals from Omega Ray? They came.

When it was his turn, Bolton stepped out onto the field. The stands stretched to the sky. The contestants filed into a line in the center of the field. Bolton noticed the man from the bar, but he hadn't caught his name when the announcer introduced the contestants.

In the bottom rows, people dressed in bright colors and wore jewels. Higher up, features were less distinct. The sea of faces swirled above him. Bolton's eyes darted to the ground to avoid the coming nausea.

"Bolton. Lightning Elemental." The announcer paused. "This must be a mistake."

Out of the corner of his eye, Bolton noticed a group of people on the sidelines. They wore silver bands around their arms. *Resistance Fighters. Why are they here?*

"Bolton hailing from . . . the Insula Somnia Perpetua?" The announcer's voice was uncertain.

"WHERE?" Sara asked. She, Rodan, and Spire sat on the benches above the field.

"An island," Rodan said. "Doesn't exist. Legend says only one man knows where the island is, and you must pay with coins that aren't made anymore so he will ferry you to the island. People have tried looking for the isle to escape the threat of Hephaestus." Rodan smirked. "Bolton told me he was from the island when I first met him."

"Where is he really from?" Sara asked.

Rodan frowned. "I don't know."

The announcer began introducing the judges.

Sara noticed the silver-banded people standing on the sidelines. They seemed disinterested in the show. They stood rigid with their hands behind their backs.

Sara turned to Spire. "Resistance fighters?"

"Yes," Spire said. "New members are banded every year. The Banding Ceremony takes place after the Games. They must be here for a little entertainment before the rite."

"Why aren't they in the stands with the rest of the audience?" Sara asked.

"They're looking for something," Rodan said.

The Resistance fighters scanned the stadium.

"Perhaps they are afraid things will get out of hand," Spire said.

The referee, a broad man in a short, blue coat strode onto the field. He held up a hand until the noise of the crowd subsided. "This round will test the contender's aim. Scores will be given. The ten highest will move onto the next challenge."

"Do things get out of hand often?" Sara asked.

"Very rarely," Spire said.

Farah stepped forward. The referee threw a colorful fist of dust into the air. Wind shot the dust toward the target where it hit within the innermost circle.

Sara clapped. Spire and Rodan joined her.

The contestants stepped forward to face the challenge in the order they were introduced. Jacopo approached the line and rolled his shoulders.

The sentiment of the audience was a mix of claps and jeers.

Jacopo tilted his head to the side and cracked his neck.

"He should be disqualified," Rodan said. "People suspect he's a member of Hephaestus's army. It's dangerous to let someone like that on the field."

"Perhaps," Spire said. "But the City Counsel of Lumina doesn't like to involve itself in politics. Anything to thrill the tourists is fair game."

"It's not politics," Rodan said. "It's a matter of safety."

Jacopo burned a hole through the bullseye.

Bolton stepped up. Sara's breath caught.

"He looks nervous." *But why?* she wondered. Bolton had always manipulated his element effortlessly.

Bolton stood behind the line and stopped. He stared toward the target. The crowd began to chatter. The referee held up one finger to quiet the audience.

Sara leaned forward in her seat.

Bolton pushed his hands out. Lightning zipped from him and struck the target. A pinpoint surrounded by black marked the center of the bullseye.

The crowd let out cries of awe. Bolton backed away from the line and joined the other contestants. The judges tallied the scores and selected ten Elementals to move onto the second round. Farah joined Bolton in the winners' circle. A third contestant joined them who Sara recognized. The red-faced man from the bar. The announcer had introduced him as Fero, a Fire Elemental from Omega Ray. He glared at Bolton as he took his place alongside him.

The referee announced the next challenge. "And now round two: Artistic Talent."

"Your dad is with the Resistance, isn't he?" Sara asked Rodan.

"Yes," Rodan said. "He's a commander."

Farah stepped into the circle. The referee offered her a bag of green dust. Farah focused. Dust shot from out of the bag and flew across the sky in the semblance of a flock of green birds.

The audience applauded.

"Impressive," Spire said.

Sara looked down at her hands. They tingled.

Lastly, Bolton took his turn on the field. He sent two bolts of lightning into the air. They got closer and closer until they clashed and sent sparks down onto the audience.

The judges selected six of the ten to enter the final round.

"Now," the announcer said, "we will pair up the contestants for the Battle Round."

Two men, each carrying a pedestal, approached opposite ends of the field. The pedestals reminded Sara of the one in the Fire sanctum. The referee strolled to the center of the field where he placed a silvery orb. The orb could fit in the palm of one's hand.

"It's the jewel orb," Spire said. "The prize we came to win."

The referee silenced the murmurs of the crowd. "We will witness the final challenge. The contestant must place the orb on his or her pedestal before his or her opponent. The contestants will fight for the orb with their elements only. No punching. No kicking. No weapons."

Sara itched her palms. "They're going to fight?"

"Yes," Rodan said. "My dad brought me to the Games when I was a child. Fire burned the side of a man's face. It melted his ear off."

Sara's head swam. She recalled when the fire engulfed her home.

"For the first bout," the referee announced, "the judges have chosen Bolton, the Lightning Elemental from the Insula Somnia Perpetua, and Fero, the Fire Elemental from Omega Ray.

Sara jumped from her seat.

"Sara?" Rodan touched her arm.

"I'm okay," Sara said. "I need to get some fresh air." She walked to the stairs between the benches and climbed down. She stood outside the Stadium. The pavilion was empty. She took out her canteen, poured water into her hand and splashed it onto her face.

They're going to think I'm weak, Sara thought.

She breathed through her nose. I have to get back. Fighting is what we came to do. If I can't witness a controlled bout, how can I challenge Hephaestus? How can I challenge him?

Sara paced the pavilion.

She jumped and dropped her canteen. The water spilled.

Three people stood in front of her.

The tall man stepped forward. "You sank our ship."

BOLTON'S hands were in fists as the announcer called him to the circle. He stood and looked out into the crowd of pulsating colors. When the announcer called out the name of his opponent, Bolton's eyes darted forward.

The red-faced man marched toward the circle. He stood at the mark.

The scattered applause dulled in Bolton's ears. He thought of the encounter in the bar, of the flames hovering above Fero's hand. His brow sweat. He thought he might vomit.

He stepped up to his mark. They stood on opposite sides of the jewel orb in the center. Fero smirked at Bolton.

"Begin!" the referee bellowed.

Sweat trailed down Bolton's brow as he waited for Fero to make the first move. But he didn't. Bolton gulped. He raced toward the orb. The field erupted in flames in front of him. Bolton jumped back.

The noise of the crowd met Bolton's ears. The sea of faces twisted and swirled.

"Kill him, boy! Kill him!"

Fero laughed.

Bolton sent Lightning through the flames. He missed Fero by a hair. The flames in front of Bolton extinguished.

Bolton reached for the orb. Smoke rose from the ground. Bolton plucked the orb up before it was engulfed in flames.

He zigzagged across the field as fire roared past him.

A fireball hit Bolton's arm, but he didn't let go of the orb. He ducked as the heat of another ball of flames careened past his head. As he approached the pedestal, flames erupted around it.

Bolton shot Lightning across the field. Fero dodged the bolt. But the next stunned him. The flames surrounding the pedestal died down, giving Bolton time to set the orb.

The crowd roared.

Bolton's hand stilled on the orb.

"All hail, the victor!" Fero clapped in slow rhythm.

Bolton turned.

Flames raced toward Bolton's head. He dropped to the ground.

The referee stuck his hand in the air. "That's enough."

The announcer pointed from his seat beside the judging booth. "Fero of Omega Ray. You must leave the circle immediately!"

The judging booth caught fire. The announcer and the three judges leapt to their feet and backed away from the booth.

Fero faced the audience. The people in the stands ran to the exits.

Bolton looked around. Fire Elementals stalked the field. Their hands glowed with flames. The other Elementals stood against them. The so-called heroes. *They've never seen real battle in their lives*, Bolton thought. *This is going to be a massacre.*

Fero stepped forward. "So, traveling with the Water Elemental, are you, boy?"

He's working for Hephaestus, Bolton thought, I should have known.

"I thought I knew you from somewhere," Fero said. "Your father won't like to find you with her."

"He's not my father," Bolton said.

"Take that up with him." Fero threw rings of fire at Bolton.

Bolton rolled away from the flames. "I didn't have a choice. This was the only way." He sent Lightning at Fero.

Something gleamed out the corner of Bolton's eye. Orka flew above the field. Her talons wrapped around the woven tie of a small satchel. The satchel hung open, and an item glistened within before the weight of it drew the drawstring tight.

Farah fought Jacopo on the opposite end of the field. Flames surrounded his body like fiery armor.

THE Resistance fighters joined the fight. They wielded weapons of steel: swords, spears, and shields. The silver-banded group focused on the battle, which turned into more of a staggering bar-fight than the strategic battles for which they trained.

Four of the contestants crawled away. Many were injured.

A woman with burnt-red hair scanned the benches as she fought.

"Mercedes." Abdiel fought beside the red-hair woman.

"Do you still see her?"

"No," Mercedes said. "She left the stands before the battle. It seems she has not returned."

Mercedes sliced through her latest opponent and left him bleeding on the ground.

THE battle drained Bolton. The nerves brought on by the contest and the subconscious fear of this man he didn't know exhausted him. He swayed where he stood.

"Come on," Fero said. "You get a free one. Take your best shot, boy.

Bolton tried to call Lightning, but all he got was sparks and static.

"Too bad," Fero said.

"What are you doing?" Bolton shouted.

"You lose. I think I'll take it from here."

Fero sent a burst of flames at Bolton. Bolton backed up, tripped, and fell to the ground. Fero summoned up the flames to put an end to him.

"Do it!" Bolton ground his teeth.

"I wouldn't, Fero." A man with a scar running down his face walked into the circle.

Fero ignored him. He sent the flames toward Bolton.

The scarred Elemental stopped the flames before they hit Bolton's face and sent them off into the open air.

"You don't know what you're doing," Fero said. "You should mind your own business. Not like last time."

"This is my business," Talon said. "You've disappointed me. Call these Fire Elementals off, before I do."

Fero gave Talon one long stare. Without taking his eyes off Talon, he announced, "Soldiers, let's go. We have what we came for."

Fero stepped up to Talon. "I called them off, *Master.*"

Talon glared at him.

The Fire Elementals stalked off the field and left the others to nurse their unforeseen wounds.

Farah ran over to Bolton and extended her hand. He took it, and she helped him to his feet.

"How did you do that?" Farah asked Talon.

Talon glanced at Bolton.

"They're afraid of him." Bolton brushed the grass from his shirt.

"Well, that's good," Farah said. "Welcome aboard, sir."

"Who said I was joining you?"

Farah narrowed her eyes at the old man. "What did he mean by they got what they came for?"

Talon scanned the field, looking from one injured Elemental to the next. He turned his eyes to the stands. "Where's Sara?"

Farah's eyes darted around. The benches where the audience sat were empty.

"Spire and Rodan must have taken her somewhere safe," Farah said. "I'll go find them." She rushed out of the Stadium.

"We should go with her," Bolton said. "He might have meant Sara. She's what he came for."

"What are you doing here, Bolton?" Talon asked.

"I'm helping a friend," Bolton said.

"A Water Elemental," Talon said.

"No," Bolton said. "A fool Earth Elemental who thinks he owes her his fealty."

"You're going back to Element."

Bolton smirked. "Are you going to make me, Uncle?"

"It's not safe with her," Talon said.

"So, didn't come to ferry *her* back to Element?"

"That has nothing to do with you."

"You can't control everyone."

"I'm trying to protect you."

Bolton tilted his head to the sky and laughed. He faced Talon. "I didn't ask you to protect me then, and I'm not asking you to protect me now. If it was up to me, I would have stayed in your over-booked prison and she would be marching to her death by herself. But plans change."

"This isn't a game."

"What makes you think I don't know that? That guy seems to have an affinity for setting people's faces on fire. He could have burned mine to a crisp if you hadn't shown up. Is that what happened to you?"

Talon turned away from Bolton.

Bolton looked down at his feet. "Sorry." He shook his head. "I don't know what you came to do, but she's set on this. This whole going to face him thing. And you can't drag her back to Element. I talked to her. She'll keep trying. You stepping in isn't going to change that."

"I didn't come to change her mind. I came to change yours."

"Well, I'm sorry. I'm going. And you can stand there and tell me all the reasons I'm as much a fool as she is. Believe me, I've run through all of them. But it's not going to change anything."

ONCE Farah left the field, she couldn't recognize the city streets. Crowds rushed to leave the city. They passed the ticket booth and ran toward the docks.

Farah pushed through the crowd. She was too short to see over the mass of people. Beyond the bridge was a sculpture of a man wearing bangles around his arms. The sculpture was ten feet high. She hurried across the marble bridge and climbed the statue.

Farah looked over the crowd. Her eyes stopped on the market square. Sara struggled in the arms of two strangers. A third man walked in front of Sara and her captors. They pulled her toward the docks.

On the opposite side of the bridge, Rodan and Spire stopped people. They appeared to be asking questions, probably pertaining to Sara's whereabouts.

"Hey!" Farah yelled from atop the statue. She waved her arms.

Spire spotted her and pointed. Rodan looked. They ran to

Farah.

Farah jumped down from the statue. "Some people have Sara over by the docks."

"Come on. We have to hurry." Spire lifted the hem of her dress and ran. Farah and Rodan followed her.

They caught up with the kidnappers in the garden behind the docks. The area was a small plot of elevated land, filled with flowers and shrubs, and surrounded by a short, stone wall. A tree grew in the center of the garden. Marble floor encircled the tree and spread to the garden. Covered stands sat within the sales area.

"Stop!" Spire shouted. She held out her hand, but the tall man turned and negated her power.

"They're Wind Elementals," Farah said.

Farah looked at Rodan.

"Right," he said. Rodan marched toward the Elementals who held Sara.

Farah looked at Spire.

"What are you doing?" Sara twisted in the arms of the two Elementals.

Rodan pulled back his fist and punched one of the two in the face. The punch stunned the man. Rodan pulled Sara from the grasp of the second Elemental.

The tall Elemental stood in front of Rodan. The others surrounded him. Farah rushed forward. She leapt onto the back of the tall man and clawed his face. He spun. Farah hit the ground.

Wind tore through the sales area. The Wind pushed back and forth. Spire gritted her teeth.

Rodan held a hand out. Branches wrapped around the tall Elemental's neck. The branches came from the tree in the center of the garden.

"Leave," Rodan said, "and I'll let him go."

The tall man held out his hand, and the two others backed away. Rodan released the man. The branch curled away from him and went back to its normal length and position on the tree.

The man rubbed his neck and gasped for air. He glared at Rodan.

"We have friends coming," Farah said. "A Lightning Elemental and a Fire Elemental in case you want to challenge all of us at once."

The tall man frowned, but his eyes stabbed her. He didn't look like a man used to being kicked. He turned to his friends, and they left.

"Are you okay?" Rodan asked Sara.

"Are you?" she asked.

"I'm the only one who fell on the hard, marble floor." Farah stood.

"You should be more careful," Bolton said.

He and Talon stepped into the disheveled sales area. Wind had knocked the stalls from their foundations. Fruits rolled across the ground. Some leaked their smashed guts onto the marble floor.

"More careful? We were attacked," Farah said.

"Even more reason to be careful," Talon said.

"Talon?" Spire turned to him.

Sara stepped away from Rodan's embrace.

"How did you find us?" Spire asked.

"The entire island of Caleena is talking about Sara," Talon said. "You don't keep secrets well."

"I'm not going back to Element," Sara said.

Talon looked at Bolton. "I was told you would say that."

"You didn't come to stop us?" Sara asked.

"I came when I heard you ran away," Talon said. "But I realize how fruitless it would be to try to stop you. If you want to face Hephaestus that is your choice. No one should tell you what to do with your power. But I must come with you."

"Alright," Sara said. "We could use a Fire Elemental."

"What do you mean?" Talon asked.

"We're taking the element spheres from their sanctums," Rodan said.

"That's a crime," Talon said.

"Yes." Spire approached him. "But sometimes taking the spheres is the only way to protect them."

"I see," Talon said.

Sara and the others stopped on an oval balcony overlooking the sea. The steps leading away from the balcony would bring them to Dustpath.

"So," Rodan said. "We think Hephaestus sent those Wind Elementals to kidnap Sara."

"But that means Hephaestus knows about me," Sara said. "How can that be? How can word have reached Omega Ray so quickly?"

"I think it was more a crime of opportunity," Spire said. "Perhaps they weren't sent, but saw you and knew Hephaestus would want you."

"How did Hephaestus find so many Wind Elementals to side with him?" Rodan asked. "A whole ship full of them attacked Caleena."

"It was the pact," Farah said. "After the Great Raid, some Wind Elementals felt safer fighting for Hephaestus."

Orka landed on the railing surrounding the balcony. A satchel was tied around her foot. Farah unknotted the string and opened the satchel. She emptied the contents into her hand.

"The jewel orb," Rodan said.

Farah put the orb into the sack on the side of her waist.

"You stole it," Bolton said.

"No," Farah said. "They're Orka's treasures."

"Treasures? How much did you steal?"

"I didn't steal anything," Farah said. "Besides, one of us would have won it anyway."

"You know what they do to thieves," Talon said.

"What?" Farah asked.

"Cut off their hands or, in this case, talons."

Farah placed a hand over Orka.

"I won't deal out the punishment," Talon said. "But I

would suggest you teach your little friend to stop stealing before you get us all into trouble."

Farah opened her mouth to say something, but Spire stopped her.

"Let's move on," Spire said. "Wyvek is beyond Dustpath. If we start now, we'll make it to the sphere sanctum in a few days."

16

FEAR

DUST rode on the breeze as the travelers kicked it up. Ruins lay on either side of the road. Buildings were lost to the sand. Footprints and wagon tracks stamped the path.

"What happened here?" Sara asked.

She and Rodan walked side by side.

"A hundred years ago this was a town," Rodan said. "The Earth Elementals who lived here called it Tosia. But they had to leave because a storm hit the town."

"Didn't they try to rebuild?"

"They did, but the storm kept coming. Crops failed. The water dried up. They relocated to the forest, founded a village, and kept the name."

"They weren't afraid of bad luck?" Sara asked.

"Bad luck is an illusion," Talon said, "a way for people to

explain their random misfortunes."

Rodan glanced at the sword at Talon's side. "You carry a weapon of steel."

"Yes," Talon said. "My father taught me how to make a blade. I made this one before my first journey to Omega Ray. It will remind me not to make the same mistakes."

"Mistakes?" Sara asked.

"We have a long walk ahead of us," Spire said. "Talking will only make us tread slower."

"Ahead of us?" Bolton walked alongside Rodan. "We just put a long walk behind us."

"There's an inn between this road and the new one," Spire said. "We can rest when we arrive. It should be nightfall by then."

Spire, Rodan, and Talon picked up the pace. Farah raced ahead of them. Bolton and Sara fell behind.

"Have you been to Wyvek?" Sara asked Bolton.

"No, why?"

"I know a lot of Lightning Elementals come from Wyvek."

"Sure," Bolton said. "But I've never been. I think my father was from Wyvek. Not that it matters."

"Where are you from?"

"The Insula Somnia Perpetua, didn't you hear?"

"I did," Sara said. "People thought it was amusing."

"I'm glad I could be the entertainment," Bolton said.

Dust wafted through the air. Sara shielded her nose and mouth with the sleeve of her dress. The dust stung her eyes, and they watered. She kept her head down.

The road curved. A wooden, painted sign sat on a cliff. The sign read: "Welcome to Dustpath Inn. Five sparklings per night. Trust Dustpath Inn for all your traveling needs."

Farah stopped by the sign. The wind died down.

Sara dropped her sleeve.

"Sorry," Farah said. "Sometimes I don't know I'm doing it."

A building sat opposite the cliff. The wooden gate surrounding the building was missing pickets. A sign above the door read: *"Dustpath Inn."*

Farah knocked. The door opened, and a booming voice announced: "Welcome to Dustpath Inn!"

Farah jumped.

A man with white blond hair smiled in the doorway. "Welcome," he said. "I'm the famous, the generous, the intelligent, and the modest Solace the Calm." He took a bow.

Sara and her company looked at each other and back at the strange man.

"The Calm? Never heard of you," Bolton said.

"You haven't heard of me?"

"Sorry," Sara said.

Solace sighed.

"Wait," Farah said. "I think I know you. Um, you're . . . you . . ."

"I invented the Independent Motion Traveler!"

"Yeah, that!"

"I knew you must have heard of me!" Solace said. "Come in." He turned and disappeared inside.

"Telling tales?" Bolton turned to Farah in the doorway.

"It made him happy," Farah said. "A little lie can be good if it makes someone happy."

"Well, in that case," Bolton said, "you're a genius."

Farah punched his arm and entered the inn.

In the check-in room, supplies sat along the shelves behind a desk. On the shelves were water canteens, ointments, bandages, imperishable foods, traveling cloaks, lanterns, matches, and boots. In the back of the room, a doorway led to the bedrooms.

Solace rushed behind the desk. Spire counted out the sparklings from her coin purse. She was short two sparklings.

"I guess I could give you a discount." Solace frowned.

"No need." Farah ran up to the counter and slapped down two glittering coins. The coins were of a larger denomination than Spire's and alone covered the cost.

*   *   *

SARA jolted from bed. The sky outside her window was dark. Farah and Spire rested in their beds. Sara's face was hot. Sweat wet her brow.

I must have dreamed of the fire again, she thought.

She threw the covers off her legs and searched the floor for her bag. She grabbed the lantern from her bedside table and tiptoed out of the room. She left the inn and walked to the cliff overlooking the ruins.

She set the lantern down and took the drawing paper and charcoal from her bag. She sketched the ruins. She turned her head and glanced toward the door of the inn.

Did Rodan forget about me?

He must have known she would come outside to escape the stuffiness of that room. Sara shook her head. When she left Element with Rodan, she imagined they would grow closer. But Rodan forgot they were friends. Sara caught him staring into the distance with that serious look on his face. He found his mission, and she had become a part of that, an important part, but no longer a person.

The door creaked.

Sara's eyes darted to the inn.

Bolton approached her. "Hey. I knew I'd find you out here."

"Couldn't sleep?" Sara focused on her drawing.

"No." Bolton sat next to her. "You were quiet on the way here. Hope I didn't upset you."

"Upset me?"

"The Insula," Bolton said.

"You think a joke upset me?"

"It's not really a—"

"Look, I get it," Sara said. "That kind of thing doesn't bother me." She looked out past the ruins. "I was little when my parents died. I ended up in Ocean's Light, and I told the girls my parents were alive and would come to take me home. I made up this elaborate story about them being on a trip across the sea, and I couldn't go because I was too young. It helped. But I couldn't forget where I was from and why my story changed."

"You don't have a problem with lying?"

"People lie for many reasons. Sometimes to protect others. Sometimes to protect themselves. But most people are good. They don't intend to hurt anybody."

Bolton stared at the sky. "You're wrong."

Sara turned to him.

He looked at her. "Sure, intentions matter to a degree. But the people who protect themselves with lies, always hurt someone in the end. They pretend to see past themselves to the greater good. But when they're at the knife, they'd sacrifice a friend before risking their own necks."

"You seem to know a lot about it," Sara said.

"I know what I'm shown."

RODAN opened the door to the inn. He stopped. Sara sat with Bolton on the cliff. Sara laughed at something Bolton said. Rodan turned away and closed the door. He shuffled down the hall to his room.

He watched the light inch into his window as the sun rose. Grabbing his bag, he made for the door.

"Good morning," Solace said as Rodan entered the main room.

Rodan glanced at the jars of preserved food. "I'll have a jar of peaches."

"Excellent choice." Solace plucked the jar from the shelf.

Rodan's eyes landed on the boots high on the shelf. He looked down at his own boots. They were worn and dirty. "Can I try the boots?"

Solace climbed a ladder to the top shelf and grabbed the boots. He brought them down and handed them to Rodan. Rodan took off his boots and tried the new ones. They didn't fit.

"Too small," Rodan said.

"Sorry," Solace said. "These are the only ones I have. Average size, you know."

"I could tell." Rodan reached into his pocket and withdrew two sparklings. "Here."

Solace took the sparklings from Rodan and held them to his chest. "Thank you, kind sir." He put the coins in a box under the desk.

"Where are you and your friends going?" the innkeeper asked.

"Wyvek," Rodan said.

"Wyvek? But, that's miles away," Solace said.

"Yeah." Rodan pointed down to his boots.

Solace leaned over the desk to look. "My, you need my invention."

Talon stepped into the room. "You ready?"

Rodan turned to him. "Solace says he has a way to get us to Wyvek."

"An excellent way," Solace said. "Please, follow me."

Solace led them outside to the back of the inn.

Talon leaned toward Rodan. "I trust my tired feet more than anything this innkeeper has put together."

Solace stopped in front of three covered objects the size of cattle. He uncovered one of them. "The Independent Motion Traveler or, for short, the IMT. I've sent the blueprints to Wyvek. They must have tons of them by now. All you have to do is push the red button and squeeze the handles to adjust the speed. Go on. Give it a try."

"I'll try it." Farah pushed past Rodan and Talon. She sat on the machine made of metal. The side panels were loose and shook as Farah sat. Two buttons were set in the bars above the handles: one red and one white. She pushed the red button.

The machine roared and zoomed forward onto the plot of land beside the inn. The metal wheels left deep impressions in the dirt. It twisted and turned under Farah's control.

"Does this thing have a learning curve?" Farah cried as the IMT zipped around a lonely fencepost. "How do I stop it?"

"Press the white button," Solace yelled through cupped hands.

Farah jabbed at the white button. The IMT came to a whip-lashing halt. Farah jumped off the machine and staggered toward Talon and Rodan.

"No," Talon said.

"Wait," Rodan said. "It's a long walk to Wyvek. This might save us time and supplies."

"It might cost us a few members of our team as well," Talon said.

"The IMT is perfectly safe," Solace said.

"He's right." Bolton leaned against the side of the building. "Farah's just a bad driver."

"I'd like to see you try it," Farah said.

"I'm not getting on that thing." Talon turned to leave.

"Please," Bolton said, "you're not afraid of a mechanical wagon. You're just stubborn, old man."

Talon turned to them. "If those things give us any trouble on the road, we're abandoning them."

Solace put up his hands.

"It's settled," Talon said.

Bolton rubbed his palms together. "You heard that, kids. We got ourselves some new toys." Bolton uncovered the other two machines. He slapped the side of one of them. The panel rattled. "Let's take them out for another test run." He swung his leg over the side and sat.

Rodan shook his head and grinned as he approached the contraption opposite Bolton's. He sat on the metal seat. It wasn't comfortable. He grabbed the handles and pressed the red button with his thumb. The machine bucked forward. Rodan squeezed the handle twice, which slowed the contraption to a reasonable speed. He pulled out onto the road. Bolton pulled up next to him.

Rodan increased his speed. Bolton followed. They raced.

Wind ripped past Rodan's ears and tore away all other sounds. He jerked the handles to the side and skidded to a stop. Bolton braked alongside him.

"These aren't too bad," Rodan said.

"Not too bad?" Bolton said. "Hope this thing has enough kick in it after I'm done with it." He zoomed ahead.

Rodan turned his front wheel and trailed Bolton.

They returned an hour later.

"Where were you two?" Spire waited at the door with her arms folded.

"We had to test the machines," Bolton said.

"We're driving them to Wyvek," Rodan said. "To save time and supplies. Talon approved it."

"Fine." Spire turned. "We have to leave. Now."

Bolton looked at Rodan and smirked.

"You're leaving with my IMTs? Good," Solace said. "All my brothers are traveling merchants. Family business, you know. If you see them, know that they come with my seal of approval."

Rodan bought another jar of preserved peaches and ate them on the stoop outside the inn while Bolton taught Spire how to operate the IMT.

Spire had more mastery over the contraption than Farah had.

Talon sat behind Spire. Bolton and Rodan mounted the other two IMTs.

"This seat taken?" Sara sat behind Rodan.

"It is now," Rodan said.

Sara put her hands around his waist. "Let's go then."

The new road did not hold the same memories as the old one. No ruins lingered to haunt visitors. Dust did not smother the patches of grass and flowers that grew along the road. The dirt that made up the path was more compacted.

They crossed a land bridge. The bridge led to the entrance of Wyvek. The cliff winded down to a grassy area at the entrance to Wyvek. The IMTs saved them a day. But the rickety mechanisms shrieked and thundered for the duration of the trip.

A wagon lay abandoned at the city gates. The doors of the entrance creaked as they swung.

The ground was rocky. The city was like a giant cave with an opening at the side. Stalactites hung from the ceiling like thorns. Rocky pillars stopped the ceiling from closing on the city like a gigantic mouth.

They stepped down from the IMTs and looked around. Rows of stone houses lie in front of them, but the streets were abandoned.

"This is weird," Rodan said.

"Looks like they all left," Bolton said.

"I shudder to think why." Spire knocked at one of the doors. "Hello?"

No one answered.

They continued down the street until they came to a fork in the road.

"This way," Spire said.

They followed her to the right of the fork and approached the temple. They crossed a bridge above dark waters. The temple was gray among brown rocks. Bolts of Lightning lifted the structure from the ground.

"He knows we have come to take the sphere," Talon said.

"Who?" Sara asked.

"The Keeper," he said. "This sphere has been stolen before. The Sphere Protector will fight twice as hard."

"When was it stolen?" Farah asked.

"A few years ago," Talon said.

"How are we going to get in?" Sara asked.

Bolton stepped forward and held his hands out. He strained to keep the bolts lowered, but the temple stayed elevated.

Rodan stepped up beside him. Vines sprouted from the rocky ground, probably for the very first time. The vines wrapped over the top of the temple. With combined effort, Bolton and Rodan forced the temple back to the stony surface on which it was built.

"Quick," Talon said. "Inside."

They rushed inside the temple. The vines Rodan called disappeared, and Bolton released his power on the bolts of lightning. The temple shook as it rose from the ground.

The stone relics of prophets and their followers decorated the inside of the temple. The lights were dim, and splashes of crimson and brown painted the walls and floors.

"They must not have been gone long," Spire said. "The temple is well-kept."

Farah cowered behind one of the statues. Orka perched on her shoulder and pressed her beak against Farah's cheek.

"The Lightning's below us," Bolton said. "It can't hurt you inside."

"I'm not afraid of what's below us. I'm afraid of what's in the sanctum. Some Lightning-shooting demon who wants to fry us into the next life."

"You don't have to come," Bolton said.

She and Orka stayed behind while the others continued up the stairs.

At the top of the narrow staircase was a doorway. Through the doorway was a long hall. At the end was a platform with a railing around it.

At their feet was a deep line engraved in the floor. The line ran down the hall and formed a circle around the platform.

"It's an energy channel," Talon said.

Bolton knelt and sent a stream of lightning through the channel. The channel glowed.

They walked down the hall and stood on the platform. The platform rose to the second floor, a loft that settled above the first room. They stood in front of an ornamented door painted in shades of gold. The element symbols marked the tiles before the door. The Lightning symbol glowed like the energy channel.

Sara, Spire, Rodan, and Talon stooped in front of their symbol and touched down on the tiles. The tiles sank into the ground. The symbols glowed. Bolton approached the door and tried the handle.

He laughed and looked back at the others. "Didn't burn me this time." He pulled the door open.

The room was oval-shaped and windowless. Bolton crept inside. He turned back to the others. "Is there a way of doing this without alerting *it?*"

"Probably not," Spire said.

"Yeah," Bolton said.

Sara casted her eyes down.

Rodan squeezed her shoulder. "It's okay." He followed Bolton into the room.

Bolton took a deep breath and stepped toward the door at the opposite end of the room. Behind that door was the element sphere. As soon as he moved, the door behind them slammed shut.

Rodan's skin prickled.

Lightning struck the middle of the floor. Bolton staggered back. A glow spread from the center of the room. A winged unicorn emerged from the light. Lightning made up the unicorn's body instead of flesh and fur. It hooved the ground.

Sara stood beside Rodan. Her eyes glistened. "It's sketched from Lightning."

Talon circled the unicorn in a ring of fire. The unicorn screeched and went up on its back legs.

"Get the sphere!" he shouted.

"It's scared." Sara's hands shook. "Look at its eyes."

Rodan looked into the creature's eyes. They reflected the flames.

Sara dropped her canteen.

Lightning zipped from the unicorn's horn. The bolt hit Sara in the chest. She collapsed.

Bolton's hand was on the door to the sphere room, but he stopped when Sara fell. He rushed forward, but the Sphere Protector stood between them.

Rodan dropped beside Sara and snapped his fingers in front of her face.

"Bolton, focus!" Farah burst into the room.

Rodan held Sara's body. He glanced toward Bolton.

Bolton tore his eyes away. He turned to the unicorn and calmed the Lightning. The creature kneeled. Rings of Lightning wrapped around the room, blocking both doors.

Farah pinned her eyes on the door to the sphere room. The door flew open, the pressure of the air bursting from the inside out.

Rodan looked toward the Sphere Protector. It was standing. With one arm still cradling Sara, Rodan thrust out his hand and focused. Vines twisted around the room and through the open door. They wrapped around the element sphere and removed it from its pedestal.

The temple fell to the ground and settled with a boom. The unicorn knelt one final time and flickered into darkness.

Bolton ran toward Sara. He skidded to the floor as he approached. "What happened?"

"It struck her in the chest," Rodan said.

The canteen of water spilled around her.

"Is she breathing?" Spire asked.

Rodan leaned over Sara. No breath came from her nose or mouth. He pressed his lips together and shook his head.

Spire stood above them. "Shock her again."

"What?" Bolton asked.

"It stopped her heart," Spire said. "Shock her again."

Bolton knelt opposite Rodan at Sara's side. He rubbed his hands together.

"No." Rodan grabbed Bolton's arm.

"She's right," Bolton said. "Let me do this. I could shock her. Bring her back. It can't wait."

Rodan let Sara's body slump to the ground.

Bolton rubbed his hands together. He pressed his palm onto Sara's chest. Lightning buzzed, and Sara's back jumped from the ground before settling down again.

Spire knelt at Sara's side and listened for breathing.

Rodan stared, unable to move.

The sphere lay abandoned on the ground.

Sara's eyes blinked open.

Bolton helped her to sit up.

She looked around the room and picked up the sphere. She examined it. "What happened?"

"You marched into a death trap," Farah said. Orka flew to her shoulder and fluffed her feathers.

"You missed it," Bolton said. "Farah came barging into the room at the last second."

"You were in the room with the Protector?"

"Sure," Farah said. "Looks like you all need me more than I thought."

17

THE NIGHTMARE

RODAN handed Farah the Lightning Sphere to store in her canvas bag. Her bag was heavier, but it was heavy with more than element spheres. Orka stole valuables from all the towns they visited, and she found a few treasures in the abandoned city of Wyvek.

The rocky terrain ended in a dirt road with grassy borders. The path widened. Orka chirped as birds called in the distance. They picnicked in the grass alongside the path.

Spire shared food from her bag. They ate in silence.

Rodan stole glances at Sara. She almost died, but she acts as though nothing happened.

Wheels screeched and bumped along the road. Two grey mules pulled a wagon packed with crates. An old man directed the wagon down the path. He tipped his hat to them.

Rodan nodded to the man. "The road narrows further

back. I'm afraid your wagon won't make it through."

"Well, thank you for the warning," he said, "but I won't be taking that road, the store room is down the hill."

He stared at Sara. He took off his glasses and wiped them on his shirt. He looked from Sara to the others and back again.

"Excuse me, miss. But are you the Water Elemental?"

"How did you know?" Sara asked.

"The skipper who delivers my crates told me of you. He told me how you saved Caleena. It's amazing there's still a Water Elemental alive. After all these years of hoping, here you are."

"Here I am," Sara said.

"Do you know why the people of Wyvek came this way?" Talon asked the man.

"No. I saw them though. A few days ago. Didn't stop to ask them."

"Were they running?" Talon asked.

"No," he said, "passing through, or should I say *marching* through. Every man, woman, and child was in the troop." He looked out toward the road. "Well, I better get these crates to the store room before the captain arrives for the next shipment. Good luck to you. Hephaestus won't know what's coming to him." The man swiped at the reins, and the mules led the wagon down the hill.

THAT night, they camped away from the road. Bolton and Rodan gathered some branches, and Talon sparked a fire. Talon took some bread from his bag and passed it along. Everyone broke a piece and ate.

"The people of Wyvek came this way," Talon said, "and they weren't forced. They must be headed for Omega Ray to fight."

"What makes you think that?" Bolton asked.

"If they were interested in hiding," Talon said, "they would have gone in the opposite direction."

"They brought their children," Spire said.

"Perhaps they feared Hephaestus would come for them if they lost the battle," Talon said. "They'll probably try to leave them at Tosia. The people of Tosia may take the younger ones."

"But why now?" Rodan asked. "They could have fought years ago."

"Word has spread of a Water Elemental on the road to challenge Hephaestus," Spire said. "Perhaps they plan to meet us on the battlefield."

Sara stared at the fire. "What makes them think I can beat him?"

Spire looked at Sara.

Bolton glanced up from his bread. His chewing slowed.

Why did I say that? Sara wondered. They'll think I'm weak. Am I weak?

"I know Hephaestus fears Water Elementals," Sara said. "But he's killed so many of us. What makes me any different?"

"You don't have to do this," Talon said. "We can go back to Element."

"We can't turn around now," Bolton said. "Not when we've announced to the world of Sara's existence. He'll hunt her down. The time to make this decision was weeks ago."

"He's right," Sara said. "I have to be what the people expect me to be. I have to win."

Spire nodded. No one looked at Sara.

I did this to them. I made them think I was ready.

When the sun rose, they continued down the dirt path and came to a forest. The path went through the trees and ended at the turn. They stopped at a lake that blended with the horizon. The water was dark blue. The Lake de Somnia.

"There's a small dock not far from here." Talon scanned the area.

He walked on, and the others followed.

"Why do they call it the Lake de Somnia?" Sara asked.

"If you fall in, you dream," Talon said, "but the dreams aren't always pleasant."

"Nothing ever swims in the Lake de Somnia?" Rodan asked.

"Nothing can," Spire said.

"But why?" Sara asked. "What makes people sleep when they fall in?"

"The mushrooms along the banks," Spire said. "They have medicinal properties that induce sleep.

"What about the Nightmare?" Bolton said, "the Dark Water?"

"The Nightmare?" Farah asked.

"A myth," Spire said.

"What's the story?" Farah asked.

"No reason to frighten anyone," Spire said.

"If it isn't true, what is there to be afraid of?" Talon asked. "The Nightmare is an ancient shadow, a dark cloud. It looms over the lake and waits. When someone falls into the waters, it drags them down, and they never wake."

"Where does the Nightmare come from?" Sara asked.

"It's been too long to say," Talon said, "but some believe the Nightmare is the buildup of the bad dreams of those lost to the lake."

A boat was docked near a tent.

"The owner must be inside," Talon said.

They walked to the tent. A head popped out from the folds in the cloth. The head belonged to a man older than Talon.

"What do you want?" The old man scowled. His skin looked like it could tear.

Rodan approached the man. "We were wondering—"

"...if you could borrow our boat." The voice came from inside the tent.

The old man stuck his head back in to let the one who spoke walk through the folds of the tent. The voice belonged to a tall, young woman with cropped, dark brown hair. She wore a black band around her left arm.

"I apologize for my father," she said. "He's bitter because

we haven't been getting customers. No one wants to travel on the Lake de Somnia anymore."

"Maybe he's chasing all the customers away," Bolton said.

"They're afraid," the woman said.

"Of the lake or of your father?"

"Both," she said.

"Rai, what do they want? Directions?" the old man shouted.

"No, they want to cross the lake," Rai said. "I've got it. You rest."

Rai led them to the boat.

"Step lightly," Rai said. "You don't want to fall in."

One by one they stepped into the boat, floating above the deadly waters.

"Orka, you're not coming," Farah said to the little, green parrot sitting on her shoulder, "I want you to fly over this lake and meet me on the other side."

Orka chirped and flew away. Farah watched her disappear into the distance and got down into the boat.

"She's safer than we are," Bolton said.

In the boat were four oars. Rai took the first oar, and Talon, Rodan, and Bolton each took another.

They rowed across the lake. The waters were calm but an eerie calm like the waters were waiting, waiting for someone to fall in.

Rai, Talon, Rodan, and Bolton rowed along. The water waved as the boat passed through.

"So," Rai said, "why did you choose to cross the Lake de Somnia?"

"We're very daring," Bolton said. "We're doing this on a bet."

Rai smirked, but asked no more questions. As she rowed, she noticed Talon staring at the black band around her arm, and she turned her eyes away from him.

"What was the trouble?" Talon asked her.

"What are you talking about?" she asked.

"The black band around your arm," Talon said. "You've been jailed or marked for something."

Rai looked away again.

"Never mind," Talon said. "Your secrets don't belong to us. I was merely inquiring into who our escort is."

"It was a mistake," Rai said. "I was young."

No one uttered another word.

Farah scanned the skies for Orka. The little, green bird flew down toward the boat. She landed on Farah's shoulder and chirped loudly.

"Orka," Farah said, "get away from here!"

The oar in Bolton's hand was jerked into the water.

"I'll get it," he said.

He reached out over the water in attempt to recover the oar.

"Bolton, no!" Farah shouted. "I think Orka—"

The boat rocked, throwing Bolton into the water.

THE sun burned on a large house-boat on the coast of the Insula. The sky was blue with hazy, pink clouds lining the horizon. The ripples in the water rocked the ship.

Bolton woke. He was on the deck of the houseboat where he used to live when he was a child.

The houseboat looked the same as when he was forced to leave it. The railing around the steer was engraved with a line that wrapped around the wood. The boat was painted sky blue, yellow, and orange. Every door had a circular window at the top. The wood on the deck was well-worn. On the side of the ship was the symbol for Lightning and alongside it, the symbol for Fire.

Bolton turned in a circle. Seagulls passed overhead.

A breath of flame and a spark of lightning appeared on either side of Bolton's head and right above his shoulders. The fire roared and the lightning snapped. His mother and father used to play this game with him. Which element would he possess when he grew up: Fire or Lightning?

"Mom?"

He looked for her, eager to see her again, if only in a dream. His hand was on the door to his parents' room. He imagined her there, arms open to him, but the dream turned.

Bolton waited in a void. Images trickled in.

He stood on the roof of a skyscraper. A city sprawled below him. The night was starless. The only light was the light from a far off gray moon. It was cold with an eerie stillness.

He glanced over the edge of the building. Down below, the darkness swallowed everything.

It was a colorless world, a world of gloom and shade. The world was wrong and unnatural. Shadows seemed to move of their own accord, and the wind sent harsh whispers through the air.

He stared at the shadows twisting in the street.

"Bolton." The wind whispered his name.

Bolton turned. Behind him, on the opposite side of the roof, a figure stood hidden in the shadows. He moved in the dark.

"Show yourself," Bolton said. Was the figure consumed by the shadows, or was it a shadow itself?

The figure stepped into the dim light. His face was pale, aged, with a slim nose and amber eyes. A face that might belong to a temperate man, but Bolton knew better. He was a man who never saw the sun.

The figure dressed all in red. He was an immense part of Bolton's nightmares.

"Why are you here?" Bolton tried to keep his voice steady.

"To ensure you do not stray," the figure said.

"I was attacked," Bolton said, "by Fire Elementals from Omega Ray."

"I've grown to understand that people need constant motivation." He approached Bolton and touched the medallion around his neck.

"Don't be blinded," he said, "like your mother was."

Bolton looked away. His hands were in fists. "When the

time comes, I'll do what I have to do."

BOLTON fell into the water. Rodan dropped his oar into the boat. His hands gripped the edge. He was ready to jump in, but Talon stopped him.

"You can't," Talon said. "You'll fall into a dream too."

They all stood in the boat, except Rai.

"You should sit now before we all fall in," she said. No one heeded her warning.

"We have to do something." Farah looked at Sara. "Maybe you could use the water to throw him back into the boat."

Sara concentrated on the water, but it would not move. "It won't listen to me," she cried. "I don't feel its essence."

Spire stared into the water. "It's real."

"What?" Farah asked.

"Something else is commanding the water," Spire said.

"You must stay calm," Rai said. "Panicking won't help."

Bolton sank into the water. A shadow swam across the lake.

"The Nightmare," Rai said.

"I thought that was a myth," Farah said.

"No," Rai said. "The Nightmare takes over your dreams and envelopes you in darkness. It drags you to the bottom of the lake never to return to the surface alive or dead. We have to get him out."

The shadow closed in. It wrapped around Bolton and shaded him in a veil of darkness. The shadow dragged him into the dark abyss.

"What are we going to do?" Farah asked.

Rodan sent vines into the water.

Sara leaned over the edge of the boat.

The Nightmare had dragged Bolton so far down that they couldn't see him. Slowly, Bolton appeared through the cloudy water. Shadows and vines encircled him.

Rodan pulled, but the Nightmare pulled back: a tug of war between life and death.

Rodan doubled the number of vines.

The shadow released Bolton, and the vines brought him closer to the water's surface. From within the shadow a face formed. The boat shook. The Nightmare sank into the water.

Rodan sent more vines and thickened them. They swam through the water surrounding Bolton. The vines pulled him up, and Bolton broke the surface of the lake's dark depths.

Rodan sent away the vines and went to the edge of the boat to pull Bolton in.

"Is he alright?" Farah asked.

Bolton lay still on the floor of the boat. He clenched the medallion. He jerked up and coughed water.

He gulped in air. Once his breathing slowed, he said: "Okay, who do I owe?"

Sara helped him up.

"Are you alright?" she asked.

"Fine. How long was I under?"

"That was stupid," Farah said, "reaching out to get an oar. What were you thinking? Of all the dumb, thick-skulled things to do."

"I'm sorry I inconvenienced you." Bolton coughed.

"You're lucky Rodan found a way to save you."

Bolton glanced over at Rodan. "Thanks."

"No problem," Rodan said. "I fished your oar out for you too." He threw Bolton the recovered oar.

"You expect me to row after what I've been through?"

They continued to row with Bolton's help.

"You didn't tell me you were Elementals," Rai said.

"We weren't aware that we needed a permit," Talon said.

"No, but if you had mentioned it, I would have told you I'm one too."

She snapped her fingers, and a flame appeared.

"I know why you're crossing the lake," Rai said. "You're going to Omega Ray, and she's your secret weapon." She motioned to Sara.

"Not a secret anymore," Spire said.

"I won't say anything," Rai said.

"All of Caleena and Lumina knows," Farah said.

"If we could get all of them to make the same promise," Bolton said, "we wouldn't have a problem."

"Maybe it's good that everyone knows." Sara thought of the Lightning Elementals of Wyvek. "It will bring them hope."

"But we don't want that hope to be false hope," Spire said.

Sara rubbed her palms with her fingers. I shouldn't have said anything to make them doubt me. Spire doesn't think I can do this. But it's too late.

Talon stared at the black band around Rai's arm. "What crime have you committed?" he asked again.

"A crime of stupidity," Rai said. "My mom was sick. We needed money for food and medicine. Business wasn't booming at the lake. It never was.

"I became a pickpocket. But it wasn't enough. I heard people were looking for the spheres, and I knew they would give anything to get them. I didn't know they were Hephaestus's men. I travelled to Wyvek Temple. I went up to the room of the Protector. I didn't get far before I was hit with a jolt of lightning. It felt like my organs were cooking, and I could smell roasted meat and burnt hair. I blacked out. When I came to, I saw a beast standing over me. Its body was made of Lightning. It took pity on me. It kept its head down as I walked to the Sphere Room. When I took the Sphere off its pedestal, the beast turned to dust. I hadn't meant to kill it.

"I was discovered running from the temple with the sphere clenched to my chest. The citizens of Wyvek beat me in the street. When the Resistance came, I was banded. My mom died after that."

Rai took in a deep breath, looked to the sky, and blinked to keep the tears from falling. "I could take it off." She touched the black band around her arm. "The Resistance hardly has reason to come to the lake, but I keep it on to remember."

"You didn't kill him," Sara said. "The Sphere Protector

was alive."

"Was he?"

"You should have known better than to steal a sphere," Spire said. "The Protector is a lot less trusting now."

"You think I don't know?" Rai's eyes narrowed. "I can sense it. I don't know why, if it's the lightning running through my body or the guilt through my soul, but it haunts me. I know where the sphere is, and it's no longer in the temple."

"How did you get into a sphere sanctum without a balance of the elements?" Rodan asked.

"I had help." Rai took a jar from beneath her cloak. Inside the jar was a small, pulsing being. The being was transparent and gel-like. It floated in a sphere shape.

"What is it?" Farah asked.

"An Aether," Rai said. "It can summon any element." Rai concealed the jar beneath her cloak. "We'd better row faster before the Nightmare regains its strength."

When they made it to the opposite side of the lake, Spire paid Rai. They stepped out of the boat. A large bell hung from a post near the bank.

"Good luck," Rai said. "Ring that bell when you need to cross back."

18

THE GEMSTONE

HEPHAESTUS turned in his sleep.

In the world behind his eyes, he drifted. He was young and in the room where he had been kept in his childhood. The room was more of a cell. It was small with cold floors and no windows.

"Sicilia?" He nudged the sleeping girl next to him.

She turned. "What's wrong?"

"I had another nightmare."

She sat up on her sleeping mat and took his hand. "It's going to be okay. I have the nightmares too, of the time they took me away."

"It was because I burned down the village," he said.

She squeezed his hand. "It wasn't your fault. You couldn't control your power." She gave him a smile. "I can make Water dance for you." She turned his palm up, and with her finger made a swirling motion above his hand. A tiny string of water came from her fingertip and swirled in the air.

Hephaestus tried to pull himself from this subconscious world.

"Sicilia, I got you something." He reached into his pocket and retrieved a small stone in the shape of a raindrop. The stone was light brown.

"Where'd you get this?"

"I found it before I was taken. I kept it. I thought it was an old rock, but look." He clenched the stone between his finger and thumb, and sent heat into it. The stone changed from muddy brown to clear blue. "It's a gemstone. I shaped it for you."

It was the last time he saw Sicilia smile.

Soldiers and a man in long robes came. "That one." The robed man pointed to Sicilia.

As they took her away, he reached for her hand.

"Sicilia. Sicilia!"

"Why are you trying to erase me from your heart?" she whispered.

PERDITUS shook Hephaestus from his involuntary slumber on the armchair. "Wake up, father, you're dreaming of her again."

Hephaestus flinched out of his sleep.

"You! Don't call me *father*." He glared at Perditus.

"Who is she?"

Hephaestus slapped him across the face. "Never ask me that! You're always crossing the line, boy."

Perditus's bony hand rubbed his stricken cheek. Blood issued from his busted lip.

"You're like your mother, always asking questions."

"You were shouting down the hall," Perditus snared. "I don't understand."

Perditus looked small, broken.

He averted his eyes. *Was he afraid?*

But his lips pressed together. Perditus's eyes shifted back to him.

Hephaestus straightened in his chair. "I want a war, Perditus, I've been needing one."

19

PROPHECY

T HE path from the Lake de Somnia continued through a
forest. The trees swayed and trembled, but no wind
passed through.

Hums or chants sounded in the distance.

"Can you hear that?" Farah asked.

"What?"" Bolton asked. "Can you talk to trees now?"

"Shut up, and listen," Farah said. "Where is that coming
from?"

"I can hear them too," Rodan said. "It must be the
Tosians."

Sara walked alongside Rodan. "Why are they chanting?"

"It's their ritual," Talon said. "Walk slower. We don't want
to interrupt it."

Before Sara could ask, Spire said, "In reverence for the
Creator. No outsider has seen it."

The path winded through the bending trees and led to Tosia. Tosia was a town in the hollow of a large tree. From a distance, as far as Lumina, one could see the leaves of the great tree over the horizon. The Earth Elementals of Tosia had aided the tree in its growth and made it their home. It was made from nature, and the people were like hermits to the outside world. They never left Tosia and were not very welcoming of strangers passing through their homeland.

The great tree was the last testament of the Tosians's power. They believed it was wrong and against the natural order to bend nature to their wills. Defying nature could only bring destruction.

"The Tosians don't like other Elementals," Farah said.

"It's not that they don't like other Elementals," Spire said. "They have certain beliefs. Because they are Earth Elementals, they feel they have a closer link with the Creator. They believe that without Earth, no other element could exist."

"Don't use your elements around them," Talon said. "They'll find it disrespectful."

"What if someone attacked Tosia?" Sara asked. "And they couldn't fight because they refuse to."

"It's unlikely that anyone would," Spire said. "They are a very placid people, and they have nothing Hephaestus would want."

"And they don't like strangers," Talon said.

"Well," Bolton said, "let's be sure to introduce ourselves quickly."

The path ended at an arched doorway with green ivy growing up to the top. Sara looked up at the leaves hundreds of feet in the air and the massive trunk, large enough to hold the entire town of Caleena at its base.

"It looks so much smaller from a distance," Sara said.

In front of the door was a small, round courtyard. Tree roots grew over the floor, made of pure, green crystal. Beside the door grew two more tree trunks. The door was covered in ivy so thick that only the doorknob showed.

Rodan tried the door. The handle felt alive in his hand. This door opened for him.

"For people who don't like strangers," Farah said, "they don't have good security."

"The door is made of wood that still lives. It senses our purpose."

Inside Tosia were more trees of a lesser size. Houses and shops were made out of the living trunks. A sloping tree trunk made a spiral slope to the second floor where more homes and shops were located.

On the first floor was a place known as the Domum Fidei where people of Tosia went to meditate and stay in touch with nature. The Domum Fidei was protected by a huge, violet door covered in tree roots. The people of Tosia often went to the Domum Fidei to show reverence for the Creator of the element spheres.

On the second floor was another sacred place: The Cliff of Broken Promise. Those who went to the Cliff did not go in search of hope.

"Why does everyone look so sad?" Farah asked.

People dressed in cloaks with hoods passed them. Their heads bent down. They glided as they walked. Several of them had bands around their arms, much like the ones that Rai and the Resistance soldiers wore. Only, these were green.

"They're all wearing green bands," Sara said. "Rodan, is that what you were talking about on the ship?"

"It's how Earth Elementals show veneration to the Creator," Rodan said. "Without the Creator, the element spheres wouldn't exist, and therefore, we would not exist, not with the gift of our power at least."

"Come," Talon said.

He led them to a door near the entrance. They could not be sure if it was a house or a shop because everything looked the same from the outside. No signs marked the paths. The citizens had made no effort to welcome visitors to their village. Tosia was a place where only those who knew the way could find their way.

Talon turned the ivy-covered knob on the leaf-green door which opened without a sound.

Shelves, stocked with goods and supplies, packed the room. A counter made of woven tree branches sat in the corner. On the counter were dried herbs and ointments in small glass bottles. A few silver coins were scattered in the center.

Behind the counter stood an elderly man dressed in a silver and green robe. The dim light shined off his bald head, and between his eyes a small inverted triangle was etched into the skin with a line running through the center.

He looked like he had been standing for a long time and seemed to be in a trance. He crushed herbs into a powder with a mortar and pestle. When Talon walked up to the counter, the man blinked twice and looked up.

"Talon?" His eyes were wide. "I thought you'd be dead."

"No," Talon said, "I'm still half-alive."

Sara and Rodan exchanged puzzled glances. How did he know this man, and why were they here?

"Last I saw you," the man said, "you and your friend were undertaking a task that could only end in death. But here you are standing before me. Is there anything I can do for you?"

Talon grabbed his arm and leaned in close. "Aldo, I need you to grant me the same favor you did last time," Talon said.

"Are you sure you want to do that?" Aldo asked.

Talon gave him a look like he had better change the subject.

"I know why you ducked in here."

"We need a place to stay."

"Last time it was only the two of you. It was easier to house you then. But now . . ."

"Never mind," Talon said. "Sorry we bothered you."

"I have news, would you like to hear it?"

"Not interested." Talon turned to leave.

"But it's about Hephaestus's son."

Talon stopped but did not turn back to Aldo. His eyes

were calm, but his mind was darting.

"Hephaestus has a son?" Farah asked.

"Next of kin would be more accurate," Talon said.

"He's in Element, enlisted as a spy," Aldo said.

"And how would you know that?" Bolton asked.

"Travelers know," Aldo said. "I hear them talk. You don't have to be one of Hephaestus's sympathizers to get into Omega Ray as long as you sell the right goods. Travelers pass through to rest, and Hephaestus's men come through from time to time. Though their occupations as murderers are never said out loud, you can always see death in their eyes. From them, I have heard rumor of Hephaestus's *next of kin*."

"Hephaestus's unfortunate *relative* isn't up to anything," Talon said.

"It wouldn't hurt to hear what he has to say," Farah said. "Maybe his son, I mean next of kin, *is* up to something."

"We're far from Element now. He isn't any of our concern," Talon said.

No one challenged him.

"Come on," Talon said. "It's going to be difficult to find a place to stay. Tosians aren't the most welcoming of people."

Farah folded her arms, but followed the others without a word.

SARA, Rodan, Bolton, and Farah took a tour of Tosia. Spire went to visit an old friend she hadn't seen in over ten years, and Talon left and didn't say where he was going.

Aldo helped them find a place to stay the night. A cousin, he said, had some rooms available, but she had glared at them as they walked in. What had Aldo done to earn such a favor?

Their rooms were much like the rest of Tosia, made of trees and ivy. The bed posts were made of twisted branches, and the beds themselves were so comfortable they seemed to be filled with fresh rose petals.

Flowers grew against the trees, and curling branches and vines wrapped around trunks. But the scenery could not take their minds off Talon's strange behavior.

"What do you think Talon's up to?" Farah asked.

"He knows these people," Rodan said. "He's been comfortable everywhere we've gone because he traveled a lot in the past."

"He's hiding something," Farah said. "I wonder what his story is."

"Maybe he needs time," Sara said. "Maybe he's afraid of what we'll think of the truth. Perhaps he's waiting for the right time to tell us."

Bolton looked at the dirt floor. *She's a fool*, he thought, *to trust someone blindly.*

"But what if it's something we need to know *now*?" Farah said. "What was Talon hiding when he stopped that old man from telling us about Hephaestus's next of kin?"

"He's not a threat," Bolton said with his eyes to the ground.

"How do you know?" Rodan asked.

"I heard he was dead," he said not moving his eyes from the earth and lowering his head still more.

"Dead?"

At least on the inside he is, he thought. To do what he must do, you'd have to be dead on the inside.

"You must be the strangers." A girl approached them. She was younger than Farah. Her head was hoodless, revealing her long, black hair. Her dark eyes shined within their depths.

Without waiting for a response, she started again. "Madame Dawn told me you would come. She doesn't usually like strangers very much, but she said you were special, like the others. She said it would be an honor to meet you. And she wants to give you her blessing."

"Wait a minute," Bolton said. "Who are you?"

"I'm Lucerne. Madame Dawn is anxious to meet you. Come, this way." Lucerne ran up the slope to the second floor.

Sara stood. "Could be interesting."

They followed the girl.

"She must have had one too many dragon fruits," Farah said as they ran after Lucerne. "This girl's got enough energy to light up all of Lumina."

They followed her past shops and houses covered in ivy, lavender and mountain flower sprouts, and up the sloping branches of the large tree.

"Wait, you run too fast," Farah shouted.

"Now you know what it's like to follow behind *you*," Bolton said.

Lucerne stopped. She stood in the middle of the pathway. To her right was another door covered in ivy, and to her left was an open archway. The floor under the archway glittered with crystals.

When they had caught up, Rodan asked, "She's through there?" He motioned to the archway.

"Oh, no. That's the Cliff of Broken Promise," Lucerne said.

"What's the Cliff of Broken Promise?" Sara asked.

"You don't want to go there." Lucerne went to the door covered in ivy and lily buds and opened it without knocking.

"Madame Dawn," Lucerne called, "the strangers are here."

"Invite them in," an old, throaty voice said from behind the ivy door.

The room smelled earthy, like freshly tilled dirt. Roots ran along the floor, and the ceiling was a canopy of leaves. In the center of the room on a satin, green cushion sat an elderly woman. Her skin was the color of red mud while her hair was as white as sea foam. Her eyes were of the lightest blue and translucent.

"Please, sit," she said.

They sat on the green, satin cushions near Madame Dawn. Lucerne sat on a sloping branch in the back of the room.

"I knew you would come," Madame Dawn said, "Earth Turner, Wind Carrier, Lightning Caller, and Water Nymph." As she said each element in turn, she looked to the one that possessed that element.

"How could you know that?" Sara asked. "This place is so isolated."

"It is," Madame Dawn said, "but there are other ways of knowing things besides what you hear."

"Why did you call us here?" Rodan asked.

"I know of your journey and of what you plan to do," she said. "I am interested in humans who would undertake such a task. Like those before you."

The old woman sat higher than they did, like a goddess overlooking the people below. She was here to watch her creations play.

"Those before?" Farah asked. "Who?"

"Ten years ago, a young man and a woman undertook the same journey with friends of theirs. They wanted to protect the Water Sphere and to find its essence in the hopes of fostering more Water Elementals. I warned them that their journey would only end in tragedy.

"In the years before them, two men took the journey. It did not end well for them. One of them lost his nephew while the other lost his life."

Bolton looked away.

"That is all I can say," Madame Dawn said.

"You can't tell us who they were?" Farah said.

Orka chirped.

"What's the Cliff of Broken Promise?" Bolton asked.

"A hopeless place," she said. "It's where one goes to end their worries."

"You jump," Rodan said. "That's how you end it?"

Madame Dawn nodded.

"That's suicide," Sara said.

"No," Madame Dawn said. "You will lose your worries in an endless freefall."

"I'm tired of hearing of hopeless places." Farah sighed.

No more responsibilities, Bolton thought, no more loyalties.

"Are we in any danger?" Rodan asked.

"You will have many worries," Madame Dawn said.

"We already *have* many worries," Bolton said, "getting enough sleep being one." He rose to leave.

"You are right," Madame Dawn said. "You must go, but first I would like to bless your journey."

Madame Dawn closed her eyes and sat with her hands resting on her knees palms up. She bowed to the ground. After a few moments, she looked up. "It is done. My blessing is upon you. I hope that it will help you in battle."

Sara, Rodan, and Farah stood.

Madame Dawn rose to see them out. When she got up from her seat, the bones in her knees popped. As they left, she stopped Sara and wrapped her long, knobby fingers around her arm.

"Sara, a chink lies not in your armor, but in your army. But no matter what, stay on the path you have chosen. It will lead you to the right ending and the right beginning. Never let your guard down, and do not offer your trust to him. It is what's best for the both of you that the lesson be learned."

Madame Dawn seemed upset, like a child that had meddled in things she wasn't supposed to.

"I don't understand."

"You don't have to, not yet."

They returned to their sleeping quarters. Outside their rooms, Sara stopped. Rodan walked over to her. Bolton looked back at them.

"Sara, don't worry about what that woman said. She's probably a little senile in her old age, or maybe a fanatic trying to worry you."

"I don't think so," Sara said. "She was trying to warn me."

The lights dimmed, and Tosia was full of leafy shadows.

While the other slept, Bolton left his room. He had to know what Talon tried to hide.

He wandered through the darkness to Aldo's shop. As he touched the doorknob, he heard steady footsteps coming toward him. He hugged the side of the building against a tree trunk hidden in the shadows. He waited.

The footsteps belonged to Talon. He opened the door to Aldo's shop and walked inside without noticing Bolton.

Bolton breathed a sigh and relaxed his muscles.

ALDO stood behind his counter. He had been waiting for Talon's arrival. A cup of clear blue liquid sat upon the counter. He handed the cup to Talon.

"Here it is," Aldo said, "straight from the waterfall at the Cliff of Broken Promise."

"Thank you." Talon raised the cup to his lips.

"You are brave," Aldo said, "to want to see your future. It is not always a good one."

"I have to make sure I am doing what is right." He drank the liquid, which burned his throat.

The drink's unworldly effect made his eyes water and his brain burn. Talon shuttered as images from the near future flashed within seconds before his eyes.

After the images had passed, Talon gasped and put a hand on the shop counter to maintain his balance. "Brina!" Her name escaped his lips in a rush of air.

"I'm guessing it was not good," Aldo said, "same as last time."

Talon held his hand to his throbbing forehead.

"You tried to change it before, did you not?" Aldo said. "You can't change the future, Talon, just like you can't reshape the past."

BOLTON watched Talon leave. He wondered what had gone on in the shop, but not for too long. He had more important questions to ask.

Bolton opened the door and walked inside.

Aldo stood behind the counter. Bolton leaned over the counter and grabbed Aldo by the collar of his robe. Aldo's eyes widened.

"What is it that you know of Hephaestus's nephew?"

"*Nephew?*" The old man choked. Bolton loosened his grip but kept his hold on Aldo.

"What do you know?" Bolton shouted, but he instantly regretted raising his voice, thinking Talon might not be far enough away yet.

"He has plans," Aldo gasped, "from Hephaestus to lead the Water Elemental to her death. He's very close. He talks of friendship but hides a future betrayal. I tried to warn them, but Talon said he changed paths. I don't believe that." Aldo glared at Bolton. "I believe he will be their undoing."

"Nonsense!" Bolton hissed.

He released Aldo and pushed him against the back wall. Aldo staggered and fell, bringing down shop supplies from the back shelves with him.

Bolton turned and left the shop.

Rage boiled in him that he did not understand. He paced. I must tell her, he thought. She'll understand. But Talon . . . he won't. He'll think I'm foolish, a foolish coward for turning back to him after what he's done. No, no, I can't!

He changed direction, arguing with himself. He tried to organize things in his head, but his anger only caused further confusion. *I can't do this anymore*, he screamed inside himself.

He was near the crystal path under the archway. Music called to him from inside. He stepped onto the path, walking slowly now. With each step came the click of his boots upon the crystals, and the music grew louder. It was a melodic moaning like the sweeter side of despair—the part that says there is nothing left to lose.

Specks of light on the ceiling and the walls glimmered, reflecting the crystal flooring. The path winded up without pattern, like a jeweled ribbon carelessly tossed on the floor.

Bolton walked up the winding path, which led to another archway and on to a bridge. On the bridge, he glanced over the railing. Misty fog rested below.

Is this what they fall into? he wondered, a misty nothingness?

Stairs led away from the bridge. Crystals lined the sides of the steps. Bolton crept up the stairs. What lie beyond was the last place he would ever see.

It was a cliff, flat and brown. It was very plain and unwelcoming, unlike the scene that lay before it.

Beyond the cliff was a field of red flowers in full bloom and a waterfall colored with pink, blue, and purple light. The sky was pale cerulean and cloudless. *A paradise. Emptiness. The chance to no longer feel.*

He had come to the cliff with every intention of jumping from its edge, but he could not. *What now?* he thought. *What should I do?*

Bolton was not sure how he would fix what he started, but he was sure of one thing. He ripped the silver medallion from his neck and threw it into the abyss.

20

THE MARCH INTO DARKNESS

THE next morning, Lucerne had questions for the travelers. She wanted to know all about Elementals' war powers and the dangers that Sara and her friends had faced and would encounter on the journey ahead.

Sara, Spire, Rodan, and Farah answered her questions. Talon was quiet and reserved as usual, but Bolton was acting differently, like a cloud had passed over, and he was anticipating rain. He leaned against a thick wooden and knobbed column with his arms folded and his head down.

Bolton's change in behavior did not go undetected by Sara.

They stood at the exit of Tosia to the north. Lucerne had followed them to ask more questions. "How were the Elementals created?" she asked.

"What do you mean?" Sara asked.

"How did they . . . come to be?"

The question had come to Sara's mind often, especially when she was young. "I don't know," Sara said.

"The Creator," Rodan said. "He made the element spheres through which Elementals obtain their power."

"But who was the Creator?" she asked.

"Not much is known of him," Spire said. "Everyone has a different view of who the Creator was. In Wyvek, they have statues depicting the Creator as a giant god with the head of a bear. Here, in Tosia, they believe that the Creator is nature itself."

"Madame Dawn has explained that one to me many times," Lucerne said. "But it doesn't . . ."

". . . satisfy your curiosity," Talon finished.

"Besides . . ." Lucerne folded her arms. "I think she's lying to me."

Talon bought lanterns. "We'll need them in D'arkadia."

"Is Madam Dawn your grandmother?" Sara asked.

"No," Lucerne said. "I wasn't born in Tosia, and I'm not an Earth Elemental in case you were wondering."

"Where are you from?"

Lucerne shrugged. "Don't remember. Hephaestus burned the place down. My mom hid me in a ditch. A merchant found me and brought me here so Madame Dawn could heal my burns." Lucerne pulled up her sleeve and turned her arm. On her forearm, the skin was marbled and pink.

"I'm going to leave here someday," Lucerne said. "To see the world like you."

Talon stood at the entrance to D'arkadia. He handed a note to a messenger. "To Brina in Elementa. Get it to her as soon as you can." Talon sighed.

No light shone across the barren land of D'arkadia.

After several attempts to bring light to D'arkadia, efforts ended.

Decades ago, the Wind Elementals of Breeze tried to set up a trading post because the land was near Vella City, which was, at the time, prosperous and worthy of trade. The Wind

Elementals set up huge columns that radiated light all over D'arkadia. Some say they were the first and only ones to see the D'arkadia that lie beneath the darkness.

The next day the columns had been mysteriously destroyed. They had been crushed in, and only a few were still standing, absent of any luminescence. The damage could have only been done by something of great size.

That is when the stories began of the Beast of D'arkadia. People said it was the rogue Protector of an ancient element sphere. The sphere that it guarded was said to be a broken sphere, a lost element.

When someone had destroyed the sphere, the Beast went mad with rage.

It broke the laws of the Sphere Protectors and attacked people who did not threaten the sphere. No one had ever seen the Beast, but they had heard its rough, sand-papery growl.

Those who were lucky were only frightened off by the Beast, but those who were not as lucky never returned from D'arkadia.

The pathway from Tosia was steep, and it became darker with every step. The ground was rocky and jagged, and they could not see any more than four feet in front of them by the light of their lanterns.

"Do not lose your lanterns," Talon said.

Farah tied her lantern to her waist and sheltered Orka with one hand.

"How long will we have to travel through here?" she asked.

"Two days at the least," Talon said. "And that's if we hurry."

"Days?" Farah said. "How can we tell day from night?"

"You'll get tired."

Sara kept pace with Bolton behind the others.

"What happened to your medallion?" Sara asked him. "I noticed you weren't wearing it when we left."

"I lost it," he said.

"Was it important to you?"

"No. Not anymore." He stared at the barren ground as he walked.

"Is something wrong?"

"Why would you think something's wrong?"

"You seem lost," Sara said, "and you're trying to figure a way out."

Bolton looked ahead into the darkness.

"There is something I've been trying to figure out," he said, "but I'm not sure how to explain it yet."

"Can you tell me more about the Insula?" she asked.

"It's an island," he said, "and everyone who lives there goes around the island telling people that the land under their feet doesn't exist."

"What if I said, I believe you?"

Bolton turned to her. "Do you?"

"I've had time to consider it."

"The Insula is very hard to find, but still it is surrounded by bright blue water, and the sun hits it like a spotlight. On the east side, a lagoon leads to a cave. The ceiling of the cave shines with crystals. When I was younger . . . You don't want to hear all this."

"Yes, I do." Sara said. "Go on, please."

"When I was younger," Bolton said, "I hid a box of treasures under the waterfall behind the bridge so when I returned, I could remember all the adventures I had and all the people I had gotten to know. My parents and I had to leave the island. My mother . . . I remember she was so scared to stay. She never wanted to stay in one place for too long. But she cried when we left. It was so peaceful. It was home."

"You make it sound so real," Sara whispered.

"What?"

"Tell me more about your parents," Sara said. "What made your mother so afraid to stay?"

"My parents died a long time ago. I don't remember much."

"I'm sorry. Is that why you haven't returned to the Insula?"

"No. I wanted to go back for a long time. I had friends, and I love living on the water. But, I can't go back. Only one man knows the way. He's a captain, and he charges people a lot of money to get to the island. Not just any kind of money, but glistenings."

"Glistenings? But they're not used anymore."

"I know, but that's what he wants. My parents went to the island because they thought we'd be safe. I've made a vow that I will get the money and go back. I don't want to be tied here anymore."

Sara looked at him.

"Anyway," Bolton said, "have you decided on what you're going to do once this quest is over?"

"I've decided I want to go to the Insula Somnia Perpetua," Sara said.

"When I get the glistenings, I'll take you." Bolton wanted to bite back his words.

"Promise?" she asked.

Bolton hesitated. "I . . ."

"Keep up," Talon yelled to Bolton and Sara. "We have to stay together."

Talon held his lantern out into the darkness.

"If you see anything, don't scream," he said.

"Why did you have to say that?" Farah kept her hand over Orka. She had wanted Orka to fly over D'arkadia, but she was afraid the little, green bird would lose her way.

"He's right," Rodan said. "We have to look out."

"For what?"

"The Beast of D'arkadia."

"Beast?" Farah's eyes darted. "What Beast?"

"You've never heard of the Beast of D'arkadia?" Bolton said.

"Sara, have you heard of this beast?" Farah asked.

"No," Sara said.

"Sara was cut off from the rest of the world for three years," Rodan said.

"Well," Farah said, "I'm sorry my dad didn't try to scare me with creepy bedtime stories like *your* parents did."

"It's not a story," Talon said.

"Okay, so tell." Farah folded her arms and stopped in her tracks.

Orka chirped.

"All right, but keep moving," Talon said. "Tell her."

"The Beast of D'arkadia protects a broken sphere," Rodan said.

"A broken sphere?" Sara asked. "What was its element?"

"It's lost," Spire said. "No one remembers it."

"But the Beast still protects it," Rodan said.

"How is that possible?" Farah asked. "As soon as the sphere is taken off the pedestal, the Protector disappears."

"But the sphere was never taken off the pedestal," Bolton said.

"It still rests there," Rodan said, "and the Beast still thinks it must protect the sphere. But because the sphere is broken so is the Beast's mind. It attacks those who mean the sphere no harm."

Talon searched the ground with the lantern. A three-lined symbol was etched into the ground. "Let's rest."

"Rest! I want to get out of here as soon as possible." Farah moved Orka from her shoulder to her hand.

"We're halfway to the Crystal Forest," Talon said.

"How do you know?" Rodan asked.

"The path's marked."

Talon put down his lantern and pulled twigs from his canvas bag. "I'm lighting a fire. You can put out your lanterns." Talon snapped his fingers, and fire sparked the twigs.

They all put out their lantern flames, except Farah. They settled around the fire.

"Do we need the broken element sphere?" Sara asked.

"No," Spire said. "It isn't part of the circle anymore. Its

power has faded."

"Where's the next sphere?"

"In Demlama."

"But in Jetty Verte," Farah said, "We get two spheres in one. The Earth Sphere is in a dungeon near the center of the city, and the Water Sphere is in a cave over the bridge."

"I never understood why the Earth Sphere rests in a dungeon," Rodan said.

"Earth Elementals have abandoned their sphere," Spire said.

"Not every sphere finds its place somewhere sacred," Bolton said.

"What," Rodan said, "like the static terror the Lightning Sphere was in?"

"Yeah, but how challenging will it be to get the Earth Sphere?" Bolton said. "I wonder what the Protector is. A weed?"

A branch wrapped around Bolton's neck. Rodan smirked.

Bolton laughed. "You don't want me to do that with lightning."

"Settle down," Talon said. "This isn't a playground."

Rodan sent the branch back, and Bolton stopped laughing.

"Talon?" Sara asked.

Bolton touched her hand, and when she looked at him, he shook his head.

"Let her speak," Talon said.

"It wasn't—"

"No, ask it," Talon said.

Bolton looked at him like he had gone insane. Talon had kept his secret for so long. *What are you doing old man?* he wondered. *You have more than* your *secrets to protect.*

"I wanted to know," Sara said, "how Aldo knows you and why he said that you should be dead. I want to know why, years ago, when you brought me to Element, Brina thought the same thing."

Talon put his face in his hands. When he looked up all

eyes were on him, except Bolton's. Bolton looked off into the distance, afraid of what Talon would confess. Bolton was not ready to own up to his own past yet, and he did not want Talon telling his secret for him.

"I knew I would have to tell you," Talon said. "But you all must understand that I can't tell you everything. Some things aren't mine to tell."

"You don't have to tell us at all," Spire said. "Your secrets are yours alone."

"After coming this far, you deserve to know," Talon said. "I grew up with a younger sister, Ana, and an older brother, Eli. My family lived in a small village east of Lumina.

"Ana, Eli, and I used to be very close. When I got my element before Eli, he became angry. He always wanted to be the best. He began concentrating more and more on attaining his element. One day, he got it. But he was so strong, so uncontrollably strong. He set fire to our village. People we knew died. Eli cried for days and refused to leave his room. They came for him. Soldiers. They took him from us.

"Eli never got to grow up with his family. My father was never able to teach him how to forge swords, like he taught me. My mother died of grief. She wouldn't eat, and she lay in bed all day. With Eli gone, our family was not whole.

"I found out that the people who took him from us were known as the Council, and they brought him to a place where they took all children who were extraordinarily gifted in their elements. They locked them up and tested them, made them use the extent of their powers. They tortured them physically and mentally, curious to find out their limits.

"No one knew what they were looking for, but I believe they were trying to find out how their powers worked. But their cruel experiments did not go on for long. The building where they operated caught on fire. Very few got out. Eli was one of them. But he had changed. He was no longer the little boy who would cry over the dead.

"The Council went underground, and Eli went away, bent

on forming a kingdom among ruins. We never heard from him till the wedding.

"When Ana came of age, she married. Her husband, Benn, was a Lightning Elemental. Eli attended the ceremony. I could see the hate in his eyes for Benn. I don't know why my brother hated him so much, but I think he wanted to keep our family as pure as the fire.

"He was very outspoken at the wedding. Everyone feared him. He said that their marriage was an abomination and that they would pay for it.

"Ana was so happy to see him, but when she heard of his distaste for her husband, she didn't know how to react. He was our brother, but he was a stranger to us.

"Six years later, Eli had them murdered and took their five-year old son to claim him as his own. He killed my sister. I had to do something.

"I used to train apprentices, but I left my position at Element to find my older brother and fight him. I took a friend, a Water Elemental, who wanted to stop him as much as I did for the sake of his family. I didn't tell anyone else where I was going.

"We traveled to the place my brother named his kingdom. But the fight didn't end well. We were beaten and left for dead. We stumbled and dragged ourselves back to Jetty Verte. People gave us food and shelter, and we recovered.

"After that my friend went back to his family, but I couldn't return to Element. I could no longer train apprentices. I had forsaken my responsibility, left the ones I cared for, and I had led my friend into a battle we couldn't win. What's more, my most accomplished apprentice turned on me and joined my brother's followers. So, I hid on an island where I hoped no one would find me. It was the one Ana had told me of.

"Years later, I learned that my brother was killing again. He was murdering Water Elementals. At the wedding, he had confided but a few words to me that those who called Water had haunted him.

"It was a massacre. Within a year, Water Elementals became few in number. I feared the friend that had journeyed with me was in danger. So, I returned to Elementa, but I was too late. His house had been burned to the ground. I thought all of them were dead, but I heard a muffled cry through the rain.

"Behind the cottage was a small child. Instead of bringing her to Element, I took her to Ocean's Light. I thought she might be saved from the curse of being one of us."

"It was you." Sara's voice was a whisper.

Talon nodded. "Seeing my friend's daughter made me think of my nephew, Ana's son.

"I remembered Eli dangling him in front of me, claiming him as his own. I spent nearly two years questioning whether it was wise to take on Eli again. Perhaps it wasn't, but I couldn't let my nephew grow up like him, so I decided to go back. This time I did not come to fight. I didn't make my presence known. I came in cloaked, and by the cover of darkness, I stole away my nephew and ran.

"He didn't remember me. He was in denial about his parents. I told him that his mother and father were dead. He cried and shocked me."

Talon laughed. "He wasn't half my height at the time.

"But I couldn't hide him away. His element was too strong and evident, so I told him that I was bringing him to Element.

"I had two people to worry about in Elementa: my friend's daughter and my sister's son. I had to make sure that Eli wouldn't come for them, so I stayed in Elementa, and worked the streets in the market.

"Eight years later, I saw a young girl dancing on water. She was much older, but she had her mother's face and her father's eyes. I brought her to Element too.

"I knew that someday she would go on this journey and have to face him. No matter how much I want to keep her safe, she isn't safe from Eli. Nor is anyone else because my brother's new name is Hephaestus."

They stared at Talon, realizing that he was ready to kill his own brother because of the evil he had done. Everything connected. Some knew more connections than others.

The fire crackled. The world stood still for that moment, yielding to it as if it was the only thing that existed.

"So, you saved me twice," Sara said. "My father faced Hephaestus. You took me from the forest and brought me to Element."

Talon nodded.

"But what happened to your nephew?" Farah asked. "Wasn't he the one Aldo was talking about, Eli's next of kin? He said he was up to something. What's his name? If he went to Element we might know him."

"That's someone else's secret," Talon said.

Farah folded her arms. "I'm tired of secrets."

"How bad was it?" Rodan asked. "Are we marching to our deaths?"

Talon was silent.

"I'll take that chance," Sara said, "but that doesn't mean that anyone else has to." She bowed her head. "Anyone who wants to is free to leave."

"I'm not leaving," Rodan said.

"We all knew what we were getting into," Farah said. "I didn't come all this way to back down at the last moment."

Orka chirped.

"I've fought this battle once," Talon said. "I am trapped by my past, Sara, and I realized that your father would have wanted me to protect you from being trapped by your own. That is why I didn't try to stop you in Lumina."

Someone sighed.

"Bolton?"

"Maybe we shouldn't fight," Bolton said.

"What?" Farah asked.

"What if he wins?" Bolton said. "Maybe this sphere hunt was a bad idea."

"It was *your* idea," Farah said.

"I know, but I was wrong," Bolton said. "I don't want anyone to die."

"Then we'll fight," Rodan said, "because a lot of people will die if we don't."

"He's right," Spire said. "Hephaestus won't stop until someone stops him, permanently."

"Can you hear yourselves?" Bolton asked. "Why are we out here?" A nervous chuckle escaped his lips. "It's all noble isn't it until someone dies? We shouldn't be out here, risking our lives for the rest of the world. What do we owe them?"

Rodan narrowed his eyes at Bolton.

Bolton glared at him. "Look, I know this is your mission, okay? But I've had a lot of time to think. This is stupid, all of it. We go back to Element, right? We live our lives. Let someone else deal with Hephaestus."

"Who else?" Sara asked.

"The Lightning Elementals of Wyvek are way ahead of us. Let them handle it. Let them fight."

"And sit by?" Sara stared back at him. "You can go, you know?"

Does she want me to go? Bolton wondered.

"I'm not saying this for me," Bolton said.

"I won't stop," Sara said. "My whole life was built on this. He killed my parents. He's the reason I've been locked in a room for three years. I want to do this more than I've ever wanted to do anything in my life, and I'm scared, but I don't want to rely on someone else. This is mine. It is what I was born for."

Tears were in her eyes, and she wiped them away, hoping no one would see them in the dark, but they all could hear them as her voice trembled.

Rodan put his hand on hers. "We're all with you. No matter what."

THEY slept in a circle around the firelight. Bolton dreamed. He cringed against his nightmares.

Mom?

His hands were as small as his voice as he clenched the rail of the worn boat. He came back from playing beneath the waterfall. He heard a voice behind him.

"Hello, little Bolt."

Bolton turned around to see a tall, pale man dressed in red. Several other men stood behind him.

"Where are your parents?" He scanned the foremast of the boat.

Bolton's mother emerged from the cabin. She had been hiding, praying that her husband and son would not come back until this man had left.

"Don't you dare touch him, Eli!" Ana cried as she burst onto the deck.

The man in red smiled, and two of the other men took hold of Ana.

Young Bolton watched as his mother screamed for his life.

"Don't you hurt him, Eli!" she shrieked, struggling to break the grip of the men.

"Let her go to her son," Eli said.

The men released Ana with a hard shove. She kneeled, grabbed Bolton, and held him as if her loving arms would protect her son from the red-suited man.

"Oh, how sweet," Eli said, "mother and son together for the last time, but where's the father?"

Bolton and his mother stood huddled together against the boat's wooden rail. Bolton's father was on the other side of the cabin, out of Eli's line of sight. Ana stared at him. He stood, unable to move from the spot, as he gazed into her eyes.

"Separate them," Eli demanded.

The men pulled Bolton and Ana apart. They brought Bolton to Eli and left Ana at the railing. Ana gazed back at her husband and mouthed the words: Run, Benn. Go!

"Pull up the boat's anchor and let it drift out to sea," Eli commanded.

Benn looked back at his wife, begging him to leave. He

looked down at the wavering water as the boat drifted farther from the coast. His glance darted away from Ana, unable to witness her pain. He jumped over the railing into the sea and swam away. The men heard the splash, and Eli turned to see Benn in the distance, swimming from his death.

"Follow him!" Eli told three of the men.

They dived into the water in pursuit of Benn.

Ana's cries drifted out to sea. "Let my son leave before you do it, Eli. Please," she pleaded.

"Take him around to the lifeboats," Eli said, "and wait for me."

The remaining two men led Bolton away. His mother must have bit her lip for his sake as Eli burned her because no more than whimpers escaped her. When Eli met them at the spare boat he had blood and ash on his hands. His eyes were glassy. He commanded the men to lower the boat into the sea. The men lowered the boat and took the two oars from under the wooden seats. As they rowed away, Eli snapped his fingers, and the boat, which Bolton had called home, caught fire.

Bolton sobbed and shook. He was not the little boy on that boat anymore. His mother was dead and his father, the coward, he thought, probably died before sunset.

ORKA screeched, waking everyone. Farah looked around several times. She held the lantern up to search the darkness.

A low growl carried through the air.

"Did you hear that?" she asked.

"What?" Rodan blinked.

"That!"

"That, what?" Bolton asked.

Farah held the lantern out farther. "I know I heard something. Orka heard it too."

"Calm down," Rodan said. "Nothing's out there."

"Besides," Bolton said, "there are scarier things than the Beast."

"What could be scarier than a rogue Sphere Protector?"

Farah asked.

"What about the Maledixit?"

"What's that?" Sara sat up. Her eyes were heavy with sleep.

No one could see Spire's look of disapproval, but Sara could feel it.

"You can tell us some other time," Sara said.

"What better time than in complete darkness," Bolton said. He began his tale. "The Maledixit was once a man, a man who went on a long journey to find food for his village after harsh weather had destroyed their crops. He and four others set out to find the next town. This was before reliable maps had been drawn up. They never returned.

"Later, the bones of the men were found far away from the village. The bones were licked clean, but only four skeletons were recovered. The body of the fifth man was never found.

"One night, a villager swore he saw a monster. The creature was seven feet tall, half-man, half-beast, and stunk like something dead. The creature was one of the travelers, the fifth man.

"The men were lost and could find no food. Starvation can make a man do desperate things. The man ate his companions and became cursed to wander the earth as a creature separate from mankind. Anyone who survives the Maledixit's bite is doomed to suffer the same fate as the Maledixit itself."

"That's enough," Spire said. "We don't have time for imaginary monsters when we are dealing with real ones."

"Real monsters?" Bolton said. "No one's ever seen this Beast."

Farah scanned the blackness. She imagined things taking shape in the dark. Her breath caught in her throat. Two glowing, yellow eyes stared back at her. The eyes were surrounded by thick, black fur, but the snout was bare to the nose with wrinkled, pink skin.

The Beast snarled, revealing a mouth with two rows of razor-sharp teeth.

Farah screamed and jumped up as something five times her size rushed past her.

"Stop!" Talon said. "It's blind, but it hears you, and it feels the heat of the light."

"So why are we holding lanterns by the light of a fire?" Farah asked.

Orka chirped.

"Keep that bird quiet." Talon extinguished the fire light and eased the light of the lanterns. "We'll have to travel in the dark for a while."

"You know the way?" Spire asked.

"Yes."

She put a hand on Talon's shoulder to guide her.

Sara felt a hand wrap around hers.

"Bolton, is that you?"

"No, it's me," Rodan said.

"Farah, take my hand."

Farah put her hand in Sara's.

"Is everyone together?" Talon asked.

They all announced their presence, Farah with her voice shaking. She reached up to her shoulder to ensure Orka was safe.

"Alright. We're going to walk north," Talon said, "stay together."

They walked along the uneven road. Hours crept by slowly.

"How soon?" Farah asked.

"We're going away. That's all it wanted," Rodan said.

A low growl echoed.

"If that's all it wanted why is it following us?" Farah asked.

They could feel the course fur as the Beast brushed past them.

"What does it want?" Farah cried.

"It doesn't matter," Talon said. "Run!"

The rocky ground was hard to run on. For Farah, it would have been no problem, except fear had her nerves on edge.

Her foot hit a jagged piece of rock, and she stumbled to the ground.

"Farah! Wait!"

"What happened?" Rodan asked.

"She let go of my hand. I think she tripped," Sara said.

"Farah!"

"Farah!"

A scream echoed in the dark.

Bolton broke the chain and ran from the group.

"Don't be stupid!" Talon shouted.

Bolton suspended a bolt of lightning into the air. The bolt illuminated the area, ten feet on all sides, and surrounded Bolton in its glow.

The great expanse of land was empty. It was full of rocks and jagged peaks. It was as barren in the light as it was in the dark.

A few paces away Farah was crouched in a sitting position. She sheltered Orka in her arms. The Beast circled her. It could hear her heavy breathing.

"Hey," Bolton yelled, "come over here, you big ugly floor mat!"

The Beast turned and stuck his big, naked nose into the air.

"I guess you're stupid too," Bolton yelled.

The Beast growled and charged in the direction of Bolton's voice.

Farah picked up her head and ran to the others with Orka still in her arms.

"That's right!" Bolton said. "Come and get me!"

"Bolton, stop!" Sara yelled.

The Beast rammed him, and the lightning bolt went out.

"No!"

Lightning flashed. The beast pinned Bolton to the ground. Bolton sent a bolt into the Beast's stomach, and it jumped back. The light zipped into darkness.

Talon sparked a flame with his fingers. Sara ran to where

Bolton and the Beast had fought. Bolton lay on the ground with three shallow cuts in his chest where the Beast clawed him.

The cuts dripped with blood, but still he tried to sit up. Sara rushed to his aid and helped him into a sitting position.

"You're lucky," Talon said.

"Lucky?"

"Lucky it didn't tear you to pieces."

Rodan and Sara helped Bolton to his feet.

"We have to go," Spire said.

"Don't worry." Talon put his hand on Bolton's shoulder. "I brought supplies to bandage you up. Aldo's medicine will keep it from getting infected."

They walked on. Talon kept a flame lit but dim so it would not attract the Beast. Everyone was silent. Orka didn't dare to chirp. She sat on Farah's shoulder and was so quiet that Farah had to reach for her to make sure she was still there.

The tension from Talon's story was replaced with fear that seemed to radiate through D'arkadia. It lurked in the shadows and waited to reach out and take them. The very rocks became threatening. They all darted their eyes, looking out for the Beast.

A faint light shined in the distance. Crystals glowed at the edge of a forest.

"Look!" Farah ran to the safety of the light's glow.

"Hurry!"

Bolton had his arms around the shoulders of Sara and Rodan. Their steps were slow as they were burdened with the extra weight. The burning cut on Bolton's chest made it difficult for him to concentrate on anything else, especially walking. But seeing the light gave him the adrenaline to press on.

Spire and Talon were a few paces away.

Farah beckoned them to run faster. "Come on, you guys!"

"We're moving as fast as we can," Rodan said.

A growl reverberated, and a bulking mass charged toward them, but stopped. The Beast clawed the ground, but could not advance.

At the forest edge, Farah held her hands out. She pushed the Beast back. The Wind ripped through its fur.

They hurried into the light. Once they were safe, Farah let go and knelt from exhaustion.

The Beast walked back and forth. The light casted its long shadow. But an invisible wall stopped it from crossing.

Orka stared at its yellow eyes from the safety of a nearby tree. She flew down to Farah's shoulder.

"It won't come into the light," Talon said, "not in the Crystal Forest."

Farah stood and backed away among the trees. "Let's go. I don't want to take any chances."

21

CHOICE

BOLTON cringed as Spire put the ointment on his wounds. The strange green substance stung and reeked.

"What is this stuff?" Bolton asked.

"Aldo gave it to me," Talon said. "He said that it'll heal cuts and burns."

"Did he say anything else?" Bolton asked.

"No." Talon diverted his eyes.

They sat in a clearing surrounded by crystals and trees. Spire wrapped bandages around Bolton's chest to cover the gashes. As Spire bandaged, she caught a glimpse of Bolton's exposed shoulder. A pink and bumpy scar went from his shoulder blade to his elbow.

"An old scar? It must have hurt. Where did you get it?"

Talon shuffled his feet.

"It was a long time ago," Bolton said. "I was a kid. I got

into things. I don't remember it."

"Seems like it would be a hard wound to forget."

Talon coughed.

"Where's Sara?" Bolton asked.

"By the lake," Spire said.

"*On* the lake," Rodan said. "I think she wants to be alone."

He had a defensive edge to his voice. Bolton didn't like it. It made them strangers.

"Now why would she want that?" Bolton got up and put his shirt on. He said it more to get a rise out of Rodan than anything. They had been on two separate islands for this entire journey. He wanted his friend back, but he didn't know how to do that.

"Sara needs time," Spire said. "She has a lot to think about. Besides, you should rest."

"I'll go check on her," Bolton said. "Make sure she's okay."

"Right." Farah rolled her eyes.

Bolton left the clearing.

Talon followed him.

Once they were out of earshot of the others, Talon turned Bolton around by the shoulder.

"What are you doing?" Talon asked.

"I'm going to talk to Sara."

"You know what I mean. Aldo told me you threatened him, and I have no reason not to believe him."

"So, you wouldn't believe me if I said I didn't. Why bother asking?"

"I trust you, Bolton, but he still has a hold over you. You didn't have that medallion when I took you."

"And I don't have it now."

"I'm giving you a chance. It's not too late." Talon let him go.

Bolton turned to walk away.

"Wait!"

Bolton faced him.

"There's something you should know," Talon said. "I know . . . well, I know it might not matter much now. He told me not to tell you, but you deserve to know. You're old enough to understand."

"What is this?" Bolton asked. "Got used to telling all your secrets?"

"This one isn't mine," Talon said.

Bolton waited. Talon looked at Bolton as the words left his mouth, the words Talon thought Bolton must hear before it was too late for Talon to tell them.

"Benn's alive," Talon said.

Bolton stared at Talon. He never expected to hear those words together. They were foreign to him. But he realized what the words meant. He whispered at first, but his voice became more agitated with each word. "You knew this? My father is alive and you kept that to yourself? He's my father. You had no right!"

"But he did."

"No! No. He left my mother and me. My mother died because of him, don't you understand? And he never came back? The coward. He's more of a villain than Hephaestus."

Bolton put his hands on his knees and looked at the ground. *He left us*, he thought. *He left us to die.* He sighed and stood. He looked away from Talon as he spoke. "You're right. It doesn't matter much now, does it? He can't be alive, not after what he's done. He won't come back. If he did, he wouldn't be welcomed."

"I know it's hard," Talon said, "but are you ready for this?"

"None of that matters anymore. I've changed, and I'm not a coward like my father."

Bolton looked at him like a caged animal, trapped and not knowing how to feel, not understanding this strange world around him.

"I'm sorry," Talon said.

"I don't care. Why tell me now?"

"Because if I die, I don't want it on my conscience."

"This is for you?"

"What your father did, he did out of fear. A man will do a lot of things when he's afraid. And they seem right at the time."

"I'm not going to forgive him."

"That's not why I'm telling you this."

"Then why?"

"You have every right to be afraid of him."

"I'm not my father." Bolton disappeared among the trees.

SARA stood on the water of the lake and looked down into it as the fish swam beneath its surface. *I'll never see this again*, she thought. She did not feel like dancing. She thought of Talon's story and wondered if she would have to hear Bolton's soon.

Everyone kept secrets. She could feel Bolton wasn't being honest with her. Madame Dawn said not to trust *him*. Could she have meant Bolton?

"Sara."

Bolton waved to her. Sara walked across the water to meet him.

"Are you alright?" she asked.

"Yeah, Talon got some stuff from Aldo. I think it's working," Bolton said. "It stinks though."

She smiled. "I'm glad you're okay."

He looked around. "This is a nice place. How did you find it?"

"I looked around."

"So how does it feel to run away again?"

"I didn't run far this time." She grinned.

Bolton looked away. "Maybe you should," he said.

"What?"

"I don't know what they told you, but you don't have to do this," Bolton said.

"No one told me to do anything."

"You could run away again, leave all this mess behind."

"And hide?"

"I know how it sounds, but Hephaestus has hundreds of Elementals on his side. You'll die if you try to fight him, and you know that. I can see it in the way you've been looking at places, like you'll never see them again. You don't have to stand up to him. You can have a normal life."

"Maybe," Sara said, "but this is all I've ever known."

"It doesn't have to be," Bolton said. "I'll take you to the Insula."

Sara walked back onto the water. Bolton stood at the edge beside her.

"Maybe I will go and leave this all behind." She looked at the water.

"Yeah, you should," Bolton said.

Sara thought. "But what would everyone think if I give up now?"

"They'll understand. And if they don't, this is *your* life."

She walked out into the water and let her feet become submerged in it.

"It sounds like it would be wonderful, to let go," she said.

"It would. We could watch the moon rise over the sea on the coast of the Insula," Bolton said. "The water turns deep violet and sparkles in the light. You could dance on the lagoon. It's ten times as big as this lake. I know you'd love it. And you wouldn't have to look at it like it's the last place you'll ever see."

"I'd like to see it," Sara said. "Maybe one day. I don't know."

"But you can," Bolton said.

Sara struggled to hide the tears welling up in her eyes. "I can't. I can't go." She buried her face in her hands.

Bolton walked up to her. "Sara?"

She looked up at him. Bolton pulled her closer, out of the water, and held her to him as a light rain surrounded them.

22

REGRET

O N a mountain's peak, an evil leader sat on a throne of cold marble in his deserted palace of stone. He wore a red cloak and a gold medallion bearing the element symbols, each etched atop the other. His golden eyes, like embers, were closed. Memories haunted him.

"Eli, please, let my son leave before you do it!"

He let the men take little Bolton away from his mother. Eli knelt beside her. "I'm not here to kill you or your child. I want you to leave that monster's spawn you call husband and join me in Omega Ray."

"I won't have you kill Benn, not for whatever his father did to you." Tears ran down her face.

"Not to *me*!" Eli shouted.

Ana screamed as his thoughts scorched her, knowing he

couldn't control his emotion, like when he was a child.

He wept as she burned, and the tears were hot against his face.

A rat scurried across the stone floor of Hephaestus's castle. He singed the end of its tail as it tried to escape through a crack in the wall. He heard the tortured squeaks as the rat burned alive.

Perditus listened from behind the wall.

The large door to the front of the castle opened, and a soldier walked in. He was a soldier without armor or a sword. His weapon was Fire.

"My lord, I have news."

Hephaestus opened his fiery, golden eyes.

"What news, Fero?"

"Our spies in Elementa have sent a message. Ships are being docked and crowded with apprentices."

"They're coming here?"

Fero looked into the eyes of his leader. "I can send men to Elementa to stop them."

"Why should I bother with them?"

"Because the Water Elemental is close. She is headed to the Crystal Forest as we speak."

"How many spheres has she obtained?"

"She's been through Caleena and Wyvek, so two so far. She's nearing Demlama. She'll have to back track once she gets to Jetty Verte. That should afford us enough time. But if the apprentices of Element are headed for the city now, the timing would mean they'd make it here before we returned."

"I can't have that."

"I'll send the men."

"Wait . . . I'll accompany them."

"I wouldn't suggest that."

Hephaestus leaned forward on the throne and whispered to Fero, his voice was taunting like someone who had gone mad. "We have nothing to fear. The boy will make sure they remain near the tower until I arrive."

"He is distracted. He might betray our cause."

"We'll speak of this no longer. Gather the men. Prepare them for their mission. I want you to go to the Crystal Forest. Remind him of what he promised."

Fero bowed and left his master to his thinking.

Perditus crept from behind the wall. "Let me go with you," he said.

"You are weak and defective, like your mother," Hephaestus said. "You would be of no use."

Perditus stared at the man on the throne for some time. The corner of his lip upturned. He left the room and stormed down the hall. He beat the walls with his fists. He tried to send Fire, but all he got was smoke. He beat the stone walls harder. His knuckles bled.

23

CALLING WATER

"WHERE did the rain came from? I don't see any clouds," Bolton said. "Did you . . ."

"No." Sara's voice was soft.

Bolton and Sara sat by the lake.

"What's this?" He picked up the papers beside her. A piece of charcoal slipped from inside one of the folded pieces and fell onto the ground.

"Oh, it's nothing. Just my drawings."

Bolton unfolded the papers. "You drew me? When was this?"

Sara's face warmed.

Bolton smiled and continued to look through the drawings. "Is this you?"

"No, it's my mother."

"She looks like you."

"I've always wanted to look like her. So, you meant what you said before?" she asked.

"Of course."

Sara looked out into the gentle water of the lake. "I want to go. I do," she said. "At first, I was doing this for myself. I knew he killed my parents. I wanted revenge, and I wanted freedom. But now everyone believes in me. If I were to turn back now, I would be turning my back on them, everyone whoever hoped I would succeed. I can't do that. I know what will happen if I fail, but if I give up now, I could never live with myself. I could never forget."

"But . . ." Bolton said. "I mean, I know how it feels to have someone depend on you, and I know how it feels to disappoint someone."

Silence lingered between them.

"Come on," he said. "There's something you should try."

Bolton took Sara's hand and led her away from the lake into the clearing among the trees and crystals.

"Concentrate," he said. "What were you thinking of when the rain fell?"

"The rain?" Sara said, "but I told you. I didn't do that. I couldn't."

"Why not? Because you think you're not strong enough." Bolton took both her hands in his. "You are."

Sara closed her eyes, pressed her lips together and looked up at him. "I'll try."

"That's all I ask. Focus on what you were thinking of when the rain fell."

Sara concentrated. "The night my parents died. The rain, it's so comforting to know that it can put out the fire. It feels safe. I wanted to keep my family safe, to protect them from the flames."

"Think of that. Think of all the people you'll be protecting." Bolton tightened his grip on her hands. "You can do this."

Sara closed her eyes and thought of her mother and father

and all the people whose lives depended on her strength.

Bolton felt a drop of water hit him under the chin. He looked down. Droplets of water rose from the ground. "You're doing it! Keep trying!"

Sara focused harder.

The water came up from the ground around them.

"Sara, look." His voice came out in an awed whisper.

Sara opened her eyes. A wall of water glistened around them. The water flowed from the ground to the sky, like a watery cylinder.

"You did it! You called Water!" He reached out to touch the glistening wall. The water flowed through his fingertips as if he had dipped his hand into a stream.

His eyes caught hers, and he felt an overpowering pull inside himself. He leaned closer to her, and his lips touched hers. Something changed between them, never to be reversed.

A loud chirp echoed from among the trees.

The wall of water collapsed, splashed around them, and trailed down the bank of the lake. Sara looked around.

The chirp came again.

"It's only Orka." Bolton spotted the little, green bird among the trees. "Come on. They're probably wondering where we went off to."

TALON, Spire, Rodan, and Farah set up camp in a crystal clearing. Talon set a fire. They settled around it on the soft ground.

"So, your own brother gave you that scar?" Farah asked Talon.

"No, it was that apprentice of mine who betrayed me. But Eli has scarred people in much the same way."

"It looks like Bolton's," Spire said.

Talon glanced up at her. She did not go on.

"Who was your appren—" Farah stopped.

Bolton and Sara walked into the clearing.

"Where have you two been?" she asked. "I sent Orka to

keep an eye on you."

"Thanks," Bolton said. "I'm sure if we were attacked, Orka would have made the perfect defense."

"Oh, yeah, joke about it," Farah said, "but if you were in trouble who would've saved you?"

Orka chirped. She landed on Farah's shoulder.

Farah petted the little, green bird.

Bolton sat near the fire.

"No, no, no," Farah said, "I have something to show you. Rodan and I found it."

"What is it?"

"You'll have to see for yourself."

Sara and Bolton followed Rodan and Farah out of the crystal clearing.

Once they were gone, Spire spoke. "I'm worried."

"You have a right to be," Talon said.

"Why's that? Do you still know something that I don't?"

He was silent.

"I know you sent a letter to Brina back in Tosia. It's okay to miss her."

"REMEMBER that tree slope we passed on the way to the clearing?" Farah asked. "It winds through the trees. That's where we found it."

"Are you leading us into danger?" Bolton asked.

"Of course not."

She ran up the slope. "This way!"

They walked on the sloping branches that connected the trees. At every intersection was a collection of crystals that grew from the ground like flowers. The crystals shined in the absence of sunlight. The many facets glowed and created a variety of colors that played on the branches.

The Crystal Forest was once inhabited by people, but they never hunted on the land. They journeyed far for their food to protect the sanctity of the forest. When others had tried to settle the land, they found that they could not hunt. Their weapons and elements could do no harm to the beasts. The people abandoned the forest, but as deserted as it might appear, it was never empty.

A song drifted through the trees. The tune was faint at first, but deeper into the forest it grew louder and made the heart beat in time.

"Do you hear that?" Sara asked as they walked along.

"Yeah," Rodan said, "we heard it on the way."

"Orka was the first to notice it," Farah said. "She started whistling the tune."

"Where's it coming from?" Bolton followed close behind them.

"We don't know." Farah jumped over a tree root. "That's still under investigation."

"It's so beautiful," Sara said, "the sound."

The branches sloped down into another clearing, bordered by trees and crystals. The music was loud in the clearing.

"Here it is!" Farah said.

"What?" Bolton asked, "an empty piece of land?"

"It's not empty." Rodan ambled into the clearing.

"Be patient." Farah stared into the center of the glade.

Something started to form. It was semi-transparent, clear like a crystal. It formed in small droplets. Once it was fully fashioned, it spun around Sara and returned to the center of the clearing. It never kept its shape. Sometimes it was round, and sometimes it was flat as a board.

"What is it?" Sara asked.

"I call it a Sporadagon," Farah said, "because it keeps changing shape, and you never know what it will turn into next."

"Real sporadic. Do you know what it is?" Bolton asked Rodan.

"Hey!" Farah said.

"It's an Aether," Rodan said. "Like the one Rai showed us in the jar at the lake. They are made of a material between the earth and the sky. They were created when the elements were fused into their separate spheres. They can control all elements."

"How do you know?" Bolton said.

"Because I listened in class. Master Todd taught it. You were asleep."

"It's not controlling anything right now," Bolton said.

The Aether sent a ribbon of lightning around itself.

"Whoa." Farah giggled.

"Oh, when it calls Lightning you think it's cute, but when I call Lightning you run to the nearest hole in the ground."

"I thought that no one could control all the elements." Sara stepped closer to the Aether.

"Humans can't," Rodan said, "but Aethers can, including the lost elements."

"The lost elements," Sara said, "the ones from the broken spheres?"

"Right."

"How is that possible?"

"Aethers have the ability to recall the essence of the sphere," Rodan said, "because a part of that essence remains with them long after the sphere is destroyed."

"I can see that," Bolton said as the Aether changed shape and weaved around them. "It's so . . . strange."

The Aether disappeared.

"You scared it away!" Farah folded her arms and frowned.

"What did I say? Are you sure it could hear me?" Bolton said.

"Of course it could!"

"Come on," Rodan said, "let's get back to camp. I'm tired." He turned to leave.

Farah made a face at Bolton.

"Wait!" Sara said. "Listen. The music stopped."

"What's that supposed to mean?" Farah asked.

"I think it means it's time for us to go," Bolton said.

"No. Look!" Sara stepped forward as the others backed toward the trees.

A swirling mist formed in the middle of the clearing, where the Aether disappeared.

"Bolton's right," Rodan said, "We don't need to get into any unnecessary battles."

"I don't think we have anything to worry about," Sara said.

Two figures appeared from the swirling mist. One of the figures had a small mouse-like face. His slight, little hands hung at his waist and his tail wrapped around a flute. The second figure looked like a lizard, but he stood upright and his belly was puffed out like he had consumed an oversized meal. His three-fingered hands rested on his large belly. Both wore robes that touched the ground. They were not small as a mouse and lizard should be, but matched the height of the humans before them.

Sara approached them. Bolton took her arm to keep her from coming any closer to the strange creatures.

"Were you the ones who made the music?" she asked.

"Let's get out of here." Bolton still had his hand around Sara's arm, but she wouldn't move.

"We play a song to keep the forest strong," the mouse said.

"Who are you?" Farah asked.

"I am Milbill, and this is Omar. We've lived in the forest a long time and have taken many forms."

Other animal-like creatures emerged. All carried instruments. "Together we are the guardians of the forest."

Omar nodded.

"So, this music, it keeps people from killing in the forest?" Farah asked.

"The music sooths the human heart. While it plays, they cannot cut down one branch, dislodge one crystal from the ground, or turn their arrows toward any creature."

"So why did you stop playing?" Sara asked.

"Founten quieted us. He sensed a presence very great. He needed to see."

"Who's Founten?" Farah asked.

Mist swirled behind Omar and Milbill.

"I think we're going to find out," Bolton whispered.

From out of the mist, a robed figure emerged. He was three times the height of the others. He had a silver, feathered head and held a harp. The harp had golden strings that vibrated though the harp wasn't being played.

Farah and Rodan backed up further until they were among the trees, but Sara stood fast, and Bolton's grip on her arm tightened.

The tall figure stepped in front of Milbill and Omar and overshadowed them.

"I am Founten." He looked down at them with his owl-eyes.

Sara stepped forward. "My name is Sara."

Founten nodded. "I know. You are the Water Elemental. And these are your protectors?"

"My friends."

"It is good that you have come. I heard you speak in the forest. You are determined." He took a golden string from his harp. "For luck." He handed the cord to her.

"Thank you."

Founten stooped until his large, round face was level with Sara.

This time Sara backed away. A cloud of dust swept toward them as he bent.

"An evil lives where you are going. Don't go down into the dark." His breath was musty and hot.

"What do you mean?"

His large eyes blinked at her, but he said nothing. His form faded back into the forest along with the other creatures that had emerged.

The clearing was empty except for Sara and her friends. Bolton loosened his grip on Sara's arm. He hadn't realized how tightly he held her.

The music played again.

24

An Unexpected Visitor

SHIPS docked near Elementa. Workers loaded food and supplies. Two ships had set sail, their hulls filled with apprentices and trainers.

The people watched as the ships filled.

Brina rushed the remaining apprentices from the halls of Element. She had put all school funds and anything else she had into this endeavor.

Apprentices shouldered their bags and hurried out the doors of the school and toward the ships. The townspeople watched from windows and doorways as apprentices trooped through the streets.

Brina's knuckles were white as her fingertips pressed into the doorframe. In her other hand, she clutched Talon's letter. The delicate paper wrinkled in her grasp. She hadn't put the letter down since the messenger delivered it.

Her palms were sweaty, making the ink that had long dried run. Her hand was black with it.

Her thoughts were not far from Talon as she packed her bags. She remembered a man who once promised her the world, but got lost in it. The one who had kept secrets from her, ones she knew were important. She had tried to write letters to him, but kept the letters because she did not know where to send them. She wondered where he was now.

Talon had tried so hard to keep her safe. He tried so hard that he didn't tell her who he was hiding her from. She knew nothing of his family or his past, and she knew little of his present. Years ago, he brought her to Element. He said he wanted to protect her. He thought that with all the Elementals of Element around her, she would be safe. She became like a fixture in Element, as much as the high stone walls or the vines that lined the building.

Ink smeared on the clothes as she tossed them into the suitcase. She tore open the wardrobe door and pulled out the small box. She opened it and made sure the contents were inside. She spotted the ring and stopped.

Her heart hammered as she took the ring from its place. She put it in her pocket.

Closing the box, she put it in the suitcase too.

Her mind raced.

Oh, no. The sphere!

Brina abandoned what she was doing and rushed to the groundkeeper's house across the training field. She had to hurry. She couldn't have a ship full of apprentices waiting for her when they should be setting sail. They didn't have much time.

Brina yanked open the door to the little house. The room was dusty with things left untouched.

Where is it?

Brina rummaged through everything. Pulling the pillows from the couch. Tossing the wood from the fireplace. Her mind was frazzled, and her hands were dark with ink and ash. Her eyes darted around the room.

Where could it be?

She rushed to the bedroom and ripped the sheets from the mattress. Lifting the corner of the mattress, she looked underneath. As her feet moved across the floor, a soft creak resonated through the room.

Brina stepped back.

The floor groaned again.

Dropping to her hands and knees, her fingers explored the floorboards. One of them was loose. She pried it from the others. Underneath was a small crevice, and inside was a box.

Brina's breath caught in her throat.

She removed the box from its hiding place and lifted the lid. Grabbing the glowing sphere inside, she clenched it to her chest and breathed a sigh.

The air had grown chill as Brina hurried back. Only a few apprentices and trainers remained in the halls. They were too rushed and worried to see the object Brina clenched to her chest.

As her palms sweated anew, Brina placed the sphere into her cloak pocket. As she neared the entrance hall, a loud knock came at the door.

Her heart skipped a beat.

Talon?

She froze in the entrance hall.

The knock came again and again in that familiar, irregular rhythm that she had grown to know so well.

Brina ran to the door and swung it open. "Talon!"

But it was not Talon. Brina's smile faded. An army stood outside the door. Hundreds of men crowded the steps of Element, and their leader was the one who knocked.

"So, you know my brother."

25

A WARNING

TALON stared into the flames. Spire sat on a flat-headed crystal and waited for Sara and the others to return. She broke the silence. "I remember this place."

Talon looked up. "You came to the forest?"

"Once."

"What are you two talking about?" Farah asked as she, Sara, Rodan, and Bolton walked into the clearing.

"Did you find what you were looking for?" Talon asked.

"More," Rodan said.

"We found out who's playing the music." Sara took her mother's blue gem stone off the worn woven cord and put it on the golden one. She tied the cord around her neck.

"Animals as tall as men." Bolton shivered.

"The Old Tribe," Talon said, "the creatures that calm the hearts of men. I'm surprised they showed themselves to you."

"They knew of us." Sara sat next to Spire.

"I'm not surprised," Talon said. "What did they want?"

"They said not to go down into the dark. There's an evil where we are going But I didn't know what that meant."

Spire's brow tensed.

"They are wise and ancient," Talon said. "Sometimes they forget that we are not."

THEY slept in the clearing around the fire that night. Orka slept on a branch overhead. Quiet footsteps intruded on the sounds of the music and the crackle of the fire.

Orka watched as two people entered the clearing. They walked over to Bolton, and one of them put a hand over his mouth to keep him quiet as they dragged him from the clearing.

After they were gone, Orka flew down to Farah and tapped her on the nose to wake her.

"What is it?" Farah asked.

The little, green bird chirped, and Farah got up. She scanned the clearing to find Bolton gone.

"What is he up to?" Farah said under her breath. She left the clearing and crept through the forest.

The two men dragged Bolton into the forest and pinned him against a tree. Farah stopped when she saw them and crouched among the leaves.

"Orka, we have to think fast," Farah whispered, planning Bolton's rescue.

The man took his hand from Bolton's mouth.

"Fero. Are you insane?" Bolton asked. "What are you doing? They could have seen you."

"Fero," Farah whispered. As she looked again, she could see the red mark on his face. But she didn't recognize the other man. She strained her ears to hear what they were saying, but she couldn't make it all out.

"So, you remember me now. Do you?" Fero held Bolton's shoulders against the tree. "He wanted me to have a little chat with you."

"Why didn't he come talk to me himself?" Bolton asked.

"You would have preferred that?"

Bolton looked away.

"He had other business to attend to," Fero said, "but he's concerned about you."

"Right," Bolton said, "if he's so concerned, why did he send you on a mission to kill me in Lumina?"

"I should choose my words more carefully. He's not concerned *about* you. He's concerned about any ideas you might have picked up in your time with the Water Elemental. You're not the hero. You're with us."

"I have no idea what you're talking about."

"Well, let me enlighten you," Fero said. "He only suspects, but I know that you've gone soft, and it didn't take long. You're still that scared little boy on that ship, crying out for your mother."

Bolton lunged at him, but Fero held him fast.

He let out a grunt of frustration.

"Tell him that his suspicions were right. I don't work for him anymore. We'll gather the spheres, but they will never touch Fortress Tower's threshold."

"We?" Fero said. "Listen to me. I'll make this easy. No one has to die. Not you and not them as long as you do as promised, understand me? He only wants to toy with her. She's the last Water Elemental, after all. But . . ." Fero leaned in. ". . . if you decide to be a hero, she'll pay for it."

They threw Bolton to the ground.

After they left, Farah watched Bolton.

He didn't get up.

Farah rushed over to him. "Are you alright?"

He got to his feet, "How did you know I was here?" He looked around.

"It's just me," Farah said. "I thought I heard something."

"Did you see anything?"

"Nothing, I saw you lying on the ground. That's all."

"I must've been sleep-walking or something." Bolton rubbed the back of his head.

"Or something," Farah muttered.

"What?"

"Nothing." Farah walked a few paces. She turned back to see if Bolton was coming.

"I'm going to stay out here for a little while," he said.

"Out here? In the dark? I'll stay with you."

"No. That's okay."

Farah sauntered back to camp. She debated with herself whether she should hide among the trees and keep an eye on Bolton.

Should I tell the others what I saw? Bolton was her schoolmate. The class clown. Not the kind of guy Hephaestus's men would waste time on. *But they did come.*

Why didn't Bolton say anything to her about Fero threatening him in the woods? She wished she could hear their conversation, but she only caught bits and pieces, not enough to get the big picture.

"What is going on?" she whispered under her breath.

26

STOLEN

THEY journeyed from the Crystal Forest to Demlama. Snow covered the ground. The air was cold, and ice frosted the buildings. The sky was a pale blue-violet with specks of falling white flakes.

"It's so cold," Farah said.

"Deal with it," Bolton teased.

"Or I can take it out on you."

"Stop fighting," Spire said. "You'd think you two are related."

"The shrine is up ahead," Talon said.

"The shrine of who?" Sara asked.

"Of Clara," Rodan said. "An Elemental and youngest daughter to King Rogard. He sent her away because he was afraid of her, but when the tyrant, Bennett, attacked the kingdom, she came back and waged war against him to earn back the favor of her father."

"Did they reconcile?"

"No," Talon said. "Her father held his army back while she fought. He let them destroy each other, and he cleaned up the rest. By the time his army arrived, the only Elementals who remained alive were weak after battle."

"What was her element?" Sara asked.

"We don't know," Spire said.

"Bennett was a Dark Elemental," Talon said.

"It's a lost element." Spire said. "Some say it's the void from which all other elements came, but it's been gone so long that no one knows."

"So, Clara died here?" Farah asked.

"She and Bennett both. They died on the battlefield."

"What were they fighting over?" Sara asked.

"The same thing you and Eli are fighting over."

"I don't like the sound of that," Farah said.

They stopped at a path without borders. It was a clear drop into the chasm of the mountain, and the walkway was narrow.

"Do we have to walk on that?" Farah asked. "I don't trust it."

"Is that the shrine?" Sara pointed. At the end of the path was a marble temple suspended over an abyss.

"I've never seen it before," Rodan said. "What's holding it up?"

"Faith and hope," Talon said.

"Great, two things I'm lacking in right now," Bolton said to himself.

"So, we do have to take this path," Farah said.

"After you." Bolton made an exaggerated gesture with his hands.

They made their way along the path.

"Orka," Farah said to the little, green bird on her shoulder, "it's going to be okay. Just don't look down."

The path widened into a courtyard in front of the shrine.

As soon as she set foot in the courtyard, Farah knelt into the snow. "Land, safe, secure land!"

"This is where they died." Talon entered the courtyard.

Farah jumped up and brushed the snow off her.

"Stop being so dramatic," Bolton said.

"Hey, I'll show you dramatic."

"I'm getting a lot of death threats today," he said.

"Stop it," Spire said, "this is not the time or place for joking. People died on this land."

"Are we going in?" Rodan stepped forward.

"What's that?" Sara asked.

Something rose from the snow, yet did not disturb it. The thing was human in figure, but was misty and transparent.

"What is it?" Farah asked. "I don't see anything."

"What are you looking at, Sara?" Rodan asked.

"You don't see it? It's a woman. She's beckoning to us."

"Clara," Talon said, "she knows."

"Of us?" Sara asked.

"Do you see her?" Spire asked Talon.

"No," Talon said. "But Sara sees her."

"She's right in front of me," Sara said. "Could it be her?"

"Many strange things exist near the forest," Spire said. "It is a place of boundless energy. Whatever you're seeing isn't Clara. It's what she left behind, her life force."

The ghost of Clara wandered into the temple and disappeared behind its walls.

"We must have awakened her," Spire said, "by taking on a cause like her own."

"Well, can't she go back to sleep?" Goosebumps rose on Farah's skin.

"Perhaps when we are gone."

They approached the temple.

Something glanced off the sun's light. It twinkled in the snow. Bolton knelt and picked it up. It was a looking glass.

"Bolton, are you coming?"

He pocketed the mirror and met the others on the stone

steps of the temple. They walked up the steps leading to the temple door and went inside. The main room was empty. The floor was tiled, and the walls were made of a deep colored marble. Two hallways led out of the room.

"To the left, you'll find the shrine," Talon said, "to the right is the element sphere."

"Should we go to the shrine first?" Rodan asked, "to pay our respects."

"That is up to you."

They all went to the shrine except Talon, who waited in the entrance room. The hallway was lined with candles.

"How do they stay lit?" Rodan asked.

"The same way you can sprout flowers from your fingers," Bolton said.

"You *want* someone to murder you," Rodan said.

Sara got in between them. "What's wrong with Talon?"

"What do you mean?" Rodan asked.

"Everywhere we've been? Wyvek, Tosia. He's made a point to pay his respects, but now he doesn't want to. Why?"

"Maybe he's tired." Bolton shrugged.

"I don't think so."

"I think we've all done a bit of reflecting," Rodan said. "I'm sure Talon has too. Maybe he can't find a reason to do it anymore."

Spire opened the door at the end of the hall, and they walked into the room. The room was circular. A statue of Clara sat in the center. She wore armor and raised her sword into the air. One stone hand extended, palm up as if waiting to receive something.

"They used weapons of steel," Rodan said.

"She looks so brave." Sara bowed her head, and when she lifted it, Clara's life force was in front of her. The ghost gazed at her own statue. She looked back at Sara. Her eyes glistened.

Sara didn't know energy could feel sadness. She had always thought of energy as power, something to be used, not something that could feel. But she realized it was how the energy was harnessed that mattered. In the vessel of Clara, it could feel and remember.

Sara was afraid to die. Where would she go after everything went dark? What would her life force be used for?

They met up with Talon in the entrance room. His head was bowed, and he whispered something to himself. As they approached, Talon lifted his head.

"Are you ready?" he asked.

"Yes," Sara said.

They proceeded down the adjacent hall and entered the sphere room. The door was open. The element symbols were aglow. The room was big and decorated with engravings and statues of great birds. The sun shone through an opening in the ceiling.

"Where's the Sphere Protector?" Rodan approached the center of the room. "The door wasn't sealed. Someone must've opened it."

Bolton walked around the room and tried to make their presence known. "Hello!" he shouted. "We've come to fight you!"

"I don't think that's going to work," Spire said.

"Hey," Bolton screamed, "isn't there a sphere you're supposed to be protecting?"

"It's not coming out," Sara said.

"Look," Bolton shouted, "we've come to take the sphere. Aren't you going to try and stop us?"

"Something's wrong," Talon said.

"Don't you dare sneak up on us!"

"Stop it, Bolton," Farah said. "It's not going to come out."

"We'll see about that." Bolton focused, ready to use his element.

"No, it's not here!" Farah shouted. "Just stop!"

"What do you mean?" Rodan asked.

"It was taken a long time ago before I was born."

"Taken by who?"

"My dad," Farah said. "My dad and the people of Breeze

stole it."

"Why?" Bolton asked.

"Because they wanted it, and they could."

"You captured a Sphere Protector?" Talon said. "That's a crime."

"It wasn't me," Farah said. "It was my dad. What? Are you going to tell on him? Besides, isn't stealing the spheres an equal felony?"

"We're taking the spheres to stop an evil man," Spire said, "not for the fun of it."

"Can we stop fighting? Look at it this way," Rodan said, "now we can take a break from battling Sphere Protectors."

"Not exactly," Farah said. "He did install some security."

"Security? Like what?"

"Well, he couldn't take the Sphere Protector and leave the Wind Sphere unprotected."

"What are we up against?" Bolton asked.

"I don't know."

"You don't know?"

"It's not like I was here, okay?"

Bolton walked to the sphere room door.

"Bolton, wait!"

When his hand touched the door, the temple shuttered.

"What was that?" Bolton asked.

The wall in the back of the room crumbled as if something was tearing it down from the outside. The wall fell away. Behind it was a giant, twelve feet tall. Its entire body was made of metal, and it held a large iron hammer.

"What is that thing?" Rodan asked.

"It's a machine?"

"A what?"

"I don't know what else to call it. It's a machine. They make them in Breeze. It's one of my dad's prototypes," Farah said.

"That's no prototype," Bolton said.

From behind the massive machine, two smaller metal creatures crawled in. They were the size of cats, but shaped like insects. They had metal stingers on their scorpion tails.

Sara backed away. "What do we do?"

"Kill it." Talon hit the machine with a long stream of flames. But the metal didn't melt.

The machine swung its hammer at him. Talon moved away in time.

"Farah, Wind!" Spire shouted. They both sent Wind at it, but it didn't falter.

"Again!"

The clinking of metal feet prickled in Farah's ear. It lunged at her. The cold metal appendages pressed into her skin. The metal needle raised and poised to sting her.

Farah wrapped her hands around the skinny, metallic body. "Get off of me!" She threw the bug across the floor. It flipped in the air and skidded on its thin legs.

It scrambled back toward Farah and Spire.

Vines wrapped around its body. Rodan pulled it back. Its metal legs scraped across the floor.

The cold sweat on his back had turned colder.

"Rodan!"

But the needle was in. When the creature withdrew its metal stinger, Rodan collapsed to the ground.

Talon stood and unsheathed his sword. The sword met the steel handle of the hammer as it descended, but the heavy hammer forced Talon's blade to the ground.

"There has to be a way to stop it," Bolton said.

"Bolton," Farah shouted. "Maybe you can short circuit it. Hit it with Lightning."

Bolton sent Lightning, but the machine kept going.

"It didn't work."

"You have to get behind it. Get on its back and fry its brain!"

"I have to get on top of that thing?"

A metallic scorpion headed for him.

Bolton leapt, his foot touching down on the insect. He

launched off it and grabbed hold of the back of the massive machine.

The machine faced Talon with its hammer raised. Talon backed up, tripping over the uneven floor. The machine raised its iron hammer above its head, ready to smash him.

Bolton climbed up its back and to its neck. He reached into the space between its neck and the metal helmet that protected its brain. He sent Lightning into it.

Its body buckled. The machine froze while Talon was under the shadow of the iron hammer. Talon moved out of the darkness.

Bolton jumped down from the back of the machine.

As the jolt went through the machine, its movements slowed. Its heavy hammer made cracks in the ground every time it fell. The steel monster leaned over and stopped moving.

Spire kicked the metal insect that clicked along the floor toward her. The two scorpions faced her.

Sara stepped in front of Spire. A rush of water hit the two scorpions. She swept them away into the hole from which they had come.

Bolton rushed to the opening. The current forced the scorpions off the cliff.

"Sara!" Spire stared at her. "You didn't tell me."

"I didn't know I'd be able to do that," Sara said.

She put a hand on Sara's shoulder. She walked across the floor and opened the door to the Sphere Room. She retrieved the sphere. She felt the familiar pull of the sphere's essence as she took it from its pedestal. She felt her own power stir inside her.

"The Wind Sphere." She handed Farah the sphere. "Let's go."

Bolton ran over to Rodan. He shook him.

"It injected him with the venom," Farah said. "Don't worry. It was only to make him sleep long enough to get smashed by the big one's hammer. He should wake up soon."

Bolton put Rodan's arm across his shoulders and lifted

him to the ground. "He's even heavier than he looks."

They left the shrine and walked back out into the snow. Before they stepped onto the path, Clara appeared. She nodded to Sara, and Sara nodded back.

Clara's mouth stretched open. It was impossibly wide. A voice echoed through the cold. They all heard it.

"His army is rising!"

"What does that mean?" Farah asked.

"Who said it?" Bolton looked around.

"Behind us!"

From the snow in front of the temple emerged clusters of rotted bones—the skeletons of hundreds of soldiers laid to rest in the ice. They held swords and shields.

"Run!"

They rushed down the path.

"They're getting closer," Farah yelled.

"We woke them," Spire said.

"Maybe we should put them back to sleep," Bolton said.

"They're dead. They can't be stopped. Their bones are being animated by all the dark energy in this place."

"Maybe we can keep them back," Sara said.

"It's useless," Talon said.

Sara tripped in the snow. Talon helped her up. The dead soldiers made their way down the path. Bolton ambled with Rodan at his side. Talon rushed to help them.

"We can't keep running from them," Sara said.

"Call Water," Spire said, "and wash them off the cliff."

"I don't know if I can do that right now."

"Farah," Bolton said, "give Sara what's left of the water."

"That's not enough to take out a whole army," Farah said.

"No," Sara said. "Talon, melt the snow."

"You overestimate me."

"Do what you can."

Beneath the soldiers' feet, the snow melted to water. Sara lifted the water. It was a wall between them and the undead.

"Quickly," she said to Spire and Farah, "send cold wind to

freeze it."

The water hardened to ice with a few skeletons half through it, struggling to get out.

Sara stared up at the wall of ice. It was twice as tall as the chapel.

"Come on," Spire said. "They may still get through."

As they ran through the snow, a large bird landed in their path. It had a hooked beak and wings that spanned out over their heads. Its feathers held a silver lining, and its feet were scaled and clawed. On its back was a dome-like structure as big as a house. The hatch of the dome opened, and the bird leaned down.

It cawed at them. They backed up.

"What in the world is that?" Bolton asked.

"Chill out," Farah told the bird. "These are my friends."

"You know it?" Bolton asked.

"This is Thermal," Farah said. "He's extremely bad-tempered."

Thermal let out a shriek.

"See," Farah said.

"Where did it come from," Bolton asked.

"It's the Sphere Protector." Spire's eyes were wide.

"Yep," Farah said.

Orka chirped.

"Shouldn't you be dust or something?" Farah asked Thermal.

"He's probably forgotten the sphere," Spire said. "He no longer has a connection to it. He is not its guardian anymore."

"Get out of the way!" Farah said to Thermal. "What do you want?"

Thermal cawed.

"No, forget it," Farah said. "I'm not going with you. I don't care if Dad sent you. I'm on a mission, and you're disrupting it."

Farah tried to walk past Thermal, but he blocked her path with one clawed foot.

"Hey, move!"

Thermal cawed at her again.

"It's not going to let you pass," Bolton said.

"I can see that." Farah tried to dodge her way around him, but he blocked her every time.

"Farah," Bolton said, "maybe you should listen to it. Those dead men are breaking the ice."

The undead soldiers chipped away at the ice with their swords and war axes.

Farah stomped her foot but climbed into the dome. Her friends followed. Inside the metal dome, windows lined the walls, and seats were bolted to the floor.

"Where are we?" Rodan lifted his head.

Bolton sat him down on one of the metal seats. Rodan's eyes were half-lidded, and his head lolled to one side. He looked like he might vomit.

"You alright?" Bolton asked.

"What happened?"

"Farah got us into trouble."

Farah braced herself between the window and one of the metal seats.

"Hold on to something," she warned. "Trust me."

Thermal jolted up, and the dome shifted side-ways.

"This is going to be a rough ride."

27

FAIR

NO sun shone in the smoke filled skies of Elementa. The smoke was so thick that even as it shifted, one could not see a glimpse of the sun passing through. It was blacker than night without the moon and stars. A dark nightmare surrounded the townspeople.

People hid behind the closed doors of their houses, but that didn't help. They tried to soothe the burns with water. It was in vain. Their burn wounds gaped open and bled. The wounds got dirty as they fell in the mud and struggled to get to safety.

The few apprentices who remained fought for their lives. A clash of lightning cut across the sky. The harsh howl of the wind rushed into their ears. In places, the earth quaked and cracked the ground beneath their feet. The fire roared loudest.

Balls of fire sailed through the air like missiles, falling on houses and people as they rushed through the streets.

Those without elements armed themselves with what they could find: kitchen knives, axes, broomsticks, but they weren't fighters. Challenging Hephaestus's followers only served to get them killed the sooner.

Hephaestus's men stalked the streets like hellhounds sent by their master to seek out their prey. Their eyes were unfeeling. Soot and ash covered their faces and made their teeth glow from the darkness.

When the victims weren't coughing on the smoke, the smell of burning flesh soured their noses. It was unlike any meat they had ever smelled. It was nauseating. In every whiff of it they could smell their doom.

Between heartbeats were long stretches of silence that wrenched at the emotions of every man, woman, and child. These moments were the most jaw-clenching of all, for in these instances they could imagine their own deaths to come.

The copper smell of blood built in the air, so much so that they could taste it.

Inside of Element, Hephaestus's men tore open every drawer and rummaged through every closet in search of valuables they could take as spoils of war. But in their rough quest for treasures, they broke many things of value.

When Brina saw the face of Hephaestus staring back at her. It was like her soul had left her body and looked down on them from some great distance.

Her mind raced with his words, *my brother.* Talon. Was he taunting her?

At first, she couldn't see how this tall, thin man had any relation to the man she loved, but her mind traced the outline of his face, his eyes, his nose. He did resemble Talon.

There was something about his eyes, not the color, but something else that reflected Talon's image back at her. Maybe it was her reflection in those eyes.

Brina's mind raced back to her body.

This man came for the sphere, and it was in her cloak.

Brina darted into the library. She closed the door and turned the key in the lock. She backed up toward the wall. With each footstep, the floors creaked, reminding her of the sphere. She wanted to reach into her pocket to make sure it was still there, but she was too afraid.

The doorknob rattled, and the door shuttered.

Brina closed her eyes and concentrated. She concentrated so hard that she squeezed the tears from her eyes. Vines burst through the wooden floor, crept up the door, and sealed it to the door frame.

The men shouldered the door. The vines broke against the strength of the men.

One of the men grabbed Brina's arm and threw her to the ground. They kicked her as she screamed.

"That's enough!"

Hephaestus knelt beside Brina's beaten body. "Who are you to Talon?"

"Nobody," Brina cried.

"You're his girl, aren't you?" His breath smelled musty and stale. But his eyes were worse. Those eyes . . . it looked like he had gone mad. "They killed my girl. And Talon, he let them take me."

Brina didn't know what he was talking about, and she hadn't been Talon's girl for a long time. Now, she was an old woman who had locked herself up waiting for him. She could sense her own doom. Her fear sealed her lips.

"*His* girl," he said, "for *my* girl, wouldn't that be fair?"

28

BREEZE

TALON stared out over the desert through the small window of the dome. The sand was white against the sun. The grainy hills shifted in the wind like people shuffling through a large city.

"Where is this thing taking us?" Talon asked.

"Home," Farah said, "to Breeze."

"That's out of our way." Talon moved away from the window.

"Don't worry. I'm going to convince my dad to make Thermal fly us back. Well, not to that specific spot."

"And what if you can't convince him?" Rodan. swayed. Talon couldn't tell if he was still dizzy from the sleeping spell or from the flight.

"Don't worry. I will."

"We're flying over a desert." Sara looked out the window.

"That's the Windy Desert," Farah said. "Breeze should be close now."

Thermal slowed his speed and hovered toward the sand.

"We'd better sit," Farah warned. "Thermal is landing."

Sara sat next to Bolton on one of the metal benches lining the walls of the dome. Farah put a hand over Orka.

The dome shuttered as Thermal's claws cut through the sand. They leaned back until the momentum slowed. Thermal used his wings to decelerate.

The dome stilled. The hatch squealed open like a thousand screaming mice.

"We're here?" Rodan asked.

"No." Farah rushed to the window and scanned the area. "I wonder what's going on."

The others followed as Farah left the dome and walked out upon the sand. She looked around. "We're in the middle of the desert. Home is miles that way." She pointed west.

"Hey," Farah shouted at Thermal, "what's the big idea? We're not home yet."

The hatch closed.

Farah rushed to it. "Wait, what are you doing?"

But she was too late. The hatch had shut, and Thermal glared at them. The bird cawed and lifted his massive wings into the air. He propelled his wings up and down, causing great waves of wind and sand to fly into the faces of the onlookers. He hovered over the sand and flew west.

"What are you doing?" Farah shouted into the distance. "You can't leave us! Come back!"

But Thermal was gone. He looked like a much smaller bird in the distant skies.

"Stupid bird!" Farah stomped her foot.

"What are we going to do now?" Rodan asked.

Talon saw only desert and sky.

"Guess we'll have to walk," Bolton said.

"Through the desert? Are you crazy?" Farah peered into her canteen.

"You live here and you've never walked through the desert?"

"Yes, I have, twice, and both times I was nearly eaten." She scanned the ground.

"By what?" Sara followed Farah's eyes.

"You don't want to know."

"So," Bolton said, "we're going to wait for him to come back? That may take a while."

Farah looked out across the desert stretch. She shielded her eyes with one hand. She thought she could see the leafy balm of a tree where the desert met the sky. "Fine, we'll walk."

"How far?" Sara asked.

"I think we're only a few miles from the next oasis and maybe a day's walk to Breeze," Farah said. "We have to hurry though. The coyotes come out at night."

"You're not sure?" Rodan asked.

"She's right," Bolton said.

"How do you know?"

"I've traveled to Breeze before."

"When?"

"When I was eight."

"That was ten years ago," Rodan said.

"I remember it like it was yesterday."

"Ten years ago? The Great Raid was ten years ago," Farah said.

"The Great Raid?" Sara asked.

"Breeze was attacked."

"By who?"

Farah looked at Bolton.

"That was a long time ago, I don't remember much," she said. "We should start walking."

Orka rode on Farah's shoulder.

As they walked, they neared an oasis with trees and balmy plants offset from the desert sands. A deep pool of water was among the leafy palm trees.

Orka flew from Farah's shoulder to the water's edge. She

drank from the pool and flew into a palm tree to rest.

"Gather as much water as you can carry," Spire said.

"It's not that far." Farah took off her boots and emptied the sand from them. "If we're lucky we won't run into anything that might eat us."

"What's out there?" Bolton asked.

"Lots of things. Coyotes, scorpions, Custos plants.

"Why should we be afraid of a plant?"

"Because they're harvested from the Earth Sphere sanctum. They're parts of the roots that grow there."

"From the Sphere Protector?" Sara asked.

"Yes."

"So, they're like a mini version of the Earth Sphere Protector?" Bolton asked.

Spire gave Farah a disapproving look.

"I don't know," Farah said. "It's not like I've seen it before. All I know is that my father harvested them so they could protect the perimeters of the city. I guess after the Great Raid, he felt like he needed them."

"Why did Thermal leave us?" Rodan asked.

"It's my dad's way of punishing me for leaving Element. A friend of his recognized me in Lumina. He helped organize the Games. That's why they announced me as Heiress of Breeze. My dad sent Thermal to track me and now this."

"This is his punishment?"

"We'll be fine," Farah said, "and my dad knows it. He probably told Thermal to stay close by." Farah looked at the skies. "You heard that Thermal! I'm on to you!"

Orka flew back to her shoulder.

"This would be a good place to train," Talon said.

As evening approached, they stood outside the oasis to train. Although Sara called rain in the forest and used her element in Demlama, she had not yet mastered the art of calling Water.

"You can do this," Spire said.

Sara concentrated, but no water appeared. "I don't understand. I did it in the forest when I was with Bolton." She looked at Bolton from across the sands, and he smiled at her.

Spire saw the look between them. "Sara, focus."

The stolen gaze did not escape Rodan's notice either. While they gazed at each other, he summoned a wall of sand between her and Bolton.

Bolton looked at Rodan, and Rodan glared back. Bolton summoned bolts of lightning to hit the sands. The heat of the lightning fused the particles of the sand together and created grainy glass-like tubes within the wall of sand.

Rodan let the wall fall. He closed his eyes and forced the grainy glass from the surrounding particles. The sand glass circled him as he caused the grains to separate. The glass shattered in the air, but Rodan held the particles still, broken, hovering above the ground. Rodan turned on his heel and thrust his arm toward a hill of sand several paces from where he stood.

The glass jetted toward the sand hill and cut into it. Grains of sand at the peak of the hill slid down over the pits created by the glass.

Bolton stared at the hill where his glass creations were buried and broken. "Hey, we should try that again. That would be perfect in battle."

Rodan took one look at him, and left the field. Bolton followed him.

Rodan moved among the trees as Bolton kept close behind him.

"Hey, I was messing around," Bolton said.

Rodan faced him. "This isn't a game."

"You're sore about me and Sara."

Rodan rolled his eyes and looked away.

"Look, I didn't mean for it to go this way. But it's not like you made it clear."

"We were friends, Bolton," Rodan said. "What are we now?" He walked away, and Bolton no longer followed him.

"Seriously," he shouted to Rodan as he departed. "Over

this?"

Bolton shook his head.

When the sun was too low in the sky for training to continue, they took shelter in the oasis. Rodan had not yet returned.

"Bolton, will you come with me?" Sara asked. "I want to explore."

Bolton followed Sara through the trees and balmy vegetation. She stopped near a cliff. As Bolton pushed back the leaves and stepped forward to meet her, his eyes grew wide.

"It's beautiful, isn't it?"

Beyond the cliff's edge was a waterfall. The water plunged from the cliff into the ravine below where it gathered into a small pool surrounded by plants and fruit.

"How is it that you always find these places?" he asked.

"I can sense water's presence," Sara said. "Can't you sense when lightning is on its way?"

"I usually bring the storm," Bolton said.

Sara walked along the cliff until she found a less steep path down to the water. She stepped onto the first flat stone and travelled down.

Bolton followed.

When she made it to the water's edge, Sara sat among the plants surrounding the bank. She took off her shoes and let the water glide over her feet.

Bolton sat next to her. "I got you this." He held out an object wrapped in cloth. "I found it in the snow near Demlama, and I thought you should have it."

"Oh." Sara took the gift and unwrapped it. It was a small mirror. When she brought it up to her face, she saw her mother in it.

"I wanted you to be able to see how much you look like her."

Sara looked at her own reflection, her mother in the glass. "I do look like her." She looked at Bolton. "Thank you." She put her arms around his neck and hugged him.

As she hugged him, Bolton understood why Rodan was angry. But he didn't take this from Rodan. Sara had chosen Bolton. She had drawn him from her window.

The next morning, they prepared to leave. Rodan returned in the middle of the night. As they got ready to go, he put his canvas bag on his back without a word.

Farah stared out into the desert. She couldn't see Breeze over the sand, but she knew they were close. "Let's go home, Orka. It's been a long time."

As they made their way to the city, the desert wind swirled, picking up bits of sand.

"Walk carefully," Farah said, "and watch out for scorpions. They won't attack you as long as you don't get too close."

"I'm more concerned with these shifting sands," Bolton said. "They could bury us."

"Step away! Back up!"

The sand around his feet slid downward as if something was pulling it in.

"Walk around it, far around it," Farah said.

They made a wide circle around the pit that formed as the sand got sucked in deeper. From beneath the sand, emerged a creature with a mouth of razor sharp teeth. It had a thick, rounded head, covered in scaly skin.

"What is it?" Rodan asked.

"We have to back up further!" Farah said.

The creature stuck out a purple, vine-like tongue and caught Bolton's leg. It reeled him in. Bolton summoned Lightning and zapped the creature's tongue, but to no avail. The creature persisted. Its tongue was like acid burning through the leg of his pants and searing into the skin.

Bolton clenched his teeth and threw his head back.

"Give me a second," Farah said.

She pulled a dagger from her canvas bag and leapt into the pit. Farah severed the sand-paper tongue that held Bolton.

The appendage unwound from Bolton's leg and sank into

the sand while the rest of the tongue recoiled. The creature retreated.

Farah helped Bolton climb out of the pit.

"Where did you get that?" Bolton asked.

"Sometimes you need more than your elements out in the desert." Farah helped him sit up in the sand.

"I'm guessing that was one of your mini-Sphere Protectors."

Talon got out the bottle of ointment and some bandages.

Spire knelt beside Bolton and ripped off the damaged fabric of his pants, uncovering the wound.

Bolton rolled his hand into a fist and bit into one of his fingers as she pulled away the fabric that clung to his wound. Spire spread the smelly ointment onto the wound and made quick work of the bandaging. "Can you stand on it?"

Bolton nodded. "Probably." Talon and Rodan helped him to his feet. The warm desert breeze brought the smell of the ointment to his nose. "Man, I'm going to be repellent."

Talon held his finger to his lips.

"What is it?"

A roar sounded in the distance, an inorganic roar.

"Should we back up?" Bolton searched the ground.

A strange vehicle zoomed in front of them and stopped. Its driver wore a helmet that shielded his face.

"It looks like an IMT," Sara said.

"It's much more sophisticated than that," Farah said, "but the driver, now that's another story."

The vehicle was narrower than an IMT and only rolled on two wheels. The driver of the vehicle removed his helmet. He had wide, green eyes and hair as yellow as Farah's.

"Farah, what are you doing out in the desert?" the driver asked.

"I'm on a mission," she said.

"Uncle Tag doesn't like your mission."

"Since when do you care?"

"I don't, I just pretend to. Now when are you going to be

polite and introduce me to your friends?"

Farah pouted and stood in silence.

"Well?"

"Fine. This is my cousin, Thatch."

Thatch waved to them. It was a sarcastic gesture like he was only playing a game.

"Look," Farah said, "could you give us a ride back to Breeze. We're tired."

"Well," Thatch said, "though you asked me so nicely, I have to decline. I don't have enough vehicles for all of you."

Farah folded her arms.

"You're so persuasive," Thatch said.

He reached into his pocket and took out a small cube. He threw the cube on the ground. It unfolded until it was an exact copy of the vehicle Thatch rode on.

"Buckle in."

THE city of Breeze loomed ahead. To some, it looked like a pile of haphazardly arranged scrap metal, but to Farah and many Wind Elementals it was home. The Wind Elementals of Breeze excluded themselves from others. They spent their time inventing machines and stirring ideas.

Breeze was a city of technology. The city had a collection of old books that the citizens did not share with the rest of Mirmina. The books were hundreds of years old. They were from a time when machines were the norm. Machines did everything for humans, warmed their houses, transported them, and entertained them.

Even if the people of Breeze did share the books with others, very few had the resources to build such contraptions, much less the education to make them work.

Thatch had three expanding vehicles. The vehicles blasted through the sand toward Breeze. They stopped at a steel door. A wall of tempered metal surrounded the city.

They got off of their vehicles. Someone leaned against the steel door to Breeze.

He was a little older than Farah, but had the same green eyes.

"Where have you been?"

"Why is the door closed, Shift?"

"I asked you first." He picked dirt from under his fingernail.

"I've been at Element training."

"Liar." He unhinged himself from the door. "That's where you were supposed to be, but instead you're making a mess of things as usual."

"Let me through. Dad wants to see me," Farah said.

"Are your friends Wind Elementals?"

"Not all of them."

Farah stepped forward, but Shift held up his hand.

"You know I can't let them through."

"It doesn't matter if they're not Wind Elementals. They're going to save the world."

If Shift had been the type to roll his eyes or say something sarcastic, he would have, but that was not his way. Instead, he stared at Farah. His eyes did not travel to the faces of the others.

"I'm not a Wind Elemental," Thatch said. "I'm still welcomed. What are you doing at the door anyway? You knew I was going to get them?"

"You went directly against Dad's orders."

"I wasn't going to leave Farah out in the desert."

Farah stepped in front of Thatch. "If you turn my friends away, I'm going with them."

Shift pinned Farah with his glare. He looked up and gave the signal to the guard in the iron tower above the wall. The guard pushed the red button on the side of the tower, and the steel door slid open.

"Don't tell anyone they're not Wind Elementals," Shift said.

Once they were through the steel door, Rodan asked, "Who was that?"

"My brother." Farah sounded like she revealed an embarrassing secret.

Buildings climbed to the sun. The metal walls of the buildings were screwed on in large sheets. In the distance within the city's gated walls, were large metal windmills, creating the energy that fueled the city's machines.

People filled the streets. Those who rode in metal carts propelled by Wind had trouble getting past the pedestrians. Lots of yelling accompanied the constant stop-and-go.

Bolton looked around. Now that Talon had told him his father was alive, Bolton thought he might see him somewhere along their journey. He didn't know what he would say to him.

Sometimes, he looked down afraid he might see him. Other times, he felt he needed to look for him so he wouldn't find him by accident. He wanted his thoughts to be clear if he had to confront him, but he knew no matter what he did, his mind would be a bundle of thoughts and emotions, primarily anger, and he could never think clearly when he was angry.

Farah pushed through the crowd.

"Where are we going?" Rodan asked.

"My dad lives there." Farah pointed to the large castle of metal in the center of Breeze.

"The leader of Breeze. I never imagined all this."

"Well, he's the boss."

They stopped outside Breeze's main building, which was the place where the leader planned his most advantageous mechanical endeavors.

"Thatch, if you don't mind me asking, what Elemental are you?" Sara asked. "I heard what you said outside about not being a Wind Elemental."

"I'm not an Elemental," Thatch said.

"You're not?"

"My parents were Wind Elementals. Sometimes that's the way things turn out. I'm Farah's cousin, Tag's nephew. My mother was his sister. I'm good with machines. I get that from Uncle Tag. They need me for all the electrical stuff."

"You mean energy? But you're not a Lightning Elemental?" Bolton said.

"I don't deal with energy the same way you do. Only in machines with wires, like the vehicle that got you to Breeze. I'm the best at what I do."

They stood in front of the steel building in the center of the city. The metal baked in the sun, and every sheet was a different shade of gray or rusty brown.

"Well," Thatch said, "I should go. Uncle Tag's still mad at me for not getting those shipments in on time. I better lay low for a while."

Thatch took off down the steel steps.

"Your father seems harsh," Rodan said.

"You haven't seen the half of it." Farah pressed a button near the door. A voice boomed, "Do you have an appointment?"

Sara glanced around to see where the voice came from. Farah pointed to the speaker above the door.

"I'm here to see Tag," Farah said.

"He's quite busy, but if you leave your name and . . ."

"This is his daughter."

The speaker clicked, and the voice hesitated.

"Come in."

The door slid open. They walked into a tall, hollow column. A maze of steel bridges and stairs continued up twenty floors.

"He's at the top," Farah said, "putting together some new contraption. Well, his team is putting it together while he yells orders. He gets angry when things don't turn out the way he imagined."

"How far up is it?" Bolton looked up at the labyrinth of steel.

"They tried to make an elevator once," Farah said, "but it crashed to the ground. It's a good thing no one was in it. At least, I hope no one was in it."

With every step the metal stairs clanged. The sound echoed through the tower.

"Is this stable?" Bolton asked.

"Step lightly," Farah said.

Bolton looked down to the floor below. Metal sheets, screwed into place, covered the floor.

"Farah," Rodan said, "Before we got to Caleena, you mentioned someone shot lightning at you. Was it Thatch?"

"No," she said. "Thatch can't send Lightning like a Lightning Elemental. He needs machines and wires."

"But who could it have been? No other Elementals are allowed in the city, right?"

Farah shook her head. "I can't remember. It was a long time ago during the Great Raid.

"A bunch of Elementals came and destroyed everything. The Resistance Fighters showed up, and they tried to help us. That's all I remember."

They kept walking, but Bolton stopped. He struggled with his memories. The heat of the Lightning was still on his hands as Fero urged him to send bolts at her again. A young boy a few years his senior stepped in front of him with eyes the same color as hers.

Bolton shook his head, trying to force the memory out, but it lingered.

"Farah, I'm sorry." Bolton looked up at her, but her back was turned to him.

Farah stopped walking, but she did not turn around. "Thank you for your sympathy. It was a long time ago, but a lot of people died that day, people I cared about."

After ten more flights of stairs, Farah stopped at a huge steel door and pulled it open with some effort. The others followed her inside.

"No, not that one! Hey, that doesn't go there! What's wrong with you? Did you screw your head on backwards this morning?"

The shouts came from a bald man in a gray jump-suit. People worked on a machine in the center of the room. It had a rectangular shape and made sputtering sounds. Small metal arms moved automaton.

"Hey, Dad!" Farah shouted over the noise from the machine and her father.

Tag turned around. He looked tired.

"What took you? I sent Thermal out a week ago, as soon as the messenger arrived to tell me that you had left school. I knew he would find you. I don't like him, but that bird sure does have an eye."

"He left us stranded in the desert." Farah shouted over the noise of the machine. "Why did you come and get me anyway?"

"Boys," Tag said to the workers," get out. You can finish building that thing later. Maybe next time you'll do it right."

The workers left the room.

"They aren't *all* boys," Farah said.

"I don't care what they are," Tag said. "My daughter is a young lady, and young ladies don't run away from school and go off gallivanting around Mirmina. I was sick to death when I got the message from Element that my daughter, Heiress of Breeze, had run away from her schooling like some common nobody."

Farah folded her arms.

Rodan stepped forward. "Sir, we're going to Omega Ray to stop Hephaestus."

"I don't care what *you're* doing. Who are you?" Tag motioned to them. "Who are these people?"

"They're my friends."

"I don't want you playing around Omega Ray, young lady," Tag said. "You can't take the world into your hands."

"Isn't that what you do every day, Dad?" Farah said. "Take the world and shape it the way you want it. You push people around and force deals all the time."

"I don't care what I do. Do as I say, not as I do. You're staying in this city. These people can leave by any means necessary, but you are staying on my property. Understood?"

* * *

"THAT went well," Bolton said. "You really convinced him."

They sat on the metal benches outside Tag's steel castle. The benches were hot from the sun.

Farah had her face in her hands. "What are we going to do now?" She shook her head back and forth in her palms.

"Farah will have to stay," Spire said.

"No, I'm not staying." Farah lifted her head. "I'm not going to sit by and do nothing."

"Yes, you are." Shift approached them. "You heard what Dad had to say. You're not leaving."

"So, you're going to lecture me too?"

"It's dangerous."

"I know, but it's for a good cause," Farah said. "This is important."

"You don't understand," Shift said. "Do you remember what happened after the Great Raid? Hephaestus forced our father into a negotiation, a surrender. That's why Breeze still exists. They both agreed to no more battles. How do you think he would react if the leader of Breeze's own daughter marched into Omega Ray and demanded war? They'd give us war. That's what they'd do. It's better if we stick to the agreement."

Sara stood and faced Shift. "Your sister's right."

"Our silence is his comfort," Spire said.

Shift eyed Sara. "Which one of you is the Water Elemental?"

They were silent.

"This is Breeze," Shift said. "We know of the Water Elemental."

"This place is so remote," Spire said.

"It's not as remote as it seems. My dad controls most of the trade routes, the merchants, and the messengers. It wasn't long before we knew a Water Elemental was going on a crusade to battle Hephaestus and that he was bringing my sister with him. Now who is he?"

"*She.*" Sara eyed him back. "*She* is going on a crusade to battle Hephaestus. I am the Water Elemental."

"A woman." Shift shook his head. He looked at the ground and snickered. He rubbed his jaw and turned to Sara. "Take care of my sister."

"I will," Sara said.

Shift sighed. "I can't believe I'm doing this. Thermal is behind the steel scrap pile in the back of building A."

"But Thermal won't listen to me," Farah said.

"But he will listen to Thatch."

They walked down the crowded streets of Breeze. Outside their homes, people forged steel panels and tools. Children built metal toys by using screws and bolts under the heat of the sun.

"Where's Thatch?" Rodan asked.

"He's hiding from my dad," Farah said.

"I don't blame him," Bolton said.

"He should be on the west side of the city. The buildings are still in disorder. Thatch likes to lie low there when my dad is angry."

Smog and debris coated the west side of the city. It was still in disrepair after the Great Raid. One could get lost in the many tunnels and alleys, and the smoke floating through could be deadly.

"He hides in this place?" Bolton asked. "I think I'd rather face your father."

"No, you wouldn't," Farah said.

"Bolton," Talon said, "neither you nor I should use our elements. We might ignite something."

"A touch of static might blow this place to pieces," Bolton said.

"Thatch!" Farah yelled. "Don't worry. We chased away your fan club! It wasn't much of an effort."

Someone wearing a strange mask came from behind a ruined building. "Farah, what are you doing here without a gas mask?" Thatch asked.

"I'm making my escape," Farah said. "Listen, I need your help. Shift told me where Thermal is being kept."

"Wait," Thatch said, "Shift is helping you? That can't be good."

"We agree sometimes."

"That's usually when things go wrong."

"Thatch, you have to help. You're the only one besides Dad who can tell Thermal to take us back."

"Uncle Tag's going to kill me."

A rustling came from under the thick sheets of metal lining the floor, and the sounds of grumbling echoed below.

"What is that?" Rodan asked.

"The *Lacwanx*," Thatch said, "They're metal-workers who stay to themselves. They don't like any noise other than the hammering of steel. It's not wise to bother them."

The sheets shifted as the group of travelers lingered.

"Well, you can always hide out here when we get back," Farah said.

Thatch hesitated as more rustling came among the scraps of fallen metal. "Fine. Where to?"

THERMAL clawed the ground after having had his lunch. When Farah and the others approached, he stretched out his wings, turned around, and refused to face them.

"Yeah, that's right, turn away," Farah said, "after you left us out in that desert. You should be ashamed of yourself. Orka would have never done such a thing."

Orka chirped from Farah's shoulder.

"It's okay, Thermal." Thatch stepped forward. "They forgive you."

"No, we don't!"

"Do you want to leave? Speak gently." Thatch reached out and smoothed Thermal's feathers. Thermal leaned down so he could reach the full feathers of his belly.

"So," Bolton said, "here you go breaking the rules again."

"I'm not breaking any rules," Farah said. "Dad said I was

not to leave his property. Well, Thermal is his property."

"A Sphere Protector is no one's property," Spire said.

"Thermal, we need you to bring us to Jetty Verte," Thatch said.

Thermal lifted his head into the air and turned to face Thatch.

"That's right," he said. "You don't like it here much, do you? But if you take us to Jetty Verte, I'll let you run around all you like."

Thermal brought his head down far enough for Thatch to reach. The hatch to the dome opened, and Thermal leaned down to allow them access.

A loud caw shrieked through the city. Tag walked over to the large window on the twentieth floor of his steel castle where he could see where the sand meets the sky. Thermal sailed through the air and flew off into the distance.

"Shift!" Tag yelled. "Where's your sister?"

29

THE HEALING LAND

"WE'RE flying over the Crystal Forest," Thatch said. "We should be in Jetty Verte soon."

Rodan gazed out the window. "Everything looks so small. To think we covered all that land. It took us weeks."

"Thermal will cross it in a matter of hours," Thatch said. "The sky is free of obstructions, and Thermal's wings can cover ten times the land your feet could walk."

Bolton sat alone. He stared out the window. His head was full of thoughts he didn't know how to process. His father, Breeze, Hephaestus . . . What would he do if it all fell apart?

"We're landing," Thatch said. "Get ready to feast your eyes on the most wonderful place in the world, well, according to Thermal anyway."

The hatch of the dome opened to a field. A cliff overlooked the sea in the distance. The breeze was gentle and cool. The sun baked the land enough to make the climate comfortable. But, the field was scarred. Rips textured the fabric of the land.

An earthquake had shaken the land of Jetty Verte and created tears in the land decades ago. At first, the tears were very deep going all the way to the sea, but over time they closed up. The land of Jetty Verte had healed itself. Now the cracks wrinkling the green surface were no more than three feet deep, although some were several feet wide.

In the distance, smoked and darkness surrounded the mountains.

Rodan approached Sara. "That's Omega Ray. It's in the valley between the mountains."

Sara peered into the darkness.

"Are you okay?" he asked.

She nodded.

"We're all behind you," Rodan said.

"Okay, Thermal," Thatch said, "don't go scaring away the locals."

Thermal ran off across the field.

"We have to go east," Spire said.

"What are you going to do, Thatch?" Farah asked.

"I guess I'll stay," Thatch said. "I can't be much help. There's only one Sphere Protector I can handle. I'll catch up with you later."

They moved on while Thatch stayed behind to watch Thermal.

"So, how far is the sanctum?" Rodan asked.

"You mean, the dungeon, remember," Farah said. "I wonder if we'll see some convicts."

"You'd like to see some of your own kind, wouldn't you?" Bolton said.

"Your kind you mean," Farah said.

"It's empty," Spire said. "No one is incarcerated. No criminals like either of you."

"Hey," Farah said, but Bolton kept quiet.

An inn was in the distance. They approached it.

"We'll rest," Talon said. "The inn is abandoned. It might have some left-over supplies and, hopefully, lantern oil. We'll need it."

They explored the inn and found the oil and jars of preserved food.

The owner left the inn when Hephaestus built his army in the mountains. He feared for himself and his family. The only travelers who came that way anymore were Hephaestus's men and the few brave souls who wished to challenge him.

It was rumored among travelers that Hephaestus's fiends became angry with the innkeeper and killed him and his family. They left their bodies to rot in the inn.

The inn held no sign of a struggle or rotting bodies, only abandoned supplies and dusty beds.

Farah didn't want Orka to stay in a place with all that dust, so she took some of the blankets and beat them outside. She walked along the side of the inn and made her sleeping quarters. She pulled loosed boards from the fence surrounding the inn and made a T-shaped perch for Orka. She sank it into the ground near where she would be sleeping.

Orka flew down to the perch, nestled one leg into the feathers of her belly, and closed her eyes.

After the others had retired to their rooms, Sara sneaked out. She sat outside the inn with her drawing paper and charcoal, and sketched what she remembered of Breeze and the Crystal Forest.

The door to the inn creaked, and she turned, expecting to see Bolton. But it was Rodan.

She felt like she was back in Element, and Rodan was sneaking out to meet her by the lake. Those moments had made her happy. After everything that happened, those four walls from which she escaped didn't seem so terrible.

She wanted to go back. It felt comfortable, safe. Why had she ever wanted more?

Rodan sat next to Sara as she gazed at the land and committed it to memory for her next drawing. "You're always looking at places like it's the last time you'll see them."

"That's funny, Bolton said the same thing."

Rodan cringed.

"If I don't get to see these places again," Sara said. "I never want to forget them."

"You and Bolton are becoming close."

"Yes." Sara looked away with a smile.

Rodan sighed.

"What is it?"

He changed the subject. "I remember this place. When I was young, my dad used to bring me. Until Hephaestus's men started moving through and the inn closed. We used to camp in the field and not tell my mom. She was so mad when we came home. She worried for us. I don't know why my dad liked to worry her so much." Rodan looked out into the distance. "Maybe he liked to see how much she cared for him."

"Would you do that?"

Rodan paused. "No, I don't think so.

"But my dad wasn't around a lot. I think my mom resented him for that. She told me once that it was not the life she wanted. He hadn't told her he was going to be a soldier. She didn't want me to go to Element. She was afraid I wouldn't come back."

Sara put her hand on top of his. "We're all going to be fine." But as she said this, her eyes glazed over.

Rodan gazed into the dark skies. "I did this for you. I'm not a hero."

"You are a hero." Sara squeezed his hand. "If we don't get to Omega Ray, if we don't face him, you still saved me. I couldn't have done this alone, and without you, I wouldn't have had anyone. At Element, you taught me what it means to be free, and out here, I learned what it is to be alive." *I know why I wanted more*, she realized. "I'd rather feel alive and be bared to danger than live sheltered and comfortable, never knowing the world."

30

SMOKE

PERDITUS stood in front of the throne in the empty room. He held an unlit torch in his hands and tried to ignite it, but all that came was smoke.

"Maybe you're not a Fire Elemental, Perditus. Maybe your weapon is the smoke." Fero walked into the throne room.

Perditus had expected that he would be gone longer. He had hoped so. With Hephaestus and Fero gone, he was free to move around the castle. He had sat on Hephaestus's throne and mocked him. He had walked along the wall and stared into the faces of the prisoners. Their faces in the cold were crimson.

Through the dirt on Fero's face, his dark red birthmark was visible.

"That mark," Perditus said, "Were you born with it? I bet, growing up, it tormented you because people saw you as something alien, something deformed."

Fero sneered and held out his hand to summon Fire. But after Perditus made his cutting remark, Hephaestus walked through the door. A few of his men followed. They had arrived on the first ship back from Elementa.

Soot stained Hephaestus's cloak, and his eyes shone a brighter gold where the fire had kindled inside the irises.

"Did you find what you needed?" Perditus asked.

Hephaestus stepped in front of him, a warning for him to move aside so Hephaestus could take his seat on the throne. But Perditus didn't move.

"Why did you leave? You never leave anymore." Perditus busied himself with the torch. "You don't have a plan, do you? You want to die so you can be with that woman you call for in the night—Sicilia."

Hephaestus hit him so hard he stumbled to the floor. But, for once, Perditus stood back up to face his tormentor. "You never loved my mother because you never got over *her*."

Hephaestus pushed him aside and sat on his throne. "Get out of my sight, Perditus."

Perditus smashed his hands onto the floor and got up slowly. His leg felt bruised and tender, but he stood on it. He stared at his father with his head half tilted to the ground, making his gaze sinister.

Hephaestus didn't flinch nor did he look back at Perditus.

Perditus's rage stirred inside him, but it would not come out, not like the fires of his father. It wasn't fair.

His father used to slap his hands when he failed to call Fire. He slapped his hands for years until one day, he slapped him in the face, and he ignored him from that day on.

Perditus began to write. He wrote and wrote and separated himself from everyone else. He started to wear black, and he stopped bathing.

He would go outside and stick his fingers in the snow until they were deep blue. Pressing his fingers together, he would marvel at the numbness.

He thought about going out naked in the cold and making his whole body numb. Maybe if he stayed out long enough, it would travel to his heart. Maybe if he persevered, the fires would come to warm his body.

Either way it would be a better outcome than the miserable existence he was living every day.

But he never did it because he was afraid of what would happen in the dark once he was gone. He was afraid of what he might meet on his journey through death.

He heard the howls in the night, and he knew that Death was waiting to take him under its shadow. Every day he saw that shadow looming in the shadow of his father.

What did Death do to people who weren't loved? What did it do to those who were hated? Was Death equal to all?

Perditus couldn't imagine that this would be so. Why would he deserve a better death, a better afterlife just because he was tormented? It only made sense that his torment would continue.

But maybe it would be a purposeful, focused torment, not one where he was ignored. His body would be tied to a bloodied stake, and he would be looked upon, maybe not with pity, but eyes would be on him.

He had lived so long without a witness. If no one sees it, does one still live? No, he wasn't alive. People who are alive are treated as if they live.

He ripped open the door to his room and looked at his face in the dusty mirror.

It was pale against his black hair. He looked like his father. His nails tore into his skin, and from his fingertips smoke issued forth. Tears rolled the blood down his face.

He stopped.

What parts of him were his mother? He couldn't see anyone but his father when he gazed at his own reflection. Nothing, nothing . . . Perditus touched the glass, right under the reflection of his eye. The gray eye, maybe it wasn't because he was smoke inside. Maybe that was his mother.

"She would love me," he whispered.

He looked around the room.

Reaching under his bed, he pulled out a sack and stuffed clothes into it. His movements were frantic and unmeasured. He thought of his mother and where he should go to find her.

31

THE EARTH BENEATH US

THE sun rose on the small inn. Farah yawned as the light hit her face. Thermal planted his large feet in the ground alongside the gate. He cawed when Farah awoke.

"I don't need a guard bird." Farah held her finger up to Orka's perch, and the little bird descended. Farah brought her up to her shoulder and tried to walk away from Thermal, but the great bird stepped over the gate and obstructed her path.

"Get out of the way!"

"It's okay." Thatch ran from inside the inn. "Thermal, it's okay. You don't have to watch her anymore."

The great bird cawed.

"Calm down. We're in Jetty Verte."

Thermal's feet touched off the ground as he flapped his wings and left the gated area.

"Sorry. He's still hooked on Uncle Tag's orders."

"You came to the inn?" Farah asked.

"Well, yeah," Thatch said. "You didn't expect me to sleep in the forest."

"Where is everyone else?"

"They're getting up."

"Good. I want to do this."

"Farah, are you okay?"

"Yeah, why are you saying it to me that way?"

"It's just you always get so . . . passionate about things. Like the time you wouldn't eat fish for three weeks straight because you said they have more complex nervous systems than us."

"They do, and I still don't eat fish."

"All I'm saying is I hope you're not in over your head."

"I'm not."

"And you don't have to be loyal to these people because they're your friends."

The others emerged from the inn.

"Are you ready?" Talon asked.

Farah glared at Thatch. "Yeah." She went over to join them.

They walked to the end of the plain and came across a rusty iron grating over a hole in the bright, green surface. The loose dirt shifted in the wind and fell through the grating.

"It's the dungeon." Talon lifted the heavy, metal grating. A set of stone steps led into the darkness.

Talon snapped his fingers to spark a flame to light the lanterns.

"Step lightly," he said.

Dried up brown roots covered the dungeon walls and stretched to the floor. Torches lined the walls. Talon took one and lit it. The light from the torch was brighter than the lantern. He put his lantern down and proceeded with the torch.

Cells lined either side. Each cell was equipped with a wooden bench held by two chains suspended from the wall. A small hole was in the floor of each cell.

Mice and beetles darted in front of them as they walked.

"Disgusting," Farah said. "How far are we from the Sphere Room?"

Orka chirped and flew into the depths of the dungeon.

"Orka, wait!" Farah shouted and took off after her.

They followed her.

"Orka!"

Farah stopped, and the others caught up with her. They were in a round room, like the sphere rooms in Caleena, Wyvek, and Demlama, but instead of ornate floor, rich dirt covered the ground. Flowers grew across the floor, and vines traveled up the walls. Light issued from a hole in the ceiling. But darkness overwhelmed the large room.

"Orka?"

Talon swept his hand out to the room, and Fire lit the torches.

"Orka?"

Farah ran across the room toward the door.

"Farah, wait!" Sara shouted.

Farah stopped and backed up, but it was too late. She had alerted the Sphere Protector.

Moss and vines rose from the ground. The moss gathered to form a giant creature with teeth like giant rose bush thorns. The light from the hole in the ceiling hit the creature and bathed it in the sunlight's glow.

Rodan focused on negating the creature's power as it coiled a thick vine around him, pinning his arms to his sides.

Talon threw flames at the enraged monster. It screeched in pain and knocked Talon against the wall. Talon did not get back up. His eyes were closed, and he wasn't moving.

Before the others could react, the creature wrapped vines around Spire, Farah, and Bolton. As they struggled for their freedom, Sara ran to the opposite door to retrieve the sphere. She tried to open the door, but it wouldn't budge. Above the door were the element symbols.

"I can't reach it," Sara shouted.

"Call Water!" Spire yelled.

Sara focused. Water splashed against the symbol. The symbol glowed. "It worked. It worked!"

Farah sent Wind to set the wind symbol aglow. The symbols were out of Bolton's line of sight. But the creature shifted, and Bolton could see the symbols. He sent Lightning, and the lightning symbol lit.

"Fire," Sara said. But Talon was unconscious. "The torch."

The torch lay abandoned by Talon's side.

"No, Sara," Rodan said. The vines wrapped around his neck.

She stared at the torch by Talon's side. Talon had lit it with Fire. *It could work.*

Bolton couldn't send Lightning through the Protector because the circuit would run through them all. "What's she doing?"

"She's headed for the torch."

Sara ran along the wall toward the torch. The vines licked the wall, and she weaved around them. She gasped as one vine nearly grabbed her. When she made it to Talon's side, she wanted to make sure he was okay, but there was no time. "I'm sorry," she said and reached over him to get the torch.

She ran with the torch back to the sphere room. Lifting the torch up to the Fire Symbol, she activated it. She dropped the torch to the ground and swung the door open, but before she set foot inside, vines caught her around the wrist.

Sara stretched for the sphere, but it was inches from her fingers.

Talon blinked and opened his eyes. He got up and braced himself against the wall. He removed the sword from his side. He hacked at the vines and freed Bolton.

"Wait," Bolton said. "You have to get to Sara. She's almost in the Sphere Room."

Talon nodded and headed for Sara. As he rushed toward the Sphere Room, the creature shifted its weight and sent more vines. Talon cut them, and the creature screeched through its rose-thorn teeth.

"A little more," She urged herself, but she couldn't reach the sphere.

A loud caw echoed through the room. Dirt fell on them from above as Thermal broke through the earth ceiling. His talons dug into the creature's soft body.

Soft chirps sounded. Orka rode on Thermal's head as he attacked the creature.

Screaming in pain, the moss-covered being released Sara's arm.

Sara grabbed the sphere from its pedestal.

The creature turned to dust, and the vines disappeared. Rodan, Spire, and Farah fell to the ground. Orka fluttered away from Thermal as the great bird cawed and flew off into the sky.

Sara rushed out of the Sphere Room. "Is everyone alright?"

They got up from where they had fallen. Talon dropped his sword. Orka flew back to Farah's shoulder.

"Hey, what's the big idea scaring me like that?" Farah asked.

Orka chirped.

"Don't you know not to go looking for trouble?" Farah said.

"Well, if her master knew better herself," Talon said. "We learn from the wise, but we can learn from the foolish too."

"Was that an insult?"

"Not if you're the wise one," Rodan said.

"What do you mean, *if?*"

They emerged from the dungeon.

"One sphere left," Farah said. "Where to?"

"The Water Sphere rests in a cave a few miles north," Talon said.

"That's funny," Bolton said, "Spire is usually our element sphere guide."

Spire said nothing. She led the way north.

"You'd think someone would have built a temple for the

Water Sphere," Farah said, "where it could be better protect-ed."

"There used to be a temple," Spire said. "But it was destroyed long ago. The Water Sphere and its pedestal were recovered and set in a place that many dared not venture."

They passed between rocks and across a small bridge. The path curved down and led to the mouth of the cave.

"The Water Sphere is well protected in the cave," Talon said. "Spirits and hungry creatures stalk the cavern, and they don't turn to dust at the lift of a sphere."

They approached the cave, but Spire remained where she was.

"Spire?"

"Don't waste your time," Spire said. "The Water Sphere isn't in the cave."

"What do you mean?" Bolton asked.

"It's in Element."

"But how did it get there?" Sara asked.

Spire sighed. "I should have told you. It's the reason I'm so respected at Element. It's the reason I was chosen to train you. Many know that I protected the Water Sphere, but only Brina and I know that I took the Sphere from its sanctum," she said. "Eighteen years ago, I journeyed to obtain the Water Sphere.

"I went with many others, including the groundskeeper, Decca. He wasn't an Elemental, but he thought that if he could get the Water Sphere, he could summon its power and destroy the army in Omega Ray."

She reached for the ring on the chain around her neck.

"We fought hard to get the Water Sphere. We traveled up Regret Mountain to reach Omega Ray. But they ambushed us.

"Decca handed me the element sphere and fought with all he had. I was struck down. I was still conscious, but I never got up. I held onto the sphere while the fight raged on without me. I could hear the screams of my friends as I lay there, clenching the sphere to my chest.

"When everything was quiet, I got up from my place in the snow. My friends were dead, burned beyond recognition.

"When I returned to Element, I had the sphere. Brina and I hid it away. We didn't want anyone to know of the sphere, so we told them I prevented Hephaestus's army from entering the sanctum.

"But the truth is I left my friends. I left them to die. They suffered while I became the comfortable hero." Spire looked away stony-eyed. She touched her arm and felt the folds of the golden band beneath the sleeve of her dress.

"You were young," Talon said.

"I knew what I was doing," Spire said.

"But why didn't you tell us all this back in Caleena before we traveled this far?" Bolton asked.

"The sphere is safe in Element. I thought that's what we were trying to do."

"But the binding circle, it won't work without the Water Sphere."

"So, we have to go back to Element?" Farah said.

"We'll have to find your cousin to see if he'll give us a lift," Rodan said. "Or else we'll have to retrace our steps, and we're a long way from Element."

"Let's find him," Talon said.

Sara nodded to Spire and led the way. They walked on in silence.

"Wait," Talon said. "I sense Fire."

"Where are you headed?" Two men emerged from behind the large boulder beside the bridge. One of them had a red mark on his face.

"You dropped this." Fero brandished a dagger which Farah recognized as her own. "I thought I'd return it." He grabbed Sara and held the dagger across her neck.

"Leave her alone," Bolton said.

Fero smiled and pretended not to hear him. "You didn't think Hephaestus leaves his land unguarded, did you? I don't think you've met Dirge." He motioned to the man behind him.

The man was tall and broad. His face was scarred from battle. "He's an old friend of mine, a war buddy. We fought in the Great Raid together. He killed more than twenty men that day."

Farah glared at the man. He was the one in the Crystal Forest with Fero.

"Let her go," Farah said.

"Why is she so important?" Fero asked, faking ignorance. "What are you all doing so close to Hephaestus's kingdom? I could kill her. She's just a girl. It wouldn't matter."

Dirge grinned his toothless grin.

"Do that," Talon said, "and I'll turn you and your friend into a pile of ashy black bones. Two against five. The odds don't sound too good for you. You might have been a traitor, Fero, but you were never stupid."

Fero glared at Talon. The old man always played tricks like that, manipulating one to think thoughts not his own.

He removed the dagger from against Sara's neck and pushed her toward her friends.

"Are you okay?" Bolton asked Sara.

She nodded.

"Talon, that wound I gave you has settled into a nice scar, hasn't it? It leaves you with something to remember me by." Fero traced his hand along his deep red birthmark. The birthmark matched the scar on Talon's face. Fero summoned Fire into his hand. "I could do the same for all of you." He sent the flames toward them.

The flames headed for Spire and Farah. They leapt to avoid them. Bolton felt the heat of the flames against his face as he took Sara's hand and moved away.

Talon returned Fire on Fero, but Fero dodged his flame.

While Fero sent more flames toward Talon, Dirge shot flames in Spire's direction as she rose to her feet. The flames snaked up her dress.

"Get on the ground quick!" Farah shouted.

Spire threw herself to the ground, while Farah dropped beside her. Farah scooped up sand from the ground and dumped the sand onto the fire. Rodan rushed over to help Farah put out the flames.

Bolton stood in front of Sara and shot Lightning at Dirge. Dirge ducked from his attack and laughed.

Bolton looked to Farah and Rodan who were still scooping up the sand to put the fire out.

"Rodan!" Bolton shouted. Bolton summoned lightning bolts to hit the ground between himself and Dirge.

Dirge was amused by Bolton's efforts.

Rodan held a scoop of sand in his hand as he turned to see the lightning hit the ground. Looking where Bolton had injured the ground, Rodan stood. He could sense the hot, glassy earth where Bolton had fused the sand particles together with the heat of the lightning. He focused on those glassy objects, lifted them fast from the sand, and broke them in the air.

Dirge stared at the particles. Rodan sent the broken glass shooting toward him. They embedded in Dirge's face, neck, and chest.

Fero looked back at Dirge.

Dirge screamed and held his hands up to his face. He pulled shards of glass from his chest, making his fingers bloody.

Fero turned to Talon. "Not this time, teacher." Fero sent flames around them, encircling them all.

"Leave!" Talon extinguished the flames.

Fero glared at him.

Dirge stopped messing with the glass shards and grinded his teeth.

Talon went to Spire and helped her to her feet. They ambled in front of the others as they left the clearing. While they weren't looking, Bolton glanced back at Fero.

Once they were away from the clearing, Talon asked Spire if she needed Aldo's ointment.

"I'm alright," Spire said. "The flames didn't reach my skin."

The air got heavy as the wind pushed down on them. Thermal swooped into the clearing, disturbing the grass and sand. The hatch to the dome opened, and Thatch walked out.

"I saw those two men. Are you alright?" Thatch asked.

Farah nodded. "But we need to get to Element."

32

THE WATER SPHERE

THERMAL flew toward Elementa. The skies were dark, but the smoke was still visible. It polluted the sky in big bellows. The thick gray rose and covered the stars.

"What's happening down there?" Farah asked.

"Something must be on fire." Rodan moved to the window.

"Element." Talon didn't need to look.

"How do you know?" Bolton asked.

"That must be why his minions stopped us," Spire said, "to delay us from getting here to prevent this."

"Do you think they came for the Water Sphere?" Sara asked.

"That's what I'm worried about," Spire said.

"Should we land?" Thatch asked.

"Yes," Talon said.

Thermal landed on a hill overlooking Elementa. Not only was Element on fire but the entire marketplace. Roofs were ablaze, and smoke smothered the area. Ocean's Light, too, had caught fire. People suffered and died in the streets. Smoke and ash muffled their screams.

They surveyed the ruins.

"This is awful," Sara whispered. She hadn't had a family in the small town in a long time, but still . . . Elementa was home.

"We have to go down there," Rodan said. "Maybe we can help."

He rushed downhill to the destruction below. The others followed.

"Orka, you stay with Thermal," Farah said.

Orka flew from Farah's shoulder and landed on Thermal's head. The little, green bird chirped as the great one cawed.

When they reached the market place, they found people covered in soot. Some lay on the ground, and others leaned against houses and food stands. They were between life and death.

"We have to help them," Sara said.

Talon opened his sack and took out several pouches.

"Here." He gave each of them a pouch. "Apply this ointment to their wounds."

It was the ointment Aldo had given him. It would have proven more useful than he could have imagined had he not seen his future. But Talon knew what lay before him, and the next moments would be his darkest.

"And Sara, get some water and try to put out these fires."

Rodan and Bolton carried the injured to the stream where the smoke wasn't as thick. Farah, Talon, Spire, and Thatch treated the wounded. Sara doused the flames.

The smoke thinned, and a rupture of white moonlight shone through the veiled sky. They saw the wounds of the people. Some were burned to such a degree that the flesh had melted. Bloody marrow-like lesions invaded the places where skin should be. The moaning and crying grew louder until the sound deafened Talon's ears. He could taste the air like over-cooked meat.

What could he have done to stop this?

Nothing.

After a few hours, the streets were cleared of the wounded and the flames. They continued to look for survivors who could be hidden in the debris.

Bolton looked around him. This was the man who he had followed. Locked away in Element, he couldn't see it. His eyes were no longer shielded. He couldn't ignore what was right in front of him.

He walked down a narrow street covered in ash and scorched wood.

"Help." Someone called. The faint voice came from the ruins of a burnt down house.

Bolton dug through the dust and debris and uncovered a child, but before he could lift her from the ashes someone else did.

The man held the child by the collar of her dress and backed away from Bolton.

He didn't recognize him, but he knew what he was.

"Look what we've done." He laughed. "He will be so proud of all this destruction, all this pain."

Bolton stared at the man, mesmerized by his callousness. But the longer he stared, the more he felt like he was looking at some future reflection of himself.

The child coughed and choked. Her head fell to her chest, and her eyes closed. She never lifted her head again.

The man laid her among the ashes and ran. He only got past two houses before Bolton struck him down with Lightning. Bolton ran to where he fell and punched him in the face.

Talon, Spire, and Thatch heard the noise. They found Bolton hitting the unconscious man.

Talon pulled Bolton off him. "That's enough!"

The man wore a silver medallion around his neck. It was like the one Bolton threw into the abyss at the Cliff of Broken

Promise.

"He was part of this," Spire said.

Bolton knelt on the ground and sobbed. He looked at the man and saw what he could become.

"It's alright," Talon said.

"You all should go on to Element," Thatch said. "There might be more of these goons there. I'll stay and keep looking for wounded. After that, I'll go back to the dome and wait for you."

"He's right," Spire said. "They might have the Water Sphere."

"Do you think that's what they came for?" Sara asked.

"I can't imagine what else. But what bothers me is how they discovered it was in Element."

Talon stepped forward. "There are plenty of reasons Eli chose this place. The sphere is only one of them."

Again, Talon walked up the steps of Element. This time he dreaded it more. He knew what was beyond those doors. He had seen the future, the unchangeable future. But still nothing could prepare him for the reality of it. He had believed Element to be a place of safety.

Apprentice Elementals struggled to help their friends, who were sprawled on the floor, wounded. Many more had been murdered in the streets as they tried to escape to the ships.

Sara and the others stayed to help them.

"Spire . . ." Talon said.

Spire looked at him. She knew. "Go," she said. "We can manage."

Talon wandered through the halls. He could not stay to help. There was someone he needed to see one last time. He found her lying on the floor in the library alone, right where he knew she would be.

"Brina." He knelt beside her.

Burns covered most of her body and snaked up her neck.

"I was loading ships." Her voice was soft and raspy. "I

wanted to save them all."

"How did you know to do that?"

"I got your letter." Brina tried to lift her arm. The letter was still clenched in her hand.

"My letter, but how?"

"It arrived before the attack. I got the ships together as soon as I could. Talon . . . you don't know how many lives you saved."

Talon stroked the hair from her face. "I'm sorry," he said, "for leaving like I did and never coming back. I wanted to prevent something like this."

"I didn't ask you to protect me," Brina said. "I just wanted you to be with me."

"I wish I could have been. I wish I could have stayed with you."

Brina covered his hand with hers. "Do you remember when we were young? We crept out of our homes to see each other by the woods where we used to play, and you showed me the most beautiful stone I'd ever seen. I didn't know what it was. I wanted to take it, but you said to leave it so others would find it and look upon it as we had together."

Talon nodded.

"Do you think anyone else found it the way we did?"

He shook his head. "Not the way we did."

Brina moved her hand from his and reached into her dress pocket. She took out the ring he gave her, placed it in Talon's hand, and held it there.

"I feel horrible," Talon confessed.

"Why?" she asked.

"That we didn't have our time."

"Talon, every moment I was with you was special to me. That was our time."

Her grip on Talon's hand loosened until she closed her eyes. Her lips moved. Talon leaned in closer to hear her words. He could feel her breath upon his ear. "In my cloak pocket."

Talon reached into her pocket and retrieved the sphere.

He held it out.

Brina opened her eyes one last time. She nodded.

"You protected the sphere."

Tears gleamed in Brina's eyes.

Talon put down the sphere and wiped her tears away.

"What you and I had was the best thing I've ever known." It was true, and he normally wouldn't have said it. But he wanted her to know. His eyes glazed over, and he pressed his lips to hers. Her lips were still warm, but she couldn't kiss back.

SPIRE ran across the field of Element. It was quiet under the dark sky. Ahead of her was the groundkeeper's cottage. She opened the door to the cottage and went inside. The cottage had been ransacked.

Decca's belongings were still inside. A bucket, a scythe, and other workmen's tools rested at the entrance. Dirt and grass covered the tools. A worn shirt slung across the back of a chair. An old book on the art of battle by wielding weapons of steel rested on the table. Once as she cried, Spire ripped the pages from the book. Knowing how he poured over that book, she had instantly regretted it.

She walked across the room to the bed. It was still unmade as he had left it. She counted her steps away from the bed. She stared at the floorboards where her foot rested. Spire knelt and pried the boards up with her fingers. She lifted the square cut-out and set it aside, revealing a hole in the floor. Nestled within the hollow crevice was a box. Spire took the box from within the gap. She opened it. But it was empty.

Spire settled on the floor, staring into nothingness. Her fingertips pressed into the box. She remembered the time when her body was like the secret place beneath the floorboards, hiding the sphere, protecting it.

Spire rushed back to the entrance hall. Her heart pounded in her chest so hard she thought it might escape. She was a fool to think she could hide the sphere.

As she stormed back into Element, Sara and the others were still helping apprentices and trainers who were left behind. They were badly burned.

"They took it." Spire's words were soft. Her voice was caught in her throat.

"No, they didn't." Talon emerged from the library. He held the sphere.

"How did you . . ."

"It was Brina. She protected the sphere . . . with her life."

33

TAKEN

ELEMENTA'S fires dulled to dying embers, and the people of the town waited by the river for the rain to clear the smoke. Their lives could never be comfortable with the knowledge that one man with one army could strike at any time and take everything from them. Who would take his city down? Who would set things right? But most of all, when would the cycle end. The people dreamed of a day when the mighty did not take advantage of the weak, when the elements would not turn against them, and evil tyrants stopped their plunder.

"Everything is ruined," Farah said as they stepped outside of Element and surveyed the burnt land.

At the bottom of the marble stairs, Talon picked up a piece of rubble from a fallen building and held it between his fingers. *Just the way it was all supposed to happen*, he thought. *Brina dead and I no more a hero than I was when I left her.*

Ships.

Talon picked up his head.

She was loading ships. That's why they came. They thought Element was getting ready for war. He has eyes everywhere. My letter . . . It was the reason Brina readied those ships.

He got up and hurled the rubble into the distance with a curse.

"Talon?" Spire said.

Talon kept his back to them. Rage and anguish distorted his face. "I need a moment, please," he said as softly as he could.

Talon looked back toward Element. The vines died and fell from the walls. He walked further into town with his eyes to the night sky. Rain dropped onto his face.

Sara watched as Talon walked away, not sure if he would return. "I'll see how everyone is doing at the river," she said.

"Wait, I'll go with you," Bolton said.

"Me too." Farah eyed Bolton.

Rodan knelt beside an apprentice slumped on the steps.

Spire looked toward the river. "Be careful," she said. "We'll stay and wait for Talon."

Sara nodded, and she, Bolton, and Farah walked together to the river.

Not far away, they could see the river's black water, darkened from the ashes and the night. People were nursing their wounds and cradling their children.

Sara quickened her steps, leaving Bolton and Farah a few paces behind.

"Wait for us, Sara," Bolton warned.

Sara could not see anything but the suffering people. She did not notice how closely someone followed her. An unknown woman grabbed her by the wrist. She was not one of the wounded. The woman was tall with burnt-red hair and wore battle attire. She had a silver band around her arm.

Several other soldiers were with the woman. They were all dressed like her with silver bands around their arms. Another soldier took Sara by the arm.

"Let her go!" Bolton yelled.

"Hey, what's going on?" Farah asked.

The woman and her small army were silent. Sara struggled. Water pooled beneath her feet.

"Who are you?" Bolton asked.

"Hey," Farah said. "I've seen you all before. You're the Resistance. What are you doing? We cleaned this mess up. Well, almost."

The Resistance soldiers took Sara away as she fought to get free.

"Where are you taking me?" Water wet Sara's boots.

Bolton and Farah ran after the soldiers, but one of them pushed Bolton and Farah back with a heavy gust of wind. It was too unexpected for Farah to negate. Bolton rose and shot Lightning at them, but the bolt was extinguished by another Lightning Elemental in the company.

They took Sara to the river's edge, away from the injured townspeople and forced her into a small boat. The Resistance soldiers boarded the boat and rowed downstream. Wind pushed the boat carrying Sara, sending it rocketing down the river, and leaving Farah and Bolton standing at the water's edge.

*   *   *

"SPIRE!" Farah ran back to Element with Bolton behind her. "Spire, Sara's been kidnapped."

"Kidnapped?" Spire said. "By who?"

"Some crazy Resistance fighters," Farah said.

Rodan charged Bolton. He grabbed him by the collar of his shirt. "You're supposed to protect her."

Bolton pushed Rodan off him. "We did everything we could."

Rodan grimaced and stepped away from Bolton. "Where were they taking her?"

"I don't know," Bolton said. "It's not like they stopped and gave us an itinerary."

Talon returned. "We have to find her. Let's go."

They walked to the hill where Thatch had landed the dome. Thermal sat with Orka upon his head. Orka flew down to Farah's shoulder. Thatch stepped out of the dome.

"Thatch," Farah said, "we need you to help us scan the sea for Sara. She was kidnapped back at the river. Maybe we can go to the mouth of the river to find her."

Thermal flew to where the river opened to the sea, and they exited the dome. Wharfs lined the water where ships could dock. The small boat was abandoned.

Talon lifted the ropes still tied to the dock. "Sailors never leave their ropes. They must have been in a hurry. I think our kidnappers must have left by ship."

"Well," Thatch said, "I'll try to fly as low as possible. Maybe we'll be able to find her."

Thermal flew near the water, and the blue-green sea touched his belly. As he passed Caleena, the villagers stared as the giant bird swept the water.

"No sign of her yet?" Thatch asked.

"No," Farah said. "Not yet."

"How is that possible?" Rodan stared out the window. "Thermal can fly ten times as fast as a ship could sail."

"They have Wind Elementals with them," Farah said. "I think they're using their energy to propel the ship."

They searched the sea and the coast for Sara and her captors. They headed toward Lumina.

"We may have to leave the dome to search Lumina," Talon said. "The city's too big. She could be anywhere in it."

"That's if they went to Lumina," Farah said. "They could have sailed on to Vella City or Jetty Verte. We could be wasting a lot of time."

"Let's talk when we get there," Rodan hissed. "We're nowhere near Lumina." Rodan's breath caught. "Look."

A ship sailed ahead of them.

"That could be anyone," Farah said.

"No," Rodan said. "It has silver sails."

"What are we going to do from up here?"

"We'll have to trail them," Thatch said. "Thermal can't land on that ship. It isn't big enough. But we'll have to fly higher above the clouds so they can't see us."

"But what if we lose them."

"We won't. I won't lose them."

It was difficult to keep Thermal in line with the ship. He kept pushing ahead. Thatch had to signal to him to hover so that the ship could move on ahead of them.

Dawn crept in. But Lumina was close. Because the ship was being propelled by Wind Elementals, it moved faster than a normal ship. By the time the sun was up, the ship with the silver sails docked in Lumina.

Thermal landed in Lumina Port on one of the docks alongside the trade ships. The sailors looked up when the shadow of the huge bird warned them of its coming. Some dropped their crates and took cover as the wind from Thermal's wings pushed the ships aside in the water.

"Why did we land so far from them?" Bolton exited the dome.

"It was the only empty dock," Thatch said.

Bolton ran through the streets to find Sara, leaving the others behind. The streets of Lumina City were crowded.

"It'll take too long to search for her," Rodan said. "We'll never find her before they take her somewhere else."

"Wait, look," Farah said as they walked out of the port. "That ship. It's the one with the silver sails. Look at the symbol on it."

A larger ship docked away from the trade ships. The ship bore the image of an element sphere crossed by a sword etched into the ships side.

Farah rushed up to the ship and boarded. She tore the cabin door open. "There's no one here."

"They can't have gotten far," said Rodan. "Come on."

"They're here somewhere," Bolton whispered to himself, taking off into the city. He didn't know where the others were, but he didn't look back to see if they were following him.

"Look," Farah shouted. "I'd know that yellow hair anywhere. It's Bolton." She raced toward him, and the others followed.

Bolton ran through the city streets, bumping into people and knocking over goods. The others tried to keep up with him, but he was moving too fast.

Bolton neared Lumina Stadium. Alongside the Stadium were rental rooms for visitors. The Resistance woman from Elementa entered the hall leading to the rooms. He ran and caught the door before it closed. He took the woman by the shoulders.

"Where is she?" Bolton asked her.

The other Resistance fighters heard Bolton's shouting and entered the hall from a room inside.

"I asked you, where is she?" Bolton shouted again. Worry fought against the anger in his voice. "Tell me now!"

As he interrogated the woman, Talon and the others caught up with him.

"Let her go, Bolton," Talon said.

"She knows where Sara is," Bolton said.

"She won't fight."

Bolton released the Resistance soldier, and she took a step away from him. He recognized the group as the Resistance fighters from the Element Games.

"What do you want with Sara?" Spire asked. "Do you work for Hephaestus?"

"Of course not," the woman said. "I am Mercedes, a mercenary of the Resistance. We are protecting the Water Elemental."

"Protecting her?" Farah asked. "What does kidnapping have to do with protecting?"

Bolton eyed Mercedes. What are they up to? he wondered. If they weren't working for Hephaestus, what did they want?

"Too many Elementals have fought to their deaths against this man," Mercedes said.

"Hephaestus?" Bolton said.

"Not only him," Mercedes said. "This man, this type of man: a power-hungry element tyrant. You know the kind. Since their creation, the element spheres have been the object of battles, wars fought over their power, only to end in death. Not one other Elemental will die for that cause. There must be another way."

So, they are saving her, Bolton thought, by holding her back.

"We understand your take on it," Talon said, "but Sara must fight. The rest of Mirmina depends on her."

"The rest of Mirmina can handle itself," Mercedes said. "You call yourselves her friends. Why don't you tell her how the world is? It's a tired and cruel place, and it will be that way still after Hephaestus is defeated. Another will take his place."

They're right, Bolton thought.

"Who will fight him?" Rodan asked. "Who will stop him?"

"We will," Mercedes said. "It is our job to fight for the people of Mirmina. It is not the job of vigilantes. The rest of the Resistance wants to reward them, but the more they are rewarded, the more they are encouraged. We will fight Hephaestus and his army. But there will be no more death marches to Omega Ray."

"You're insurgents," Talon said.

"You need a stronger force than yourselves to fight him," Spire said. "As well trained and groomed for battle as you are, you can't change the way you think. Water Elementals are different from Fire Elementals. When he knows of Sara's presence in the battle, it will insight fear in Hephaestus and weaken him. If we don't stand up to him, it will mean letting him have Mirmina. You want to bring order to the system, but Hephaestus has torn that down. If we want order again, we must stop him together."

"But why should she have to go," Bolton interjected.

"Why should Sara have to die? Why can't we wait? Is that so hard? Or better, get all of Mirmina to join us before we march into Omega Ray with a few dull heroes and a canteen of water."

"Bolton, we can't do that," Talon said. "This is the way things have to be."

"Why?" Bolton asked. "Why?"

"Because," Spire said, "we'll be waiting all our lives, however long or short they may be."

"Why Sara?" Bolton asked. "She's the last Water Elemental. They're right. She should be protected."

"It's not that simple." Talon stepped forward. "Sara needs to do this for Mirmina and for herself. Do you understand, Bolton? You would be asking her to give up her freedom again."

I know but . . . Bolton thought, but it would save her.

"Show us where she is, Mercedes," Talon said. "You can't keep her here."

Mercedes glared at him. "You are making a mistake." She asked the Resistance fighters to move aside. Her eyes rested on Bolton. She gave him the key to the room.

Bolton stared at the silver key, heavy in his hand, as if weighing his options, but he only had one option, the only one that would make Sara happy. Bolton walked to the door.

"Think about it," Mercedes cautioned.

Bolton paused at the door. He looked down at the key. With a sigh, he put the key in the lock and turned.

This was the second time he would release Sara from her cage. But this time it wouldn't be for him. It would be for her.

She wouldn't give up no matter what he said. And if he was the one to keep her locked away, she would resent him for it.

He removed the heavy key and turned the knob of the door. As the door swung open, Sara rushed to meet him. She put her arms around his neck and hugged him.

"I'll stay with you," he whispered, "till the end."

34

SICILIA

HEPHAESTUS curled his fingers around the arms of his throne.

"You messed up."

Fero bowed his head to his leader. "Yes."

"You let them see you."

"I didn't have a choice. Talon sensed me. I couldn't have stayed hidden, and if they found me, they would have known we've been spying on them. It would have ruined everything."

"What could have ruined everything was your hastiness. You got too close."

"I know."

"You know?"

Fero lifted his head. "It won't happen again. They don't know anything."

Hephaestus's skin got hotter. His body temperature rose

with each word, but Fero looked steadily back at him. "When you came to me you were a boy, dreaming of becoming a man. You said you were tired of a world where Elementals did not harness their fullest potential. You thought of Element as a playpen and the trainers as puppets, serving no purpose but to hide the ball. I agreed with you, and that is why you are here.

"But you've gotten cocky. The men look at you and wonder if they can get away with such things too. I can't have an army of rebellious juveniles. It's time to grow up."

"What would you have me do?"

"Burn."

Fero didn't flinch. "Where?"

"In the streets at noon tomorrow. If you run—"

"I won't run."

HEPHAESTUS swung a fiery whip, but the whip wasn't real, only the flames.

The crowd heard the crack as the flames erupted in lines across Fero's back.

Fero clenched his teeth, but he didn't move. No one restrained him, only his willpower. His shirt was removed, and the onlookers could see his skin bubbling with every stroke.

His arms were not huddled across his chest nor were they hanging limply at his sides. He had them raised, crucifix-like against the cold wind.

The cold did sooth his fresh wounds, but only made them more biting. He felt the energy behind each lash as Hephaestus summoned it from the depths of his soul.

Hephaestus did not wear a grin on his face. His lips were pressed together, and his eyes were focused.

The whispers started.

"Try harder!

"I know you could do more. You burned that village down, boy!"

The lashing became faster and sharper.

Fero kept his arms raised, but his knees shook. The slight

shudder did not go unnoticed.

The flames stopped.

Hephaestus was not looking at his work, but beyond it.

A howl sounded through the air, and it was much deeper than the cry of a coyote.

The black creature lurked in the distance.

The fire of the torches magnified the blackness around them. The light would serve the dark, casting its shadow across the plain.

In his wildest nightmares, he had dreamed of the creature in the darkness. No matter how much he tried to conquer his city with light. The darkness snaked across the valley. When you live in the dark long enough, no amount of light can set you free of the things you saw there.

HEPHAESTUS slept in the worn armchair near his dusty bed. The sleep was accidental. He had tried to avoid it.

He could feel Sicilia's hand in his. It was so cold against his warmer skin.

"How long will they keep us?" she asked.

"Don't worry, I'll keep you safe," Eli promised. He held onto her hand as they fell asleep on the floor mats.

"Wake up," the man ordered, his voice unfeeling. "Come with me." He took Sicilia by the arm.

"No." Eli rose from his mat.

"It's okay," she said. "I'll be safe."

Hephaestus turned in his sleep.

"Eli, what's wrong?" she asked.

"My hand." His hand was red and enflamed. "They forced me. I couldn't stop."

Sicilia took his hand and sent Water to bathe it. "Does that feel better?"

Eli clenched his teeth. "A little better. Can I see more?"

She took his hand and twirled her finger above it until a stream of water swirled in tiny, clear strings above his burnt palm.

"It's amazing."

Hephaestus struggled in the worn chair. His face was full of pain.

Eli snuck into the room where they performed their experiments. He watched from around the corner of the hall. Sicilia stood in the middle of the room.

"Try harder, girl!" The man wore long robes and sat in the audience in front of her. All these people had come to watch her be tortured so they could test her limits.

"I've tried. I can't do more."

"You must!"

Sicilia concentrated. Her eyes squeezed shut. Water spilled from her mouth. It rolled down her chin in a puddle on the floor. She was drowning.

"Stop!" Eli rushed into the room and caught Sicilia as she collapsed from exhaustion.

"Get them out of here!"

The guards dragged them to their cells.

"Sicilia."

Sicilia opened her eyes and gave him a weak smile. "I'm okay, see." She sent Water whirling in his hand, but soon the Water whirled no more and fell onto his palm.

"Sicilia, we have to get out of here. I have a plan."

Hephaestus shook his head in his sleep.

Eli and Sicilia made their way through the fire.

Sicilia tried to put out the flames as they moved along, but the fire was too fierce. "Eli, what have you done?"

"We have to leave. We needed a distraction."

The inhabitants ran. One of the robed men fought the flames that snaked up his cloak, and Eli smiled. They were rushing everywhere as the ceiling of the building began to collapse. Paint melted off the walls. Sicilia choked on the smoke. A child's body lay on the floor.

"Come on."

"Stop!" A voice came from behind them. He sent a bolt of lightning toward Sicilia.

Sicilia turned, and the bolt hit her in the chest.

Hephaestus jolted from his sleep as if the lightning had struck him instead.

35

FORTRESS TOWER

WHEN they returned to the dome, Thatch promised to bring them to Vella City.

Farah petted Orka as the little bird perched upon her shoulder. She had her fears, but she was ready for the fight. She would make sure Orka kept her distance, and she would keep an eye on Bolton. She was glad she left home to continue the journey. The battle would be dangerous, but to her it was better than being Breeze's steel palace princess any day.

Rodan glanced toward Sara and Bolton, sitting together on the metal benches near the window. *I'm responsible for this*, he thought. If he had reasoned Sara out of it, if he had suggested that they run away together instead, would he be the one sitting next to her? In the end, would he feel instrumental in her death?

Spire touched the ring on the chain around her neck. She couldn't decide if she was doing this more for Sara or for Decca. She had wanted to wear his ring, but it shamed her as did the golden band, which was meant to honor her. She wondered if Talon felt the same about Brina. Did he blame himself now?

Talon reflected on his past. All the things he thought he was doing for the best turned out wrong. All that time was wasted. Brina was right. He should have spent less time running and more time by her side. But there was no time for his regrets. He would finish his story. He hoped Bolton's story would end differently.

Bolton placed his hand upon Sara's. He wasn't sure what his next move would be, but he knew one thing: he had to tell the truth. He had spent too much time being in his uncle's shadow. He needed to take a stand even if it would be his last. He wasn't like his father. He wouldn't run.

Sara looked out the window at the places they had travelled. She wished she could believe Water was the answer, that it could wash away everything. But in the depths of her mind, she thought she was missing something. She might die in the fight, but the thought was surreal, and she felt numbed by it. *I can't die*, she thought. *I haven't seen enough yet.*

"We'll have to land in Jetty Verte," Thatch said. "Thermal can't land in Vella City or the forest, too many buildings and trees."

When Thermal landed in Jetty Verte, it was still dark. Stars dusted the sky. They walked out upon the grass, which turned a deeper color in the night.

"Good luck," Thatch said as the hatch door closed.

Thermal kicked off the ground, the wind from his wings nearly throwing them backwards.

They went back to the Crystal Forest and took the road to Vella City.

The buildings of Vella City stretched to the skies, but it had been abandoned for many years. It used to be the wealthiest city in Mirmina. But the inhabitants fled the city because of a great flood. Some were just in time, and others were not so fortunate. The waters stopped at the forest, and when they washed away, the buildings were all that was left. Now, the city was empty and full of echoes.

As they turned the bend, the woods opened up to a cliff. A waterfall filled the chasm. The cliff and the waterfall reminded Bolton of the Cliff of Broken Promise and of his vow to change his fate.

"We should rest," Spire said. "It has been a long day."

Talon, Spire, and Rodan sat by the waterfall. Farah ran off into the forest in search of Omar and Milbill. Sara and Bolton went for a walk; he said that he had something to tell her. Rodan watched them walk away.

"I don't want you to go to Fortress Tower," Bolton said once they were out of earshot of the others.

"Why not?" Sara asked.

Bolton stopped walking and took her hands in his. "Sara, this is going to be a lot to ask, but please trust me. I don't want you to go. Let us do it. You can stay in the forest."

"I don't understand."

"Please, just trust me. When I come back, we can go to the Insula and forget about all this."

"What about Hephaestus?"

"He won't matter. We'll be free like you wanted."

Sara shook her head. "But I told you. It's more than that now. I have to stand up to him."

"Please, do this for me."

His eyes pleaded with her. But the words of Madam Dawn echoed in her head. *Do not offer your trust to him.*

"If you think something bad will happen, I want to be there for my friends. I won't let you all go alone."

"Please, Sara, you're making a big mistake."

"Maybe, but the last thing I will do is hide." Gently, Sara let go of his hands. "I'm sorry." She left him and walked to the lake.

After she had gone, Bolton walked back to the clearing. He saw Farah's canvas bag resting against a crystal. He reached for it.

"Hey!" Farah ran up and snatched the bag. "What do you think you're doing?"

"I thought you ran off into the forest."

"What do you want with the spheres?"

"Have you lost your trust in me too?" he asked.

"What?"

"I was going to take the spheres to Fortress Tower myself. There's no reason why we all should go."

"What are you talking about? What do you know?"

"I don't want Sara anywhere near Fortress Tower."

"And why is that?" Farah asked.

"I have my reasons."

"Make them known or you're not getting the bag."

"Look, all we have to do is give him the spheres. That's all he wants. He'll leave us alone."

"We're not giving him the spheres. If that's why you were taking them, forget it." Farah hugged the bag to her chest. "You're going to have to decide how important your secrets are to you."

Bolton sighed. Playing the hero was not his strong suit. He had to tell Sara. It was the only way. He didn't want her to hear it from anyone else but him.

Farah stood, watching him go. *He's up to no good*, she thought. She petted the little, green bird perched on her shoulder. "Orka, I need you to do something for me."

SARA stared into the calm waters of the lake. She ran her fingers through the cool surface and watched her reflection waver. Bolton's reflection came into focus next to hers.

He sat on the bank with her and put his feet in the water.

"Everything's going to be okay," she said. "I know you're scared for me."

"I am."

Sara put her hand on his and squeezed.

"Sara . . ."

"What is it?"

Bolton looked down into the water. Something in his voice had changed. "Those things I was saying before . . . I wanted to protect you."

"I know."

"But you don't understand. I want to protect you from something I *know* will happen."

Sara leaned in closer to him. "What are you talking about?"

Bolton bowed his head further. "We need to leave. All he wants is the spheres."

"Why are you saying this? This has been our plan all along. In fact, you said it back in Caleena. We have to set the spheres. It's the only way he'll never get his hands on them. He doesn't know what we're doing. If he's heard of us by now, he'll think we're coming to him."

Bolton shook his head. "No, he doesn't think that."

"How do you know?"

"Look, I just do." Bolton stood and grabbed her hand. "I'll tell you everything, but first we have to go, all of us."

Sara stood next to him. "Bolton, how do you know?"

Bolton still held her hand. "Because I was asked to do something."

"What?"

"To make sure you got to Fortress Tower . . . with the spheres."

"Why?"

"So, he could take them from you."

Sara stared at him.

Bolton's grip on her hand tightened. "He would have never gotten them on his own. He needed a Water Elemental who was willing to do it. If you thought you were doing it to keep them from him, you would have done so willingly."

Sara stepped back, but her hand was still clenched in Bolton's. Her eyes glazed over. "You work for him." Her shocked voice came out in a whisper.

"I'll explain everything. Just come with me."

Sara shook her head. She pulled her hand out of his grasp. She didn't say anything. She wasn't ready for this. It was like Bolton had gone away, and she was faced with a stranger.

"I don't know you." She backed away from him.

"Sara, please."

"Does it even work?"

"Please."

"Setting the spheres in the tower, does it work?"

Bolton nodded. "I think so."

"When is he coming?"

"I don't know." A look of realization dawned on his face. "No, you can't go alone."

Sara shook her head. "Leave." It hurt her to say it.

Bolton opened his mouth to plea with her, but she didn't let his words come out.

"Turn around and leave. Go, and leave me and my friends alone."

Bolton looked at her with one last pleading gaze, but her heart was stone. The only semblance of caring were the tears that dropped from her cheeks.

SARA put the hood of the cloak over her head. It shadowed her face.

She clenched Farah's bag in her hands.

The buildings of Vella City were taller than those of Lumina. Intricate designs in faded colors decorated them. Water flowed from balconies overlooking the sea.

Fortress Tower was a tall, cylindrical building near the center of Vella City. It was made of plaster and bronze, and each element symbol was outlined around its top.

In the topmost room of the tower was a place for each element sphere. Their placement formed a ring, a binding circle.

Sara walked along the ancient tiled walkway to Fortress Tower. The tower loomed over her. A heavy, brass door marked the entrance to the tower.

Sara kept her head bowed as she hastened her pace. It wouldn't be long before her friends realized she was gone. If she could only keep them out of danger and set the spheres before Hephaestus arrived. She needed to hurry.

Sara opened the heavy door. Its pull was like that of the Earth Sphere when she had lifted it from its pedestal. The room was large, circular, and full of columns running around the perimeter.

Sara walked out into the center of the room. A staircase hid behind the columns. It winded along the interior of the tower wall in a spiral until it reached the top.

As Sara gazed up with the canvas bag clenched in her hands, the door to Fortress Tower opened. Her heart jumped.

"What are you doing?" It was Talon. He was followed by the others.

"I told them what you were trying to do." Bolton walked in.

Before Sara could respond, Rodan asked, "Why would you go alone?"

"I thought it would be easier."

"Without us?"

Talon tilted his head and looked around the room. "We need to leave."

But it was too late. Dark figures emerged from behind the columns. They enclosed Sara and her friends in the center of the room.

"Don't try anything," Fero said. "There are more of us than there are of you this time."

"He's right, brother, don't do something you'll regret." Eli came out from behind one of the columns. He wore his scarlet robe which flushed against his pale skin. His orange eyes darted around the room.

Rodan and Bolton stepped in front of Sara and shielded her from Eli. Eli's fiery eyes searched the room and rested on Farah's canvas sack clenched in Sara's grasp. Fire licked Sara's hands, burning the flesh above her knuckles. She flinched and dropped the bag.

"No!" Bolton shouted.

"I believe that is mine," he said.

Bolton grabbed the bag from the floor before Sara could reach for it. He threw it to Eli. Eli opened the bag and looked at the gleaming spheres. He counted them in silence.

"They're all here," Eli said. "You've done well." Eli tossed Bolton a small pouch. Bolton caught it. The pouch strings loosened, revealing the golden coins inside.

"Glistenings?" Sara said.

"Bolton?" Rodan said. "For money?"

Bolton closed his eyes and lowered his head.

"Oh, that's right," Eli said, in pretend realization. "You don't know. Bolton, why don't you tell them?"

Bolton looked away and remained silent.

"Go on," Eli said. "Tell them how you've been watching them for me since you came to Element. And wasn't it your idea to come to the tower, the idea I put into your head."

"Stop it." Sara kept her head down.

"Why?" he asked. "Don't you want to know the truth? It was all a pretense to get close to you, to find out your secrets. What a wonderful actor he's been." Eli didn't look at her.

Fero grinned.

"And now he has led you to Vella City, the Council's city." Eli sneered. "And you're going to be my prisoners for a long time. Now step aside, boy, and let me look at the last Water Elemental." Eli strained to see Sara over the shoulders of Bolton and Rodan, but couldn't quite see her face.

Sara shook her head. She failed to stop the tears from falling down her face. Heavy raindrops fell.

"We'll fight," Talon whispered to Sara. "But you need to run."

But Sara did not move. Eli stepped toward her, sparking a flame to threaten Bolton and Rodan out of the way.

"Rodan, get her out of here," Bolton whispered.

Spire sent Wind, knocking Eli's soldiers against the wall. Farah tried to take the bag from Eli, but he slapped her to the ground. Talon took out his sword.

Amidst the chaos, Rodan took Sara's hand. She hesitated. She stared at Bolton's back. He never turned to look at her.

"Come on, Sara," Rodan said.

The waves crashed like thunder.

"You can't stay. The water . . . it'll drown us all."

The raindrops continued to fall, and the sea rose above the cliff's edge.

Sara remembered when Rodan pulled her from the water. She allowed herself to be taken back to dry land. Her feet moved on their own. She had been a puppet for so long without knowing it. She thought this journey had been a step toward freedom, but it was only a step further into the cage.

Rodan tore her eyes from Bolton, who could not look back at them as they ran out the door.

"Get her!" Eli shouted. "I'm not done yet."

36

FALLING TO SAFETY

F IVE men armed with their elements followed after Rodan
and Sara. The stomp of their boots against the tiled floor
was thunderous—the thunder of lightning ready to strike.

For Sara, it *had* struck. Bolton lied to her, and he tried to
destroy the one thing that was important to her: her freedom.

Rodan did not think of the future or past, he just ran. That
moment was the only one that existed for him. As he grasped
Sara's hand, he knew one thing: he had to get her to safety. He
ran with purpose and without looking back.

Sara did look back.

The water of the sea rose. It hung over the city, its shadow
inching over the marble buildings.

Sara had to get her emotions in check or that wave would
come crashing down on her friends, but she could feel the Water as if it was filling her, and she was choking on it.

As they neared the Crystal Forest, the men threw Fire. The flames passed Sara and Rodan. One flew inches from Rodan's face. He could feel the heat of the flames but kept his eyes forward.

Sara looked back several more times, which slowed her down. She was afraid of the rising waters, of what she couldn't control. Rodan held her hand and encouraged her to keep pace.

"Don't look back," he said.

As they entered the forest, flames leapt up, blocking their escape. Rodan and Sara tried to jump over the fire, but Sara did not make it. One leg was licked by the flames. Rodan pulled her away from the fire. He lifted her from the ground.

With tired effort, he kept going, carrying her in his arms, but three men caught up with him. He dodged them, but they ran ahead of him and blocked the path to the forest by the waterfall. There was only one way out.

"Rodan, be careful. The cliff!" Sara warned, but that was Rodan's answer.

He reached the cliff and allowed Sara and himself to fall.

The wind roared in their ears as they rushed through the air. The rocks below where the water gathered made the drop threatening.

Sara's arms clung to his neck as Rodan lifted one arm from around her. From the edge of the cliff sprang a vine which he clasped onto.

With a sharp jerk, Sara and Rodan hung suspended in the air. They dangled halfway down the cliff's side and could feel the spray from the waterfall.

After a while, things became weightless and cold. Rodan used the vine to swing to a ledge in the cliff. He and Sara fell forward onto the ledge, and the vine disappeared.

The men looked down from above.

"They jumped."

"Down there? Did you see the bodies?"

"No."

"They may have washed downstream."

They could not hear the boots of the men upon the softer ground, but their talking became distant.

Rodan caught his breath and sat on the edge of the ledge, and Sara sat with her back against the cave wall.

Sara looked down at her hands.

"Let me see it," Rodan said.

Sara moved her hands out into the light. Rodan took her hands. Beads of blood issued from the sores on her hands. A sore reddened the front of her leg and was surrounded by inflamed, red-pink skin.

"It looks bad," Rodan said. "It will be fine though."

He ripped the sleeve of his shirt and tore the fabric into long strips.

"Do you have any water to soothe the burns?" he asked.

"I dropped my canteen along the way."

"You know what I mean."

Sara shook her head. "I can't."

"Try," Rodan said.

Sara concentrated on the rushing falls, but her will was gone, and she could not make the water move. She certainly couldn't call it. "I can't"

"Okay." Rodan leaned out and let the spray from the waterfall wet the strips of cloth.

Sara hung her head, while Rodan wrapped her hands in the bandages. He had a coldness toward her that she did not detect because other thoughts filled her mind. The future with shattered hope seemed a fragile thing.

"What will we do?" Sara asked.

"Continue," Rodan said as he bandaged her hands.

"Without them?"

"We have to." Rodan sighed. He closed his eyes. "He brought so many men, and I'm sure they were all Elementals. At least we were able to divert a few of them."

Tears painted Sara's face. "It's all my fault. I shouldn't have gone to Fortress Tower."

Rodan put his hand on her shoulder. "You can't think about that right now."

"What if I fail?" Sara asked, "like I failed back there?"

"I don't know," Rodan said. "I don't know what happens next."

"He has the spheres that means he won."

Sara stared at the water falling to the river below. She shouldn't have left Element. She shouldn't have been so trusting. But Bolton . . . he played it so well. She would have never suspected. She still didn't believe it. She wanted to go back, back to the times when she was happy in her travels, back to who she thought he was. But he had helped Hephaestus. He had helped him defeat her.

Rodan shook his head. "He didn't win."

"What are you thinking?"

"We're going to Omega Ray. We're going to fix this."

"How?"

"You're the Water Elemental. He's afraid of you."

"He didn't seem too afraid of me." His orange eyes. She didn't think that fire could ever go out.

"Would you reveal your greatest fear to your enemy?"

Sara looked up at him. "Rodan . . ." It wasn't just Sara who had been hurt by Bolton's lies. Rodan had thought he was his friend all those years. She watched them from the window. They played and bantered. It looked so real.

"What?"

A sack fell into Sara's lap. She opened it. Inside was a round orb filled with spiraling blue mist.

Sara picked it up. It was cool in her hands like water in a spring. She felt a pull on the sphere like it yearned for its pedestal. The closer they got to the sphere sanctum, the stronger the pull would be.

"The Water Sphere."

"But how?" Rodan asked.

Orka landed on the ledge and chirped. Tied to her leg was what remained of the bottle of ointment Aldo had given them.

37

THE CLEAR PATH

ELI sat at a stone table on the seventh floor of Fortress Tower. His fire red cloak was laid aside on the table. He had Farah's canvas sack in his hands. He was alone.

Fero and the rest of his army kept watch in the dungeon where Talon, Spire, and Farah were being held. Instead of killing them, Eli decided that they should be kept imprisoned until the Water Elemental returned for them. He would be waiting. They were in separate cells rank with dirt and rats. They were tired, but none of them dared to sit on the foul floor.

Bolton found an empty room in the tower and locked himself inside. What he had been dreading happened, and all he kept thinking was—why didn't he do more to stop it. He wondered why he had not jumped off the Cliff of Broken Promise. He had broken all his promises. He had vowed to no longer be controlled by his uncle, and he had promised never to become like his father.

All his life his uncle made him feel like he had a purpose, a corrupt purpose, but still a purpose. Sara made him feel like he had a purpose too, only it was a virtuous one. She made him feel important, like something would be missing if he was gone. He had destroyed that by being a coward.

Eli never made him feel significant, he only used him. Since he was young, he did what Eli told him. He knew no other way. Once he was out of Eli's grasp, Eli still had his hold on him. Talon had never been around, never told him that he came from something good. He was Eli's slave, but it was his fault now. He had had a choice. He now knew who Eli's enemies were, and they were not Bolton's enemies. They were his friends. Yet, he delivered them into danger.

And Sara. She thought he was a snake. He would never again be able to sit close enough to see the specks of green in her eyes or to hear her laugh at his lame, sarcastic jokes.

A deep curse came from the floor above him. Bolton looked up. He stood, unbolted the door, and raced up the steps.

ELI counted the spheres in Farah's bag. The room was quiet and empty, which Eli liked. He had no concern for what was being done with the prisoners or for his depressed nephew. He was content with examining the collected spheres.

With them, he could rip the Council out of hiding. He would do it for Sicilia, and after that he wouldn't have to be reminded of the girl he couldn't avenge.

He took the spheres out one by one and marveled at their beauty and hidden power. He reached into the bag without looking, and every time he picked up one of Farah's stolen treasures, he threw it over his shoulder.

The first sphere he removed was the Wind Sphere. Inside the sphere was a white, twirling mist. Eli set the sphere on the table.

He picked up the Lightning Sphere. Inside pulsed tiny, vibrating strings of energy. As he held the sphere, he remembered the man who took Sicilia from him. In the eyes of that man, Eli saw Benn and Bolton.

"Hateful lineage." He put the sphere aside on the table.

Now that he had the spheres, no Elemental would ever come against him. He would use the spheres as leverage to form a new nation with himself as the leader. He could eradicate all that caused him pain. He could weed out the Council and get justice for Sicilia.

He pulled out the Earth Sphere. A flower bloomed at its center. He shook his head. From what he had seen of Earth Elementals, the delicate flower did not do them justice. But the spheres showed only the beauty of the elements and not their true natures. He put the sphere on the table alongside the others.

He lifted the Fire Sphere from the bag. The sphere's heat matched the temperature of his hand. Spiraling flames circled inside the sphere. He held it longer than the others and marveled at the spiraling energy.

Eli reached into the bag once more. Four spheres rested on the stone table in front of him. There was one more sphere to pull: The Water Sphere. He longed to see the power he had so long sought to extinguish. He didn't want to be reminded of the love he had lost. He thought it would destroy him and make him too weak to battle his enemies. Now, he yearned to remember Sicilia's gift.

He lifted the last sphere from the bag. He held the sphere to his eyes. Something was wrong. The sphere did not hold the same power as the others. In fact, it was devoid of life completely. It was a jewel orb.

Eli held the orb to the light and struggled to see the sphere's essence. He shook it in desperation, but still the essence did not appear. He soon was forced to realize this was not the Water Sphere.

He turned the canvas sack upside down and dumped the remainder of Farah's treasures onto the table. No other spheres lay among them. *No,* he thought, *NO!* He had been fooled. Eli let out a loud curse.

BOLTON stood outside the door. He tried the knob, but Eli had latched the door shut. Bolton put his ear to the door and listened to the stomping and cursing within. It stopped. Bolton backed away from the door.

A click sounded as Eli unlocked the door. The knob turned, and the door swung open. Eli stood, unmoving, as the swinging door revealed his presence. He walked out of the room, and never taking his eyes off Bolton, he closed the door behind him.

He moved past Bolton. Bolton held his breath as his uncle passed. When he thought it safe to breathe again, Eli turned. He took Bolton by the shoulder, put one hand around his neck, and slammed his back against the cold, stone wall. "Where's the sphere?!"

"What do you mean?"

"The Water Sphere, where is it?"

"I don't know," Bolton said.

Eli tightened his grip around his neck. He glared at him, but he could tell Bolton wasn't lying. "The Water Nymph must have it. That is why they told her to run. She won't get far."

He let go of Bolton, who collapsed on the floor and gasped for air.

"I didn't want a chase. Did you know of this?"

Bolton was still recovering on the floor.

Eli knelt. "Don't be a fool. If you try anything while I'm gone, I'll kill all your friends, and I'll let you live a life of pain. I'll burn you."

Bolton didn't say anything. He sat motionless with his eyes to the floor.

Eli rose. "Remember that." He turned and walked away, his robe sweeping across the dust on the floor.

Bolton sat staring at the clear path before him and wondered why his father couldn't see such a path. He knew what he had to do.

38

THE FLAWED HERO

FARAH sent Wind, but all she could do was rattle the bars of her cage. She paced from one end of the cell to the other. The burn on her arm was hot, and the skin was itchy. "They're not watching us," Farah said. "Any ideas?"

No one answered her.

Talon and Spire stood in the cells facing hers.

The dungeon was cold and smelled of rats. The guards found the atmosphere unpleasant. As soon as they heard Hephaestus had left, they abandoned their posts and had not returned.

"Don't waste your time," Talon said. "We can't escape."

"You're trying to punish yourself," Farah said. "You feel guilty that you trusted him, that you gave him a second chance."

"How do you know that?" Talon asked.

"I listen."

"Stop it!" Spire said. "I don't want to hear any more of this. These might be our last days. Don't spend them fighting. It will do no good. We all made mistakes. Now all we can do is hope that we live to make plenty more of them."

Farah and Talon became quiet. After the echo of Spire's argument faded, the only sound was the scurrying of rats across the dungeon floor.

Rushed footsteps broke the silence. A long shadow was cast on the floor. Bolton appeared. He held a ring of keys. Without a word, he set to work finding the keys to their cells.

"What are you doing?" Farah asked.

"What does it look like?" Bolton said.

"Escorting us to our execution?"

"The opposite."

"That's what I hoped."

Bolton found the key to Farah's cell. The guards had not returned.

"Not that I'm complaining," Farah said, "but shouldn't they be watching us. I mean, they know how dangerous we are, right?"

"They're upstairs," Bolton said, "and they're knocked out, or probably dead. I hit them with Lightning. There were only a few. Hephaestus and the others are gone."

"He left?" Farah asked. "Good way to lose prisoners."

"I don't think he considers us much of a threat," Talon said. "He only used us to get the spheres."

"Well," Farah said, "he could've never gotten the spheres himself, not without Sara."

"Eli has always liked to toy with people," Talon said, "and this time Bolton was his pawn."

Bolton unlocked Talon's cell. "He's looking for Sara," Bolton said.

"What? Why didn't you try to stop him?" Farah asked.

"You know I can't do that alone." He opened Spire's cell.

"We can talk later," Spire said. "We have to find Rodan

and Sara before Hephaestus does."

Bolton was glad everyone was caught up in the moment. He didn't want to feel like a stranger in front of his friends.

He led the way up the stairs. The four guards were slumped on the floor. Their chests did not rise and fall. He thought maybe he did kill them. But he didn't think it in sorrow or regret. *These are the first people I ever killed*, he thought, *and they won't be the last.*

39

WEAKENED BUT NOT SPENT

SARA clenched the sphere. She was afraid to let it go. It
felt like it was being pulled away from her. She thought if
she loosened her grasp, the energy might pull it back to its
pedestal. And what if Hephaestus's men found it before it got
there? She tried to banish the silly thought from her head, but
it lingered. She wondered how silly it really was.

The trees did not grow as close together where they were.
The sun was near the horizon, giving the forest an orange
glow. Sara and Rodan spent the day on the ledge by the waterfall. The sounds of Eli's men crossing the path had put their
nerves on edge. But Rodan knew if they didn't climb up before
nightfall, they would have to sleep on the ledge.

"I know you've climbed before." Rodan couldn't stop the
smile from lighting upon his face.

Sara looked up at him. "There were a lot of footsteps.

We've waited so long."

"Talon is skilled, and Spire faced them before. Farah's ferocious as hell."

Sara bit her lip, but it did not stop the tears from coming to her eyes.

Rodan held out his hand to her. "You're strong, Sara. You're the strongest person I know."

She swallowed and let the remaining tears dry on her face, but cried no new ones. She took Rodan's hand.

It felt so warm as if it was giving her life.

Rodan sent a vine up over the cliff.

"We have to hurry."

Sara put the sphere in the pocket of her cloak and with both hands gripped the vine. She got a foothold and climbed up. Her burnt hands ached from her firm grip on the vine. Sara's arms strained as she hoisted herself over the edge of the cliff.

Rodan wasn't far behind her. His fingertips dug into the ground as he pulled himself up. The vine disappeared.

Sara spotted Orka in a nearby tree. The little, green bird had one leg nestled in the feathers of her belly. Her eyes were closed. She looked so peaceful, like she knew everything would be okay.

"The trees are too thin," Rodan said. "The ground is worn from travelers. We'll be easily spotted. Come on."

She followed him as he retreated into the forest. Night was falling. They had been walking since the sun lingered on the horizon.

"We're getting too far from the tower," Sara said.

"A little farther," Rodan promised. "We don't want to be too close or we could be spotted. Those guards might still be out looking for you."

"I can barely see. What is that?"

"What?"

Sara peered into the darkness. "That."

Two eyes glowed among the trees. A hulking mass stood

and growled.

"It's a bear," Rodan whispered. "Walk slowly."

But the bear was on all fours now. It charged them.

Rodan grabbed Sara's hand, and they ran. Sara couldn't see where they were going, but she could hear the heavy, patted footsteps of the bear. Rodan turned and darted left with Sara's hand clenched in his.

Sara had never seen a bear before. She wasn't quite sure if she could count this one. Its fur was so black it blended with the darkness surrounding it. All she had seen was its eyes, and they didn't look like the eyes of a bear.

She tripped on a tree root. Instant pain shot up her leg.

Rodan still held her hand. "Are you alright?"

"My ankle."

Rodan helped her up, and Sara limped behind him through the trees. Rodan tried to keep pace with her. They no longer heard the stampeding feet of the bear. They slowed to a walk, which was a great relief to Sara as she limped along.

"I've never known a bear to react like that. My father and I used to travel these woods," Rodan said. "I've seen bears, but not like that one."

"Did you see his eyes?"

"What about them?"

Sara struggled to walk. "They weren't animal eyes. They looked like human eyes."

"It was too dark."

"I saw them. I thought at first it was a man."

As they walked deeper into the forest, Rodan stayed near Sara's side. Sara wanted to tell him she was fine, and that of all the things to worry about she should be at the bottom of the list, but she knew he would continue to worry about her just the same.

"Now what do we do?" Sara asked.

"Well, you were right. We can't leave them," Rodan said, "but I think I should go alone."

"What?"

"You won't get very far with a sprained ankle."

"I'll be fine. I don't think I sprained it. It only hurts a little," Sara said.

"Not only that. We can't take the sphere back. It's too great of a risk, and someone has to watch it."

"How can I defend the sphere if I'm not strong enough to rescue my friends?" She thought she was the strongest person he knew. Maybe she didn't understand the way he meant it.

"Don't be difficult." Rodan had never spoken to her that way before.

"Difficult?" Sara glared at him. "I'd hate to make any part of this easy."

Rodan's eyes hit the ground. "I'm sorry. Look, I'll walk with you deeper into the forest."

"I don't need an escort. I can manage."

"Sara . . ." Pain rose in his voice.

She tried her best not to be difficult. "Okay, but we have to move quickly. I don't want anything to happen to them."

They walked further into the woods before stopping.

"This should do," Rodan said.

Sara refrained from sitting to prove Rodan wrong.

Rodan took both her hands in his, being delicate because of the burns. "You'll be okay?"

Sara nodded. "Promise me you'll find them."

Rodan sucked in the air through his nose. "I promise." He pressed his lips together into a smile. He let go of her hands. "I'll be back as soon as I can."

Sara nodded, and Rodan turned to go.

"Wait, Rodan, one more thing."

"What?" He turned to her.

"Be careful."

"I'll try."

Sara could not see him go, but the sounds of his footsteps faded, and she knew he was gone.

She settled down against a tree and put the hood of her cloak over her head. She looked around. Few crystals graced the ground. She removed the necklace from beneath her cloak and clenched the raindrop gem.

Bolton was not far from her mind although she tried not to think of him. She wanted to believe it was all lies. She didn't want to believe the truth.

When she was a little girl, she used to think that her parents weren't dead, that they only left to protect her from the people who attacked their home. But as she grew older, she realized that was a fantasy.

She understood now that anything good she thought of Bolton was just a fantasy too.

Sara shook her fantasies away.

She heard movement through the trees and the sound of voices getting louder as they approached. Her heartbeat quickened and her breath was caught in her throat. She couldn't make out what they were saying, but she thought she heard "Water Elemental" and "checking downstream."

Eli's men were back. But the voices were many and of different pitches and tones.

Sara couldn't count the number of men in the group from the voices, but she guessed that the number was large. She wondered if Eli had discovered that the sphere was missing, and now he was on the hunt.

She wished they were near the center of the forest where the Old Tribe played to calm human hearts, but part of her doubted they could calm Eli's.

The footsteps grew louder. What would she do if they found her?

She removed the sphere from the pocket of her cloak. Maybe its energy could help her. She closed her eyes and tried to block out the voices.

She kept her emotions bottled to stop the sea from rising on Vella City, but now she let out all that disappointment and pain.

Heavy rain fell on the trees. It was so loud, she could hear it from miles away. Fading voices mingled with the sound. The voices became quieter and quieter until they dulled to nothing.

40

THE BROKEN PROMISE

FARAH felt the spray of the waterfall on her face. She picked up a small bottle from the ground. It was no bigger than her pinky finger. "Look. It's Aldo's ointment. Sara and Rodan must have dropped it."

"It's empty," Talon said.

"Sara's hands," Farah said. "Eli burnt them." Her eyes turned to Bolton.

He couldn't hold her gaze. A million thoughts raced through his mind of what he might say to them, but none of them sounded good enough. Now, he realized it didn't matter what he said.

Spire looked at him. "All of this is your fault!"

An unnatural gale threw Bolton to the ground. He tried to get up, but the wind pushed him back down again.

"You lied to us. It was your idea to gather the spheres, to

bring them to the tower. You led us straight into danger blind-folded."

With each remark, a gust of wind pushed Bolton closer to the edge of the cliff.

"Did you care? Did you for once think of someone other than yourself? You got us thrown in a dungeon, and what you did to Sara was heartless."

"That wasn't a lie," Bolton managed to say before the next sharp gust would have pushed him over the edge.

Spire narrowed her eyes.

"Spire, stop!" Farah stood between them.

Rodan emerged from among the trees.

"Rodan!" Farah ran up and hugged him. "Where's Sara?"

"She's waiting for me. I asked her to stay behind so I could come for you," he said. "Glad to see I didn't need to." He noticed Bolton lying on his back. "What is he doing here?"

"Rodan, no!" Farah pressed her hands against his chest. "He let us out."

Rodan glared at Bolton.

"Let's be civil for one minute," Farah said.

Rodan let out a sarcastic, breathy laugh. "There's nothing civil about leading your friends to the slaughter. What were you . . ." Rodan put his hand on his head and turned around.

"I'm sorry." Bolton got to his feet. "I didn't know what to do."

Rodan faced him. "You didn't know what to do?"

"Stop!" Farah shouted. "Let's get out of this clearing before he puts us back in those cages."

"Alright," Rodan agreed, and he looked at Bolton. "You're not coming."

AS the moon rose, the light found its way through the trees, Sara's head lulled against the tree trunk. Her heavy lids closed, and sleep started to pull her into a dream.

A twig snapped. She prepared herself.

Rodan stepped from among the trees.

Sara wanted to rush to him, but she stood on her sprained ankle clumsily.

When Talon, Spire, and Farah followed him out from the cover of darkness, her heart leapt. "You're okay? I didn't want to leave you."

"You did what you had to do." Talon settled down and laid the flat of his sword across his knees. "We'll go to Omega Ray—"

"Wait," Farah said. "We're not going to talk about this? About Bolton?"

"What is there to say?" Spire asked.

"He let us go," Farah said.

"He lied to us," Spire said. "He led us to Hephaestus without saying a word."

"No." Sara's voice was a whisper. "Bolton told me not to go, but I wouldn't listen."

"Why didn't you say something?" Spire asked.

"I couldn't. All I knew is that I didn't want to put any of you in danger. So . . . I went alone."

Orka chirped from a high branch among the leaves.

Bolton emerged from amongst the trees.

"You followed us?" Rodan hissed.

Bolton bowed his head.

Sara took a step toward him. "Bolton?"

"Can I explain?" He reached for her arm. The bandages around her hands were in tatters.

Rodan stepped in front of Sara. "What do you want?"

"To talk. That's all."

Sara could tell Rodan was battling in his mind. He couldn't believe it either. Bolton was a loyal dog that had turned into a wolf.

Rodan turned to her. "Sara . . . you can't."

"I can fight my own battles."

Rodan saw the determination in her eyes, the same determination she showed the night before they left Element. She wasn't his secret anymore.

Sara approached Bolton.

"I should have told you the truth long before this," Bolton said.

"You told me your most terrible secret."

"You don't know all of it." He reached for her hand.

When she drew away from him, his breath caught.

"I'm sorry," Bolton said. "I should have told you. Hephaestus is my uncle. He took me from my home when I was a boy."

"Was everything he said true?" she asked.

"No, I didn't get close to you because he asked me to. I didn't want to get close. But it happened."

"Are you sure that wasn't part of the plan?" she asked.

"Of course not." Bolton shook his head. "I didn't like lying to you."

"What did you . . . think of me before all this?"

"I didn't know you."

"But you were willing to have me killed?"

"He said no one had to get hurt if I followed his plan. He said that he wanted to meet you. But I knew that was a lie. I thought I could protect you."

"Like you did in the tower?"

"I wanted to," he said.

"Why didn't you?" Sara's voice calmed, and she looked at him as he struggled inside himself for the answer. "Why didn't you stand up to him and tell him you weren't his puppet anymore?"

"I'm afraid of him."

She had never heard truer words escape his lips. "What did he do to you?"

"He hated me," Bolton said. "He told me my mother abandoned me. He said I would be his apprentice. But once he saw I wasn't a Fire Elemental, like my mother, he turned on me. He kept me alive, although I think part of him wanted me dead. He used to burn me when he was angry.

"But . . . after I spent years under Hephaestus's shadow,

Talon got me out. He told me the truth about my parents, but I didn't believe him. I was afraid of my uncle, but I also had a great deal of respect for him. I trusted him and was slow to let go of what he had told me.

"When Talon took me to Element I felt out of place. No one had treated me with kindness in a long time. I was confused by it.

"Every night, I lie awake in my bed. I was exhausted all the time. I don't think I truly slept since I was taken from my mother. I saw the shadows when they took me and carried me into the forest. Eli's men. One had a red birthmark on his face. They gave me that medallion. They said that the weight of it would remind me of what I had to do. I had to find the last Water Elemental.

"As the years went by, I forgot my uncle. I felt normal. I had friends. Then you came. I found out about you before anyone else could, even Rodan. I sent you the notes and the key. I wanted you to have a taste of freedom so you would crave it. I didn't know you. I've never known anyone who made me feel needed in a good way. Once I got to know you, I told Fero plans had changed, but he threatened your life if I didn't obey. I thought I could convince you to leave this all behind. When that didn't work, I thought I could be brave and stand up to him."

Bolton bowed his head further. "I hate him because he used me to get to you."

Sara felt pity for him. "He burnt you." An ache rose in her chest. "Like Talon."

She looked up at him as he pulled the neck of his shirt down to the shoulder to reveal the discolored and uneven skin. He covered it up again.

"That's my worst one," he said.

Sara had the urge to look away.

"But that's in the past," Bolton said. "It's not an excuse."

"The glistenings. You wanted to go home."

"Yes." Bolton sighed. "I can't keep my promise to you."

"What promise?"

"That I would go with you to Omega Ray, that I would not leave your side."

"I can't have you at my side or at my back."

"I know."

Sara's eyes glistened.

The tears were coming, and she tried her best to hold them back. She didn't want him to leave. He thought that would make him happy, but it only made him sadder. He had forced her to hate him.

This goodbye was going to be forever.

41

PREPARED

BOLTON turned to Rodan. "I—"

"I think you've said enough," Rodan said. "I don't need you to say anything to me."

Rodan tried to erase the years from his mind as his once best friend disappeared among the trees. Rodan leaned against a tree and slumped to the ground.

Talon sat in the shadows. He didn't want to look up and see accusing eyes on him. He had given his fallen nephew a second chance. Was he wrong?

Farah sat with her elbows on her knees and her chin resting in her hands. Orka perched on her shoulder. Farah kept wondering if she should send the little, green bird with Bolton. Would Hephaestus's men would come looking for him after he had helped them? She didn't trust Bolton, but she still cared for him.

Sara had her back to them. She stared at the place where Bolton had stood.

Spire sat on a flat-topped crystal. "I should have seen it. He always gave me a bad feeling."

"We should get him back," Farah said.

"He's a snake!"

"He's my nephew," Talon said, "and he's never broken my trust until now. I believe he is trying to make amends for it."

"Don't forget, Spire said, "he is Hephaestus's nephew too, and I think his loyalty lies with him, not you."

"I have no doubt. He was raised by Eli for seven years. He was tortured, ridiculed, and hated. That usually does a lot to someone, but I don't think he follows Eli anymore."

"You don't *think*. It's all well and good that you can think that he's reformed, but I can't trust him."

"Stop it!" Farah said. "Doesn't it come down to whether Sara believes in him? This is her fight. Everybody keeps telling her how important she is in this whole thing. Shouldn't she get to choose her army? How could she forgive him, in front of you?"

They all became quiet.

Spire shook her head. She wasn't finished tearing Bolton apart, but she settled for the rips she did get.

"This journey," Spire began, breaking the silence. "So much time has been spent, wasted. People have died. Deaths that could have been avoided if we had never gotten involved. Was it all worth it?"

"Of course, it was," Rodan said, "Caleena still stands because of us, and many other villages and cities will remain standing once we defeat him. Many people have died, but many others will live."

"It seems an unfair trade."

Sara's shoulders rose and fell.

Spire stood and placed her hands on Sara's shoulders.

Sara's voice came out in a whisper only Spire could hear. "I thought I had something to fight for. Maybe the only true freedom is in death."

"Come on." Spire led Sara to the flat-headed crystal, and Sara sat. The crystal had lost all light.

"Eli won't stop," Talon said. "If we don't do something, he will enslave and kill thousands more."

"But," Spire said, "look what we have done. We haven't helped anyone. We played right into Hephaestus's hands. We gave him what he wanted. Now all the element spheres belong to him."

"No," Rodan said. "We have the Water Sphere."

"What?"

"Orka dropped the sphere down to us when we were on the cliff."

Orka chirped, drawing all eyes to Farah. "I knew it was a good idea," Farah said.

"But he counted them. I saw him count them," Spire said.

"I switched it."

"With what?"

"Remember the Element Games? When Orka took the prize orb? Before we got to the tower, I switched the Water Sphere for the jewel orb and gave the sphere to Orka."

"How did you know to do that?"

"I had a bad feeling about Bolton," Farah said. He was acting strangely before we left. He tried to take the spheres, and when I questioned him about it, he said all Hephaestus wanted was the spheres."

"You should have said something," Talon said.

"What was I supposed to say? You trusted him. I thought you would defend him like you did when Aldo tried to tell us about him in the first place," Farah said. "I thought it was the best way. If nothing bad would have happened, I could have whistled, and Orka would have come with the sphere. I wanted to play it safe."

Rodan looked at Sara. Her head hung so low it seemed as if she had fallen asleep where she sat. Rodan knelt next to her. "Sara?"

"Bolton's gone."

"I know."

Sara looked up. She shook her head.

"She's in shock," Spire said.

"I'm fine." Her voice sounded unsure. She stood. Pain shot up her leg, but she tried not to flinch.

"Maybe you should sit," Rodan said.

"No," Sara said. "I have to go. I have to fight."

"Rest, first," Spire said.

"No!" Sara said.

The crystals glowed, and the tree shifted.

"Perhaps, she's right," Talon said. "If we go now, it'll be a surprise attack."

"We should wait," Spire said. "We can't. Not with Sara in this state."

"I'm not in a state," Sara said, but she hardly believed that herself.

"You're not clear-headed. You won't be able to use your element," Spire said.

Sara lifted the water from their canteens, causing the canteens to rise into the air. She allowed them to drop to the ground. "My element is fine."

"I should remind you," Talon began.

Sara turned to him.

"Omega Ray is devoid of a water source . . . at least, not one that isn't far beneath the ice. I hope that won't be a problem.

Sara was not sure if she could call Water, if she would be able to summon the power as she had with Bolton. But her emotions would drive it from her. Controlling her power would be another matter.

"I will call Water," she said. "I can do this."

42

MOTHER

ELI slumped on his stone throne and thrummed his fingers against the side of his chin.

The room was dim, and the ashy air floated in through the cracks in the old building. The thundering sound of the door signaled the entrance of Fero.

Fero approached and bowed to Eli.

"Has the Water Elemental been found?" Eli asked.

"I am sorry, sir, but no. I have men patrolling the forest, but no sign of her yet," Fero said. "I came across something more pressing on the way. That's why I have returned."

Eli left his seat and stood over Fero. "I decide what is most pressing. Finding the Water Elemental is of paramount concern to me. She has the Water Sphere, and I need it."

Fero, unflinching, stared into the eyes of his master. "Lightning Elementals from Wyvek are headed this way. The lookout saw them marching through Jetty Verte. I think they've come for war."

"A few Lightning Elementals are nothing. We'll execute them quickly."

"But that's not all," Fero said. "The Wind Elementals of Breeze claim we have Tag's daughter. That means we have breached the treaty, and they wish to settle it."

"Well, we do have his daughter. She is that little nothing of a girl we imprisoned in the dungeons. She reminded me a lot of her father: small, but forceful and quick to jump to conclusions, and foolish as well. They'll be no problem either, but at least they are trying." Eli laughed.

"Should I rally the guards and have the soldiers prepared for battle?"

"What for?"

"What if they come all at once? We'd certainly have a problem on our hands, sir."

"Fine, Fero, but tell the men to take lots of interesting prisoners. Perhaps," Eli said, calling a flame to burn on the tip of his finger, "we can make them more interesting "

His leader's reaction puzzled Fero. *Does he want to lose this battle?* Eli had always been unstable, but never suicidal. He wondered if his leader had gone truly mad.

Perditus entered the throne room.

"Where have you been?"

"You told me to leave your sight, father."

Eli cringed at the word.

"I went to find mother. She told me I was a *poor* boy."

"I never told you that you could see her."

Perditus stepped closer. "Well, I did. She's an old beggar with a hobbled leg. She hadn't bathed. She hadn't eaten in days. And she called me *poor* boy.

"You abandoned her." He stepped in front of Eli. "You tried to replace me. You took another son. But he wasn't good enough either, was he? He betrayed you. Yet, if he came back to the fold, you would accept him with open arms like last time. Oh, sure, he gets his share of father's punishment. Yet, he is praised like he is something more than he is. He had an important task to fulfill, while my only task is to scurry like a rat through this castle and wait to get my tail burnt."

Eli's expression changed from indifference to disdain. "At least you know your place, Perditus. You are my son, and, yes, I never loved your mother. I used her to block someone else from my heart. It didn't work, so I tossed your mother aside. I hoped you could be my soldier, but you are weak. You could never be of any use to me. So, you can go now. For good."

"I know why, father," Perditus said with a smug smile on his face. "You think I'm worthless and dim, but I listen. Sicilia, she was one of *them*, a Water Elemental, right? You want to kill everything that reminds you of what you can no longer have."

Eli glared at him. Perditus's leg burned from the inside. He could feel the searing in the marrow of his bones. His eyes glazed over, and he wailed. Eli stared at him until the pain forced him to kneel.

43

FROM THE FOREST

BOLTON pushed the leaves aside. The lake sparkled by the light of the crystals. He sat by the water's edge. The canopy covered any chance of sunlight and brought eternal night to the forest.

He ran his fingers through the cool water. It was strange. The feeling was different, but still he recalled the strands of Sara's hair through his fingers.

He questioned whether he should go back and try to convince Sara he was worth trusting again. *But he would use me to hurt them*, he thought. *He would find a way to do it.* The world was against him and, at the same time, crumbling right in front of him, and there was nothing he could do.

Like father, like son.

"I'm a coward," he said. "Talon should never have trusted me."

Feet unsettled the ground. The movement through the trees grew louder.

Bolton turned around.

Three of Eli's men walked into the clearing. They must have heard his cry and came to silence it.

Bolton stood. He hadn't eaten. He was tired. But something surged inside him when he saw those men.

One laughed. "Where is she?"

Bolton glared at them. He didn't know what he was in for—Fire, Wind, or Earth. But he knew neither one was a Lightning Elemental.

"You have your money. What are you still doing here? Shouldn't you be on some imaginary boat set for seas unknown?"

They laughed.

The man in front approached him. Costa, if he remembered his name right, but he wasn't sure.

"I saw that look in your eye," Costa said. "You wanted to save the Water Elemental. Been away for too long. And you know where she is, don't you?"

"I'm on my way out," Bolton said. "Why would you think she would have anything to do with me?"

"Well, you see we've been walking for hours. No sign of her. But I have a feeling that even after your betrayal, she'll still come running if she hears you scream."

The other two approached.

Bolton grabbed Costa's shoulder and pushed him into the lake.

Zap!

Lightning came from above and hit the head of one of the men. He slumped to the ground never to rise again.

Bolton's back erupted in a searing burn like he had laid on hot coals. And he did scream then. Costa waded through the water toward him. The remaining man charged him, and the burnt skin of Bolton's back hit the ground. Pain spread.

The man was on top of him. He punched Bolton in the

face while he was still dazed from the pain. Bolton rolled with the man. He was able to loosen himself from his hold. He kicked the man in the chest.

Splash!

He landed next to Costa.

Bolton scrambled away from the edge. Fear gripped him. He didn't want to be burned again.

Energy swept through the lake, lighting up the water in flashes of singing voltage. The men spasmed in the water until their bodies slumped.

Bolton was breathing heavy. He cringed. His back felt like one big sore, and it was still burning.

After the lake went dark, Bolton crawled into the water. He sighed as the coolness soothed his burns.

He looked up over the water's edge.

Ghostly figures stood in the lake. They pulled something from the men. It was transparent, but in that moment, Bolton could see it.

Two figures stood in front of Bolton. Two ghostly monsters. A lizard and a rat too big to be real.

"Talon wasn't the only one who trusted you, but the time for regret is over. You need to return to your friends."

"Who are you?" Bolton tried to see them through blurred eyes. "You don't understand. They're better off without me."

"You need to get up."

"What am I supposed to do?" Bolton laughed, but soon the laughter turned back to frustration.

He looked up at the two strange creatures before him.

An Aether appeared and floated to Bolton's side. Bolton didn't understand. What could he do? But he thought of his father. He could see him swimming away, leaving him and his mother. *I can't do the same*, he thought. *I won't be like him.*

Bolton stood in the water. The pain urged him to sink back down, but he didn't. Water saturated his heavy clothes, pulling him, and yet he stood. "But how—"

From the mist came many animals, carrying instruments.

And from their midst walked a creature taller and greater than any of them. An owl, taller than the trees themselves stood before him. The owl carried a harp.

Bolton tilted his head to the great bird.

"You have been lost," Founten said, "but you are not the only one. Not even the music of this forest can calm the heart of Eli the Fire Elemental. Only one thing can still his tortured soul."

"What is that?" Bolton asked.

Founten pointed to the Aether. "It will give the answer. You must lead it to the Water Elemental. It will give her strength. This will be but the first of her battles. She will weaken him, but not in a way she will expect."

"I don't understand."

"You may never, but that is not what's important."

Bolton blinked, and they were gone. He stared at the Aether. It glowed with an unnatural light.

44

THE BROKEN TREATY

THE ash in the air receded across the burnt plain. An unknown wind pushed it away. The heavy smell retreated.

The army of Wind Elementals waited outside the ruined, stone castle as the dark clouds loomed. They were armed not only with their elements, but with weapons of steel.

The Wind Elementals of Breeze set up camp in the mountains surrounding Omega Ray. The city below them was crumbling and empty of soldiers. Workers repaired the stone wall that served as the city's only remaining protection.

"Hephaestus, you will release my daughter!" Tag stood in front of Eli's throne. Several of his men surrounded him, including his son, Shift.

Shift had his spear ready.

Eli's only guard was Fero. Hephaestus's men were scattered across the many regions of Mirmina.

Fero didn't know why his leader was being so careless. He had sent for the men, knowing of the battle that would surely come while Eli lounged on his throne and ignored the threat to his kingdom.

"What makes you think I have her?"

"She was traveling this way," Tag said.

"Now why would she be traveling to my city? Was she looking for trouble?"

"That's none of your business!" Shift shouted.

"Shift, please," Tag hissed. He turned to Eli. "By capturing my daughter, you have broken the treaty."

"Are you sure she wasn't coming to break the treaty herself with a foolish attempt to kill me?" Eli said.

"The people of Breeze do not wish to make an attempt on your life, and I'm sure that was not my daughter's intent either," he said. "Where is she?"

"She's locked up at the moment."

Shift took a threatening step forward, but Tag stopped him.

"Save it," Tag said. "I honor my treaties, and I don't stab my enemies in the back, no matter how vile they may be, so this is a warning. The treaty is broken. Release my daughter or the battle begins at sunrise."

Eli watched with unfeeling eyes as the Wind Elementals left his stone castle. He slumped further into his throne, saying nothing.

"Sir, your army is spread to the far reaches of Mirmina," Fero said. "I can't be sure our men will make it back before dawn to ready themselves for battle. Perhaps you should negotiate for more time."

Eli stared into the distance.

"Sir?"

"I want to see her."

"Who?"

"The Water Elemental."

45

PAIN

BOLTON traveled through Jetty Verte and the snow of Regret Mountain. He had not met Sara and the others yet. He kept the Aether at his side.

He knew a shortcut to Omega Ray through a cave near the mountain's peak. Perhaps if he could not catch up with them on the path, he could scope out the area instead and give them the details when they arrived.

"Not far now." Bolton spoke to the Aether. "It's through this cave."

Bolton sparked Lightning. The cave was musky like someone had died inside.

The cave was the home of a Maledixit, a hairy giant who did not like intruders. One bite or scratch from the Maledixit would turn a man into a beast, afflict him with leprosy, and turn him into an eater of human flesh.

Bolton knew it would be dangerous travel through the cave. He would have to be careful not to encounter the monster.

Once Bolton had turned the first bend, he could see the light from the cave's exit. The ash of Omega Ray blocked out the sun, but the light was brighter than the darkness of the cave.

When he saw the glow, Bolton hurried toward it without being quiet or careful. He tripped over a jagged piece of rock, and when he hit the hard ground, he let out a loud curse. The Lightning he had called went out, and darkness surrounded him.

As Bolton lay on the rocky ground, the pebbles on the floor rattled. The ground vibrated under his body. Heavy feet echoed through the cave, followed by a deep roar.

Bolton scrambled to his feet and sparked Lightning. He scanned the darkness on all sides. From the glow of the Lightning, he did not see the dark cave abyss. Taking up his field of vision was a wall of thick matted fur. It shook as the Maledixit issued forth another roar.

Bolton stopped breathing and stood still. But when the beast growled again, Bolton was shot back into realization. He backed away.

The Maledixit had thick, bear-like claws, and hair covered its body. It had a face like a man's, and its physique was the shape of a man's, but it was over seven feet tall and smelled like the dead.

Bolton turned to run, but he tripped again. He turned over on his back as the beast approached, snarling and growling. He was conscious of the searing pain running up his back from the burn.

In his fear, Bolton had let the lightning bolt fade out, so that he was in blackness again. His thoughts were at a standstill. He shook the fear. He had to find a way out.

From out in the darkness, came a deep, sinister laughter. The Maledixit wailed in pain. Bolton gained the strength to summon another bolt to see what was happening.

The creature was being sucked into a black, oozing muck, and laughter came from the very blackness pulling him in. The Aether glowed with an unnatural light as the muck sucked the Maledixit into the ground.

The Aether was using the Dark Element, one of the lost elements. The element had disappeared long before Bolton was born. Some believed that it was nothingness, devoid of life.

The Maledixit clawed the cave floor and tried not to be sucked into the darkness, but the nothingness was stronger than the monster. The darkness, like black bile, consumed it.

Once the Maledixit had been sucked into the gloom, Bolton tried to get back up. He stared at the ground where the darkness remained. It was darker than the cave itself. Bolton stayed far away from it and stumbled toward the light at the exit of the cave. He came out into the light and took a deep breath.

He stood on a high ledge at the mouth of the cave, over looking the city of Omega Ray. He looked down at the streets between the ancient, ruined buildings. He saw no soldiers preparing for battle, in fact the streets appeared empty.

"Good. We'll have the element of surprise." He grinned.

He turned to make sure that the Aether had made it out of the cave, but it was gone. Bolton called for it, not knowing if it had the ability to hear. "Aether?"

"Aether," he called into the cave, but he didn't dare to go in again.

Bolton sighed and leaned against the side of the mountain in defeat.

"So, the prodigal son returns," a familiar voice said.

Fero stood at the foot of the ledge. He blocked Bolton's entrance to the slope along the mountain. Bolton had no way out but a piteous fall from the ledge or a journey back into the cave.

"Welcome back."

As Fero stood dangerously near the edge, Bolton wanted nothing more than to push him over, but he knew he lacked the strength to challenge Fero alone.

He knew where Fero would take him, and it would not be pleasant. He had been there before when he was younger. It was the place where he had gotten his scars.

Yet, Bolton did not need to be dragged into Eli's stone castle. He strode in front of Fero. He felt he deserved whatever happened to him now, not for the reasons Eli thought he did, but because he betrayed his friends. He was afraid, but he wanted to face him. He didn't want to be like his father.

Eli stood at the end of the marble hallway. Bolton approached him with pretended confidence, but as soon as he met Eli's eyes, he stopped.

Eli tried to look at him with indifference, like he was an annoying maggot rather than a threat, but a deep seeded hatred flared in his eyes, not only for Bolton but for his father and his father's father. The hatred spilled over not for what he had done, but for who he was and where he had come from.

"You know where to take him," Eli said.

Bolton summoned the courage to speak. "No. You killed my mother. You won't kill my friends. You're as much of a monster as that thing in the cave."

Fero and another man grabbed a hold of Bolton. He struggled out of their grasp and sent a bolt of lightning toward Eli. Fero brought his elbow down hard on Bolton's back. The pain caused him to lose focus on the bolt of lightning, and it disappeared before it met its mark.

Fero kicked Bolton while he was down, trying to exhaust his energy. Once Bolton lay motionless on the stone floor, Fero picked him up and dragged him down the cold stone stairs and to an underground room.

The room was bare except for a set of iron shackles hanging from chains high on the wall. No devices of torture were present. The room looked more like a prison cell than a torture chamber, but Bolton knew better.

The second man removed Bolton's shirt and his bandages from the attack in D'arkadia. The gashes had not yet healed. They made him stand on an old battered stool as they chained his wrists to the wall. Fero kicked the stool from under him, and Bolton cringed as the shackles yanked at his wrists.

"I warned you," Fero said. "No one had to get hurt as long as you did what you were told. You helped them escape, didn't you? How long did you think it would take us to find out? And what happened after you helped them? They threw you away like a piece of rotted meat."

Bolton did not respond to Fero's taunting, instead he kept his eyes narrowed.

"You seem angry. Well, in a way, you're lucky. The mind usually forgets pain."

Bolton snarled. He remembered all the pain he had suffered in that room and out of it.

Eli came in, his face pale like stone, but threatening. "You're trying to have me killed aren't you, Bolton?"

"Yes," Bolton said.

"Though you are a Lightning Elemental, like your worthless father, I thought you could still be of use to me," Eli said. "You failed to prove that."

"So, I die today," Bolton said.

"Your crime is far too great for a mere death sentence," Eli said. "I'm going to let you live with what I'm going to do to you. I'll have Fero scar your face like he did my brother's."

Bolton lashed out in vain at Eli's words. The chains held fast.

"Don't worry. I won't damage you too badly. I want you to be alive enough to witness the death of your friends."

The skin of Bolton's chest reddened. In thin layers, it peeled back and smoked. He screamed. It was ten times as painful as he remembered.

Another white-hot burn crept along his jawline and more scorched his arms and shoulders. The burns dripped blood as he screamed.

The minutes crept by as the torture continued. When it ended, Bolton was light-headed, and the throbbing pain still remained. His breathing was heavy, and his ears pounded as the room shifted before his eyes.

Eli spoke to him. "I wanted to remind you of this, of how it feels. This will happen to all of them, but I promise you, the Water Elemental will be the last. I want to savor her pain."

46

HER ARMY

THE air was frigid, but the snow wasn't too deep. The rocky ground was visible through the flaky, white ice. The pathway twisted up the mountain with steep slopes and treacherous curves.

As they traveled, Spire remembered past mistakes. She never went back for Decca. She had loved him, but love was not as important as duty. Her duty had been to keep the sphere safe, and Element had praised her for following her duty. She had regretted not following her heart. She watched Sara as they made their way up the mountain.

Spire had first thought her journey and Sara's were the same. Now, she knew that Sara's journey was different. Sara was following her heart.

They walked in silence for hours.

"Sara, I was wrong," Spire said. "Maybe not about Bolton,

but it wasn't my choice to make. I was angry. Fear is a strong emotion. I remember the battle on this mountain and how I had to protect the sphere, how I never got up to help my friends. I said it was my responsibility. It still hurt, but what hurts worse is that duty was the last thing on my mind. I was afraid. I traded Decca's life for mine. I should have been more understanding."

"You were trying to protect me," Sara said. "I made my own choice."

"Look, tracks!" Farah shouted.

Thin, long, narrow tracks ran through the snow. The tracks had deep ridges in them.

"A machine made these tracks," Talon said.

Rodan ran ahead of them. "I don't believe it," he said.

"What?'

They rushed up the slope. In a cluster of snow were hundreds of IMTs.

"It's Solace's design," Rodan said.

"He gave the plans to Wyvek," Talon said.

"Orka," Farah said, "fly above the mountain and tell us their position."

The green bird left Farah's shoulder on its new mission.

The wind was biting as they continued their journey past the abandoned machines.

Sara wrapped her cloak around her. The wind battered her face as she looked toward the mountain's peak. This journey began as a quest for her own freedom. A concept she could latch onto easily. It was to want something for herself. But she didn't feel like she was fighting for herself anymore.

Freedom was necessary for happiness, but it wasn't enough.

As the wind died down, Orka flew back and reported what she had seen in a series of chirps and whistles. Farah read the pattern of her chirps.

"They're not too far from us now," Farah said.

She took off through the snow. Sara, Spire, Rodan and

Talon followed.

As they turned the next bend, Farah was talking to a Lightning Elemental of Wyvek. Sara and the others were still breathless from the run.

"These are my friends: Sara, Talon, Spire, and Rodan, oh, and this is Orka." She touched the small, green bird on her shoulder.

"Pleasure to meet you." The man was dressed in a silvery cloth.

"So, you're the Water Elemental." He turned to Sara. "I'm Waviel. We would like to join you in battle. Omega Ray is beyond this pass. With your leave, we shall continue."

"Have you been looking for me?"

Waviel nodded. "We have. We thought you had gone by boat from Caleena. We wanted to follow you, but the cliffs of Wyvek are too high above the sea. We needed to journey further, but we didn't want word to get out that we were marching on Omega Ray. So, we decided not to travel from Lumina Port. Our army would have been spotted immediately."

The Lightning Elementals all wore the same silvery cloth. The hundreds of men and women looked to Sara.

Sara could not believe her journey had banded so many people together. She had given them hope. Now she would fight with them on the same battlefield. Hephaestus would have to fall.

This . . . this is what I'm fighting for.

Hephaestus was an oppressor. He hurt people. That's what they wanted to stop. They were dedicated and strong. They were right.

Sara had lost focus. It wasn't ever about her. None of it. This was about the people of Mirmina. It wasn't only her freedom she was fighting for. It was theirs.

Sara took one final look at her army. They were eager. They were ready. She was their beacon. Her voice rose over the crowd. "You have my leave."

47

THE BROKEN SON

THE men left Bolton hanging from the wall. The shackles made his wrists bleed, and his body was caked in blood. He was numb apart from a dull throbbing in his head.

A stranger entered the room. He carried a basin of water and towels, and the most gracious item in his possession: a key.

The man's eyes were kind, the frown did not fit naturally on his face, but it seemed to have been forcibly set for many years. He was very tall and powerfully built, but even the strong could be easily enslaved by Hephaestus.

He unlocked Bolton's shackles and caught him before he fell to the ground. He rested Bolton against the wall by the basin and cleaned his wounds. "They did a number on you. I could hear the screams from across the city."

Bolton tried to focus and stop his head from spinning.

"Do you work for him?"

"Not by choice. I rebel and accept the consequences. I've been burned and beaten, but I've never looked as bad as you do now, my friend. I'll get myself into a lot of trouble helping you."

The stranger helped Bolton to the floor beside the basin of water. "How did you get here?"

"You could say that my friends and I sought to kill him," Bolton said.

"That's a brave undertaking, my friend."

He touched the raw wound on Bolton's shoulder with the cool rag, and Bolton flinched.

"Not that brave," Bolton said. "I betrayed them. I deserved this."

"Were they killed?"

"No, they're still fighting."

"Well, it's a good thing I'm helping so you can join them and make amends, yeah?"

"Thanks."

"What's your name anyway?"

"It's Bolton, and yours?"

"Decca."

"Decca? *The* Decca?" Bolton recalled Spire's story.

"The? You're head still spinning, man?"

"No." Bolton tried to sit up taller. He cringed against the pain. "She thinks you're dead. Spire . . ."

"How do you know her?" Awe was written on Decca's face. He hadn't heard her name aside from in dreams.

"Element . . . she's a trainer now. We were going to fight him."

"Spire's coming here?"

Bolton nodded.

"I tried to go back to her, but this place is impossible to escape," Decca said. "The walls may be crumbling, but they guard them well."

"The battle should offer enough distraction," Bolton said.

"We have to make it to the surface."

"Right. They know me, the soldiers. They've become used to me. Maybe I should go ahead."

"Okay." Bolton hugged the wall. He was still light-headed from the pain. He stood at a crossroads between two hallways. One Decca journeyed down. The other was in darkness.

A figure stood in the darkness. "Hello, Bolton."

Bolton thought he recognized the voice. "Perditus?"

"Yes, your brother or should I say cousin? I remember when father brought you here. You were a sniveling, little boy, but he loved you because you were stronger than me."

He remembered Perditus, his older cousin. When he recalled him as a child, he always thought that was with hate looked like.

"What are you doing down here?"

Perditus limped out of the darkness. He dragged his leg after him. "I wanted a reunion. I wanted it to be a bit bigger than this. I wanted father and mother to be here, but father won't let me invite mother. Besides she couldn't hobble all the way here anyway, could she?"

"What are you talking about?"

"My mother, the beggar. You haven't met her? My father tore me from her arms just as he ripped you from the arms of your dear mother."

Bolton looked down at Perditus's lame leg. "Look, this isn't a good time."

"You're trying to prove yourself to father?"

"No."

"Well, father would be ashamed." Perditus pulled out a knife.

"What are you doing?"

"What he would want me to do, or, perhaps, the opposite? He doesn't talk to me."

"Perditus, put the knife down."

"Why?"

"I don't want to—"

"You won't kill me. You're the weak one now." Perditus lunged at him with the knife.

Bolton sent a bolt. It hit Perditus in the chest. Perditus fell to the ground. His body twitched.

"No!" Bolton knelt beside him.

"What happened?" Decca returned. He looked from Bolton to the body of Perditus lying beside him.

"I didn't mean to." Bolton shook his head.

Decca grabbed his arm and helped him onto his feet. "Come on. We can take them."

Decca led Bolton through the underground of the stone castle where, years ago, he had loosened the stones of the worn wall. Decca removed enough of the stones so he and Bolton could make it through.

Out in the cold air, Eli's army was coming together, marching through the mountain pass to the north. Hundreds of men flooded into the city.

48

WATER AND FIRE

SARA and her friends traveled with the Lightning Elementals of Wyvek to Hephaestus's city. The IMTs could not make it through the mountain pass.

"Solace should have made those things narrower," Farah said. "He could take a few lessons from Thatch."

"I hope Thatch is okay," Sara said.

"I hope your father didn't murder him," Rodan said.

"It's likely." Farah walked through the snow.

Waviel handed them each a shirt made of the same material as the clothes he wore. "It will protect you from the fire," Waviel said. The silvery cloth was made of carbon fiber, and it was resistant to the flames.

The city was dark. The scent of smoke prevailed. The city was in ruins, the only building that was whole was the one in the center, Eli's castle. The castle stood awkwardly among the rubble, out of place and time. The stones that made up the building's walls were hauled from the cliff, and the clay roof was melted into place.

Omega Ray was built on the ledge of Regret Mountain, and no water rested in or around the city. A chasm lay at the edge of the cliff, an empty void.

"You were right, Talon," Sara said. "This will be difficult." She clenched the canteen.

"Don't doubt yourself," Talon said. "You can call it."

They stood on a stony slope where they could survey the city.

"We should all stay at the entrance." Waviel pointed. "On that wide expanse of land. We should not separate, we are stronger together."

"Look," Farah said. "I think someone's beaten us to the post." She didn't get a good look at them before she turned to Waviel.

An army of people gathered toward the city. They wore gray jumpsuits. Some stood at attention, while others greased the joints of three massive machines.

"Farah," Spire said. "I think you know them."

"Isn't that your father up front?" Rodan asked.

Farah recognized the bald man in the jumpsuit leading the army. "Dad. I hope they're not here because of me."

"Who else?" Spire asked.

Tag shouted commands across the large expanse. "You, to the front! You, left, left! Straight lines, we're not a bunch of savages! No, no, not like that! For goodness sake, regroup! Alright men, it's time to get my little girl back."

"Well," Farah said, "he's certainly not going for a surprise attack."

The sun was a white scar in the sky. The dark gray clouds streaked across it.

The street filled with light. Flames moved through the alleyways and streets.

"We'd better get up there," Talon said.

Sara led her army up the slope. They gathered on the higher ground overlooking the city as the flames rushed in.

"Push them back!" Tag screamed.

The Wind caused many of Eli's soldiers to fall to the ground and extinguish their flames. The Lightning Elementals of Wyvek struck several men down.

As they fought, flames flew into the crowd. People were burnt, some so badly they fell unconscious. The Wind Elementals of Breeze pushed against the Wind Elementals in Hephaestus's army, traitors after the Great Raid.

"Take the roof off his stone castle!" Tag shouted.

"You heard him. Let's go." Farah positioned herself between the two allying armies.

"Farah?" Tag looked over at his daughter.

"Dad!" She reached out to hug him.

They embraced. Tag pulled away from her. "You scared me to death, girl. All of this because you decided to go against my orders. You've got nerve."

"We need to help, Dad. We're all here, so let's do this."

"Right." Her father turned to the stone castle. "The truce is broken."

With the help of the Wind Elementals of Breeze, Farah and Spire concentrated on the air around the clay roof of the stone castle. They could feel the pressure of the wind beneath the roof, lifting it from the four walls.

"Push!" Spire used her memories of Decca to fuel the force of her element.

The roof peeled back from the stone walls, crumbling as it lifted from its base. Fragments of the roof fell into Eli's cold throne room and upon the dusty bed, breaking the legs, and sending dust and debris gusting out as thick as the smoke.

Fire Elementals approached. They threw balls of flames at the attackers. In the distance was Dirge, his face gashed and wrapped in bloody bandages.

Flames landed in the crowd, unable to be stopped. Several in Sara's company went down, being burnt by the flames. Their forces were weakening. The Wind was no longer keeping Eli's men back.

"Sara, you must call Water," Spire said.

"I'm trying." Sara's eyes were closed. She tried to remove herself from this place. It was the only way she would be able to concentrate.

Sara focused, but it would not come to her, and the enemy was getting closer.

A Fire Elemental sent flames her way. Sara was so focused that she hadn't noticed, and everyone else was so immersed in the fight that they were oblivious too.

Only one perceived the danger. Strong hands pushed her out of the way and caught her moments before the flames hit.

Surprise ran through her as she fell, but arms stopped her descent. Opening her eyes, Sara looked up at a familiar face. "Bolton, you came back."

"With help."

Decca stood behind Bolton, and when he saw Spire, his eyes lit.

Spire felt an emptiness inside her recede. "Decca."

He grabbed her wrist and pulled her into his arms.

"What have they done to you?" Sara asked Bolton.

Blood dripped from the raw, open wound running along his jawline and down his neck.

"I'll be fine," he assured her. He looked over at Rodan.

Rodan grimaced. Bolton looked back to Sara.

"Bolton," Rodan said as he looked toward the battle. He walked down to where Bolton stood. Bolton turned around to meet him as Rodan held out his hand. He stared at the hand for a moment, and he took it.

Rodan knelt to the floor, put his hands on the ground, and concentrated. The ground erupted and was swept over with sand. The sand replaced the thin layer of snow in front of them. He looked up at Bolton. "You know what to do."

Bolton sent Lightning down to strike the sand, forming glass beneath the surface. Rodan concentrated on the grainy glass and lifted it from the sand. The glass broke in the air, and he sent the shards shooting toward Hephaestus's army. The glass embedded into the faces of two men, stunning one and forcing the other to kneel in pain, holding his bleeding face in his hands.

Rodan looked at Bolton. He couldn't reconcile the man before him and the traitor he knew he was. It didn't matter anymore.

"Sara," Talon said, "we need Water. You can do this. You called the rain to save your parents. We all believe in you. Shape your destiny, and believe in yourself."

A Fire Elemental who had exhausted his element grabbed Bolton and rained a sea of punches upon the fallen hero.

"Bolton!"

Bolton drew his arm back and punched the man in the face. "Sara, don't worry about me! Do what you have to. You can do this. I know you can."

Sara focused and summoned the strength. Her thoughts flowed back to the Crystal Forest, back to the lake outside Element, back to her parents' cottage. She never wanted to forget.

A wall of water formed in front of them. It crossed the entire expanse from one side of the valley to the other. It wavered between the two armies. It flexed and reflected the light of the fire.

Bolton was on the other side of the wall with the enemy.

"Bolton, cross the water!" Spire shouted.

Sara's eyes remained closed as she held up the wall.

Bolton pushed away from the Fire Elemental and through the watery wall. Holding his breath, he felt like he was swimming through a forceful stream, but he wasn't swimming away like his father. He wasn't like him.

They all went silent as the wall towered over them. Both armies were in awe.

A deep roar sounded as the top of the wall bent forward onto the enemy's side. They ran, but as the wall came crashing down, they had no time to escape.

The water flooded the alleyways and streets of Omega Ray and rushed down the ledge, bringing with it many of Eli's followers.

Sara opened her eyes. Nearly the entire city was swept clear. Three feet of water filled the city streets as it made its gentle roll down the eastern cliff. A roar of cheer went through the crowd.

But a line of fire drew a boundary between them and the city. Some of Eli's soldiers had made it through the wave and were regrouping.

"We have to find Eli," Sara said.

Talon nodded.

Sara, Talon, and Bolton approached Eli's castle, but two soldiers blocked their path. One brandished a rotted piece of wood. They had exhausted their elements.

Talon set the tip of the wood on fire. The man grinned. Now, he thought his weapon was worth something. But the fire spread down the wooden stick and burned his hands. He jumped out of the way to tend to his scorched fingers.

Talon threw Fire at the second man, but he dodged it. He screamed as large talons bit into his shoulders. Thermal tossed his body out of the way.

"Thought you could use some help," Thatch said.

He sat on the back of Thermal. The dome the bird carried was gone. Thatch took off on Thermal's back. Thermal picked off a few more of Eli's followers. He launched them over the cliff as their screams echoed through the city.

Waviel and the other Lightning Elementals of Wyvek continued the fight. Their flame-resistant armor helped them to stay in the battle where others had fallen.

But the Wind Elementals of Breeze kept pace.

"Fire!" Tag shouted after the soldiers of Breeze had loaded their machine with scrap metal. The machine propelled the pieces of metal into the crowd. The sharp metal bit into the bodies of the men in Eli's army, forcing them to halt their advance.

Spire and Farah fought together, sending Wind to tear through the remaining enemy forces.

"Well, isn't it our brave little warriors from Lumina?" Sandel and his small militia approached them.

"You're a bunch of traitors," Farah said.

Sandel and the others negated Spire and Farah's powers, but Decca, wielding a heavy stone from Eli's broken wall, swung the stone across Sandel's face.

49

INTO THE SHADOWS

ELI went down to the dungeons to find Bolton. His men were fighting, and he didn't want Bolton to miss when his friends' bodies slumped to the ground.

The guards at the door had been beaten. Their faces were bruised and their noses bloodied.

"Wake up, you drunkards!"

The men came to and followed Eli into the dungeons. "My lord!"

"I don't want to hear your sniveling excuses . . ." He stopped.

Perditus's body rested on the floor. His hands had been placed across his chest.

Eli knelt beside his son. His face held a frozen look of horror.

Pressure filled the walls of Eli's chest. He waited as the

pressure built, anticipating the explosion. But the explosion never came. Instead the pressure left, leaving him with an unfilled emptiness that grew in the depths of his body in a region he could never reach.

He stared at Perditus, confused that the fool would take chances Eli had never expected he would take. Confused because he had grown and degenerated in ways Eli never anticipated.

The pressure built again, this time behind his eyes, causing his face to tense up. Little hands reached out to him, as he was torn from the arms of his mother.

He gazed down at Perditus, broken like his mother, driven like his father.

"My lord, the battle."

Eli turned his cold eyes to the floor. "He was my son. Leave, now!"

The soldiers left, while Eli mourned. "I'm sorry," he whispered as he looked down at the body of his neglected child.

SARA, Talon, and Bolton entered Eli's stone palace. The throne room was open to the sky after the Wind Elementals of Breeze had swept off the clay roof. Debris covered the throne. Some of the columns stood. The floors were cracked and covered with rubble.

Sara stepped ahead, but Talon stopped her.

"Wait," he said.

Talon strode forward. "Brother?" Talon called into the emptiness.

"Talon, be careful," Bolton said.

Talon took another cautious step. This is it, he thought. It ends here. "Eli."

And another step.

"Brother . . ."

And another.

Eli came from behind a column. The tears he shed for his son stained his face. He pulled the sword from Talon's side and pushed it through Talon's chest. "I would never kill you with Fire, brother," Eli said.

Talon collapsed as Eli tossed the sword aside.

"No!" Bolton screamed.

He charged into Eli. The sack of element spheres at his side fell to the ground. The spheres rolled out onto the floor.

Eli knocked Bolton to the ground as Sara hastened to his aid. She tripped, and the Water Sphere went rolling to join the others.

When Sara looked up at Eli, he stopped. He looked from her familiar face to the gemstone necklace. "Sicilia?" Eli reached out to touch her face.

Sara moved away from his touch. "You knew my mother."

Eli stared at her. "She was mine."

Sara grimaced. "And you killed her."

"But," Eli said, "she was dead. When I left her—"

"No," Sara cried, "she had a family. She lived."

Eli shook his head. "I never went back. I thought she was dead. I never went back." Flames burned the palms of his hands.

"Don't!" Bolton cried. He reached out his hand, and a bolt of lightning zipped through the air and struck Eli in the chest. He shook and fell to the floor.

"Sicilia."

She was surrounded by light.

"Make Water dance for me," Eli pleaded. Tears streamed down his face.

Sicilia shook her head.

Eli blinked and opened his eyes. He rose to his feet. "It can't be." He turned to Bolton. "Lightning killed her!"

"Stop!" Sara glared at Eli. Something in her eyes scared him. She was thinking about Talon, Bolton, her parents, and everyone Eli had hurt.

He could see Sicilia in her, but her eyes were different. He tried to escape her, but Talon lifted his head once more, and with his final store of energy, he drew a ring of flames around

Eli. While Eli tried to extinguish the flames of Talon's last will, Sara concentrated.

Eli gasped in horror as the water was pulled from his body. He gazed on in shock. A watery outline of himself glistened before his eyes. Eli's body shriveled as the water was pulled from it. His throat and mouth were dry, making it hard to breathe.

Sara watched him suffer, but something made her stop.

Eli's watery shadow flooded back into his body, and he fell to the floor on his hands and knees.

Talon could hold on no longer. "Now it's our time," he whispered. His head fell once again, and his flames faded.

Eli looked up. "Do it," he said to Sara. "Kill me!" Eli faced the truth: Sicilia had lived, and her daughter stood before him. "You can't? You are your mother's daughter. You'd have to tear up your heart and swallow it first. I killed her. Kill me!"

A pool of water formed beneath Eli's feet. As Sara called Water, Bolton prepared to send Lightning through it, but Eli set Bolton's outstretched hand on fire. "Let her do it on her own!"

Bolton screamed and Sara panicked. She doused the flames that burned Bolton's hand. Eli summoned more flames to stop Bolton. But something went wrong in Eli.

Eli's light went out.

"What happened?" He looked at his hands.

The Aether stood between Sara and Eli. The Fire Sphere glowed.

"It absorbed my power," Eli said, still looking at his hands.

The sphere went dark.

"We have to get out of here!" Bolton yelled.

He got up, took Sara's hand into his unharmed one, and pulled her toward the door.

A pool of darkness surrounded Eli. From out of the dark mass came the shadow of a man. "Perditus!" He began to pull Eli into the darkness.

"What is that?" Sara asked.

"I'm not sure."

Bolton rushed over to Talon. Talon's eyes were closed. Bolton shook him, but he did not wake. The warmth was starting to leave his body.

Bolton wiped the tears from his face. "Come on. We have to go."

Eli screamed as the shadow of his son drew him into the darkness. His hand reached out, clawing the ground, but the darkness was too strong. It had consumed his heart long ago, and now it came for the rest of him.

The battle pushed Sara and Bolton deeper into the city, but they met up with the others again.

"Are you okay," Spire asked. Farah, Rodan, and Decca were beside her. "Where's Talon."

"He's gone," Bolton said.

"No." Farah shook her head.

Sara looked back. He was her mentor, her savior. It was his warm hand that guided her to Element, and now it was cold.

"They're setting the buildings on fire," Decca said.

"Their own homes?" Sara asked.

"They'll do anything to get us out. It's best to stay low till we get our strength back."

"Especially you, Sara," Spire said.

"The smoke's getting thick." Farah coughed between words. "We should get out of the city."

Fallen buildings and burning debris blocked the streets leading back toward their army. They ran to the edge of the city, hoping to escape the smoke. When they reached the cliff, Fero was waiting for them.

"You obviously haven't learned your lesson have you, Bolton? I told you it could be easy, that you could save your friends. But no, you'd rather play the hero."

Fero stood at the cliff's edge and held a sphere.

He looked at Sara. "Oh, and you must have dropped this."

He tossed the Water Sphere into the air and caught it with his other hand. He pressed the sphere in both hands and summoned Fire. Fire filled the sphere and created a damaging pressure. A crack ran down the Water Sphere's center extinguishing its essence.

"Now, Water Nymph, you're mine."

Before Fero could send flames to harm Sara, Bolton rushed into him.

He thought of all the things he had done, of how much it was worth it to change. He hadn't been a coward.

As he and Fero fell from the ledge, he felt rain. Or maybe tears.

Sara reached out over the cliff, lunging for Bolton moments after he fell. Rodan grabbed her hand to stop her from falling too. As she leaned over the cliff, the drawings of all the places she visited, of Bolton, of her mother, were stolen by the wind and drifted down to the misty chasm.

50

NEVER FORGET

SARA looked out over the sea. The sun was high in the sky, and seagulls flew overhead. She stood on the docks of Lumina Port. She tried to keep her mind empty of mournful thoughts. The salty-smelling air, unburdened, swept through the strands of her hair. A light spray from the sea dashed against the wooden pillars of the docks and sprayed onto her skin only to be dried by the sun.

"Sara, they're ready for you." Spire wore her golden band unhidden, along with her engagement ring. She no longer wore black.

Sara nodded and left the dock with Spire. They walked into the Stadium where a crowd of people waited in the stands. The Stadium's domed ceiling was let down for the event, and the stands were open to the sun.

Sara and Spire climbed the marble stairs inside the Stadium's entrance room. The steps led them to the announcement stand, a small wooden balcony high above the rows of seating.

The audience quieted as Sara walked onto the balcony. Spire, Rodan, and Farah stood beside her.

Sara looked out into the immense crowd. It must have taken all Mirmina to fill the seats of the Stadium.

As she gazed into the crowd, she caught herself searching.

Sara glanced over at her friends. Rodan smiled at her and Spire nodded in encouragement. She looked back out into the crowd.

"We all have lost something. We've lost homes, loved ones, and hope. But now Hephaestus is gone."

Cheers erupted from the audience.

"Our hope is renewed."

The people continued to celebrate.

"I know you all believe it was my efforts that saved Mirmina." Sara paused. The crowd remained quiet.

"But the truth is much more than that," Sara continued. "I started this journey thinking I would face Hephaestus alone. But I learned something I hope you have all learned as well— nothing can be done alone. I thought everyone depended on me, but there were people who I depended on too. I couldn't have done it without my friends beside me."

Sara gestured for Spire, Farah, and Rodan to join her.

"Cherish those who stand by you, and never forget the ones who died and fought for this very moment."

She gazed into the crowd and hoped to see his face. "Now, I know it will be hard, but we can build a new Mirmina together with all our friends beside us."

Sara looked out at the cheering crowd, and all the people they had saved. Tears came to her eyes.

Months later, in Elementa, the people had begun to rebuild. Element was not what it once was, but the building was being repaired and apprentices had come back to train.

Sara sat by the lake in Element and stared out into the water. Rodan settled down beside her. He wore a silver band around his arm.

"You'll be leaving soon?" she asked.

"Yes," Rodan said. "I heard they asked Farah too."

"Did she join?"

"Farah . . . join an organized group of patrol soldiers? No, I don't think she'd like it."

"No. I guess she wouldn't."

"Hephaestus's followers are still out there. The Resistance needs us."

Sara looked away.

"I'm sorry," Rodan said.

"I don't know why they let me stay. I'm not an Elemental anymore."

"They owe you. If you hadn't been brave, none of this would have happened."

Sara looked back out into the water. She still felt the insurmountable urge to make the water move, to summon it, to dance on it again.

"I have to go," Rodan said. "If you should ever need my help . . ."

"I'll send for you," Sara said.

Rodan held out his hand. A seed appeared, and from the seed a flower blossomed. He handed Sara the white flower streaked with gold.

EPILOGUE

MIST settled at the bottom of the gorge as the rain fell. It covered the ground with ghostly mystique and swept down from the summit of the mountain. The vapor was a cold and permanent fixture of the chasm with its many misty arms, embracing those who had fallen and awaiting those who would plunge.

Lying on the rocky ground was a cracked sphere and a broken medallion. The sphere's essence flowed over the medallion and caused it to glow as the mist swept over it.

Two men lie at the bottom of the gorge. One was dead. The other, worn and weak, struggled to breathe in the cold air. The scarred man lie face down. His burnt hand reached out to the sphere.

Here is a preview of the second volume
of the Elementals Trilogy

THE COUNCIL

L. M. Peralta

Now available in Kindle and paperback

SARA danced on the surface of the lake, surrounded by crystals. Ripples danced through the clear water as she twirled upon its surface. She delighted in the cool lightness beneath her feet as the water wavered like silk in the breeze.

This moment was long forgotten. Sara stopped when she felt a hand upon her shoulder. Arms hugged her and blond hair brushed against her cheek.

"I missed you," she whispered.

His arms loosened their grasp, and the scene faded. As wakefulness pulled Sara from the dream, two voices sounded.

The first was Talon's: "Your story is not over."

And the second . . . "You're not alone."

Sara woke. She closed her eyes and tried to return, but her body was refreshed and sleep would not come back to her.

She pushed her light brown hair from her face. She combed through her hair with her fingers and got out of bed.

She went to the window. The sun peeked over the mountains, and the training field was deserted. But soon, the apprentices would have their breakfast and meet their trainers on the field. Fewer apprentices attended Element than in the years previous.

Element's lack of apprentices was the fault of Morica

Council. The Council had gone into hiding when Hephaestus gained power. They hurt many Elementals, including Sara's mother. They blamed Elementals for the imbalances of nature, the thirst for power, and the destruction.

Parents refused to send their children to Element for fear that the Council meant to do something more than political containment. Many trainers had left as well to join the Resistance, hoping to get into the graces of the Council.

The Resistance was now the Council's military strong arm. Both claimed to be devoted to the protection of Mirmina and its people. Most of their influence remained in Lumina, but the Council was spreading its ideals to the out-lying regions.

Sara looked across the field to the lake. For three years, no one had danced there. The water was still, sleeping. Not even the branches of the low-hanging tree disturbed its surface.

Now that Brina was gone, Sara took on her duties: making sure Element was well-maintained, keeping the schedule, and waiting, waiting for someone like Talon to disturb her waters.

Sara sat in Brina's library when a knock came to the heavy oak door of Element.

She went into the entrance hall, and opened the door. A girl stood outside. Her canary yellow hair was piled atop her head. Her skin was tan.

A little bird perched upon her shoulder. Green feathers surrounded her small, black eyes. The bird chirped.

"Farah!"

Farah grinned.

Sara led her into Brina's library where they sat in large armchairs.

Farah sank deep into the armchair with plenty of room on either side of her. "Ah, comfort," Farah said. "You wouldn't believe the things I've had to sit on in the last few weeks."

Farah's boots were well-worn.

"Have you been traveling? I thought you were still in Breeze."

"I couldn't stay in that steel prison for another minute. All my dad wants to do is talk about politics and how we all should get on Morica's good side. From what I've heard, those no-good cowards ran at the first sight of danger."

"How is your father doing otherwise?"

"He's been off on *business*. Wouldn't say what kind. So, at the first sight of a clear opening, Thatch, Shift, and I took off."

"Shift went with you?" Sara remembered how unwilling Shift had been to disobey his father.

"Shift's not so bad. He just needs the right kind of guidance. Besides, Dad made him really mad when he told someone else to manage the city while he is away. After all, it is Shift's birthright."

"Why would Tag do that?"

"Shift hasn't been right since the battle in Omega Ray. He's having trouble calling Wind."

"Oh." Sara could sympathize. Since Fero's destruction of the Water Sphere, she had not been able to call Water.

"I have so much to tell you, but first, do you want to say hello to the guys?"

"Sure. Where are they?"

"Well, Thatch couldn't land in the city."

"Land? You mean the dome?" Sara recalled the large metal contraption that rested on the back of Thermal.

"Not exactly. Thatch's new toy is much bigger than the dome."

SARA followed Farah through the streets of Elementa. No Elementals performed in the market or outside the alleyways. They followed the trail up to the mountains. Beyond the cliff, on the beach, Thermal dug his long claws into the sand. Thermal raised his ashy gray beak and cawed. Attached to his back was a harness, and a wagon-like structure four times as large as the dome trailed behind him.

The structure had wheels like a giant carriage. Where the driver would sit, holding the reins, a glass covering tilted downward.

"What is it?" Sara asked.

"Thatch calls it our Flying Chariot," Farah said.

As they approached, the hatch door opened and a ramp unfolded.

Sara looked up.

"Don't worry," Farah said. "It's completely safe. A lot safer than the dome."

That's not saying much, Sara thought.

She led Sara up the ramp and into the carriage. Inside the large structure, various metal contraptions spun on axels, and gears moved in circles.

"This is the engine room," Farah said. "Wait until you see the rest."

They walked to the elevator in the center of the structure, which brought them to the upper floor.

"Thatch worked hard to get this thing together. He's been working on it for years, gathering materials from the ruined streets of Breeze."

The elevator doors slid open to the control room. Machines lined the walls. Steps led to the cockpit. Three seats faced the big glass panels overlooking Thermal's head. At one seat was a blue monitor streaming with little white words falling across its face. In the middle was a wheel to navigate the structure. Pipes and wires lined the right side of the room. Monitors clustered against the opposite wall.

Sheets of metal covered the floors, walls, and ceiling, which curved up.

"Hey." Thatch spun in his seat at the blue monitor. "It's been a long time."

Shift sat in the driver's seat. He turned to look at Sara as she approached.

"What do you think?" Thatch asked.

"I've never seen anything like this," Sara said.

"I hope not. It's an original design. Shift's the pilot. That wheel controls Thermal's direction. It pulls the reins connected to Thermal's harness. I'm the navigator. These numbers on the screen here—they're coordinates."

"Coordinates?"

"A map of Mirmina. Like in the books I've studied. The books from the old world. Up there," Thatch pointed to the sky, "there are structures that can pinpoint any location. This machine can communicate with them to create a map."

"Tell her what you do," Shift said.

"Me?" Farah asked. "I sit at the window over there and point when I see something interesting and say: 'Oh, oh, land there!'"

"Yep, that about sums up what she does."

"Hey, I do more than that!" Farah said. "I handle negotiations."

"What negotiations?" Shift asked.

"Like when I talked to Lord Fletzi about allowing Thermal to land in Lumina Port. For a price, of course."

Orka chirped.

Shift shook his head and turned back to the windows.

"So," Sara said, "if Thermal flies the Chariot, what are the machines for?"

"Well," Thatch said, "the ones up here are location-trackers. They find places, things, people."

"People?"

"Well, provided they have a tracking device on them."

"Oh," Sara said.

"And," Thatch said, "the ones you noticed downstairs are engines. They not only run the locators, but they also power the Chariot, to a certain degree, which is a lot less strain for Thermal. I wish I could get them strong enough to power the whole structure, but that may take some time and a huge jolt of energy."

"Where's Stan?" Farah looked at the cluster of computers and the empty seat in front of them.

"Yeah," Shift said, "I was wondering where that little buzz-can got off to myself."

Thatch held down a button on the arm of his chair and spoke: "Stannum, report to the control room."

Buzzing and crashing echoed from the back of the room.

The sliding door opened and an oversized metal beetle with skinny steel arms flew into the room. Sara ducked as it zoomed past her. In the center of the room it stopped and shook itself until something rattled inside its head.

Its metallic body gleamed in the light, but its skinny arms showed signs of rust. An orange light blinked in the center of its body as it hovered in the air.

"You called?" The floating machine's voice was monotone and high-pitched.

"I wanted you to introduce yourself to Sara," Thatch said.

"Hello, Sara." Stannum floated over to her and extended one small steel hand. "I am Stannum. It is nice to meet you."

"And you as well." Sara shook its hand.

Stannum's eye turned deep orange. He tilted his eye up and down until the light scanned Sara from head to toe. Stannum's glowing eye projected a small holographic image of Sara. "Lady Sara, former Water Elemental. Three years ago, she spearheaded the group of Elemental fighters that waged a battle against Hephaestus, a Fire Elemental and tyrant. His tyrannical reign lasted approximately twenty-four years before the battle, where he then perished."

Shift sighed.

"Excuse me?" Stannum said.

"Shift, why did you have to start?" Thatch asked.

"Start?" Shift turned to face the room. "I didn't say anything."

"You never appreciated me," Stannum buzzed.

"Appreciate you? You're a metallic piece of junk."

"You are an organic piece of junk who will not admit that I am superior in every way."

"Shift, it's just a machine," Thatch said.

"With an attitude, which you gave it," Shift said. "I wish I would have never built it. Why did you feel the need to finish putting together this heap of junk?"

"Heap of junk?" Stannum buzzed. "I will be ticking long after you are gone."

"We'll see about that." Shift made a move to get out of his seat.

"Please," Thatch said, "we need Stannum. He's a machine and a helpful one at that. But his thoughts, feelings, and reactions are programmed, and you made him that way, not me."

Stannum's glowing eye turned a pale shade of orange, and his arms hung at his sides.

"Shift made Stannum when we were kids," Thatch said. "But he failed to make the right connections in Stannum's brain network. Stannum went haywire and destroyed some very valuable prototypes Uncle Tag had been working on. Shift got in trouble for it. He was frustrated with Stannum so he locked him up. One day, I found Stannum, half-smashed in a supply cabinet, and I salvaged him. It took years for me to fix him, but now he works fine."

Stannum zoomed over to the blue-screened machines and pressed buttons, his long arms stretching over the control panels, allowing his skinny steel fingers to reach the keys.

"Stannum analyses objects we find on the locator. He's working on a link right now.

"A few nights ago, we picked up a reading on the locator. A strange landmass appeared far out to sea, but as we got closer to it, it blinked on and off the map until it disappeared. It was strange. Something that big coming in and out like that. We couldn't find it again.

"Stannum is scanning and analyzing every map from Lumina's library. We hope we can send him to scan the maps in Element."

"We asked around," Farah said. "No one's heard of an island that far out. Neither Caleena nor Lumina Port has ever shipped there."

"I don't think it will come up again," Shift said. "Probably a mishap with the locator. I think all this map scanning is a waste of time."

"Don't say that," Farah said. "We'll find it. I know we will."

"Why?" Sara asked. "You think it could be the Insula?"

ABOUT THE AUTHOR

L. M. PERALTA graduated from the University of New Orleans with a degree in English and holds a law degree from Tulane University. Always an avid reader, her love for fantasy led her to begin writing her debut book, *The Elementals*, at the age of seventeen. She lives with her family in Violet, Louisiana, and is looking forward to completing the second book in the Elementals trilogy.

Follow L. M. Peralta on Facebook
www.facebook.com/authorlmperalta

Follow L. M. Peralta on Twitter
www.twitter.com/l_m_peralta

For free content, updates, and
behind the scenes information,
visit www.lmperalta.com

www.ingramcontent.com/pod-product-compliance
Lightning Source LLC
Chambersburg PA
CBHW050536260626
47157CB00002B/312